Evelyn Hood is an ex-journalist and has been a full-time writer for many years, turning her talents to plays, short stories, children's musicals and the novels that have earned her widespread acclaim and an ever-increasing readership. She also writes under the name Eve Houston.

For more information about the author and her books, visit www.evehouston.co.uk and www.evelynhood.co.uk.

McADAM'S WOMEN

Evelyn Hood

SPHERE

First published in Great Britain in 1994 by Little, Brown and Company
This paperback edition published in 1995 by Warner Books
Reprinted by Warner Books in 2000
Reissued by Sphere in 2012

A CIP catalogue record for this book
is available from the British Library.

ISBN 978-0-7515-5099-3

Printed and bound in Great Britain by
Clays Ltd, St Ives plc

Papers used by Sphere are from well-managed forests
and other responsible sources.

MIX
Paper from
responsible sources
FSC
www.fsc.org   FSC® C104740

Sphere
An imprint of
Little, Brown Book Group
100 Victoria Embankment
London EC4Y 0DY

An Hachette UK Company
www.hachette.co.uk

www.littlebrown.co.uk

1

Although she had been watching the doorway intently for the past five minutes, Isla felt a sense of shock, like a fist slamming into her breastbone, when the girl she had been expecting arrived. They had never set eyes on each other before, but she would have known immediately who the newcomer was, even if they had only glanced at each other in a crowded street in passing.

From beneath a black cloche hat clear blue eyes swept the busy tearoom, halting as they reached the table in the corner, and Isla's tentative, half-raised hand.

They flared, just as Kenneth's did whenever he was astonished. Black-gloved fingers reached out to grasp the door-frame for a moment, and then, wiping the shock from her face with a deliberate effort, the girl came across the room, skirting tables, side-stepping waitresses.

Isla had intended to rise to meet her, but instead she stayed where she was, pinned to the small chair by this reminder of her recent loss. The paralysing agony had hit her several times since Kenneth's death; just as she thought that she had accepted it and come to terms with it, sudden realisation and a wave of desolation swept anew through her.

Now her first sight of Kenneth's daughter – his older daughter – had revived it.

The girl had his clear, steady, somewhat pale blue eyes, though in her case they were fringed with gold, instead of Kenneth's more stubby lashes. She had his strongly marked brows, his mouth – without, of course, the red-gold moustache above it – his straight neat nose. Beneath the black velvet hat she wore, Isla glimpsed hair the vibrant glowing bronze of autumn leaves. The colour Kenneth's had been. Her face was oval, her chin neatly rounded where his had been square. Slim and straight, dressed in a high-necked black knitted suit, black stockings, black shoes, she even had Kenneth's walk, lithe and quick and easy, though constricted at that moment by the tables in the room.

Isla's throat tightened, and for a moment tears prickled behind her eyes. She fought them back, telling herself sternly that she was not going to let herself weep in this public place, in front of this young woman who looked so familiar to her, yet was a stranger.

Swallowing hard, she regained her own self-control as the girl arrived beside her table, suddenly hesitant and unsure. 'You can't be—' she began, then stopped, folding her mouth round the next two words as though to hold them back.

Isla got to her feet. 'I'm Isla Mc—' She hesitated, then said clearly, 'Isla McAdam.'

The girl's eyes flared again, this time with arrogant anger, and she ignored the hand that was held out to her. 'You've got no right to that name!'

'Please believe me when I say that I thought I had,'

Isla said steadily, letting her hand fall back to her side. 'And you're Ainslie.'

'But you're so young!'

'I'm twenty-six.' Twenty-six for the past week. Her birthday had come one short week after hearing of Kenneth's death.

'My God!' There was anger in Ainslie's voice. 'You're only five years older than I am – and he was forty-six!' She swayed slightly, groped for the back of a chair, found it, and sank into it.

'I knew Kenneth's age, but I never felt that it mattered.' Isla took her own seat again, still fighting to keep her voice level. She had made up her mind that she wasn't going to be afraid of this girl, but despite herself, the fear was there. Without knowing it, she had been part of a terrible wrong committed against Ainslie McAdam and her mother and brother.

Colour rose to Ainslie's cheeks and contempt honed her voice. 'How could he do this to – to us?'

It was numbing to look into eyes so like Kenneth's, yet cold in a way his had never been. Under his daughter's antagonistic stare Isla might well have given way to her grief and her terror of the unknown future, but it was the contemptuous note in the girl's voice that saved her from possible weakness. She wasn't to blame for what had happened, she had nothing to be ashamed of. She would not allow this young woman to make her feel like a criminal.

'Ainslie – Miss McAdam, it was you who suggested this meeting. If you've changed your mind, you're free to go, though I've ordered tea for us both.'

It arrived just at that moment, brought to them by a

middle-aged woman so plump that her small white frilled apron looked like a postage stamp stuck on to her black dress. She deftly transferred the cups and saucers and the nickel-plated teapot and sugar bowl and milk jug to the spotless white table-cloth, then scurried to a huge sideboard and brought back a tiered plate-stand filled with plates of cakes and biscuits. Her eyebrows rose and she looked hurt when Ainslie McAdam impatiently flapped a hand at her and said, 'Take these away!'

'Madam? The cakes've just come up fresh from the bakery below . . .'

Isla forced the corners of her lips into a placating smile. 'They look delicious, but I don't think we're in the mood for them today.'

The woman's eyes swept from one to the other, taking in Ainslie's black suit and the black armband on the sleeve of Isla's grey woollen coat. Her own face fell into solemn lines.

'Of course, madam,' she murmured, and went off, leaving them alone and silent in a roomful of chattering, brightly dressed women.

Ainslie McAdam watched, her brows drawn together in a straight line above brooding eyes, as Isla drew off her gloves and began to pour tea. She shook her head when Isla lifted the milk jug, and pulled her own gloves off, lifting a hand to flick the flowing end of the black silk scarf that served as a hatband back from her shoulder.

Carefully, aware of the unblinking gaze opposite, Isla poured her own tea, added milk and more sugar than she would normally have taken, and stirred the liquid. The hot sweet tea helped to steady her nerves.

'This is very difficult for us both,' she said as she returned the cup to its saucer.

'I asked you to meet me here because I won't have you calling on my mother. She's never been strong, and now she's ill with worry and shame over this – this business. I'll not have her upset any further!'

'I've no intention of forcing myself on your mother, or on any other member of your family.'

Ainslie's eyes said that she didn't believe that. 'Why would you come here to Paisley if you weren't out to make trouble for us?'

'I came at my—' Isla stopped herself just in time from saying, 'my husband's,' and changed it to, 'your father's lawyer's invitation. There are matters we have to discuss.'

'You – talk to his lawyer?' Ainslie's voice rose, and one or two people at neighbouring tables turned to look at the two sombrely dressed young women. She noticed the curious glances, and lowered her tone. 'But there's nothing to talk about. You weren't his wife!'

The words stung against Isla's cheeks like small stones, raising spots of colour. 'I thought I was.'

'You thought wrong!'

'I know that now. And I didn't ask Mr Forbes for this meeting – as I said, I'm in Paisley at his invitation.'

'I don't see why,' Ainslie McAdam said with open hostility.

'Nor do I, until I see him.'

Ainslie's right hand, having dealt with the troublesome hat-ribbon, was rubbing nervously at the third finger of her left hand. Her gaze dipped to the gold band on Isla's wedding finger, and her mouth tightened.

'Mr Forbes said' – she hesitated, then went on as though the words were wrenched out of her throat, 'he told me that there were – children.'

'We – I have a four-year-old daughter and a baby son.'

The girl's eyes darkened. She drew in her breath sharply, then said in a burst of anguished rage, 'I wish he knew how much misery he's caused with his selfishness! I wish I could tell him! He's ruined everything for me – for us!'

Tears sparkled among her lashes, diamonds in a mesh of gold, and Isla automatically stretched a comforting hand across the table towards her. Ainslie jerked back, rising to her feet with an awkward motion that set the china on the table jangling and the tea slopping in the cups.

'Don't touch me!'

'My dear—'

'Keep away from my mother! Keep out of Paisley!' Ainslie McAdam blurted the words, her face crumpling, then almost ran out of the room, heedless of the faces that turned to watch her go then swung back to where Isla sat, alone, at the table.

She reached for her cup and discovered that she was trembling so much that she had to use both hands to lift it from the saucer. Head bowed, she sipped at the tea again, but now its warmth held no comfort for her. The waitress appeared as she put the cup down, her face creased with concern.

'Is something wrong, madam? Isn't your friend coming back? She's scarcely touched her tea.'

'No, she's not coming back.'

'Oh dear, your saucer's wet. I'll fetch a clean one.'

Her fussing was irritating, yet comforting. Nobody had fussed over Isla, until Kenneth came into her life. She smiled her thanks at the woman when the clean cup and saucer arrived, and after she had poured out more tea she opened her envelope handbag and drew out a single, folded sheet of paper. The letter had been handed to her by the solicitor when he came to her home to break the news of Kenneth's death – and the news about his other wife and children, living in Paisley.

Although she knew the few words off by heart, Isla smoothed the sheet out and read them slowly, carefully, one by one.

'My darling Isla,

By the time you read this you will know the truth about me. Please, my dearest, forgive me for what I have done, and what I must now do. I can see no other way. You have given me more happiness in the past few years than I have ever known before, though you will know now what I always knew – that I had no right to it. Kiss the children for me, and I hope that you can find it in your heart to let them think kindly of me.

I love you all, Kenneth.'

The letter had been in her possession for only fourteen days, but already the creases where she had folded and refolded it were beginning to bite into the paper, and the fainter lines, where she had impetuously crumpled the page up and thrown it away in the first angry throes of her grief, were fading.

She smoothed it yet again, carefully, before tucking it away in the small pocket that held her return train ticket to Gourock, the Clydeside town where she lived. Then she signalled to the waitress to bring the bill.

After fumbling in her purse for the necessary coins to pay the smart, aloof cashier in her raised box by the entrance, she went into the ladies' room, unable as yet to face the busy pavements. The mirror, lit discreetly, reflected a thin face, normally with a smooth olive glow to the skin, inherited from her Italian mother. Since Kenneth's death, the glow had gone, leaving her skin almost sallow. Her brown eyes, tilted slightly at the outer corners in an almond shape, were large and expressive, and her surprisingly full mouth, her best feature, was pale. She stared intently into the glassy depths, noting that grief ill became her, thinking of Ainslie McAdam's creamy skin and blue eyes against the unrelieved black clothes she wore.

Fumbling in her bag, she found a pale pink lipstick that Kenneth had bought for her. Isla had never made her face up until she met him, but he had persuaded her to try some lipstick, and she had to admit that it enhanced the colour of her skin and improved the mouth that she had always considered to be too large, but Kenneth had described as beautiful, and eminently kissable.

The memory of his words almost brought tears to the surface again. She forced them back and applied the lip colouring lightly, but it didn't do as much for her as it had in the days when she had been happy and fulfilled, a woman in love, a woman who knew that she was loved in return.

8

After tidying an errant strand of black hair away beneath her plain woollen cloche hat, she went downstairs and through the bakery on the ground floor, wondering, as she stepped out on to the pavement, how the May sun could shine, the small fluffy clouds drift calmly across the sky, the people around her go about their business as though nothing had happened. How could a world suddenly robbed of her beloved husband's presence – for to Isla he was still her husband, despite what she now knew of him – continue to function?

Even the discovery that she was not his legal wife couldn't dull the edge of her love for him, her need of him. She felt like a widow. She was a widow, no matter how the law stood in the matter.

A clock chimed. She looked up and saw it atop the imposing Town Hall on the other side of the wide bridge spanning the river that ran through the town centre on its way to the Clyde. It was a quarter to three, and her appointment with the lawyer was at three o'clock. She had already ascertained that Moss Street, where he had his office, was only a short distance away. A few minutes would take her there.

Taking advantage of a break in the traffic, she made her way to the other side of the bridge, mildly curious as to what lay beyond the stone balustrade edging the opposite pavement. The Town Hall was to her left, rising from the river bank; on the opposite bank, to Isla's right, people walked through well-laid-out public gardens, or sat on the wooden slatted benches facing the bright flower beds. A handsome statue of Queen Victoria stood on a plinth in the middle of the gardens, her back to Isla.

She smiled faintly at the stone figure, thinking that it was little wonder that even the likeness of the dead Queen should be turned away from her. She was a fallen woman now, with no right to the gold band that Kenneth had put on her finger. She briefly touched her left hand with her right, and, under the material of her glove, felt the ring's outline. She wasn't going to take it off; she had decided that almost as soon as she heard that their marriage had been bigamous. Even the thought of that word, harsh and ugly, made her wince.

Below, a stick, once part of a tree or a bush, circled lazily in the water and was almost caught in the long grasses fringing the river. It broke free at the last moment, disappearing beneath the bridge, drifting with no will of its own. Isla sympathised with that stick. She too was drifting, alone and with no power, it seemed, to control her own life.

She would have liked to go down the stone steps further along the pavement and into the gardens, moving among the flowers, perhaps sitting on a bench, defying Queen Victoria's stony disapproval, but there was no time for such luxuries. Instead, she turned away from the water and re-crossed the road.

Thin strands of music met her as she neared the handsome war memorial on open paved ground. A handful of men stood below it, faces hollowed by lack of nourishment. One played a penny whistle, one had an accordion, another beat on a child's toy drum with a stick. A fourth man jigged from foot to foot in a pale imitation of a dance as he played the fiddle. Lying upside-down on the ground at their feet was a well-worn cloth cap. They were almost certainly ex-servicemen, learning the hard way that their country's gratitude for their service during the most appalling war the world had ever experienced didn't stretch as far as guaranteeing them the right to earn their own livings once they returned home.

Pausing to search in her purse, Isla thought of her own adored father, who had been killed in action in April 1915, shortly before her twelfth birthday. Her mother had died three years later, an early victim of the great influenza epidemic that shadowed the ending of the war.

She tossed a coin into the cap and the man with the drum said hoarsely, 'Thanks, missus.'

It might well be the last time she would be able to help poor souls such as these, Isla thought as she went on her way, passing another group, this time idling on a street corner, hands in pockets. A grim smile twisted her mouth as she pictured herself entertaining people in the streets in order to feed and clothe her children. She had no musical talent at all, unlike her father, with his rich baritone voice, or Aunt Lally, his sister, who had taken her into her Edinburgh home after she was orphaned.

It struck her that while it had become commonplace in the 1920s to see men playing musical instruments or singing in the streets in the hope of making a few pence, she had never seen women taking it up. Surely there must be many women in the position she now found herself, alone and destitute, with small children to care for. They tended to work for their more fortunate sisters, taking in washing or sewing, or scrubbing stairs and other women's houses.

Isla wondered if that was what she would have to do. If so – she drew a deep breath and squared her shoulders – she would do it. She would do anything, rather than lose her children, all that was left to her of the happy years she had spent with Kenneth.

The words 'Forbes and Son Limited' glinted at her from a polished brass nameplate on the wall of the building she was passing. She walked through the close and up the spotlessly clean stairs, whitewashed in two broad strips down the sides, to find out what lay in store for her.

12

2

The woman in the reception area looked at Isla with more than passing interest when she introduced herself.

'Take a seat, Mrs – er . . .' she said, a sudden flush coming to her face as she stumbled over the name. 'I'll tell Mr Forbes you're here.'

She disappeared into one of the rooms flanking the square hall. The door closed quietly behind her, then opened again a moment later. A fair-haired young man came out, looked at Isla with unexpected hostility, then walked past her without a word and disappeared into another room. She was still staring after him, puzzled by his attitude, when the receptionist said, 'Mr Forbes will see you now.'

After the hostility she had encountered from Ainslie McAdam – and from the young man who had recently left this office – Isla felt that Gilchrist Forbes, coming round his large desk to meet her, hand outstretched, was an old friend. He had been remote and stilted early in their first meeting, but once he had realised that she was completely unaware of her husband's other life he had mellowed, treating her with a comforting courtesy that was still evident in his manner as he seated her, then went back to his own place behind the desk.

'You found your way here with no trouble?' As before, the well-educated voice brought a lump to her throat. He spoke just like Kenneth. Kenneth's voice had attracted her the very first time they had met in the ward of an Edinburgh hospital, where he had been admitted with appendicitis after being taken ill on a business trip to the city, and she had been undergoing her nursing training. 'It's fortunate that we're only a short distance from the station.'

'I arrived by an earlier train. Kenneth's daughter had written, asking me to meet her first.'

His thick brows, dark and speckled with grey, rose sharply. 'Ainslie contacted you?' His voice was disapproving.

'I presume she got my address from you.'

'Yes, she did wheedle it out of me.' Gilchrist Forbes frowned down at the papers on his desk. 'But I advised her to leave matters be, and I thought she had agreed. I should have known better where Ainslie's concerned.'

'I imagine that her curiosity got the better of her,' Isla remarked dryly, drawing off her gloves. 'She'd got it into her head that I might call on her mother and cause trouble.'

He glanced up with a quick motion of the head, concern in his eyes. 'You'd not do that, surely.'

His reaction, coming on top of Ainslie's attitude, suddenly angered Isla. 'I assured her, and I can assure you, Mr Forbes, that I have no intention of doing such a cruel thing,' she said sharply. 'I may not have been legally married to Kenneth, but I believed that I was. I love—'

her voice broke and she brought it under control at once, digging her fingernails into the palms of her hands. 'I loved him,' she corrected herself, and saw embarrassment in his eyes. This man didn't belong to a generation that spoke of love. Neither had Kenneth, though with her he had managed to overcome his reservations. 'I would do nothing to harm him or his family. I even stayed away from his funeral, though that was very hard. I shall always regret not being able to see him laid to rest.'

'I'm sorry, my dear, but, like you, I'm in a very difficult situation. Kenneth McAdam was one of my closest friends. Our two wi— our families know each other well, and it came as a great shock to me to learn first of his death, then of your existence.'

Isla nodded, smoothing her gloves out on her lap. The fingers of her right hand stole across to touch her gold wedding band for comfort. She was reminded of much the same movement made by Ainslie a short while earlier.

'Would you like some tea?'

'I'd rather attend to our business, then get back to my children.'

'Of course.' He cleared his throat, and rustled the papers on the desk. 'I'm afraid that I can give you nothing but bad news.'

'I expect little else, these days,' said Isla, then listened intently while he explained that Kenneth had taken an overdose of laudanum because the hitherto comfortable Glasgow-based business he had inherited from his father had crashed due to financial problems. She had already been given that information, on his earlier visit to her home, but then she had been too distraught to take it all in.

'Why?' she asked now. 'Why should he have been in such distress that he could see suicide as the only way out? It wasn't like Kenneth. At least, not the Kenneth I knew.'

Gilchrist Forbes paused, compressing his lips tightly together, reluctant to betray his dead friend.

He had glossed over the situation when talking to Catherine McAdam, and she, wrapped up in her own thoughts, had accepted what he said without question.

Ainslie, however, had come to his office later and insisted on hearing in detail about her father's financial troubles. Forbes found himself thinking that Ainslie and the young woman now facing him had a lot in common. They both had a way of looking directly at him, of wanting to know everything, no matter how much it might hurt them. They even shared the same expression in their eyes, one of deep loss, and a determination to survive. Neither would turn away from the truth, however hard it might be. He wondered if Kenneth himself had ever noticed the similarity between daughter and consort.

Isla's brows tucked down in a slight frown as the silence lengthened. 'Mr Forbes?' she prompted, and the solicitor was jerked back to the present.

'I'm sorry – I was trying to think of how best to explain matters to you.'

'I believe that the time to soften blows is long past, Mr Forbes. I know very little about business, but I'm sure I can deal with a straightforward explanation. I understand that my husband was an insurance broker, though he never spoke of his work.'

'He was well thought of in the city, but to be frank,

it would seem that he had taken to speculating some-what rashly with his clients' money.'

'It can't have been easy, running two families. I wish,' Isla said, 'that he had confided in me. It's hard for me to know now that he was so worried, and I did nothing to help because I was in ignorance.'

Forbes blinked at her. Her attitude was so unlike Catherine McAdam's that for a moment he floundered. Catherine had turned her head away when he tried to explain about Kenneth's financial problems, had flatly refused to accept a word of it.

'Under the circumstances,' he said at last, 'he could scarcely have confided in you, of all people.'

'If he had, I would surely have tried to understand,' Isla told him steadily. At least she would have heard the truth from Kenneth's own lips of why he had drawn her into an illegal marriage, and how he had managed for five years to live a lie. Now she would never know the answers.

She said aloud, 'I imagine that there is very little money for anyone to inherit. And of course his legal family will have first right to anything he left – includ-ing the house my children and I inhabit.'

'That, like most of his estate, will be sold and the proceeds will go to his creditors. Catherine, his . . .'

The man's voice faltered, and Isla said clearly, 'His wife.'

The papers rustled sharply. 'As you say. Catherine has money of her own, enough, perhaps, to cushion the worst of the blow. Do you yourself have private means?'

'I have nothing. I was training to be a nurse when I met Kenneth.'

'Is there no family to assist you?'

'I was an only child, and my parents both died several years ago. I have an aunt, but I'm quite certain that she only has enough to support herself.'

She was relieved that Aunt Lally, in Edinburgh, was too far away to know anything of the situation. Not that she had ever been interested in Isla's problems. 'If I'd wanted a man and children you can be sure I'd have got them,' she had said often during the few years Isla had lived with her. 'But I'd no intention of tying myself down. Life's for living, not for fretting about others.' It was quite impossible to imagine Aunt Lally, who loved spending money, having any savings.

'There's a tenement block here in Paisley, in George Street, that Kenneth owned. I handled the purchase for him, years ago, and the rent collector's a man I use myself for other properties. It seems that Kenneth signed the building over to you several months ago. Did he not tell you?'

Isla looked at him in astonishment. 'Not a word.' Then, with sudden hope, 'Does that mean that the rent it has made since he signed it over will come to me?'

He cleared his throat, and a slight flush appeared over his cheekbones. 'Kenneth re-invested the proceeds in his company – I assume that he did it on your behalf, to make the money work for you.'

Isla saw her hopes of a nest-egg fade away. 'But it would have been lost when the company folded.'

'Sadly, yes. The rent it has made in the past few weeks is yours, of course, but it amounts to very little, because it's an old property and the tenants don't necessarily pay promptly, though I can assure you that the collector we use is very conscientious.' Gilchrist Forbes riffled through the papers before him until he found the right one. He studied it, stroking his chin. 'One of the dwelling-houses is lying vacant at the moment, but I'm sure that we can find tenants for it. I could put the building on the market on your behalf.'

'How soon would you expect to find a buyer?'

His brows lifted slightly at her forthright question and she knew with grim amusement that because of her youth and her accent, more broad than his own prim, educated speech, he had instantly assumed that she was no businesswoman.

'Frankly,' he said after a slight pause, 'I wouldn't be too optimistic. Businessmen are finding these times hard, and it is, as I said, an old building. But there's no harm in searching for a buyer.'

'Then we must do so,' said Isla briskly, adding as an afterthought, 'that empty flat – I could live there in the meantime.'

Concern flashed into Gilchrist Forbes' eyes. 'I scarcely think that it would be the most suitable place for your children.'

'There's nothing wrong with tenements, Mr Forbes. I was raised in a Glasgow tenement, and I survived the experience.'

'But – but this is an old building—' Consternation made the man stammer over his words. 'And with Catherine and her children already living in this town—'

'How much time do I have before I must move from the house we're in now?'

'No more than another month, I'm afraid. If I can manage to sell the tenement for you in that time you

could use the money to buy somewhere else to live –
perhaps in the area where you live at the moment.'

'And if not, I've no option but to move into the
empty flat. I'd be grateful if you would retain it for me,
just in case. I must keep a roof over my children's
heads somehow,' she reminded him as he opened his
mouth to argue.

The Town Hall clock could be heard chiming the half
hour, and he automatically consulted the watch pinned
across his waistcoat. Isla, suddenly feeling stifled, got to
her feet. 'I must go.'

'But there are still some matters to discuss.'

'Perhaps we can meet again. Next week?'

'Certainly. I'll call on you – shall we say Wednesday,
at three o'clock? I'm sorry, my dear,' he went on, going
ahead to open the office door for her. 'This must be
extremely difficult for you.'

'I shall manage.' Then, as they crossed the hall, she
asked, 'That young man who was in your office when I
arrived – who is he?'

'My son, Colin. He and Ainslie McAdam are' – he
paused, then said – 'were to be married.'

Recalling the way Ainslie had touched the third finger of her left hand, feeling for the consolation of a ring
that was no longer there, and the girl's bitter, 'He's
ruined everything for me!' Isla felt a flash of contempt
for the young man who had cared so little for his
fiancée that he had abandoned her at the first whisper of
scandal.

'Indeed? I take it that he ended the engagement
because of her father's shameful death?'

Something of her condemnation must have sounded

in her voice, because Gilchrist Forbes was cool when he retorted, 'Indeed not. It was Ainslie who ended it, very much against my son's wishes.'

The rapport that had been growing between them had vanished with her criticism of his son, and his voice was formal when he wished her good day and closed the door behind her, leaving her to walk alone down the stairs to the street.

Emerging from the tearoom after her disastrous confrontation with her father's secret 'wife', Ainslie McAdam walked aimlessly along the street, weaving her way around pedestrians without seeing any of them. Someone called her name, and she looked up to see a former schoolfriend, her round, rosy face suitably solemn, but her eyes bright with curiosity. Clearly she had heard the rumours that had begun circulating despite all Gilchrist Forbes' attempts to keep the details of Kenneth's suicide quiet.

'Ainslie, I meant to write to you. I was so sorry to hear about your father.'

'Thank you, Christine. I'm – I'm in a terrible rush,' Ainslie said, and hurried on, knowing full well that Christine was gaping after her, taken aback by her coldness. But she couldn't talk to anyone while her mind was filled with pictures of the woman she had just left. She had expected – had hoped – to see someone much older, a plain elderly spinster, perhaps, who had somehow embroiled Kenneth McAdam in her clutches. Instead she had been confronted by a young woman only a few years older than herself. At that moment, for the first time in her life, she hated her father with all her heart.

She was glad that he was dead, she told herself fiercely, swinging round a corner and almost bumping into a great crowd of women straggling along the pavement, moving in the opposite direction from Ainslie herself. Young, old, fat, thin, all dressed in working clothes with scarves wound round their heads, they talked and laughed and called to each other loudly as they poured along the pavements past her. Drifts of cotton clustered on a coatsleeve here, a mop of hair there, and Ainslie realised that she had walked right through the town and was nearing Ferguslie Mills as it was disgorging its workers at the end of a shift.

She glanced at her watch and discovered to her astonishment that, somehow, the afternoon had passed, and she should have been home an hour earlier. She turned the next corner and kept walking, this time with purpose, past the cricket ground and the neat double row of back-to-back housing built to accommodate some of the mill workers, then under the railway bridge and up the hill to where a row of comfortably large houses stood back from the road, separated from it by their neat gardens.

Her heart sank when she saw the small car, its chocolate-brown paintwork and chrome gleaming in the late-afternoon sun, standing in the driveway of her own home. Letting herself in quietly at the front door, she tried to escape upstairs to her room, but her mother's voice called her name as she passed the drawing-room's closed door. Ainslie hesitated, then decided to pretend she hadn't heard the summons. Just as she gained the staircase the drawing-room door opened.

'Ainslie?'

She stopped, turning towards the man she had once promised to marry. 'Hello, Colin.'

'Your mother wants to see you.' His voice was gruff, and his hazel eyes, when she met them, still carried the hurt of her rejection.

There was nothing else for it. Ainslie stepped back down into the hall and walked past him and into the room.

'Ainslie, where have you been?' Catherine McAdam wanted to know as soon as her daughter appeared. She lay on a chaise longue, a rug over her legs and cushions piled behind her back. The windows were curtained against the daylight, and fringed standard lamps glowed feebly in the twilight within the room.

'I went out for a walk. I thought you were resting in your room, Mother.'

'I was, but I had to come downstairs to see to some business.' The rings on Catherine's limp hand sparkled in the electric light as she indicated the open desk. Colin moved to it and began to gather the spilled papers together neatly, his back towards mother and daughter. 'I could have done with your help,' Catherine went on reproachfully.

'What d'you want me to do?'

'It's too late now, I had to see to it all myself, with Colin's help. Now I'm trying to persuade him to stay for tea.' A warm note crept into Catherine's voice. She had been delighted when her daughter and Colin Forbes became engaged, and furious when, only days after her father's death, Ainslie had taken it upon herself to return the handsome diamond and emerald ring that had been specially made for her.

'I expect he has to get back home.'

'I've already explained that to your mother,' Colin said stiffly, turning away from the desk. 'Goodbye, Mrs McAdam.' He took Catherine's hand in his for a moment. 'Remember that you only need to telephone myself or my father if you need help. Goodbye, Ainslie.'

'Goodbye.' She opened the door for him, and her mother said sharply, strength coming into her voice, 'Ainslie, have your manners deserted you entirely? You might at least see Colin to his car, since I'm not fit to do so.'

'I expect he remembers where he left it.'

'Ainslie!' A cushion tumbled softly to the floor as Catherine, outraged, struggled to sit upright.

Colin's face had gone quite white. 'I can find my own way out, Mrs McAdam. I know this house well,' he said, looking at Ainslie, who glanced away. Still shocked by her meeting with the woman who had been part of her father's secret life, she didn't feel strong enough to deal with Colin's pain as well as her own.

'Nonsense, Colin, I hope that we've not entirely forgotten our manners in this house, despite all that's happened.'

Catherine put a hand on the rug over her legs as though about to throw it back and escort her guest to the door personally, and Ainslie said, 'Stay where you are, Mother. I'll see Colin to his car.'

3

They walked through the square hall and down the stone steps in silence, blinking as they emerged into the sunny garden. The familiar scent of petrol and sun-warmed leather upholstery filled Ainslie's nostrils as Colin opened the car door; his car was so familiar to her that she knew just how hot the leather passenger seat would feel against her calves on such a day.

He tossed the brief-case into the car then straightened and said, his hand on the door-frame, 'Something's troubling you.'

'My father's killed himself and left us with the shame of knowing that he had another wife and family hidden away,' she retorted tartly. 'Is it any wonder that I'm troubled?'

He reddened under the sting of her sarcasm. His fair colouring and his tendency to flush easily was a great burden to him, Ainslie knew. It was one of the qualities that had once endeared him to her. 'I mean that something else is troubling you. I was at the window, I saw you charging in the gate and up the drive as though you were about to do battle with some poor soul. Your eyes' – he hesitated, then swallowed and

25

said, 'Your eyes are very bright, and that means that you're angry.'

She bit her lip and scuffled the toe of one of her smart black strapped shoes in the gravel, heedless of scratch marks. 'I met her this afternoon.'

'Who?' The question was automatic, followed immediately by, 'You don't mean your father's—'

'His *woman*!' Ainslie spat the word out. 'Colin, she's quite pretty. And she's young, not much older than I am!'

'I know. I saw her outside my father's office. That's why I had to come here, instead of him. He'd arranged to meet with her.'

'You didn't tell Mother that, did you?'

'Of course not – d'you take me for an utter fool? I said he'd had to call on a very old client who needed his advice urgently.'

Ainslie gave a bark of harsh laughter. 'Scarcely a very old client. How could he? How could he take up with someone not much older than I am?'

'How did you happen to meet her?'

'I wrote to her, when I heard that she was coming to Paisley to see him. We had tea together.'

His jaw tightened. 'You shouldn't have done that, Ainslie.'

'I had to see her for myself.' She rushed on, her voice suddenly choked, tears gathering behind her eyes, 'They even had children together, Colin! A girl and a boy, just like Mother had. Only they're still very s-small—'

His hand closed over her arm. 'Come for a spin – we can talk about it, away from here.' He looked beyond her bent head to the drawing-room window, worried

26

that her mother might see them and assume that he was upsetting her daughter. But there was no movement in the narrow space between the curtains.

Ainslie drew away from him, shaking her head. 'Mother would only think that we were making up. She'd start expecting me to wear your ring again.'

'Would that be so terrible?' His voice was low, but vehement. 'Ainslie—'

'The past is past, Colin. Nothing can ever be the same again. Everything's changed!'

'I see no reason why we should change too. I love you, Ainslie, yet you've not even given me the chance to—'

'Hello, Colin,' Ainslie's young brother called cheerfully from the gate, and Colin, inwardly cursing, turned to smile at the boy as he and his closest friend, both in the neat blue blazer and striped blue and silver tie of Paisley Grammar School, came up the short gravelled drive.

'Hullo, Innes – Gordon.' He hoped that the boys would continue on round the side of the house to the back door to coax something to eat from the cook, but instead they stopped, letting their schoolbags drop to the ground, their hands and eyes hungrily reaching out to the car.

'I'm going to get one just like this when I'm old enough,' Innes announced, and Gordon gave him a scornful look.

'You're only eleven! By the time you're old enough to drive, this'll be out of date. I've got a cigarette card of the new Delage sports car. That's the sort of car I'm going to get when I'm old enough.'

'You didn't tell me! Why didn't you bring it to school?'

'And let everyone put their grubby fingers on it? I'm keeping it at home, in my album.'

Ainslie, who could have kissed the boys for arriving at just the right moment, saw that her young brother's eyes were bright with avarice.

'What would you swop for it? I'll give you my Swift open tourer card.'

'And your Alvis?'

The boys began wrangling, and Colin, with a resigned shrug, got into the car.

'You couldn't take us for a run, could you?' Innes asked at once. Colin started to shake his head, but Ainslie cut in.

'Go on, just a short spin.'

'Your mother—'

'I'll explain to Mother,' she said, and with whoops of glee the boys jostled their way, schoolbags and all, into the rear seat.

Colin shot an angry look at her and then, resigned to his fate, started the engine. Ainslie waved as the car reversed down the short drive, then went back indoors to where her mother was still lying on the sofa.

'You took your time – the two of you must have had quite a lot to talk about.'

'Innes arrived, with Gordon. Colin's taken them both out for a short drive. We didn't think you'd mind.'

Catherine shifted restlessly. 'He's such a nice young man. I can't think why you gave him back his ring.'

'I told you, Mother – this isn't the time to think of marriage.'

A sharp note came into the older woman's voice. 'Don't be so silly, girl, it's the perfect time. The Forbeses are comfortably off, and one day Colin will take over the business. A connection with them just now would put us in better standing with the town than we are at the moment, after what your father did. Anyway, I can't afford to keep you indefinitely, you know that. Not now that I've got Innes's school fees to see to.'

'You won't have to keep me. I shall find a job.'

'You're not trained for anything other than marriage!' Catherine said irritably.

'I'll find something.'

'You sound more like your Grandmama McAdam every day! She was always a difficult, stubborn woman. I can't think why your grandfather married her.'

It was a chant that Ainslie had heard over and over again. 'Won't you let me open the curtains? It's such a lovely day—'

'Leave them!'

'Very well.' Her hands dropped from the curtains. 'I'll take the tray to the kitchen, and find out how dinner's coming along.'

'Tell Cook not to make anything for me. I don't feel like eating.'

'But you must eat, Mother.' Ainslie regarded the older woman with concern. Catherine's greying fair hair was drawn back tightly, accentuating the harsh lines of her face and the droop of her mouth. Her cheekbones jutted sharply beneath her pale skin. 'You have to keep your strength up.'

'I can't think why,' Catherine said bleakly. 'There seems to be little point, now.'

As Ainslie carried the tray out of the room, she marvelled that her mother hadn't realised why she had given her engagement ring back to Colin. After what her father had done, she herself no longer had any desire to marry, to become tied to a man, dependent on him, open to the humiliation and hurt her mother was suffering. She had loved her father, almost worshipped him, despite the fact that he showed little interest in her. Now, she would never trust men again.

Although she had told the lawyer that she had to hurry back home, Isla turned away from the station when she left his office. She walked back towards the Cross, where she asked a passerby for directions to the cemetery, and was directed to one of the tram-stops. The ex-servicemen were still playing their reedy music as she passed the war memorial. Only a few coins lay in the pathetic cap.

Paisley, she realised as the tram rocked along, was built on three terraces. The High Street ran along one of them, with all the streets on Isla's left swooping downhill, and the streets on her right running uphill. She glimpsed a handsome church with a great broad sweep of steps leading from the pavement to the arched doors; it was very like a church she had seen in Paris, where she and Kenneth had spent their honeymoon.

And all the time, a small voice whispered in her ear, Ainslie and her mother and brother had been going about their lives here in Paisley, no doubt believing that Kenneth was away on business. Was that what he had told them? She tried to close her mind to the malice in the voice, not wanting her precious memories to become soured and blackened.

The conductress tapped her on the shoulder. 'This is the cemetery, hen,' she said cheerfully, pointing. 'Just across the road there.'

Inside Woodside Cemetery's stone gates Isla made enquiries at the small office, then walked up the wide driveway between the gravestones, some of them so elaborate that they were like miniature war memorials. Kenneth's grave had yet to be marked by a headstone; the earth was still raw above him but the dead funeral flowers had been cleared away and someone – Ainslie? The real Mrs McAdam? – had recently put some carnations into an urn at the foot of the grave.

Isla stood for a long time looking at the mound. She had expected to weep, had wanted to weep, to ease the pain that had been gnawing at her ever since Gilchrist Forbes, hat in hand, face sombre, had come into her comfortable home to tell her that Kenneth had left her for ever. But her eyes remained obstinately dry. The man she had loved, still loved, wasn't really here, in this quiet, green graveyard where the dead slept in peace beneath the trees. He was still with her – and yet not with her.

She turned away, and started on her journey home.

After their quiet marriage in Edinburgh, Isla and Kenneth McAdam had settled in a comfortable little house in Gourock, by the River Clyde. Isla had come to the place as a stranger, and had not made many friends. For one thing, she wasn't used to having friends and therefore didn't feel the need of them, and, for another,

Kenneth didn't care to see people when he was at home, claiming that he had enough contact with others in his office.

Isla had been happy to go along with his wishes. During her training she had lived in the nurses' quarters and spent her off-duty time with Aunt Lally, a garrulous woman who usually had her tenement flat filled with people. At times Isla had ached for peace and quiet, and at last, in Gourock, she had found it.

Although Kenneth was often away – on business, he had told Isla, and she had had no reason to doubt him – she had never felt lonely. She enjoyed gardening and sewing and reading, and when first Barbara and then Ross were born, she had had more than enough to do.

Grace, the maid, opened the door as her mistress went up the front path between the hydrangea bushes. 'How are the children?' Isla asked as soon as she got indoors.

'Miss Barbara was frettin' for ye, but she got over it. Pearl took them both out for a walk this afternoon. I'll make ye a nice cup of tea.'

'I don't want—' Isla began, but Grace had already vanished into the little kitchen at the rear of the house. Wondering why it was that the Scots felt that everything could be cured by tea, Isla hung up her coat and went upstairs, towards the sound of splashing and squealing. Barbara loved bathtime.

Before going in to see her daughter she opened the door of the small nursery. The room was quiet and smelled of baby powder and clean clothes airing before the guarded fire. The coverings were folded back invitingly in Barbara's small bed in the corner, and Ross was already in his cot, clean and contented, almost asleep. She bent over the cot, resisting the temptation to lift him into her arms and bury her face in him, and he lifted heavy lids to smile drowsily at his mother, his lips parting to reveal four pearly little teeth, then slid back into sleep.

He was his father's child, fair-skinned and red-haired and blue-eyed. And very like his grown half-sister, Isla thought, as she straightened up from the cot. Kenneth had taken such delight in his children, claiming that it was because he was so much older than the average father, and had had longer to wait.

Isla wondered if he had been as devoted to Ainslie and her brother as he was to his second family. Part of her mind told her that she should hate him for deceiving her, trapping her into a tissue of lies, then leaving her with two children who were, in the eyes of the law, illegitimate. One day, perhaps, when she could look back over the years to this time in her life, she would feel anger against him, but not now, not yet. Now, she knew only terrible loss.

The bathroom was steamy and smelled of the floral soap Barbara loved. Pearl, who had come to help Isla after Barbara's birth, was lifting the little girl out of the water.

'Mummy!'

Barbara wriggled with excitement, reaching dripping hands out to her mother, and Pearl shrieked, 'For any favour, bairn, will ye stay still. Mind yer mammy's nice clothes, ye'll get her all wet!'

'Never mind about my clothes, they'll dry.' Isla dropped to her knees and gathered the plump, towelswathed body close. Water trickling from Barbara's hair, making it look much darker than its usual fiery bronze, ran down beneath the collar of Isla's blouse, but she paid no heed to it.

'Did you bring Daddy back with you?'

'Not this time, darling. He'll be away for – for a long time,' Isla said, and over her daughter's wet head she saw Pearl's eyes fill with sympathetic tears.

'I missed you,' Barbara said into her ear. 'I cried for you.'

'You knew I'd come back, surely.' Isla squeezed her eyes shut to fight back her own tears. She didn't want her own grief to touch her children. 'You know I'd not leave you and Ross,' she said. 'Not ever, whatever happens.'

4

At the end of June Isla's home was repossessed to pay
Kenneth McAdam's debts, and as nobody had bought
the tenement building he had left her, she had no
option but to move herself and her children to its empty
ground floor flat.

She left her home without looking back. Although
the house was small, it had been the grandest she had
ever lived in. She had loved having a garden, and a
front door that opened on to a path, instead of a landing or a close. Now she was returning to tenement life.

Mr Forbes had warned her that the building she
now owned was old, but even so, she hadn't realised
just how old, or how small and cramped it would be.
Her parents and Aunt Lally had lived in modern tenements, with tiled closes and stairs that were scrubbed
down each week then carefully edged with white pipe-
clay to give them a smart appearance, but this building
was small and sad and neglected.

The outer wall, facing on to the street, looked dark
and damp, and when Isla ventured in, Ross clutched in
one arm, her free hand holding Barbara's, she saw that
the stone floor of the narrow close was cracked and

broken and uneven. The centre of each of the steps rising into the darkness of the upper floor was hollowed almost to the level of the step below, and she was thankful that she lived on the ground floor, and didn't have to climb into that unfriendly darkness above. The paintwork on the door of her new home was faded and scratched, the wood itself furrowed with deep ravines, as though some predatory beast had once clawed at it in a frenzy. The entire building smelled of damp and stale food and too many years of human habitation. A child wailed from somewhere at the back of the close, and Isla felt that the misery in the sound matched her own feelings.

The empty flat was situated at the front of the building. When Isla released Barbara's hand to search for the large clumsy key the lawyer had given her, the little girl stayed by her side instead of running off to explore as she usually did.

The door had to be pushed hard before it creaked open. Isla, peering into the gloom before her, almost lost her nerve and scurried back to the street; she had to force herself to move forward instead, the floorboards squeaking underfoot.

The door opened straight into a small empty room. Isla went towards the only window with a sense of purpose that was put on for the children's benefit, and pulled aside the dingy curtain stretched across the window. The very touch of the material, stiff and clammy, sent a shiver down her spine, and she found herself rubbing her hand against her skirt afterwards.

The window was filthy. A cool breeze from the gaps in the frame brushed her face and she breathed it in with relief. A small sink leaned against the wall below the window as though tired out, its single tap weeping slowly and sadly. Barbara, clutching a brightly coloured rubber ball that had been Kenneth's last present to her, stood in the middle of the floor and stared round at the mottled walls.

'Where's the bedroom?' she wanted to know. There were two narrow doors, one on either side of the small fireplace. Isla opened them to reveal cobwebbed shelves, only a few inches in depth. Glancing round she saw that half of the wall opposite the window was covered by wooden folding doors. The hinges complained as the doors were pulled open, and dust showered down on her. The bed was there, a high metal frame supporting a solid wooden platform. The space below it was dark and forbidding.

'There isn't a bedroom, love. This is called a wall-bed. You'll sleep here with me.'

Barbara scampered over to stand by her mother, going on tiptoe to inspect the dark space. 'It looks dirty.'

It did. Isla remembered wall-beds as clean, comfortable places, with piled pillows and soft quilts. Her parents hadn't had much money, but they had been thrifty, and her mother had always kept a clean house and had taken great care of the possessions bought, one by one, when they could be afforded. Even Aunt Lally, who was more of a 'feast and famine' person, enjoying money when she had it, and coping cheerfully with spells of enforced poverty, took a pride in her small home.

'We can clean it,' Isla said with a cheeriness she

didn't feel. 'And we'll wash the window to let more light in, and once our furniture arrives it'll look fine.'

Barbara gave her one of her direct looks. 'There isn't a bathroom.'

'The water closet's outside, but that doesn't matter. When I was a little girl we didn't have a bathroom inside. We used a tin bath, all cosy in front of the fire.'

Now that her eyes were growing accustomed to the gloom she could make out the handle of a chamber-pot that was lurking beneath the bed. 'Look, we can use this at night if we have to, then empty it into the privy in the morning.'

With difficulty, because Ross was squirming in her arms, she bent and pulled the chipped, stained delft pot out from under the bed. A little puddle of gritty dust lay on the bottom, and Isla only just managed to smother a scream when a long-legged spider scuttled into the interior from under the rim. She set the pot down hastily on the wooden bed so that Barbara, shorter than the bed, couldn't see into it. Her daughter, head tilted back, doubtfully surveyed the bulge of the pot from below, then announced, 'We're going to have to clean that, too. We'll have to clean everything,' she added, glancing over at the filthy little gas-cooker beside the sink.

'It'll all look better when the furniture arrives,' Isla said hopefully, giving in to Ross's noisy demands and putting him down to ease the strain on her aching arm. He took two steps away from her, then fell over on to cracked linoleum that was so faded that it was impossible to see what the pattern had been. He broke into an angry roar and as Isla picked him up again, Barbara put down her ball. It rolled across the floor to disappear under the cobwebby gloom beneath the sink.

'See? It was the floor that pushed him over,' she said accusingly. Then she clutched at her mother's skirt with one hand and added, her voice suddenly uncertain, 'I want Pearl.'

'Barbara, you know that Pearl couldn't come with us,' Isla coaxed, doing her best to keep a cheerful note in her voice. 'We're going to be all by ourselves now, just you and me and Ross, all cosy in our new little house.'

Barbara stuck the thumb of her free hand in her mouth. 'I still want Pearl,' she said around it, indistinctly. 'I want to go home.'

Isla, bouncing Ross in her tired arms to calm him, looking round the small, bleak single room, agreed wholeheartedly with her daughter. But she couldn't say so, or give way to the tears that were building up in her throat. For the children's sakes, she had to be strong. She had to manage, though at that moment she didn't know how she was going to do it.

The furniture arrived a few minutes later, trundled along the street from the station on a cart. The man and the boy in charge of the cart edged the pieces one by one along the narrow stone close and into Isla's new home, beneath the interested stares of the women and children lounging around in the street outside. She had let almost all of the handsome furniture that she and Kenneth had chosen between them go with the house, and kept only what she considered to be essential. But the room was so small that when the cart was finally unloaded it was crammed.

'Ye'll have tae sell most o' it, missus,' the man observed as Isla fumbled in her purse for the money to pay him. When he had left she tucked Ross, who had fallen asleep in her arms, into the only armchair that she had brought with her, then searched the jumble of boxes until she found bedding for the cot, which was wedged into a corner beside the wall-bed. The little boy tumbled into the cot bonelessly, without waking, and she drew the blanket over him, deciding that it was better to leave him undisturbed than to try to change his napkin and wash him. It was only then that she discovered that Barbara had gone.

'Barbara?' she said hopefully, peering at the clutter around her. There was no answer, nor had she expected there to be. It was difficult to miss Barbara when she was around; almost from birth she had made her presence felt, first with a cheerful babbling, then, as she grew older, with words that swiftly became sentences, sentences that became paragraphs, paragraphs that became great spiels of continuous chatter.

Isla racked her brains, and recalled that she had last seen her daughter while the last pieces of furniture were being delivered, standing nose to nose outside the close with a ragged little girl of about the same age. They had been studying each other intently, silently, as children did when they first met.

She ran out to the close-mouth, careful to leave the door on the latch so that she could get back in, and gazed up and down the street. Groups of children played in the gutter, and the women who had come to close-mouths and windows to stare openly at the furniture being carried in from the cart had gone back to their gossiping. There was no sign of the familiar bronze curly head.

Panic-stricken now, Isla ran back through the close and burst out into the back court, a gloomy and overgrown walled-in area. The section nearest the tenement was paved with broken slabs, weeds thrusting up between them, edged on one side by a row of shaky-looking dustbins and coalsheds with sagging doors. A small outhouse opposite the bins probably housed the water closet, and just beyond it stood the washhouse. Then came two broken steps leading to what looked like a very small neglected field.

'Barbara?'

'Is it yer wean yer lookin' for?' a voice said, almost at her elbow. The window beside the back door was open and a young woman sat just inside the room, her head bound up in a scarf knotted at the top. Her blouse was unbuttoned and a small bald baby was fastened to one breast, sucking steadily and noisily. A cigarette smouldered in the woman's free hand.

'My – my little girl.'

The turbanned head nodded towards the steps. 'She's behind the washhoose there with oor Greta. She's fine,' she called after Isla as she hurried up the steps and peered round the outhouse.

Barbara was sitting on a sagging, slimy, wooden bench, her favourite doll on her knee. Beside her sat the child Isla had seen earlier, a thin little waif dressed in a frayed jersey that had been made for someone larger, and almost covered the skimpy little skirt beneath it. The two children were undressing the doll, their heads close together.

'Barbara! I was worried about you!'

Barbara looked up, unrepentant. 'Greta wanted to see Bella's frilly knickers coming off. I didn't go far away,' she added defensively, after another look at her mother's anxious face. Greta, tossing a disinterested glance over her shoulder, went back to the doll.

'Ach, leave them alone, they're no' doin' any harm – for once,' the woman's voice called from the open window, and Isla hesitated, then went slowly back to the close. As she walked past the open door of the water closet, the smell from the interior hit her.

'I suppose she's as well there as under my feet,' she said, as she reached the window.

'Ye'll have enough tae dae, with just movin' in,' the other woman agreed, hauling the baby away from her breast. It came free with a loud sucking noise, eyes and milk-flecked mouth opening wide with indignation. Before it could utter a yell, the small mouth was clamped against the other breast.

'That'll keep ye quiet,' the woman said, then, to Isla, 'Ye'll be ready for a cup of tea? Come on in an' I'll make one.'

'I'll have to get back to the baby.'

'On ye go, then, an' I'll bring the tea through in a wee minute. It's no bother,' the woman said airily when Isla tried to protest.

In the tiny room that was now their home, Ross was still asleep. Isla started trying to tidy the place, but hadn't got far when knuckles rapped at the door. Seen in her entirety, her new neighbour was small and broad, with button-bright black eyes set on either side of a button nose. She walked into the room with a rolling gait that reminded Isla of a sailor accustomed to the moving deck of a ship, and looked round with open curiosity. A mug of steaming tea was clutched in each fist and the baby, asleep now, was fastened against her breast by a shawl deftly wound round her shoulders and hips, and formed into a snug little hammock.

'Ye've got some bonnie furniture.' She settled herself in the armchair and thrust a mug at Isla. 'I put condensed milk intae it, an' two spoonfuls of sugar. Ye'll be needin' yer strength.'

Isla sipped at the tea, and tried not to wrinkle her nose. The liquid was strong and very sweet, with an underlying flavour of grease, as though the mug had been washed in dirty water.

'I'm Magret,' said her first caller.

'I'm Isla Moffatt.' Isla had decided to revert to her maiden name. She had no legal right to Kenneth's name, and neither did the children.

'Isla? That's nice. I wish I'd heard it afore we named her Daisy.' Magret indicated the bald-headed baby with a dip of the chin. 'She's cried after a flower. Have ye ever seen a daisy? Bonny, isn't it?' she went on when Isla nodded. 'Oor Greta's cried after a flower tae, her real name's Magret like mine, with a Rita added on to it. We cry her Greta because he' – she jerked her chin in the general direction of her own home – 'says her real name's too much of a mouthful for a wee skelf like her.' She hesitated, then said delicately, 'I saw ye were wearing a mournin' band when ye arrived.'

'My husband died recently.' Isla spoke with difficulty round a lump that had suddenly come to her throat.

43

Magret sucked in her breath. 'Ach, that's a shame, so it is. Where did ye used tae live?'

'Ayrshire.'

'I thought ye sounded different from most of us here. More posh.' Isla, who had been raised in Glasgow and didn't have an Ayrshire accent, said nothing. 'Don't fret, hen, ye'll be all right here. The folks is decent enough – most of them. He –' her chin gave another spasmodic jerk towards the back of the building – 'works at the mills. How'll ye keep yersel' and the bairns? Widows don't get much – the folk that pay out the money seem tae think women an' bairns can live on air,' she added, with a sniff.

'I'll need to think of something.' Isla decided to say nothing about the few pieces of jewellery she possessed, some inherited from her mother, some given to her by Kenneth. She planned to sell them to raise money for food for herself and the children. She wasn't entitled to any widow's pension because strictly speaking she had never been married in the first place. The responsibility for seeing that her children survived rested solely on her own shoulders.

'Ye could start by pawnin' some o' this,' Magret suggested, looking round the room. 'There's a pawn-shop not far from here, in Canal Street. He's a fair man tae deal with, no' like some.' She reached out a rough red hand and stroked a handsome chest of drawers. 'That's bonny, but it's out o' place here. The more furniture ye've got, the more corners for the weans tae hurt themselves on. Better tae ask at the grocer's shop for orange boxes – they're grand for keepin' stuff in. Anyway' – she lowered her voice and narrowed her

44

eyes – 'if the rent man sees this lot on top of the posh way ye talk, he'll think ye're a toff and mebbe put up yer rent. Ye'd not want that. The rent's high enough for a flea-pit like this.'

Isla, recalling that she herself was the landlady, felt a guilty pang. Her face warmed and she bent it over her tea. She had discovered that once she got used to the taste, the hot sweet liquid was comforting.

Magret chattered on, thankfully more interested in telling Isla about the other tenants than in asking questions. Isla learned that old Granny Thomson lived alone 'through the wall', and that the McNabs occupied the flat directly across the close from hers.

'He's younger than she is. Her husband drank himself tae death last year an' left her tae run their wee baker's shop, three doors down,' Magret confided, adding, 'they make good pies and she's a clean woman, and fair wi' the prices. Her new man started as the message boy in the shop, and she wed him just months after her man died. He was a bad-tempered pig, so he was. At least she never carries bruises now. There's three lots live up the stair, and it'll be your turn tae use the clothes-lines on Wednesday mornings. Don't hang anythin' out there on a Tuesday or Mrs Leach'll have the nose off ye. She's awful snappy, thinks she's above the rest of us.' She gave a sudden bellow of laughter, and Ross jumped and muttered in his sleep, though the baby on Magret's breast didn't stir.

'She does live above us, come tae think of it! I meant that she's awful snooty, but she's got more bark than bite. Here, I'd better be going, or he'll be in looking for his dinner, and me with the tatties not even peeled.'

She drained her mug, and, after a struggle, levered herself and her baby out of the chair, easing her way round the table to peep at Ross, still sound asleep. 'My, look at that head of hair! Ye could warm yer hands at it!'

When she had gone, Isla studied the furniture, knowing that Magret was right – most of it would have to go. She decided to call on the pawnbroker in the morning.

Barbara arrived, looking more cheerful now that she had found a friend, and announced that she was hungry. After a search, Isla found the food that she had carefully packed that morning in Gourock. She filled the kettle, trying in vain to turn the tap off hard enough to stop its persistent dripping, and lit the tiny gas cooker, making a mental note to start scrubbing the layers of grease off it first thing in the morning. It looked as though the previous tenant had never even attempted to clean it.

Ross was irritable when she roused him, and after feeding him and washing him sketchily, she put him back into his cot then cut the string that held the mattress firmly in a roll, and found pillows and blankets. She attacked the wall-bed vigorously with a stiff-bristled handbrush, raising clouds of dust, then made it up, and she and Barbara climbed in. It was still early, but Isla was bone-weary, and there was no reason to stay up.

'It's cosy here, isn't it?' she said when the two of them were snuggled together in the bed.

'You won't close the doors and leave us in the dark, will you?' Barbara asked anxiously.

'Of course not.' A chill crept up Isla's spine at the very thought. Heaven alone knew what might be lurking in the shadows below. She tried not to let her mind dwell on it.

Exhausted though they both were, they were kept awake by footsteps and voices and laughter as people went up and down the street outside. In the building itself, doors banged, people scuffed their way along the close, and feet tramped back and forth above their heads. Something scuttled behind the skirting board, and Barbara clutched at her mother fearfully.

'What's that?'

'Nothing, pet, nothing at all,' Isla comforted her, while the skin at the back of her neck crawled.

The two of them waited, holding their breaths, but the sound wasn't repeated. Gradually, Barbara's fingers eased their tight grip on Isla's arm.

'I like Greta,' she said, her voice drowsy. 'She's going to teach me to play peevers.' Then, mercifully, she fell asleep.

Isla, too, slept, and dreamed of Kenneth; of walking with him along the shore at Gourock, sitting by the fire with him, lying in his arms in their marriage bed. A drunken voice raised in song startled her awake during the night, to darkness, Barbara's knees digging painfully into her side, and the realisation that Kenneth was gone for ever.

She turned over and wept her loneliness into her pillow, until it and her face and her hair were all soaked with tears.

5

'I think it was most unwise of you to move to Paisley, Mrs – er—' Gilchrist Forbes paused uncomfortably.

'I'm calling myself Mrs Moffatt now. I have a right to the name, I was born to it,' Isla assured him tartly. 'And I wouldn't dream of raising my children in that tenement if I'd any other option, I can assure you of that.' She was tired after a night's broken sleep, depressed at the prospect of having to live in the old tenement. The lawyer's cool disapproval was more than she could take.

'Did my – did Kenneth know what the place was like? Did he know the conditions his tenants have to live in?'

The man looked offended. 'George Street is in an old part of the town, and the tenements there have been standing for some time. I understand that they now enjoy gas lighting and running water, and of course the rents are very low, to compensate for the lack of other amenities.'

'I'd hardly call life there enjoyable, even with gas lighting and water that sometimes won't stop running,' Isla told him, tightening her grip on Ross, who was struggling to get down from her lap. 'Barbara, don't touch!'

'I was only looking,' Barbara said at once from the desk, folding her hands behind her back. 'Not touching.'

There had been nobody for Isla to leave the children with. Now, realising the impossibility of carrying on a conversation with the lawyer while trying to cope with them both, she gave in and got to her feet, putting the little boy down, but keeping a tight hold of his hand. 'I only came to let you know that I was installed, and to make arrangements about the rent.'

'It's collected every Friday evening. I can arrange to have it delivered to you on Monday mornings.'

'I think it would be best for me to call here for it. And as I don't want anyone to know that I'm the land-lady, I suggest that your collector knows me only as an ordinary tenant, and collects rent from me every week as well as from the others. You can leave the money in the outer office on Monday mornings, then I won't have to trouble you. Good day, Mr Forbes.'

'My dear—' Gilchrist Forbes reached the door before her, almost falling over Barbara in the process. Although it was clear to Isla that her presence in his office – in Paisley, come to that – made the man feel most uncomfortable, he nevertheless seemed to be genuinely concerned about her well-being. 'It's a difficult business, collecting rents from that type of building. Many of the tenants tend to be in arrears, and I can't guarantee a fixed sum every week. How will you manage?'

'I shall have to do the best I can – like my fellow ten-ants,' Isla told him, and he bit his lip. Barbara, impatient to be out in the street again, scurried out of the door as soon as he opened it, and ran across the hall to the outer door. As she reached up for the handle, the door opened almost in her face, and she recoiled with a squeak of surprise, tripping over the edge of the carpet and landing, with a thud, on the floor.

The newcomer, the fair-haired young man Isla had seen on her first visit to the office, dropped to his knees beside her.

'Are you all right?'

'I'm fine.' Barbara sat up and beamed at him. 'I bounced like a ball.'

He laughed, and took her hands in his. 'Let's see if you can bounce back up again, then. Up you come – one, two th—' His voice trailed away as the little girl got to her feet and he looked beyond her to see Isla.

'This is my son, Colin. Colin, this is Mrs . . .'

Gilchrist Forbes hesitated, and it was left to Isla to say shortly, 'Mrs Moffatt. I've decided to return to my own name.'

The laughter had gone from Colin Forbes' face, and as he let go of Barbara's hands Isla was fixed, once again, by an unfriendly look. She returned it as their hands touched briefly, then fell apart.

'I like the one that knocked me down,' Barbara said as they went down the stairs to the street, 'but I don't like the old man, 'cos he doesn't like us, much, does he?' Then as they emerged on to Paisley Cross again, she asked hopefully, 'Can we go back now? Greta's waiting to teach me how to play peevers.'

Before returning to George Street they called in at the pawnbroker's in Canal Street, where Isla arranged for someone to come and have a look at her furniture. She then spent most of the money she had left, buying food and cleaning materials, and when they got back to the tenement she settled Ross in his cot with his toys while Barbara scampered out to play. Isla rolled her sleeves up, put on an apron, tied her hair up in a scarf, and tackled the gas stove.

The pawnbroker arrived two hours later and arranged to take most of the furniture off her hands for what seemed to be a very small amount of money. Half an hour after that, two boys arrived with a handcart and almost all the furniture left from the Gourock house was taken away.

The women standing round the entrances to the closes watched, their sharp eyes appraising every item and judging its value, probably to the penny, Isla thought. She smiled nervously at one or two of them, and received blank stares in return. Someone made a remark about snobby folks who liked to show off their possessions, and there was a general snigger of agreement.

'Pay no heed, missus,' the man with the cart muttered. 'Some folks is just jealous of everyone else.'

Isla bit her lip, and tried to ignore the stares.

'Folk never take kindly tae new neighbours,' Magret told her when she called in, Daisy tied to her by the shawl, and a cigarette – the same cigarette as yesterday, for all Isla knew – in her free hand. 'They'll come round in their own good time. Just don't be snobby with them when they dae talk tae ye. Ye'll need tae try tae redeem yer furniture when the ticket falls due, then just leave it in and take out another ticket. That way it stays yours. That's what we do with a bonny clock his auntie gave us when we got married.'

By now Isla had realised that the mysterious 'he'

51

Magret kept referring to was her husband. Magret sighed, then said wistfully, 'I'd like fine to see that clock on our mantelshelf just one time, but it's never been there, for we can never afford tae bring it out. The money's always needed for somethin' else.'

· Daisy was less flower-like than any baby Isla had ever seen. Beneath her bald little pate she studied the room with close-set black eyes, clearly inherited, along with the snub nose, from her mother.

Magret puffed at her cigarette and looked on while Isla scraped at the stove with a broken knife she had found lying near the dustbins in the back court. Ribbons of solid grease peeled off and fell on to the newspaper she had spread out on the floor.

'I don't know why ye're botherin', hen. It'll only get dirty again. That's what I hate about housework – it always has tae be done again.'

Daisy whimpered, and Magret settled herself in the armchair and opened her blouse, chattering on over the baby's head about the time when she had worked in Coats' mill, not far from George Street.

'It was nice, the way we all worked taegether. That's where I met him. It was noisy, right enough, and the fluff went for some of the women's lungs, but everyone was pally and we all had a good laugh. I'll mebbe get back there some day, when Daisy's older.'

'You might have another baby by then,' Isla ventured, and Magret gave a husky laugh.

'No' me, hen, not after the time I had with these two. I'd tae stay in the Infirmary for a week when I was carrying Daisy, and I near lost her the way I lost the two that came after our Greta. It's the rickets, ye see.

The nurse said the rickets was making it awful difficult for me tae carry weans.'

She hauled up her skirt unselfconsciously to reveal curved, vein-clustered legs, and Isla realised that the young woman's rolling walk and solid stocky body were due to the cruel disease, brought on by malnutrition, that distorted growing young bones.

'They said there'd be no more weans for me,' Magret explained, pushing her skirt down again.

'I'm sorry.'

'Ach, it suits us fine, for weans cost money and we've scarce got enough for the two we have already. He doesnae get a big pay. See my sister Agnes? Six weans she's got – and there'll be more afore she gets too old for it. She's never done carrying an' birthing weans, and worryin' about where their next meal's comin' from.' Magret shook her head and took another puff at her cigarette. 'I'd not want tae be her, poor soul. Anyway, I'd not want tae go back into that Infirmary – there was a terrible smell stingin' at my nose all the time from all that disinfectant they used. Cleaning like dafties day and night, so they were!'

'How could you agree to such a thing?'

It had been a long day. At the end of days like this, Gilchrist Forbes wondered if the time had come to hand over the business to his son and retire to the soothing pleasures of his books and his garden.

'I didn't agree to it,' he said wearily. 'There was no question of that. The woman owns the building and she has a right to live there if she wishes.'

Colin glared at his father across the over-furnished

drawing-room. 'But here in Paisley – scarcely more than a mile from the McAdams' home! She could have chosen to live anywhere in Scotland – why settle so close to Ainslie and her mother?'

'It takes money to buy or rent a place to live, and Kenneth McAdam left nothing but debts.'

'Surely she has money of her own – or family she can turn to?'

'Apparently not.' Gilchrist filled his glass almost to the brim, then tilted the decanter enquiringly. When Colin shook his head, his father set down the decanter and sipped at his own whisky.

'I find it hard to believe that she's entirely alone in the world.' The younger man's normally cheerful face was set in hard lines, his eyes stormy.

'There's an aunt in Edinburgh—'

'Well, there you are, then!'

'But Mrs – Mrs Moffatt tells me that she has no wish to throw herself and her children on this woman's mercy.'

Colin snorted. 'No doubt she'll have no hesitation in throwing herself on Mrs McAdam's mercy.'

'She claims that she has no intention of doing so.'

'And you believe her?'

Gilchrist took another swallow of whisky and tried to keep his own temper under control. 'Colin, I don't know what she has in mind. Nor do I have the power to order her out of her own property.'

'You must reason with her, Father! Point out that it's wrong for her to—' Colin stopped abruptly as his mother came into the room.

'What's wrong for who?' Phemie Forbes asked at once. She loved gossip and had ears as sharp as a bat's, particularly when it came to things she wasn't supposed to hear.

'Nobody, my dear,' Gilchrist started to say, but Colin blurted out, 'We were talking about Kenneth McAdam's . . .' Under his father's suddenly hard gaze he paused, biting back the words he had been about to utter, then said sullenly 'Kenneth McAdam's other woman.'

Phemie's round, good-natured face wrinkled with concern. 'Poor Catherine, all those years as a good wife to the man, and now this terrible shock on top of his death. It's changed her beyond recognition, Gilchrist. She's refusing to put a foot over her own doorstep, convinced that the whole town's whispering and pointing.' She sat down in her usual armchair by the fire and reached for her embroidery. 'I keep telling her that folk forget quickly, but she'll not listen to me.'

'I'm wondering if they really will forget, with the woman moving to Paisley,' Colin said.

'Moving to—' Phemie, about to plunge her needle into the heart of a half-stitched rosebud, plunged it into her own finger instead, and gave a choked shriek of pain. 'Look what you've made me do!'

She held her hand well away from the material in the embroidery ring and her husband hurriedly set down his glass and dropped to his knees beside her, whipping a crisp white handkerchief from his breast pocket to mop the bead of blood from her finger.

'Gilchrist, you'll ruin your handkerchief!' Phemie pulled her hand back and sucked at the injured finger. Round it she said, 'In Paisley? In this town?'

'In a tenement building in George Street that Mr McAdam left to her,' Colin confirmed.

'But surely the property should pass to Catherine?'

Gilchrist Forbes' knees cracked like winter twigs as he straightened up. 'Kenneth signed it over to her legally some time before his death. I can't force her to give it up, or to move away from the town.'

'But what'll happen if poor Catherine gets to hear of it?'

'The young woman's calling herself by her own name – Moffatt. I don't think she intends to make life difficult for Catherine.'

'I'd not be so sure about that,' Colin put in, and his father glared at him.

'She has two children to support, Phemie. It's my belief that she merely wants a roof over their heads until such time as she can make other plans.'

'There are children?'

'A boy and a girl.'

Tears came into Phemie's eyes. She loved children, and had always mourned the fact that she herself had had only one. She had been looking forward to Colin's marriage to Ainslie McAdam, and the hope of having many grandchildren in the future. 'The poor wee souls, what a start to have in life!'

'She seems to be a caring mother, I'm sure she'll do her best for them.' Gilchrist Forbes stared down at his handkerchief, then, guiltily, started refolding it to hide the bloody stain.

'I think you're being altogether too kindly in your attitude, Father,' Colin told him shortly. 'The woman may well be more ruthless than you think. Ainslie's very concerned about it all.'

'If Catherine hears that this woman and her children

are here, in Paisley, it may well be the final straw,' his mother agreed. 'She's in quite a state of depression as it is over Ainslie's latest news.'

'What news?' Colin came across the room towards his mother, bumping into an occasional table in his haste. 'What about Ainslie?'

'Did you not know? She's found work for herself.'

'Where? What's she doing?'

'Let me see that handkerchief, Gilchrist.' Phemie held out a hand and her husband reluctantly relinquished the folded square. She shook it out and tutted. 'Just as I thought – you've managed to get blood on it. It must be soaked in salt and cold water at once.'

'Mother, what sort of work has Ainslie found?' Colin persisted.

'She's taken on a position at Blayne's the auctioneers in MacDowall Street. Catherine's most upset about it, but Ainslie's not trained for anything, after all, and with Innes's school fees to find, not to mention the house to run, there's little Catherine can do about it. You know Ainslie, she can be very deter— Colin, where are you going?'

'Out.' Her son threw the word over his shoulder.

'Colin,' Phemie began, but he had already gone. She sighed, crumpling the handkerchief in her hand. 'Poor boy, he's still very upset about Ainslie returning his ring.'

Gilchrist Forbes picked up his glass of whisky. 'No point in fretting about it, my dear. They must work out their own problems, as we had to do at their age.'

'We didn't have such bad problems, though, Gil.' Phemie's voice was wretched. 'Who'd have thought of a

57

level-headed man like Kenneth McAdam killing himself, then turning out to be a bigamist?'

Her husband shook his head. 'I wish he'd come to me when his business started going wrong. I would have done all I could to help. It should never have come to this.'

'What's this other woman like, Gil?'

The sound of his son's car starting up took Forbes to the window. He watched the vehicle roaring out of the gate, scattering gravel to left and right. 'Young, much younger than Kenneth. She has dignity, I'll give her that. I don't think she's out to cause more trouble for Catherine. I can't understand why he did it – took her through a marriage ceremony, I mean. I'd never dream of doing such a thing.'

Phemie, setting aside the handkerchief and picking up her embroidery, smiled fondly at him. 'I don't think you would, my dear. But this whole business has just proved that we never know what's going on behind other people's walls, hasn't it?'

He swung round from the window. 'Are you telling me that the McAdams weren't happy in their marriage?'

Phemie sighed. 'Even though she's a friend I'll admit that I've always sensed a coldness in Catherine. I think she put appearance before anything else. Kenneth, now – I'm not sure that he was strong enough for her. From what Catherine's said about her father-in-law, I get the impression that he was a much stronger man than poor Kenneth. She seemed to admire him greatly. What was he like, Gil? I never knew him well – he died not long after I became friendly with Catherine.'

'I remember him as being very able, in every way. Kenneth worshipped him.'

'Perhaps,' said Phemie shrewdly, 'he lived in his father's shadow.'

'Surely not.' Then, tiring of the turn the conversation was taking, Gilchrist Forbes said, 'As to Ainslie, I think she may well rue the day she decided to earn her own living. She could come running back to Colin yet.'

'I'd not be too sure of that, she's a very determined girl. Stubborn, Catherine says, like her grandmother.'

'In that case,' her husband returned to his chair and reached for the evening newspaper, 'we can only hope he gets over her quickly, and finds someone more suitable.'

6

Within two weeks Isla let her few remaining pieces of furniture go to the pawnshop, realising that the room was too small for them. She bought an old fireside chair from the pawnbroker, scrubbing it well before covering its slippery, worn seat and back with remnant material bought cheaply from a draper's shop. She bought more cloth to make curtains for the window, and another curtain to stretch on string across the storage space below the bed. She crawled reluctantly into the space first, poking a long-handled brush ahead gingerly, and found a dirty tin hip-bath which served herself and the children very well, once it was scrubbed out with disinfectant.

An orange box obtained from the local greengrocer made a serviceable cupboard for their few dishes, turned on its side and with a scrap of bright material hung on a string along the top to curtain it off. Searching the waste-ground at the back of the building, she found two bricks of the same size and used a piece of wood to scrape off the slimy creatures adhering beneath them, holding the bricks at arm's length as she worked, her face twisted with disgust. When she was satisfied that the bricks were free of pests, she scrubbed them with Jeyes Fluid and sat the orange-box on top of them to keep it clear of the floor.

Her own clothes and the children's clothes were hung from nails hammered into the walls, and another curtain on a string beneath the sink closed off an area for the cleaning utensils. She scrubbed the shallow wall-cupboards and lined their shelves with an unwanted roll of wall-paper bought for two pence from a paint-shop, and after finding a spider in the flour crock, made sure that all the food kept in the cupboards was well covered.

The rent money, which she collected every Monday morning from Mr Forbes' front office, was spasmodic, and barely enough, at times, to see her through the week and pay her own rent on a Friday evening, but as soon as she could, she bought paint to brighten up the warped woodwork round the window. Gradually the room began to look cleaner and brighter.

It was impossible to get rid of the smell of sweat and urine and stale cooking that had soaked into the fabric of the entire tenement, but Isla did her best, blocking up mouse-holes in the skirting and swabbing Jeyes Fluid into the cracks in the floorboards to deter the cockroaches that emerged at night and sometimes were to be found during the day, wandering across the hearth. Once, she and Barbara collapsed shrieking into each other's arms after a particularly large cockroach marched across the table before their horrified eyes during a meal.

She worked from morning to night on the small room, falling into bed bone-weary after each day's efforts. The work helped to ease her deep sense of loss;

Kenneth was never far from her mind and she cried herself to sleep most nights, longing for the warmth of his arms, and the security that his love and strength had given her. She talked about him to the children, determined that they wouldn't be allowed to forget him. But there was nobody she herself could talk to about him, and about what he had meant, and still meant, to her. So she worked instead, driving herself on.

'This place smells like the Infirmary,' Magret complained one day, fanning the air before her. Isla, on her knees in a corner of the room, brushing disinfectant into a particularly bad crack, straightened her aching back and rubbed a hand across her forehead.

'If I don't get rid of those insects I'll go mad.'

'Ach, ye'll never get rid of them,' Magret told her. 'They was here before us, and they'll be here long after we've gone. 'Sides, they don't do any harm.'

That same evening, noticing Barbara scratching furiously, fingers buried in her thick bronze hair, Isla investigated, and recoiled in horror as she saw tiny lice scurrying over her daughter's scalp, weaving through the hair like natives bustling through a jungle. She snatched Ross up from the floor, where he was placidly playing with a toy motor car, and saw that his scalp, too, was alive with vermin.

'What's the matter?' Barbara asked apprehensively, eyeing her mother's face.

'N-nothing.' Isla put Ross down and filled the kettle at the sink with shaking hands. 'I think it's time you both got your hair washed, that's all.'

'You washed it yesterday.'

'I know that.' Isla suddenly realised to her horror that

she had absent-mindedly raised her hand to scratch her own head, and snatched it back. She could have burst into tears. She had done her best to make sure that the children were clean, but now it seemed that she was fighting a losing battle. It would have done no good to insist that they stayed away from the other children. Thanks to Greta, Barbara had settled into her new life and had been accepted by the other children in spite of the fact that she 'talked posh' and wore better clothes than they did. She had learned to play peevers and spent most of her day hopping and skipping and jumping over chalked squares and symbols on the pavement.

A natural mimic, she had fallen quickly into her new friends' speech patterns, and although Isla did her best to make sure that she spoke properly in the house, she knew that Barbara had to be free to talk to the other children in their own language. The little girl had, fortunately, adjusted to the sudden changes in her life, and it would be cruel to isolate her from the rest of the youngsters in the street.

The children yelled their protests when she scrubbed hard at their heads that night. The next day she went out and bought a fine-toothed comb and a large cake of coal tar soap, which added its own pungent aroma to the strong smell of disinfectant.

Magret sniffed at the air on her next visit, and said knowledgeably, 'Nits?'

Isla stared at her in horror. 'How did you know?'

'It's the smell of the soap. No need tae look so worried, hen – all the kids has got nits round here. Some worse than others – have ye not seen the poor wee souls with the shaved heads? It doesnae mean ye're

63

dirty,' she hurried to assure her stricken friend. 'I've heard that nits can be found in grand houses tae.'

As the weeks went by, Isla got to know the other people in the building – old Granny Thomson, a tiny wizened creature, bent and twisted with arthritis, who crept in and out of her own door like a mouse and never spoke to anyone; Lena McNab, a striking-looking woman who ran the tiny baker's shop a short distance along the road, and her husband and former messenger-boy Peter, thin and clearly younger than Lena, peering at life through a pair of thick wire-framed spectacles. Lena had a warm heart, and sometimes gave her neighbours pastries and loaves that had become too stale to sell. Broken up and soaked in a mixture of milk and water, then covered with a scattering of sugar, the stale bread and pastries made a nourishing meal for the children.

Two of the flats upstairs were tenanted by the Kellys, a shy young couple, and Mrs Brown and her son, recently out of school and apprenticed to a joiner's shop. There was no sign of Mr Brown – Magret said that he had run away with 'the woman from the Co-op'. The third flat, a single room sandwiched between the others, which both had two rooms, was the residence of the formidable Mrs Leach, a gaunt widow who wore her grey hair twisted into a small tight bun at the back of her head, and made it her business to see that the other inhabitants behaved themselves.

The first time Isla hung out clothes to dry Mrs Leach came forging her way up the steps from the close to inspect them.

'Ye're not used tae hangin' out a washin', are ye?' she said with a disparaging sniff.

'I know fine how to do it,' Isla snapped back, aware that it would be fatal to give in to a bully.

To her astonishment, Mrs Leach reached up, unpinned a garment from the line, and flipped it about. 'Ye shouldnae hang yer bairn's trousers from the waist like that,' she said, her hands re-pinning the small garment so rapidly that they were blurred. 'Ye hang them from the legs, then the waistband can blow in the wind an' get dry. Here, I'll give ye a hand.'

She delved into the basket and proceeded to hang the clothes on the line, driving the wooden pegs into place so strongly that Isla expected them to snap in two.

'Ye've got some bonny things,' the woman commented as she worked. 'It's nice tae see things like that hangin' on our lines.' She wiped her hands on her wrap-around pinny and bent to Ross, who was watching, wide-eyed, clutching at his mother's skirt.

'How old is he?'

'Fourteen months.'

'He's a bonny wean.' Mrs Leach bared her yellowed teeth in a smile at Ross, who retreated further into Isla's skirt, pushing a thumb into his mouth.

'An' ye don't want him doin' that,' Mrs Leach snapped, straightening. 'His teeth'll grow in crooked.'

When Isla told Magret about the encounter her friend nodded sagely. 'If she helped ye tae hang yer washing, it means that she approves o' ye,' she announced.

It was a surprise to find that young Mrs Kelly was Mrs Leach's only child.

'That's why the wee soul never opens her mouth – she's never had the chance,' Magret said. 'They came down in the world after Mr Leach was killed in an accident at his work, and they'd nowhere else tae go but here. The lassie worked in an office, and when she insisted on gettin' married tae one of the lads she worked with, no matter what her mother had to say aboot it, Mrs Leach got them the house through the wall from her, so's she could keep an eye on them.'

She drew her breath in sharply through pursed lips and shook her head. 'Poor souls – the old woman gave them a right hard time when he lost his job last year – not that it was his fault that the place where he worked closed down. Ye'd have thought he'd done it just tae spite her, the way she went on. I think that's why they've no' got any weans yet – he must be scared tae touch the lassie, with her mother only the thickness of a wall away from their bed. If ever I treat my lassies the way she treats hers, I hope they've got the sense tae push me under a tram.'

Gradually, Isla began to settle into her new home. She managed to clear the lice from the children's heads and also managed, by dint of careful budgeting, to keep the three of them nourished and still have enough left over to pay the rent-collector when he called every Friday. He was a tall, sour-faced man who spread the coins out over his palm and counted every one carefully before stowing them away in his leather pouch and writing the date and the amount down in a large book, licking his pencil before he began. He had the look of a man who wouldn't take kindly to people being behind with the rent.

Magret had confirmed Isla's instincts from the beginning. 'Ye don't want tae get intae his bad books, hen.

He'd no' care about you being on yer lone with the weans tae look after – he'd take yer last penny out of yer hand and think nothin' of it.'

Isla grew to hate her Monday morning trip to Gilchrist Forbes' office to collect the rent-money, because she was taking money from people she knew, people who had little enough to spare and found it difficult at times to raise the rent. But she had no option, for she had her own children to care for. The little she made by keeping her furniture in pawn helped, but not much, and as the summer crept along she had to pawn first one piece of jewellery, then another, to make ends meet.

A previous tenant had left a rusty old garden fork by the bins. Seeing it lying there, Isla thought of saving money by growing vegetables. She already knew that a patch of the weedy stretch of ground at the back of the tenement officially belonged to the single room she and the children now lived in; she marked it off carefully with rows of stones so that nobody, particularly Mrs Leach, could accuse her of taking over anyone else's weeds, and carefully went over it, picking up stones and rubbish, which she piled neatly in one corner before fetching the fork.

The ground hadn't been dug for years, and it was as hard as the mysterious bits of iron she kept finding in it. Stopping to catch her breath, she saw that several people were at their windows, watching her, and even the dingy net curtain at Granny Thomson's window was twitching. Soon there was a row of children peering over the wall at her.

'Heh, missus,' one of them shouted. 'Are ye buryin' some'dy?'

'I'm going to grow things,' she told him, and the children howled with laughter, as though she had said something very funny.

After struggling for an entire afternoon Isla had made very little impact on the ground. Nevertheless, she went back to it again and again whenever time and weather permitted. Magret watched, fascinated, Daisy straddled across her hip.

'Ye'll never dae it.'

'I'm doing it now.' Isla proudly indicated a square foot of exposed earth. Magret peered at it, and sniffed.

'Even if ye dae manage tae get somethin' planted, it'll vanish as soon as it appears,' she argued, nodding towards the next tenement, where a large, rowdy father-less family was known to survive mainly on the proceeds of the children's thefts. 'That lot'd steal a dead cat out of a gutter, so they would.'

'I'd like to see them try,' Isla said grimly, plunging the fork into the ground and leaning her weight on it. 'I've got my children to feed, and nobody's going to stop me!'

At the beginning of August Barbara celebrated her fifth birthday. When she and Kenneth had talked about the forthcoming event, not long before his death, Isla had suggested buying a doll's house for their daughter.

'I used to have one when I was a little girl – a lovely house, with stairs to the bedrooms and a cook in the kitchen,' she recalled, the pleasure of playing with the dolls' house flooding back to her. 'I wish I'd been able to keep it, for my own little girl.'

Kenneth had put his arm about her. 'She shall have a new one all to herself,' he promised. 'We'll choose it between us, and you can have the enjoyment of decorating and furnishing it for her.'

Remembering, Isla blinked back tears and looked round the shabby home she now shared with her children.

There was no room for a fine doll's house here, nor the money to buy one. She must find some other gift for Barbara, something she could make herself, for she couldn't afford to buy presents.

She was working on her gift a week before Barbara's birthday when someone rapped on the door. Isla, assuming that it was Magret, called out, 'The door's on the latch,' then jumped to her feet, showering clothespegs and scraps of cloth on to the floor, as Ainslie McAdam walked in.

'What are you doing here?'

Ainslie's mouth tightened as she looked at the mourning band on Isla's arm, then her gaze travelled on around the room. She was clearly shocked by what she saw. 'So it's true – you are living here!'

'I am – not that it's any business of yours.' Isla was stung by the look on the other girl's face as she took in the shabby room. At their last meeting she had felt herself to be in the wrong, ignorant though she had been of Kenneth's other family. This time, though, she wasn't going to allow Ainslie McAdam to dominate her. 'Who told you we were here?'

'Colin Forbes.'

'I might have known. He'd no business to tell you anything about me.' Isla stooped to gather up the clothes-pegs and the scraps of material she had been working on.

'It is my business, if you're living in Paisley. I told you already that—'

Isla straightened up. Ainslie was the same height as herself and she met the girl's blue eyes unblinkingly. 'This was the only place we could come to. I had to get out of the house I was in, and I've no money of my own. Ken— your father,' she amended, seeing the way the other girl winced at her familiar use of his first name, 'left me this building. We were lucky one of the rooms was lying empty.'

Ainslie's curl of the lip intimated that nobody living in such a place could consider themselves to be lucky. 'You could have sold it and used the money to find somewhere further away,' she said aloud.

'And starved my children under some hedge while we waited to find out if anyone wanted it?' Isla's voice was scathing. 'It's for sale now, but not a soul's made an offer.' She saw that her hands were shaking, and busied them in smoothing out the pieces of cloth she had laid on the table.

Ainslie moved forward, and her foot caught against something. She bent and picked it up, her brows wrinkling as she studied the clothes-peg in her hand. A piece of white rag had been tied round the knob at the top of the peg and a face stitched on to the cloth. Round blue eyes stared back at her, and there was the suggestion of a neat nose and a smiling rosebud of a mouth.

Isla, reddening, almost snatched the peg from Ainslie's hand. 'Don't worry,' she said dryly, 'I'm not a witch, making effigies of you and your mother. It's a doll for my daughter's birthday.'

'Is that the red-haired child I saw playing in the str—' Ainslie flinched as Ross, disturbed from his sleep, shifted and whimpered from his cot in a shadowy corner of the room. Isla went to soothe him, then, when the whimpering rose to a wail, she lifted him from the cot.

'You haven't told me yet why you've called,' she said as she turned. A shaft of light from the window turned the baby's sweat-damp curls to flame as she carried him over to the chair by the fire.

'You know fine why I called. You'll have to find somewhere else to live!' Ainslie's voice was harsh and loud, and Ross, still half asleep, clutched at his mother and cringed away from this angry stranger, pushing his hot face into Isla's neck. The smell of ammonia from his wet napkin soured the air.

'It's all right, love, Mummy's got you safe.' Isla soothed him, then over his head she asked Ainslie McAdam, 'Where d'you suggest we go?'

'Anywhere but Paisley! I'll not have you upsetting my mother . . .'

'I've already told you that I've no intention of going anywhere near your mother.'

'But she might hear about you. Someone might tell her.'

'I doubt if we move in the same social circles,' Isla pointed out, and the younger girl flushed at the contempt in her voice.

'I'm working now – I don't earn much but I could probably give you some money in a few weeks' time if you—'

'Miss McAdam, you may not think much of my

home, but at least it's mine and I'm not beholden to anyone. I wouldn't take a penny of your money, not even if you were the wealthiest woman in the country and I was starving.'

'You took my father's money. You had his children.'

If she hadn't been holding Ross, Isla would have launched herself at the girl and known the satisfaction of bundling her out of the room by force. Instead, she said, her voice shaking, 'At the time, I thought I had the right, as his legal wife. Now, will you please get out of my house?'

Ainslie's fists clenched by her sides. 'Don't you care about how terrible it's been for us, for my mother, with the whole town talking about what my father did? Isn't that bad enough, without having his – his—' she choked, then rushed on, 'you living right here in Paisley!'

Her selfishness infuriated Isla. 'D'you never give a thought to the suffering he must have gone through, to be driven to do what he did?'

'Why should I? He made sure that he was well out of it, well away from the whispering and the glances!' the girl said bitterly.

'It seems to me that it must take a great deal of misery to cause any human being to put an end to his life. As to my presence here in Paisley' – Isla's voice was as sharp and as cold as an icicle as she got to her feet, holding Ross close, and swept past Ainslie to the door – 'I'm here only because my bairns and I have nowhere else to go. I'm using my own name, not your father's. I've said nothing to anyone about my past life, and I don't intend to.' She lifted the latch and the door swung creakily open. 'Now – I'd be grateful if you would just go away and let me and my children be.'

Ainslie hesitated, then walked past her and into the close. Isla closed the door at once, then waited, clutching Ross, her ears straining for the sound of the young woman walking out of the close. Eventually it came, the tap of well-shod feet moving out into the street and away.

Isla went slowly back to the fireside chair, Ross weighing heavily in her arms, and collapsed into it. The baby, frightened by something he couldn't understand, clutched at her and burst into tears.

'It's all right, pet,' Isla tried to reassure him. Then her own tears came, and the two of them wept together.

7

Ainslie McAdam was in turmoil as she left the old tenement. She had gone there with the intention of talking things out once and for all with the woman who had brought such shame down on her family, making it clear to Isla how impossible it was for her to stay in Paisley.

But as she stepped out on to the pavement she felt that she had failed miserably, and had only succeeded in making herself look foolish.

A gaggle of toddlers played contentedly in the sun-splashed gutter, most of them barefoot and wearing dirty, ragged clothing. One or two were naked from the waist down. Ainslie shuddered and averted her eyes – and found herself looking at the little red-haired girl she had seen on her way in. The child, better dressed than most of her companions, was energetically swinging one end of a rope, her brown eyes sparkling with enjoyment. Another little girl held the other end, while a third child, in the middle, leapt high with both feet clamped together to allow the rope to swing beneath her. As Ainslie watched, she mistimed a leap, and was sent sprawling on the pavement as the rope tangled her ankles, bouncing up again almost at once.

'My turn!' Isla's daughter – and her own half-sister, Ainslie realised with sudden horror – pushed her end of the rope into the defeated child's hands and took her place. 'Ready? One, two, three, a-leary,' she chanted, feet together, skirt flying as she leapt into the air, up and down, her feet scarcely brushing the pavement before she was airborne again, the rope smacking against the stone slabs beneath her.

Ainslie turned and almost ran from the place.

When she got home her mother was in her usual place, on the sofa in the drawing-room, a glass and a half-empty bottle of tonic wine on a table close to hand.

'You're late,' she said as soon as her daughter went in.

'I had some work to finish,' Ainslie lied. Crossing the carpet to kiss Catherine, she realised that compared to the small room she had recently visited, the drawing-room was enormous. She had always taken her home, with its large, high-ceilinged, carpeted rooms and its comfortable furnishings, for granted, and had never been in any other type of house, until today.

'How are you feeling, Mother?'

'Oh . . .' Catherine shrugged one shoulder, and let her voice drift into silence.

'Did anyone call?'

'Don't be silly, Ainslie, who would call on us now?'

'Mrs Forbes, for one.' Ainslie tried to keep her voice cheerful.

'She did look in,' Catherine acknowledged, reaching

for her glass, then, 'what do you mean, you had work to finish?'

'Some items that came in this afternoon had to be catalogued.' It was the truth, she had had to work very hard to make time to visit George Street, but she had managed it.

'See to the fire, will you? Your father would turn in his grave,' Catherine went on as her daughter obeyed, 'if he knew that you were working as an ordinary clerkess, after all the money he spent on your education.'

'I don't know how to do anything else. I can't type, or sew, or cook.'

'You were brought up to be a lady, and to run your own house efficiently when the time came.'

Ainslie, poking at the coals in the grate, gave a soft sigh, recognising the build-up to a spate of reproaches over her broken engagement. 'It's a lovely day, Mother – too warm for a fire. Why don't you go into the garden and sit in the sun for a little while?'

'I prefer to be indoors,' Catherine McAdam said flatly. 'That reminds me – Innes is in the garden and he should be working at his homework now. Fetch him in, will you?'

Ainslie did as she was asked, glad of the chance to escape from the stuffy drawing-room. The garden at the rear of the house was brilliant with colour from the rose-bushes her father had planted. They massed the flower-beds, filled a small circular bed in the middle of the lawn like a jewelled brooch set against green velvet, and swarmed up the red brick wall that hid the vegetable garden from sight.

Innes was crouched down by the wall, studying a

butterfly that had settled on his hand. 'Look,' he said as his sister approached. 'Isn't it beautiful?'

She bent down, steadying herself with one hand on his back, careful to avoid letting her shadow fall on the insect and startling it. The rich colour of its spread wings glowed in the sunlight.

'Beautiful,' she agreed.

'It's a Red Admiral. Look, its wings are the same colour as your hair. I wish mine wasn't so gingery.'

'There's nothing wrong with your hair.' Ainslie ruffled it affectionately, recalling that the baby she had seen that afternoon in George Street had the same fiery red head. 'Mother says it's time for homework.'

He groaned. 'Already?'

'You'd better go in.' She watched as he coaxed the butterfly on to a cluster of yellow nasturtiums fronting the flower border, then followed him as he made for the back door.

'I suppose I should let her know I'm in.' Innes trotted into the drawing-room while Ainslie went upstairs to change out of the black skirt and jacket she had worn to the auction house.

A large portrait of the first Innes McAdam, her grandfather, hung on the half-landing beside the bathroom door. He had been a handsome man, with piercing eyes below a thatch of crisp white hair, a neatly trimmed moustache and beard hiding the lower part of his face. He had died when Ainslie was only a month old, leaving the successful business he had started as an ambitious young man to his only child, her father.

'He was so disappointed to have a granddaughter instead of a grandson,' Catherine had told Ainslie so frequently that, as a child, she had believed that her arrival in the world had been the sole cause of her grandfather's departure from it. 'I wish he had lived to see Innes.'

In her room, Ainslie stripped to her petticoat and poured water from the flowered china ewer into the matching basin. As she washed she heard Innes come upstairs and go into his own room, then her mother's bedroom door opened and closed. Ainslie put on a black crêpe de Chine dress and brushed her curly hair until it crackled. The house was hushed, as always, and she found herself missing the bustle and excitement of the auction house.

To her surprise, she had discovered that she enjoyed working in the auction house. She liked the bustle of the place, and the continual coming and going. She found satisfaction in neatly listing the goods that came in and noting the possible value of each item.

She sat on the bed and picked up a fashion magazine, then tossed it down almost at once, rising to wander listlessly about the room. She was in mourning – there was no sense in looking at bright-coloured clothes that she couldn't wear.

Almost an entire wall of the bedroom was taken up by a long low bookcase topped with ornaments and toys that had been dearly loved in their day. Every book she had ever owned was on the shelves, from her first picture book to handsomely bound editions of favourites such as *The Wind in the Willows*, and the works of Dickens and Jane Austen. Most of them had been gifts from her father, who had himself been a keen reader.

Looking at them now, Ainslie wondered if the books

proved his love for her, or merely his desire that she should understand literature. She had wanted so much to be able to love her parents openly, and had always envied those school friends who talked about cosy chats with their mothers, and hugs from their fathers. Her parents' desire that she should be well fed and well dressed, their concern over her childhood ailments, showed that they cared about her, but neither of them had been demonstratively affectionate.

It embarrassed her now to remember how she had followed Colin Forbes around as a small child, desperate for any sign of kindness, grateful for it. Deep down, she knew that she had become engaged to Colin because he was the only person who had ever said that he loved her. Because of that – and because their engagement had pleased her parents.

Then, just when she had begun to hope that she could change her world, setting up a home with Colin, having children who would grow up knowing that they were loved and cherished, her father had ruined everything. And Ainslie, crushed beyond belief by his final desertion, his final betrayal, had decided that it only proved that no man, not even Colin, could be trusted.

She thought of the dark little room she had been in earlier that day, the tiny scraps of cloth on the table and the clothes-peg with a face drawn on to a piece of rag, the young woman who had criticised her sharply for not giving any thought to her father's misery. She wished now that she had kept away from George Street.

She turned from the bookcase with a swift twist of the body, and sat down again on the bed, thinking now about her mother. Catherine McAdam had always seemed to be such a strong character, a woman more than capable of standing alone. She had run her home with great competence, taken her rightful place in local society, known just what to do and what to say in any situation.

She had turned to nobody for help when her husband died, arranging immediately after the funeral for all his clothes to be sent to a charitable organisation, and packing his personal possessions away until such time as Innes was old enough to inherit them. She had had his bedroom door locked, and then, with everything seen to, she had become an invalid.

'Let your mother work through her grief in her own time,' the doctor had told Ainslie when she voiced her concern about Catherine's listlessness. 'She'll come to terms with her loss when she's ready.'

But as the weeks passed Catherine hadn't shown any signs of recovery. Sometimes Ainslie wondered if she was genuinely grieving, if she had perhaps been closer to her husband than Ainslie had thought. That possibility didn't comfort her at all, but merely added to her growing terror with the fear that her mother, too, might kill herself rather than go on alone.

She jumped up from the bed and smoothed the coverlet briskly, trying to smooth her worries away at the same time, then went into her mother's room. Catherine, in a long-skirted black evening dress and a light wrap over her shoulders, sat at the dressing-table, staring blankly into the mirror. Even in the midst of mourning, even in her depression, she insisted on dressing for dinner, although only her children were there to see her.

'Mother, would you like me to brush your hair?'

Catherine's body rippled as though a shiver had run through it. Her mirrored eyes lifted to stare at Ainslie blankly, then blinked, recognition drifting into them.

'Very well.' She sat straight-backed as Ainslie carefully removed the pins from her hair and let it drop over her shoulders, then began to draw the brush through it. The room was immaculate, as usual, with Catherine's silver-backed brushes and mirror neatly laid out on the dressing-table. The small studio portrait of Catherine and Kenneth McAdam that had always stood on the dressing-table was gone, replaced by a photograph of Ainslie's grandfather Innes and his wife, a woman with character in her features rather than beauty. Looking from the portrait in its elaborate silver frame to her own mirrored reflection, Ainslie had to acknowledge that her mother was right – there was a look of Grandmother McAdam about her features.

'Perhaps you should have a change, Mother – go away for a few weeks,' she suggested as she worked.

'Why should I want to do that?'

'It might do you good. Helensburgh, maybe. There are some pleasant hotels there, and the sea air can be very bracing.'

Catherine shook her head impatiently, almost tangling her fine greying hair in the brush. 'How can I go away just as Innes is about to start the new school year?'

'I can see to him.'

'You?' Catherine gave a short, bitter laugh. 'You've got your work to attend to now.'

'I'm not there all the time. And the servants are very

well trained, they can be trusted to look after him when I'm not at home.'

'No.' Catherine snapped the word out, then folded her lips tightly. Ainslie, who knew better than to argue, said nothing more.

When her mother's hair was pinned into its usual twisted plait at the back of her head, she went downstairs to see that the table was set for dinner and the meal ready on time. As the clock chimed seven Catherine came in to take her place at the foot of the table. Innes, his face shining from a recent bout with his face-flannel, scampered into the dining-room a few minutes later.

'Sorry, Mother, I had to finish the sentence before I forgot what I was writing about,' he said breathlessly, his bright hair introducing light and movement into the room.

Catherine smiled, and held her arms out to him. 'Come and give Mother a kiss, darling.'

As he smacked a kiss on her pale cheek, her arms encircled him tightly. Watching, remembering how Isla had comforted her own red-haired son earlier that day, Ainslie suddenly felt very lonely.

Isla made two dolls out of clothes-pegs, wrapping pipe-cleaners round them to make arms, clothing them in long dresses and giving them mob caps. She bought a small orange box from the greengrocer's and hid it beneath the wall-bed. In the evenings, while the children slept, she covered its interior with scraps of wall-paper, drawing a large kitchen range on the back wall and a dresser on one of the side walls. A circle of cardboard nailed on to an empty wooden bobbin made a table, and other bobbins covered with cloth served as stools. With Plasticine, she made some plates for the table, finishing the single-roomed house off with a curtain stretched across the front on string.

Barbara was delighted with her gift. 'It's a house just the same size as ours, isn't it?' she said in wonder, kneeling before the orange box house. 'This is the mummy and this is the little girl.'

'She's a big little girl.'

'Not as big as her mummy.' Barbara stood the two peg dolls side by side and sure enough, one was a fraction smaller than the other. 'Where's the daddy?'

'You don't get daddy dolls,' Isla told her, and the little girl's lower lip trembled.

'Yes you do,' she insisted. 'Of course you do! Where is he?'

'At work?' Isla suggested, her mind on her sewing box. There was still some white material left that would do for a shirt, and a scrap of black that could be turned into trousers, and perhaps some kind of cap.

Barbara's face cleared, and she nodded. 'All right, but he'll be coming home. He'll be coming home soon.'

'Tomorrow.' Isla hugged her daughter. Barbara scarcely ever asked about Kenneth's whereabouts now, but clearly he was still in her mind.

Magret, invited with her children to share the small dumpling Isla had made for the occasion, was enthralled by the little house.

'Who'd've thought ye could turn an old orange box intae a house, and a clothes-peg intae a dolly?' she marvelled, studying one of the dolls closely. 'It's bonny, Isla.'

'It's not difficult.'

'Not for you, mebbe, but I'd never manage it.' Magret handed the doll back to her elder daughter, who bustled importantly over to the orange box and knelt down, pushing the top half of her body into it as she replaced the doll. Catching a glimpse of skinny little buttocks, Isla realised that Greta didn't wear drawers.

When Barbara woke up the next morning the daddy doll was in residence, much to her delight. The next day, over a mug of tea, Magret asked Isla to make a peg doll for Greta.

'She's been on at me for one ever since she saw Barbara's.'

Isla sipped the tea, realising that she was now used to its strength and sweetness, and to the mingled taste of condensed milk and grease.

'I could show you how to make it,' she offered, but Magret shook her head.

'I'm not good with my hands, like you,' she coaxed, and beamed her delight when Isla gave in.

8

Isla had begun to admit to herself that in trying to wrest a vegetable patch from the weedy backyard she was fighting a losing battle, but her pride wouldn't let her give in. She well knew that almost everyone living within sight of the back court was watching her progress, and, like Magret, none of them thought that she would succeed. So she battled on, glancing up one evening to see a young lad watching her from beside the wash-house.

Isla smiled at him, recognising Mrs Brown's son Drew, and he looked away in embarrassment, then looked back at her.

'What're ye growin'?'

'Potatoes, if I ever manage to clear enough land.'

He spat on his hands, then held them out. 'I'll give ye a hand. See's the fork.'

She handed it over, stepping back to let him get to the pitifully small amount of earth she had won from the grasses. He drove the tines of the fork deep into the ground with more force than she had thought possible from his slight frame, then leaned on the handle, lifting a solid clod of earth free. It had been bound into place by generations of grass roots that stubbornly held on to it, and he had the sense to work patiently at it until all the roots had snapped. He dumped the clod on the ground and smashed at it with the side of the fork, then drove the tines into the ground again.

Isla left him to it and went into the building. When she came back with a mug of tea in each hand, he had got into the rhythm of it, and had learned the sense of trying to gain only a little ground at a time.

He straightened up and accepted the tea with mumbled thanks. Together they sipped in silence. 'It might not work,' Isla said at last, 'but I don't think there's any harm in failing as long as you've tried.'

'Aye.' The lad drained the last of the tea, his Adam's apple bobbing in his thin throat, then handed the mug back and got on with his work, digging steadily until a cloud of midges, those tiny maddening flies that persecuted Scotland, arrived and made further work impossible.

'I could do more for ye, if ye want,' he said diffidently as the two of them retired to the close.

Isla hesitated, then decided that frankness was the only way. 'I can't afford to pay you.'

'Doesnae matter. I like diggin'.'

'What'll your mother say?'

'It was her that sent me down. I'd nothin' tae dae.'

'I tell you what – if you want to help, I'll share the potatoes with you and your mother.'

For the first time, he looked fully at her, and grinned. 'Aye. That'd be fine.'

By the time Barbara started school, Isla and young Drew Brown had dug over more than half the patch of ground between them, and a succession of women up and down George Street had asked Isla to make peg dolls for their daughters, just like the dolls Barbara and Greta had been showing off to the other children.

Isla, aware of the importance of building up a good relationship with her neighbours, refused nobody, and soon almost every little girl playing out on the pavement had become the proud owner of a peg doll. Some of the women offered her money in exchange for her work, while others brought half a dozen home-made scones, or a fruit loaf, or a good soup-bone with fragments of meat still attached, or a piece of material.

By the time she started attending the West School, only ten minutes' walk away from George Street, Barbara had made a number of friends, though Greta was her closest confidante. Barbara admired Greta; in her eyes, the child could do no wrong. This led to some conflict between mother and daughter, especially over the business of underwear.

'Greta doesn't need to wear drawers,' Barbara protested after being caught playing in the street with nothing on underneath her skirt. Her rolled-up knickers were substituting for a pillow in a battered dolls' pram that Greta had inherited from an older cousin.

'She would if she was my little girl.'

Barbara's lower lip slid forward mutinously. 'Drawers just get in the way when you want to pee in the yard.'

'When you want to – *what*?' Horrified, Isla stared at her daughter. 'But you always use the privy, like a good girl. Don't you?' she added, as Barbara shrugged her shoulders and scuffed the toe of one shoe over the floor.

'Sometimes someone's in the privy and I can't wait,

and anyway, every time I use it that old Mrs Leach comes running down to make sure I didn't make a mess,' Barbara muttered, adding, 'anyway, the grass is nicer, it's not all dark and smelly like the privy, and it tickles.'

'Barbara!' It was all that Isla could do not to shake the child. 'You must never ever use the yard as a privy, d'you hear me? No matter what anyone else does. If you do, I'll – I'll give you such a smacking!'

Barbara stared up at her, wide-eyed. Isla rarely hit her, and never hard.

'D'you hear me?' Isla insisted, and the child finally gave a sullen nod. When she had been sent out to play, with firm instructions to keep all her clothes on, Isla went back to her ironing, gnawing at her lower lip, aware that it was going to be hard to continue to insist on certain standards when the children Barbara played with had their own way of looking at life. The little girl had settled in well, even accepting her new surname without question, and as far as she was concerned the future would be like the present, living in one small room playing out on the pavement or in the rubbish-strewn backyard.

Isla still hoped that one day she and her children would be able to move out of George Street and back into the sort of home Kenneth had once provided for them. It was a hope that had begun to turn into a dream, for not one person had made an offer so far for the tenement building. But she refused to accept that she and her children were going to remain in George Street for ever.

Ross, playing on the hearth-rug with a wooden toy, lost interest in it and grabbed the leg of the fireside chair for support while he hauled himself upright. He toddled across the floor, moving from one piece of furniture to the other, until he got to the door, then banged on it, whimpering.

'You're too wee to go out and play,' Isla told him. As he continued to grizzle, she fetched the bag of clothespegs and offered it to him. He snatched at it and sat down on the floor, turning the bag upside down and emptying its contents out.

'Whatever would we do without pegs?' Isla wondered aloud, lifting the flat-iron from the gas ring and putting her finger in her mouth to damp it so that she could test the iron's heat. Barbara had started walking at an earlier age than Ross, but Magret had assured Isla that boys usually took longer than girls to get on their feet. Isla saw it as a blessing. All too soon Ross would be insisting on going out to play in the street like his sister, and then there would be two of them to deal with.

She thought of the little boys who played in the gutter, naked from the waist down, and the older boys, up to all sorts of mischief, from knocking on doors then running away to stealing from the local shops. Would Ross grow up to be like that? The responsibility of raising her children on her own weighed heavily on her shoulders, reviving the aching misery of Kenneth's death. At times like this, she would have sacrificed everything in the world, except Barbara and Ross, to bring Kenneth back again.

On the first day of the school term Magret and Isla saw their daughters settled in a large classroom noisy with the wails of children thrown into panic at the thought of being abandoned by their mothers. Barbara and Greta had no such qualms. Seated side by side, they were both enchanted with the double bench and the two desks with lids that could be raised to reveal an inviting space within, waiting to be filled.

'Thank God,' Magret said with all her heart as the two women made their way home. 'I made such a fuss the first day I started school that my mammy had tae take me home again. I got a right hammerin' when we got there, too. Black affronted, she was. I never liked the school. See the very smell of the place? When I went in there today I nearly turned and ran out again, the memories of my own time were that strong.'

Isla nodded. 'It helps when they've got each other. I was sorry for that woman whose wee boy wouldn't let go of her legs.'

Their smug pleasure at having such well-behaved children didn't last long. At half-past ten that morning, when Isla answered an imperious thumping at the door, Barbara marched past her into the room. 'I'm back,' she announced, tossing the shabby little school-bag that Isla had bought from the pawn-shop on to the floor.

'What are you doing here? You're supposed to be at school!'

'I've been,' said Barbara. 'We played with boxes of sand and sang a song, then they let us out, so me and Greta came home.'

Magret burst in just then without waiting to knock, towing a puzzled Greta by the wrist. 'Isla—'

'I know.'

'What would ye make of them?' Magret asked in exasperation, while Isla explained to her daughter, 'You were only let out to play for a wee while. Then you were supposed to go back in again until I came to take you home for your dinner.'

'Back again?' Barbara asked in astonishment.

'Aye, my lass, and tomorrow tae. Isla, we'll need tae take them back, an' me with the wean sleepin' in her cot . . .'

'Tomorrow?' Barbara and Greta squeaked in unison.

'You didn't say about tomorrow too,' Barbara accused her mother.

'Hen, ye've got years o' it ahead o' ye,' Magret said with heart-felt sympathy, adding to her own daughter, 'and you too, wee imp that ye are, what's yer daddy goin' tae say about this?'

'He'll have a good laugh about it.' Isla was beginning to see the funny side of the situation herself. 'You look after Ross, Magret, and I'll take them back. You'll come with me, won't you, Greta?'

'Uhuh,' Greta said round the thumb she had stuck into her mouth, while Barbara gave a huge sigh of irritation over the contrary ways of adults.

'You didn't say anything about going back in,' she pointed out as she and Greta were shepherded out of the room and through the close. 'You should have said!'

Ainslie McAdam had never been happier in her life. Charlie Blayne, her employer, was a broad-shouldered middle-aged man with twinkling blue eyes and a head of thick curly hair that had once been rich brown and was now well sprinkled with grey.

'I see myself as a working man's auctioneer, lass,' he told Ainslie when she applied for the post as his office

91

clerkess. 'Folk die, an' their relatives want to get rid of a houseful of stuff, some of it pure rubbish. So they send for me, and if it can be sold, I'll sell it for them. Or mebbe they need a bit o' money, so they bring their granda's clock, or ornaments they never liked anyway – stuff they don't want back, or else they'd pawn it.'

He tipped his chair back and looked with satisfaction round his small office. It was filled with papers and ledgers and boxes crammed with books and spoons and pipe racks and pots and pans. A rag doll stared blankly at Ainslie over the top of one box.

'Folk all want different things. A picture frame or a nice wee ornament for the mantelpiece – or a toy for the wean,' Charlie went on, nodding at the doll. 'An' mebbe they're looking for a bit of a gamble. In a shop they must pay the price asked, but here, they might get just what they want for less, or have a bit of fun out-biddin' the next man.' He beamed at Ainslie. 'D'ye see what I mean?'

'I think so.'

'Ye never get bored in this job, lass. Ye never know from one day to the next what'll come in – or who. Now . . .' He swung his feet down from the desk and became more businesslike. 'What I need is someone to keep the paperwork tidy. There's lists to be sorted out and valuations to record, and letters to write and books to keep. There's not much to it, but I'd as soon be free to get on with the business of seein' to the sales and the stores and going out and about, valuing stuff. D'ye think ye could manage it?'

'I was good at arithmetic at school, and I can deal with lists,' she said cautiously.

'Can ye use a telephone?'

'Yes.'

'What about a typewriter?'

'I'm willing to try it.'

'Aye, well, that suits me. We'll see how things go for a week or two, will we? If ye don't like it, say so, an' if I don't think ye'll fit in, I'll have to tell ye, lass. No point in either of us wasting our time over something that won't work. I can start ye off at six shillin's a week.'

It wasn't much, but Ainslie had never worked before, and beggars couldn't be choosers. She nodded, and he ran a thoughtful eye over her neat black skirt and jacket. 'Ye'll be in the store-rooms sometimes, lass, an' it's awful mucky there. It's mucky in the offices, come to that,' he added frankly. 'That's somethin' else ye could mebbe try to see to. It's not easy keeping a place like this clean. Ye'll get into a mess.'

'I'll bring an overall.'

'Aye, that'd be wise,' said Charlie Blayne.

The offices, Charlie's and Ainslie's, both small and both cramped, stood at the end of a long gallery that ran the length of the auction-room below and was connected to it by a stair at the far end. The gallery was crammed with items, particularly before a sale, and at times there was little more than a narrow passageway between the offices and the stairs, between high walls of tea-chests and crates and tables and roped sets of chairs. Double wooden doors with a smaller door set in one of them led from the auction rooms to the cobbled yard and the street, and two other doors at the opposite side opened into the large store-rooms where the goods were kept. Before each sale it was Ainslie's job to see that the goods on offer were clearly listed and marked, so that they could be brought into the saleroom in the correct order.

A narrow door and dark wooden stairway led directly from her office to the street outside, so that she could come and go each day without having to enter through the saleroom. Each morning, as soon as she arrived, she wrapped herself in an overall she had bought for work. The old building seemed to ooze dust through every chink and crack, and a number of women were specially employed just to keep the furniture for sale dusted and polished. Ainslie saw to the two offices, sweeping and dusting and cleaning out the fireplaces every morning before clambering up on to a high stool to work at the sloping desk. When the day was done, she had to wash her hands and often her face before leaving, because of the dust.

Charlie Blayne was an easy-going employer, with the knack of turning the men and women who worked for him into a second family. From the first day, Ainslie loved her work, and after a few weeks it seemed to her that she only truly came alive while she was busy in the tiny office, or down in the rooms, lists in hand.

While she was working there was little time to think of anything else, but as soon as she stepped out on to the narrow dreary street and set off homewards she started fretting about Catherine, who was still refusing to go out or to take an interest in life again. She also refused to let Ainslie tell her anything about her work.

'If your father knew – and your poor grandfather . . .' She gave a shudder of disgust. 'Auction rooms!'

'Auction houses can be very respectable, Mother,'

Ainslie protested, more hurt for Charlie Blayne's sake than her own.

'Yes, they can. Christie's, for one, or Sotheby's – but you're not employed by them, are you?'

'I doubt if they'd want me, since I have no qualifications.'

'You have to work in some nasty little place, when you could have done so much better for yourself!' Catherine ranted on, and Ainslie held her tongue, knowing that her mother would never change her views.

Innes, who was at the adaptable age where life always goes on, was doing well at school, and clearly relieved to be back there after a summer spent in a house in mourning.

'Will Mother ever get better?' he asked his sister once, wistfully.

She hugged him. 'Of course she will.'

Innes inspected his large-knuckled bony hands. 'She says she wants me to be just like grandfather McAdam when I'm old enough. Does that mean dying, too?'

Ainslie felt a chill creep up her spine. 'Of course not. She means she would like you to go into business.'

'Work in an office?' He wrinkled his freckled nose. 'I'd rather do something with cars. Or p'raps go to Africa to collect creatures for a zoo.'

'Best not to tell Mother that. There's plenty of time yet, you might think of all sorts of things you want to do before the time comes.'

'I won't ever want to be in business,' Innes said firmly, then added, 'but whatever it turns out to be, it'll be something that makes a lot of money for us all, so you and Mother needn't worry about that.'

9

In October an Indian summer, an unexpected spell of golden warm weather, descended on the west of Scotland, and one of Ainslie's former schoolfriends invited her to a tennis-party. The invitation was waiting on the drawing-room mantelpiece when she returned from the auction rooms; she read it and stuffed it back into the envelope without comment, but her mother, watching her, asked with studied casualness, 'What was that?'

'Lena Gillespie's having some people in for tennis on Saturday.'

'I think you should go,' Catherine said at once.

'But we're still in mourning, Mother.'

'Even so, you've not been anywhere this year, and it's not right for young people to shut themselves away for too long. It would do you good to see your friends again.'

'I don't really think I want to play tennis. For one thing, I'm out of practice.'

'Nonsense.' Catherine sipped at her tonic wine – the bottle, Ainslie noticed, was almost empty. It had been full that morning when she left. 'Phemie Forbes was here this afternoon, and she recognised the envelope, because Colin got one this morning. Phemie says he's going, and she's sure he'll be happy to drive you.' A smile brushed her lips briefly. 'She and I were just recalling the tennis parties we went to when we were your age. We enjoyed them so much.'

For the moment, her interest in the forthcoming social event had brought colour to her cheeks, and a lilt to her voice. For her sake, Ainslie agreed to go.

When the day came, her tennis dress felt very light and flimsy after the sombre black clothes she had been wearing. Surveying herself in the mirror, smoothing the crisp snowy skirt over her hips, Ainslie realised with surprise that the dress was loose. She must have lost weight since her father's death. The grandfather clock in the hall – a longpiece, auctioneers called it – chimed the hour, and immediately afterwards Catherine called up from the hall, 'Ainslie, Colin's here.'

As she went downstairs, Ainslie felt rather as though she had forgotten to put on her outer clothes and had come from her room in her petticoat. But her mother, waiting in the hall with Colin Forbes, nodded approval as she reached the bottom step.

'You look very nice, dear. Don't you think so, Colin?'

Colin cleared his throat and muttered something, and Catherine picked up her daughter's racquet, waiting in its press on the hall table, as Innes appeared from the kitchen.

'Can I come?' he asked hopefully. He had been taking lessons the year before, and showed promise, but the lessons had been cancelled after his father's death.

'No you can't, this party is for grown-ups. You can

stay here, with me. We'll have a lovely afternoon together.'

Innes's face fell, and Ainslie wished that she could have sent him in her place. She had borrowed a book on furniture from Charlie Blayne, and would have enjoyed an afternoon with it.

Catherine accompanied them as far as the steps, and stood in the doorway, waving, as the car went down the short drive. Ainslie, glancing back, noticed with concern that she wasn't the only member of the household to lose weight. Her mother, who had always been slender, was now almost stick-like.

'I wish Mother would start going out again,' she said, settling herself in the familiar bucket seat. 'She badly needs fresh air and company.'

'My mother's done her best to coax her, but it doesn't seem to be any good.' Colin steered round a car parked too near a corner, then added levelly, 'It's not easy to get the McAdams to co-operate.'

Ainslie opened her mouth to argue, then closed it again. They drove the rest of the way in silence.

Lena's father owned a local engineering firm, and the family lived in one of the largest houses in Paisley. There were almost twenty young people gathered round the tennis court, and Ainslie, on her first social outing since her father's death, was greeted with squeals of pleasure from the girls she had grown up with.

Lena hugged her. 'You poor darling – has it all been terrible?' Her large brown eyes were soft with concern.

'Not too bad.'

'I heard you'd had to find employment,' someone else chimed in, a girl who had been one of Ainslie's closest friends in their final year at school. 'I can't imagine how I would manage if I had to do such a thing!' She gave an exaggerated shiver, and lifted a hand delicately to her cheek in order to show off her new engagement ring. Her fiancé, the son of a man who owned a chain of successful groceries throughout Scotland, put a protective arm about her shoulders, and she snuggled back against him – just like a kitten in a basket, Ainslie thought, wondering why she had ever admired the girl.

The afternoon dragged by. She took her turn on the court, and found that although her skill swiftly returned, her heart wasn't in the game at all. She drank tea on the flagged terrace, ate tiny sandwiches and creamy cakes, went with the others to admire the new lily-pond, then played tennis again. And at last, to her relief, it was time to go home.

Most of the others were changing in the house before driving to Glasgow to attend the theatre, but since Ainslie was still in mourning, it was not possible for her to join them. For that, she thought as they all walked round to the front of the house, she was grateful.

'There's no reason why you shouldn't go to the theatre,' she pointed out to Colin.

'Yes, why not?' Lena chirped. 'The chauffeur can drive Ainslie home.'

He shook his fair head. 'I brought her here and I'll see her home again,' he said, ushering Ainslie to where the car waited on a wide sweep of gravel.

As the others went into the house, a group of carefree moths in their white tennis outfits, he tucked her into the bucket seat then went round to the driver's door. 'Did you enjoy yourself?' he asked as he got in and switched on the engine.

'Oh yes,' Ainslie lied.

Colin eased the car between huge gateposts and turned on to the road. 'So – tell me about this place where you work.'

She described it all in an impersonal way, reluctant to let her enthusiasm show, or to let him know that walking into her cramped little office was like pulling on a cosy, much-loved dressing-gown on a winter's night. She had a superstitious notion that if she let the two very different areas of her existence get too close to each other, they might collide, and cause some sort of damage to themselves, and to her.

Colin listened in silence, his square capable hands steady on the wheel. When she glanced at him she saw that his face was expressionless, and that he was staring straight ahead, never glancing sideways at her as he had so often done in the old days.

'I'm beginning to get a grasp of the ledgers, though the first time I saw them it was like reading Greek— I didn't think I would ever be able to make sense of them. I'm very slow when it comes to using the typewriter, but Cha— Mr Blayne doesn't seem to mind, and the letters do look more official when they've been typed.'

She caught at the dashboard as the car suddenly swerved round a corner and she was thrown against Colin. He had tossed their jackets on to the back seats, and for a moment, as their shoulders touched, she felt his arm hard and warm against hers, bringing back sudden memories of another time, another life, when being with Colin had been the most exciting thing that had ever happened to her.

'What are you doing?'

'Taking another route.'

She glanced at the small wristwatch her parents had given her on her twenty-first birthday. 'Mother will be wondering where I've got to.'

'She knows you're with me. She knows you're safe,' he shot back at her, his voice abrupt. They were driving out into the country now, instead of continuing through the town. The car swerved again, this time towards a layby, then stopped.

Colin killed the engine, then turned in his seat and said, without any preamble, 'Ainslie, will you marry me?'

She stared into his eyes, only inches away from hers. They were best described as hazel, but they changed colours according to his mood. Today, they were grey, the colour of the River Cart on a stormy day. 'Colin, we've been through this before—'

'There's no harm in going through it again. I'm asking you, in all seriousness, to become my wife. And don't answer without taking time to think about it,' he added swiftly as her lips parted. 'You owe me that, at least.'

She did, but at the same time she knew already what her answer must be. She had ended their engagement, and she had no intention of changing her mind. He must have known that himself, for he slammed a hand on the wheel and said, the words pouring out, 'I hoped you'd hate that job, hate having to earn your own living. I hoped that you'd have realised by now that your future lies with me. It always has, Ainslie. I want nothing more than to look after you, and give you everything you want and deserve, and make you happy. And if you're worried about your mother and brother, there's no need, for I'll gladly take them on, too. Look . . .' He turned in his seat, fumbling in the pocket of the jacket in the back seat, withdrawing a small white box. 'I brought this with me today. It's rightfully yours.'

His hands, Ainslie noticed, were trembling as he snapped the box open. 'I love you – did I forget to say that?' Colin asked huskily. 'I love you, and I want you to take this back, because it's yours, and so am I.'

The engagement ring blazed against its white satin bed. She remembered how snugly that ring had fitted on her finger, how happy she had been to see it there. But it belonged to another world, a world that could never be brought back. Afraid that the jewels might draw her down into their depths and drown her senses until she was unable to think clearly, she looked away, to the tumble of bushes edging the road. Other jewels gleamed back at her – glossy red rosehips, fat blackberries, ripe and bursting with their sweet purple juices, set among emerald green leaves. She stared at them until they blurred and merged and she realised that there were tears in her eyes. She still loved the man by her side, but as a very dear friend, not as a future husband.

'Colin, I'm very fond of you, but I'm not going to marry you.'

'But I thought . . .' he began, then stopped, finally saying angrily, 'where's the sense in punishing us both because of what your father did?'

'I'm not punishing anyone. It's just that everything's changed.'

'It needn't.'

'But it has. There's no sense in pretending otherwise.'

'It's that damned woman's fault – the one who's come to live in George Street. If she'd kept away from the town everything would have been over and forgotten by now!'

'I don't need her presence to remind me of what my father did,' Ainslie shot back at him. Then, seeing the bleak look in his eyes, she added lamely, 'I'm – I'm sorry, Colin.'

'So am I.' He snapped the box shut, tossed it into the glove compartment. 'I've made a fool of myself, haven't I?'

'No!' She reached out to him, but he drew his hand back sharply.

'For God's sake, Ainslie, don't start pitying me now!'

She wished that she could be anywhere but where she was. 'You've always been my best friend, Colin. I'd hate it if you turned your back on me.' Then, as he sat mute, staring through the driver's window at the other side of the road, she added, 'If you'd rather, I'll walk the rest of the way home. It's not far.'

'Don't be daft!' Colin snapped, and started the car. He said nothing more until they drew up in the McAdam drive. Then, leaving her to open her own door, he said, his voice still clipped, 'I promise I won't propose to you again. I'll not make a nuisance of myself.'

She shut the door and stepped back, watching as he turned the wheel to take the car past her along the short stretch of driveway in front of the house, then reversed noisily until the rear bumpers almost touched the locked doors of the garage where her father had once kept his own car. It had been sold immediately after the funeral, despite Innes's protests that one day he himself would need it.

Throwing up a spray of gravel, Colin went off down the drive, stopping the car with a jerk at the gate, then taking off into the road to a scream of protest from the tyres.

As Ainslie turned towards the front door she glimpsed a movement at the small gap between the drawing-room curtains, and realised that her mother had been watching for their arrival. Catherine came into the hall as she closed the front door. 'Well? Did you have a lovely afternoon?'

'Yes, thank you.' Ainslie made for the stairs and started to ascend.

'Why didn't you bring Colin in for tea? You know he'd have been very welcome.'

'He was in a hurry.' Ainslie threw the words over her shoulder and kept climbing. She had just laid the racquet down when the bedroom door opened and her mother walked into the room without knocking.

'What happened?'

'We played tennis, we had afternoon tea, then I came home.'

'Ainslie, don't be annoying! Why didn't Colin come in with you?'

Suddenly Ainslie, standing before the mirror, taking off the ribbon she had used to tie her hair back, remembered Colin's reaction to her refusal, remembered him saying, 'But I thought . . .', then choking the words back. Suddenly, she knew. She turned to face her mother, tossing the ribbon down on to the bed. 'It was all planned, wasn't it?'

'What was?'

'You and Mrs Forbes decided that this would be the perfect opportunity for Colin to ask me to change my mind about marrying him, didn't you?'

A slender hand went up to Catherine's throat. Her eyes widened, and Ainslie saw that her cheeks had gone quite pink. 'He proposed? Oh, Ainslie, how wonderful!'

'No need to pretend, Mother – you knew. That's why you urged me to go to the tennis party with him.'

'Well, I – Phemie did say when she was here the other day that Colin's been pining ever since you gave his ring back.'

Ainslie felt quite sick with shame and pity as the full realisation of the situation hit her. 'Did his mother hint to him that I'd changed my mind? How could you? How could you be so cruel?'

'I don't know what you're—' Catherine's eyes fell on her daughter's left hand, bare of rings. She whimpered faintly, and sat down suddenly on the bed. 'You turned him down? Again?'

'I told him what I had told him before. What I've told you, again and again. I don't want to marry anyone.'

There was a short silence, during which Ainslie could almost hear her mother's fury crackling in the air between them, then, 'I spent the entire afternoon praying – praying!' Catherine burst out. 'Hoping that you would come to your senses and accept him. How many men have the courage to face humiliation twice? Do you realise what you've done to that poor boy – to me?'

'What I've done? I didn't lead him to believe that I had changed my mind. You did that – you and that scheming mother of his!'

'How dare you talk about my friend like that! How dare you presume to know better than your elders and betters—'

'Mother, I will not marry in order to please anyone, even you.'

'If your father could hear you!' Catherine's hand, which had gone to her throat, now moved to her mouth, as though pressing back a sob. Round her slim fingers she said, 'He was so pleased when you and Colin announced your engagement. What do you think he would make of you now?'

Ainslie linked her own fingers behind her back and took a deep breath. 'My father didn't stop to wonder how I might feel about it before he took his own life – or before he became husband to another woman and father to another family. Why should I concern myself with him?'

The colour drained from Catherine's face. 'How dare you?' she said again, in a harsh whisper.

'I'm sorry to vex you, Mother, but I'm only trying to make you understand about my own feelings.'

'Your feelings? That's been the trouble all along. You're selfish, Ainslie, you always have been, from the moment you were born. Selfish and obstinate and uncaring, just like your Grandmother McAdam. She ruined her husband's life, and now you're ruining mine. You're no better than she was.'

'Then perhaps it's as well that I've turned Colin down. I might have ruined his life as well, and I care for him too much to do that.'

Catherine gave a bitter little laugh. 'You flatter yourself, my dear. You don't care for anybody but yourself, do you? You don't care that people in this town are wondering what sort of mother I am, letting my daughter go out to work in some nasty little auction room. Or what sort of wife I must have been, for my husband to take another woman behind my back—' Her voice broke, then changed to an eerie banshee wailing. Her hands went up to clutch at her head, fingers digging into her scalp. Ainslie went to her, alarmed by such behaviour from her normally emotionless mother, but Catherine pulled away from her touch.

'Leave me be! The only one who truly cares is Innes,' she said with sudden, almost frightening dignity. 'One day he'll make up to me for everything you and your father did.'

She rose from the bed and walked, straight-backed, out of the room, leaving Ainslie shaken and confused. She and her mother had had disagreements for as long as she could remember. She recalled, frequently, occasions when she stood obstinately silent, taking the sting of her mother's sarcastic tongue, refusing to let herself weep. But they had never had such an ugly, venomous quarrel before. And never, until now, had Catherine lost control.

Guilt welled up. She had allowed herself to hit back, had behaved very badly towards her mother at a time when Catherine wasn't herself. Although Ainslie's anger was justified by the fact that Colin had been cruelly deceived by his mother and hers, she would have to apologise.

She leaned forward until her forehead was resting against the cool mirror, closing her eyes. There seemed to be no way to please her mother, other than by giving up her job and agreeing to marry Colin. But if she did that, she would betray herself. It was too high a price for anyone to pay for other people's happiness.

With a flash of insight, Ainslie realised that she had spent the first twenty-one years of her life betraying herself. She had tried, really tried, to do what others wanted – her parents, her teachers, her friends, even Colin – but she had always fallen short of their expectations, because pleasing them meant displeasing herself.

Her father's death had put an end to it. Torn from the life she had always known, cast into an uncertain future, she had changed far more than even she herself had suspected before that moment. She had become a different person, a woman who was learning, slowly and painfully, how to make her own way in the world. Independence was beckoning, and she had started the long journey towards it. Having started, she must continue, and that meant never again allowing herself to be hurt simply in order to make others happy.

Nor, she realised, did she have the right to interfere in other people's lives. She had been no better than Catherine when she went to George Street and tried to order Isla out of the town and out of their lives. Isla had been her father's business, not hers.

When the maid came to remind her that dinner was on the table, Ainslie, still in her tennis dress, sent word downstairs that she wasn't hungry. She stripped, washed, and brushed out her curly red hair until it crackled. During the day she restrained it in a long plait hanging down her back, but when she was at home she liked to leave it loose. After changing into her night-dress and dressing-gown, she took *The Wind in the Willows* from the shelves, and turning to her favourite chapter, the one about Mole and Rat seeking shelter far from home on a cold winter's night, she settled down to read.

Almost at once she fell asleep, tired out by fresh air and exercise, followed by the stress of the scenes with Colin and then her mother, then wakened with a start to find Innes standing beside her, a tray in his hands.

'I got you this from the kitchen.'

He had brought a roast beef sandwich and a glass of milk. Ainslie still wasn't hungry, but, touched by his concern, she nibbled at the sandwich and sipped the milk while Innes sat on the side of the bed and watched.

'How was the tennis party?'

'All right. I'll probably be stiff tomorrow, not having played all summer.'

'I miss it,' he said. 'I miss everything. D'you think we'll ever get back to normal again?'

'Of course we will, next year.' She put down her sandwich, unable to take another bite. 'I ate too many sandwiches this afternoon. I'm still full up.'

'I'll finish it if you like,' he offered, and ate the food as though he hadn't had any dinner at all. Innes had always had a huge appetite.

'Mother sat with a face like thunder all through dinner, then went to bed with a headache,' he said round a mouthful of bread and meat. 'I might as well be honest,

I heard you both rowing after you came back from the tennis party.'

'She's still angry because I won't marry Colin.'

'I thought you liked Colin.'

'I do, but I don't want to spend the rest of my life married to him.'

'If you did marry him, he'd probably teach you to drive his car. He'll probably give you a car of your own.'

'Marriage is about more than cars, Innes.'

'I wonder if it'll happen to me one day.' Innes licked his fingers then lay back on the bed beside her and linked his fingers behind his head. 'Marrying, I mean, not learning to drive. I'm definitely going to do that as soon as I'm old enough.'

'Time you were in bed.'

'In a minute.' He yawned, then said, 'I don't like you and Mother quarrelling, Ainslie. We've only got each other now, the three of us.'

She put her arm around him. 'I'll apologise to her in the morning. It'll be all right.'

'That's good.' There was a pause, then he said sleepily, 'Tell me again about the place you work in.' His red hair was soft against her chin and his body solid and comforting within the circle of her arm. Ainslie was tempted to drop a kiss on his cheek, but held back, knowing that he would hate it.

'Outside my tiny office there's this long wide gallery, stacked with all sorts of furniture . . .' she began.

10

Once she realised that school was a five-days-a-week occurrence, Barbara took to it like a duck to water. She loved the sand trays, where the children used their fingers to write out figures and letters, and the importance of having a desk of her own. She loved the games in the school-yard at playtime, the chanted multiplication tables, the stories and songs and poems. She and Greta played schools in their spare time, commandeering Ross and Daisy and any other small child they could get hold of as pupils.

With Drew Brown's help, Isla cleared the patch of earth in the backyard, but the soil was poor, soured by years of neglect, smoke and soot from the chimneys, and by the cats and dogs who roamed the area, using the backyards as lavatories. Every weekday morning, after she had watched Barbara and Greta run in through the school gates to mingle with the other children in the playground, Isla, pushing Ross in the little perambulator she had brought to Paisley with her, walked on past the huge bulk of the Ferguslie Mills, where the machinery gave out a continual muffled roar, towards the open moors on the outskirts of the town.

Here, while Ross toddled around, she hunted out molehills, carefully scraping them up with a battered tablespoon and stowing the rich soil away in an old shopping bag kept specially for the purpose.

'It's dung ye want tae feed the earth,' Drew said when he found Isla emptying the battered old bag over the newly dug patch, shaking it vigorously to make sure that not a speck of good soil was lost.

'Where can I get it?'

The boy shot a surprised look at her, as though wondering if she was pulling his leg. 'From the horses that go up an' down the street, of course. It's the best thing ye can use for growin' things. I'll get some for ye after work if ye want, or ye could ask any of the laddies round here tae gather it for ye in a bucket, for a ha'penny, or one or two empty bottles tae take tae the wee shop.'

Isla felt colour rise to her face. She was well used by now to the sight and sound of the great cart-horses pulling wagons and carts along George Street, but even so she had never thought of using their droppings for her vegetable bed. She gave the bag a final vicious shake, cursing her own stupidity. What sort of example could she set her own children when she didn't even remember that manure was good for growing things, she chided herself, then a giggle bubbled to her lips as she realised that not knowing about manure was scarcely likely to damage their young lives.

She followed Drew's advice the next morning, impatient to get on with planting the old potatoes she had been carefully hoarding under the bed for weeks. As soon as she stepped tentatively out of the close, bucket in one hand and shovel in the other, a grubby little boy arrived at her side.

'Is it dung ye're after, missus? I'll see tae it for ye!' He grabbed the bucket and shovel, and was off before she could say anything. Isla looked after him helplessly, convinced that she had seen the last of her precious possessions. Thieving was rife in the street, and she had been well warned by Magret never to leave Ross's little perambulator outside on its own.

'It's not all badness, it's just that some poor souls have nothin' at all, except what the weans can lay their hands on,' Magret had said. 'Folks has got tae live.'

Ten minutes later, the boy thumped on the door and handed Isla her shovel and a steaming bucket, filled to the brim with richly smelling manure. 'I kenned there was a cuddy just turned intae Castle Street,' he explained. 'I had tae run tae catch up wi' it.'

She gave him a halfpenny, which he folded tightly into his fist as he followed her through the close and into the yard. The bucket was heavy, and she marvelled at such a small boy being able to carry it all the way from Castle Street on his own.

'What're ye doin', missus?' He gave a huge sniff and swatted at his nose with the back of his hand.

'Growing potatoes.'

'Tatties? When'll they be ready, then?'

'Mind yer own business,' Magret snapped from behind him. 'Get back tae yer own close – go on, now! Ye don't want tae tell the likes of him too much,' she went on when he had gone, his bare feet slapping hard against the steps and along the close, the hems of his ragged trousers flapping about his knees. 'He'd be wantin' tae know when the tatties'd be ready for him tae steal.' She wrinkled her nose as Isla, after a struggle, managed to upend the bucket, and a solid lump of manure thumped out on to the turned earth. 'God bless us, what a reek!'

'I'll soon have it dug in.' Isla sniffed the air then said thoughtfully, 'It's a good healthy natural smell.'

Magret, used to the stink of blocked drains and broken sewage pipes and human beings crowded together in old, unsanitary housing, gave her new friend a puzzled look.

'I don't know how ye can say that – it's chokin' me,' she complained, waving her hand before her nose while Isla seized her fork and began spreading the manure over the earth.

Over the next few days Drew obtained several more bucketsful of manure for her, and helped to dig it in. 'I think it's as ready as it can be,' she said at last, and went to the house. When she brought the old tin tray out from under the wall-bed, she saw that the potatoes she had saved for the garden were already sprouting. Putting the vegetable knife into the pocket of her pinny, she carried the tray out.

'Now we need to cut each potato in half, and plant each half with the sprouting side up.'

Drew took a penknife from his pocket and reached for a potato. When they had all been cut and planted in rows, Isla fetched her bucket and Drew found an abandoned tin can, and together they carried water from the wash-house to give the soil a good soaking. Then, side by side, they surveyed the smooth weed-free bed with satisfaction.

'With any luck, we'll have good new potatoes to eat next spring,' Isla said.

Drew, now comfortable in her presence, beamed and said, 'Aye!' just as Barbara, playing in the wash-house with Greta and the peg dolls, came hurrying up the steps, her face screwed up.

'Mummy, my dolly's lost her face!' She brandished the little doll, now with an ordinary peg-head atop her dressed body.

'Bring the cloth here and I'll fasten it back on.'

'But I don't know where it went,' Barbara wailed. 'I want her face back. I don't want her to have an old peg-face!'

'Give it here.' Drew, who had struck up a friendship with the children, took the peg from her and sat down on one of the steps beyond the wash-house. 'I'll do a new face for her, if you like. I've got some wee tins of paint upstairs that'll finish her off nicely.'

Barbara sat beside him, fascinated, as he started working at the peg with the tip of his knife. 'Two eyes – and a nose – and a nice smiley mouth,' he said as he worked. 'And curly hair, too, with a bit of a fringe at the front, like yours.' The knifepoint moved deftly, the peg twirling about in his fingers, then he gave the doll back to Barbara, said, 'Back in a tick,' and hurried into the close, whistling tunelessly.

'Look at what Drew's done, Mummy.' Barbara handed the peg to Isla, who took it and was still studying the neat little bland face and the swirl of curly hair that the lad had carved from the plain wooden knob when he came back, some tiny paint tins and a brush and an old bit of rag in his hands.

'Now then,' he said, taking the peg doll back and opening one of the tins. In a few minutes the little face had sprung to life, with blue eyes, tilted up at the corners, a neat little rosebud mouth, and brown curly hair.

'Careful,' Drew cautioned as he handed it to Barbara. 'Let her get dry, or she'll smudge into all the colours of the rainbow.'

'I didn't know you were so clever, Drew,' Isla said, astonished, and he blushed, then shrugged.

'Och, it's nothing. I like making wee things out of old bits of wood. It gives me something to do with my hands.'

There had been no further visits from Ainslie McAdam, and Isla, greatly relieved, allowed herself to hope that the girl had decided to leave her alone. She hadn't seen Gilchrist Forbes or his disapproving son either, and that suited her. Each Monday morning she went to the lawyer's office, where she received a sealed envelope from his receptionist. She signed for it, and left the office as quickly as she could, feeling very like Judas as she pushed the envelope, with its ill-gotten gains, deep into her pocket.

Back home, spreading the money out on the table, she felt as though she was stealing it from them, particularly from Mrs Brown, after all Drew's help with the potato bed. But she had no option. One day, she kept promising herself, she would make amends. One day when – if – she ever had money she would do all she could to improve their living conditions, although for the life of her she couldn't see what could be done. The entire row of tenements was old and should have been pulled down long since. What these people needed was rehousing.

Often there was a brief note with the money, recording

a tenant's inability to pay the full amount, or any money at all, and informing her that if she wanted action to be taken against the non-payer she should notify Mr Forbes. She threw the notes on the fire, feeling as though she was prying on her neighbours. She had no intention of taking action against anyone simply because they were too poor to pay the rent on time. Poverty wasn't a crime, although people like Gilchrist Forbes seemed to think it was.

Often, it was Granny Thomson who hadn't paid her rent. Old as she was, the woman did some cleaning in one of the shops to augment her tiny pension, but she suffered from rheumatism and bronchitis, and often she couldn't get out of bed, let alone work. When that happened, Isla and Magret took it in turns to see that the old woman didn't starve, taking a bowl of soup or a cup of tea and a bit of bread and butter in to her stuffy, cold, dark little room until she was on her feet again. It hurt Isla to know that Granny Thomson lived in constant fear of someone else being given her job while she was unable to do it, and of ending her days in the poorhouse. Her mingled gratitude and choking shame at 'being a burden' to her neighbours almost broke Isla's heart. She wished that she could tell the old woman the truth, and assure her that as long as she owned the building, Granny wouldn't be put out. But she had to stay silent.

Sometimes the Browns were unable to pay all the rent, and once the Kellys were defaulters, because there had been a strike at the factory that employed Mr Kelly and he had been laid off. Both he and his wife aged with worry over the two-week strike, and so did Isla, on their behalf, then to their mutual relief the strike was settled and the rent money slowly made up during the following week.

It was a hand-to-mouth existence, and she often wondered if Kenneth had had any knowledge of the struggle his tenants went through simply to survive, or about the conditions they had to live in. It disturbed her to think that he might have known, and yet not cared enough to do anything about it.

November came raging in with strong, bitterly cold winds that found every chink and crack in the old tenement. Rags and newspaper had to be stuffed round windows and below doors, and at night the flames within Isla's fragile gas mantles often flickered in the draught. It rained all the time, which meant that the washing had to be dried indoors, the smell of wet wool and the steam of its drying adding to the stuffiness and humidity of the single room. It became difficult to get close to the fire, because the washing had to take priority.

'I wish I was a vest,' Barbara grumbled more than once. 'Then I'd get to be nice and cosy in front of the fire.'

All Isla's energies were concentrated on keeping the children as healthy as possible. She fed them plates of thick porridge morning and night, because it was a cheap and nourishing way of filling their stomachs. Scattering precious sugar as thickly as she dared over it, she remembered her own childhood, when her mother had poured generous spoonfuls of honey or golden syrup over her porridge, then added cream. Her father, a true Scotsman, salted his porridge, but Isla and her mother liked theirs sweet and rich.

She learned from Magret that it was best to delay a visit to the greengrocer's until it was almost closing time, when he was anxious to sell off any vegetables that might not be fit for sale the next morning. Carrots and potatoes and turnips, chopped up and simmered with a handful of lentils and barley and a bone, made a nourishing broth that lasted for a few days. If there was meat on the bone, it was carefully pared off to add a savoury flavour to platefuls of potatoes.

Survival became the centre of Isla's existence. She lay awake at night listening to the rain sloshing down the gutters at the side of the street, worrying about the cost of calling in the doctor and paying for medication if one or both of the children took ill. She didn't even dare to contemplate the thought of any illness touching her, making her too weak to care for Barbara and Ross. But the porridge and home-made soup, with fish whenever Isla could afford it, kept the three of them well.

Poor little Greta wasn't so fortunate. In mid-November she took a sore throat and had to miss school and stay at home, one of her father's socks, filled with hot salt, tied around her small neck. Isla took Ross to fetch Barbara from school, keeping an eye on the clouds racing overhead as she hurried the children out of the school gates, anxious to get them indoors before the rain started to fall again. Her clothes-horse was already groaning under the weight of drying clothes; she didn't want to have wet coats and shoes to deal with as well.

'Come on, Barbara – don't pull at me like that!'

Barbara, undeterred, gave another tug on her mother's hand. 'Mummy, that lady over there looks funny.'

Isla's eyes followed her daughter's pointing finger.

The school stood opposite West Station, and in her rush to get the children home she hadn't noticed the black-clad figure leaning against the station wall, head bowed. The woman's unfashionably long skirt hung down below her coat, and on the ground by her booted feet stood a basket. One or two neatly wrapped parcels had spilled from it.

Nobody else seemed to have noticed her. Isla pushed Ross's perambulator across the road and bumped it up on to the pavement, turning it with its back against the bitter wind.

'Are you all right?' She put a hand tentatively on the woman's shoulder and a paper-white face swung towards her.

'So silly,' the woman whispered. 'Came over faint. I'll be – all right in a minute.'

Isla looked up and down the street, but it was almost empty. Nobody wanted to loiter on such a day.

'D'you think she's going to die?' Barbara asked in her clear voice, staring up into the old lady's face.

'Sshh! Of course not!' Beneath her hand Isla felt the bony shoulder ripple in a half-laugh.

'At least I'll die with – my boots on!' the frail voice commented.

'Can you tell me where you live?'

' 'Course I can. Not stupid, just a bit – breathless. It's just round the – corner there. I'll go on in a minute, when – when I've caught my breath.'

Isla stooped and scooped the parcels into the basket, then straightened and put an arm about the woman. 'Barbara, can you manage to push Ross's chair for me while I help this lady?'

'Of course I can.' Barbara stooped in her turn, picking up a folded umbrella that Isla hadn't noticed. 'Here, Ross,' she told her brother, 'you can carry that.' She swung the chair round with a bit of an effort and began to push it towards the corner.

'Put your arm over my shoulders, and I'll put my arm around your waist.' Isla organised the old lady, who was taller than she was, and drooped over her. Slowly, they made their way round the corner, past the entrance to the West Station, then followed the road in a gentle downhill curve towards the large houses opposite the cricket ground. Barbara had difficulty in manoeuvring the push-chair, especially as the furled umbrella clutched in Ross's chubby little hands stuck out on either side and tended to hit off the wall, but she managed it, concentration making her tongue protrude beyond her teeth.

'Round here,' the woman said feebly, and Isla saw to her dismay that the road they had turned into led uphill. There were high walls on either side, and no sign of a house, and she doubted whether Barbara, or she herself, burdened as she was, could manage to keep going to the top of the hill. But there was nothing else for it but to grit their teeth and forge on. To her surprise, the old lady stopped only a matter of yards further along, outside a small faded green wooden door set in the high wall.

'Here we are. I can take the basket, my dear, if you'll open the door.'

Barbara, forsaking the pram, squeezed past her mother's legs to stare through the opened gate. 'It's a magic place!' she said with delight, and the woman laughed, a wheezy, rusty sound ending in a fit of coughing.

'That's what I used to think when I was your age,' she said when she had caught her breath again. 'I'd forgotten that.'

The gate opened on to a small quiet road. On their left, flanked by tall trees, stood the high wall that divided this road from the main road, and on the right a series of gates led to gardens and houses. Even the wind had lost some of its power in this sheltered place; while it buffeted and howled against the other side of the wall, the little road seemed untouched, only the tops of the highest trees swaying before it.

'Just a few gates along, dear – not far to go.'

When they reached the right gate, Barbara wrestled with the latch, finally managing to open it. 'Use the umbrella for the – children, or they'll be soaked – by the bushes,' the elderly woman advised Isla. 'I'm much better now, I can manage.' Isla opened the large black umbrella and put it into Ross's hands. He held it high as Barbara, her head ducked forward beneath its shelter, pushed him up the flagged path, edged on either side by dripping bushes. Between the bare twigs, Isla, taking up the rear, could see small leaf-strewn lawns on either side.

'Now I'm for it,' the woman said gloomily, edging round the pram to mount the two steps into the small, open, glass-sided porch. Her legs, impossibly thin and looking like saplings planted in the sturdy boots she wore, just managed the climb. She tugged at a brass bell-pull set by the side of the front door and the bell jangled in the depths of the house.

'Will your mummy be angry?' Barbara asked, wide-eyed, deserting the pram and skipping up into the porch, which had a bench running down each side. The woman chuckled again, and again ended up coughing and spluttering. She dug into her coat pocket and produced a handkerchief, which she held to her mouth.

'I've not got a mummy,' she said through the folds. 'I've got an Annie, and she's far worse.'

As she spoke, the door opened to reveal a stout woman with iron-grey hair curling out from under a frilly white cap. Her sturdy body was clothed in a black dress and white apron, and her round, ruddy face was wrinkled with concern.

'Miss Flora, where have you—' She stopped, her gaze travelling down to Barbara, then to where Isla wrestled with the umbrella, trying to get it down, hampered by the basket and the push chair. 'What's happened?'

'Nothing, nothing. I took a little turn in the – the street, that's all, and these young people - kindly helped me back home.'

'I told you, didn't I, Miss Flora? I told you that you weren't strong enough to go out on your own. But would you list—'

'You were right, Annie, as usual. Now,' said Miss Flora, 'are we going to stand here – all day, or are we going to get indoors out of the cold and – offer these kind people some refreshments?'

Isla had succeeded in closing the umbrella, showering herself with rainwater in the process. 'No, really, we must get home before the rain starts,' she began, but Miss Flora interrupted.

'Nonsense, my dear, you've saved my life and I insist – on giving you a cup of tea, at least.' Stronger now that she was back home, she swept into the hall, Barbara scampering after her.

11

Isla, realising that there was no help for it, began to unfasten the straps that held Ross into the chair.

'Here – I'll get it,' Annie said as she lifted the little boy out and began to wrestle one-handedly with the push-chair. She surged down the steps and lifted the chair, muttering as she did so, 'Never pays a blind bit of notice to what I say. Oh no – off she goes and what happens? She very near kills herself!'

'Come in here, my dear,' the elderly woman called from beyond an open door to the right as Isla followed Annie into the hall, 'There's a nice fire.'

Barbara stood in the middle of the room, turning slowly, her eyes and mouth open as she took in every detail of the polished furniture and the pictures on the walls.

'You should go straight to your bed,' the maid told her employer sternly. 'You'll make yourself ill again. She's just getting over a bout of bronchitis,' she explained to Isla. 'She should never have gone out on a day like this, but try telling her that.'

'I was bored. I needed the fresh air. And now I'd like a cup of tea – if you don't mind. And some bread to toast, and whatever you think the children would like to drink.' Now that she was safely home, Miss Flora's breathing was easier. 'Take off your coat, my dear, and sit down here, by the fire.'

Annie, muttering under her breath, peeled her employer and then the two children efficiently out of their coats, while Isla took her own off.

'I don't know what I'd do without her, but she fusses,' the old lady said as Annie, arms piled high with coats, went out of the room. 'I'm Flora Currie, by the way.' A large bony hand was thrust out towards Isla. She shook it and introduced herself and the children, then allowed herself to be coaxed into a cushioned chair by the fire.

Ross, intimidated by the strange room, pulled at her skirt and she lifted him on to her lap, saying automatically, 'Barbara, don't touch anything.'

'Nonsense, children need to touch things. She'll be sensible, I'm sure.' Miss Currie – Isla had noticed that both hands were free of rings – sat down in the chair opposite. She had kept her hat on; it was a woollen black turban, and its slightly Eastern look suited her hawk-like nose and angular features. The colour had come back into her face. 'D'ye see that large, pink shell, little girl? Fetch it over here, will you?'

When Barbara did as she was told, carrying the shell carefully in both hands, Miss Currie took it and held it to the child's ear. 'If you listen, you can hear the sea. Hear it?'

Barbara concentrated, frowning, then the frown faded and her brown eyes widened in astonishment. 'I can! I can hear the sea, Mummy!' She brought the shell over and held it first to Isla's ear, then to Ross's, then to her own again.

'My father brought that home for me when I was about your age,' Flora Currie told her. 'He was a sea captain, sailing out of Greenock.'

'My daddy's going to bring one just like it for me when he comes back to us,' Barbara said at once.

Miss Currie's eyes flicked swiftly to Isla's face, a mute question in them. She read the answer, then said calmly, 'I expect he will. Until then, you're welcome to come and listen to my shell now and again. It likes people to listen to it.'

Annie came in with a large tray and set out the tea things on a low table between both women. She had included sturdy mugs of milk for the children, and piled a plate with slices of bread. While Miss Currie showed Barbara how to spear the slices on a brass toasting fork and hold them close to the bars of the fire until they were browned, Isla drank the hot tea gratefully, and ate buttered toast and Madeira cake, feeding Ross, still perched on her knee, mouth open like a little fledgling.

As they ate, Flora Currie talked about her childhood, spent in the house where she still lived, and about her father and mother and two older brothers.

'I'm all that's left now – apart from some nephews and nieces scattered about Scotland and too busy to visit me.'

She asked few questions, only enough to learn that they lived not far away, in George Street.

'But it seems like a hundred miles away,' Isla told her. 'I'd no idea that this road existed so close to where we live.'

Ross, growing bolder, wriggled to get down, and she handed him over to Barbara with instructions to behave themselves.

'Oh, let them explore a little, I'm sure they won't hurt anything. My brothers and I and the other children who lived here when we were young enjoyed popping in and out through that gate,' Flora Currie said. 'After I read *Alice in Wonderland* I felt that the gate would have fitted well into the story. I'd forgotten all about that until your little girl reminded me. The road opens out at the other end, of course, so that vehicles can get through. My papa had a carriage – the double gate just a little bit along from where we came in leads into our drive and up to the carriage-house, but the gates haven't been opened in years, and the carriage-house is filled with rubbish.' She leaned forward, her eyes on Isla. 'You don't speak like the people round here.'

'I was brought up in Glasgow, then I lived in Edinburgh for several years, then on the Clyde coast. We've only been in Paisley for a few months.'

'You've still got a trace of that pretty East coast lilt to your voice. I used to love excursions to Edinburgh – it has such an air of timelessness about it.'

As though on cue, the clock on the mantelshelf chimed softly and Isla said, 'We must go . . .' just as rain spattered on the bay window behind Miss Currie.

'Better stay here until this shower passes,' she advised, just as Barbara's clear little voice called from the hall, 'Mummy, come and see this!'

'Barbara, what are you up to?' Isla jumped up and hurried towards the sound of her daughter's voice. The children were standing at an open door on the other side of the hall, towards the back of the house.

'Look!' Barbara disappeared into the room, towing Ross behind her.

'Barbara!'

'They've found my secret vice,' Flora Currie said, moving past Isla to the open door. 'We all have our failings, I suppose.' She gave Isla a lop-sided, shamefaced smile. 'This used to be my mother's sewing room, but since my parents died and my brothers married and moved away, I've taken it over as my own. Come and see.'

Isla stopped on the threshold, staring. The room was filled with dolls' houses, sitting on counters that had been built around the walls. Large elaborate houses and smaller modest dwellings jostling together, some wide, some narrow, some high, some single-storey. Barbara was moving along the counters, hands clasped behind her back, the tension in the curled fingers and small shoulders indicating a repressed urge to open each house front and look inside.

For a long moment Isla gaped, then she said huskily, 'How wonderful.'

'So you don't think I'm a stupid old woman who's never properly grown up?'

Isla turned, and realised that Miss Currie's eyes were green. 'I think you're very lucky.'

A gust of wind hurled rain against the window, but nobody noticed as, one by one, Miss Currie opened the fronts of the houses, revealing doll families in parlours and nurseries and kitchens and studies. Ross, too small to see, found a box half filled with miniature furniture and dolls and tiny animals tucked away beneath one of the counters, and squatted happily on the floor to empty it.

'I've got a dolls' house,' Barbara told Miss Currie proudly. 'My mummy made it out of a box. And she made clothes-peg dollies for me and Greta and some of the other wee girls in our street.'

'Indeed? You've got a very clever mummy.' The old woman smiled at Isla.

The grandfather clock in the hall chimed the hour, and Isla, suddenly noticing the mess Ross was making, stooped to put everything back into the box. 'We must go – I have to get to the shops.'

It was still raining, with no sign of an improvement now, and Miss Currie offered her the large black umbrella. 'You can hand it in some time,' she said, and waved from the porch as they set off into the November gloom, Isla negotiating the push-chair with one hand and holding the umbrella with the other.

'I like that lady,' Barbara said as Isla filled the tin bath before the fire that evening. 'When I'm old like her I'm going to live in a big house.' Her brows wrinkled in thought, then she said, 'We had a house like that once.'

'Something like it.' Isla refilled the kettle at the tap and put it on to the stove, then caught Ross up as he toddled past her and settled into her chair to take his clothes off. 'Come on, young man, time for your bath.'

'When can we go back to our house?' Barbara persisted. Isla looked at her over the top of Ross's red head.

'I don't know, love,' she said, and the longing that swept over her for Kenneth was so great that she had to blink back tears.

*

She returned the umbrella on the following day, intending to hand it in and then hurry away. But Flora Currie herself opened the door, the knitted turban still pulled firmly down over her ears, and insisted on giving her a cup of tea.

'Annie's doing the shopping today, so we'll have to manage on our own,' she said, leading the way through the hall to a door hidden in the shadows behind the stairs. It opened into a kitchen fragrant with the smell of baking and warmed by a large range.

'How are you, Miss Currie?'

'Oh, completely recovered from that silly nonsense yesterday. Annie's quite right, of course, I should never have ventured so far after being in bed for two weeks. But sometimes I feel the need to defy her, just to prove to myself that I'm still alive. Sit down there,' Flora ordered, and Isla obediently sat at the white-scrubbed table that took up most of the room. Ross wandered about fingering the knobs on the cupboard doors.

'Can I help?'

'No need, my dear, I know how to fend for myself.'

Flora measured tea into a small teapot then eyed the huge kettle simmering on the range, and added, 'Though I'd be grateful if you could see to that monster for me.' She held out her large bony hands to reveal swollen knuckles and some slightly twisted fingers. 'Rheumatics,' she explained, scowling at her hands. 'I might tip the kettle too far and scald myself, and then I'd never hear the end of it from Annie. She insists on being the servant, and wearing that ridiculous uniform,' she went on, setting out cups and half filling a mug with milk for Ross while Isla poured boiling water into the teapot. 'I've tried to get her to settle for a skirt and cardigan like mine, but she never will.'

She produced a plate of spiced scones, still warm from the oven. 'I have to do my baking when Annie's out at the shops. She won't admit that I've got a lighter hand than hers when it comes to pastry, in spite of the rheumatism. My mother, bless her, believed in her children learning how to cook and bake.' She slit the scones and spread them generously with butter. 'Being a seaman, my father agreed with her. My brothers could cook and sew – not that their wives allowed it, for the very thought shocked them. My brother Arnold did that.' She nodded at a framed sampler on the wall, the words, 'The Heart of A House Is The Kitchen', surrounded by neatly stitched forget-me-nots. 'In secret, when his wife wasn't around, just to prove to himself that he could still manage it.'

She poured the tea and sat down. 'I take it that you're a widow.'

'My husband died six months ago.'

Flora nodded. 'I thought as much, the way your little girl talked about her daddy. How d'you cope, with two children to look after on your own?'

'I manage.'

'I'm sure you do.' Flora Currie pushed the plate of scones towards Isla and poured out more tea for them both. 'Tell me about the dolls' house you made for your daughter.'

'It's just a wee orange box with a curtain over the front.'

'I'd like to hear all about it all the same – what you did for furniture, and how you made the dolls.'

She listened with interest, breaking in with an occasional question, as Isla described the making of the orange-box house. 'I used to try to make houses myself,' she recalled. 'But I wasn't good at it. I lack your imagination.'

Then, planting her hands flat on the table, she levered herself to her feet. 'Come and have another look at my collection. It's not often I get to show them off. Annie complains about the dust they collect, and thinks I'm a stupid old woman. It's good to meet someone who understands.'

In the room that held the dolls' houses, Ross made for the box he had been playing with on the previous day. 'Leave him be,' Flora said when Isla tried to stop him. 'It's only broken furniture and dolls that were never repaired. I'm no good at throwing things out. I'd some notion of giving the houses to my nieces, but my brothers tended towards sons, and the only two girls were given handsome dolls' houses by their parents before I got round to making the offer.' She looked round the room, and sighed. 'They should really be given to a hospital or something. They'll just be a nuisance to my heirs one day, and they're meant to be played with, after all.'

'Not that one.' Isla pointed to the grandest house, a Victorian mansion complete with a butler's pantry, and servants' quarters in the attic. 'That's a collector's item.'

'That was my own, when I was small. My grandmama gave it to me, and I was only allowed to play with it when my nurse or my mother were there to see that I didn't do any damage. I used to long to be allowed to spend just ten minutes with it on my own; I think that's why I was so determined to do as I pleased once I had the freedom.' She sighed, touching the house lovingly. 'Poor thing, it's been neglected. It was put away in the attic when I got older, and not brought out until long after my parents died. I kept meaning to have it renovated, but I never got around to it.'

The front door opened and closed. 'We're in here, Annie,' Flora Currie called, and the maid, in her outer clothes, glanced in at the door, sniffing when she saw Isla.

'You're here again, are you?'

'Mind your own business,' her mistress snapped back at her, while Isla, suddenly afraid that she was outstaying her welcome, knelt to replace the toys that Ross had taken out of the box.

'We must go.'

'Would you like to choose one of the houses as a Christmas gift for your little girl?' Miss Currie asked abruptly as they were about to leave the room. Isla was taken aback by the suddenness of the offer, but rallied.

'It's very kind of you, but she's fine with the one she's got.'

'You said it was made from a box, and I thought she might like . . .'

Isla felt hot colour surge into her face. 'She's fine,' she repeated, and regretted the sharpness in her voice as soon as she saw the stricken look on Miss Currie's face.

'My dear, I'm so sorry if I offended you.'

'You didn't. It's just that . . .' Isla's voice trailed away and they surveyed each other in an awkward silence. Ross, between them, looked up at their faces, puzzled by the sudden tension in the little room. Miss

Currie bent and scrabbled in a corner beneath one of
the tables, bringing out a shabby little dolls' house.

'This is the one I had in mind, it seemed to me to be
the right size for a child of your daughter's age. It
needs doing up, but from what you've told me, I'm sure
that you could do it very well.'

Isla wished that she had never come back to the
house. 'I don't mean to be rude, Miss Currie, but,' she
bit her lip, then said in a rush of words, 'it's just that
I'll not take anything from anyone unless I can pay for
it. And I can't afford to buy a dolls' house just now, not
even a wee one.'

The older woman's flush deepened. 'Oh my dear, I
should have realised.'

'It was kind of you to think of Barbara. No, Ross!'
Isla seized his hand, which was reaching out hopefully
towards the box. 'We have to go now, pet.' She escaped
thankfully to the hall to collect her coat and Ross's
small jacket, hating herself for depriving Barbara and for
hurting the old lady, but knowing that she couldn't,
wouldn't, accept charity.

To her astonishment, Annie, still hanging up her
own outdoor clothing, muttered out of the side of her
mouth, 'For any favour, let her give the lassie the wee
house.'

'What?'

'Go on,' the woman hissed, putting a large cold hand
on Isla's. 'She's got nob'dy of her own, and she's fair
desperate to do somethin' for somebody. It surely
couldnae do any harm to give in to her just this once!'

Isla's resolve faded as she looked into Annie's round
face and saw the pleading look in her eyes. She

swallowed hard, her hand falling away from the hook that held her coat, then turned and went back into the room, where Flora Currie stood, looking lost and alone, still clutching the little dolls' house.

'Miss Currie – if you're sure that you really mean it—'

The green eyes lit up. 'I do! You'll accept it, then?'

'Yes, but I'll not take it without paying for it. I can't afford to pay in money,' she added hurriedly as she saw the older woman open her mouth to protest, 'but I could do some renovation work on your Victorian house in return, if you want me to.'

'Oh my dear, that would be so kind of you. I accept.'

'I'll need to work on the wee house here, for there's no room in my own place.'

'Och, that's no trouble at all. I'm sure there are some wee pots of paint around that you could use – and there's the furniture in the box. You're welcome to it, if you can do anything with it,' Flora Currie enthused.

From the doorway, Annie said heavily, 'I suppose that'll mean a mess for me to clear up.'

But the faintest of smiles tugged at the corners of her mouth.

12

Because their year of mourning still had five months to run, there could be no Christmas or New Year celebrations in the McAdam household. Christmas trees, becoming more fashionable now, could be seen here and there in their neighbours' bay windows as December matured, and Ainslie, alighting from the bus each night, liked to look at the trees with their pretty decorations as she walked home.

It was a custom that the McAdams had never taken up, but Colin's family had a tree each year, and she recalled with pleasure the fresh pine smell that had pervaded their large drawing-room the year before, and the way the light from the tall red candles on their dinner table had gleamed on green pine needles. She and her mother and brother had had dinner with the Forbeses last Christmas Day, and she had become engaged to Colin on New Year's Day, at a dinner party in the McAdam house.

Her father had been present at the engagement celebration, but not at the Forbeses' dinner table, because he was always busy at Christmas. Now, Ainslie knew where he had been.

Although they didn't make much of Christmas Day themselves, the family did give gifts to each other, and it was Catherine McAdam's custom to present small gifts to the servants. Ainslie had had a generous allowance since leaving school, but that had stopped with her father's death, and it occurred to her that she might buy presents for her mother and brother from the auction house. Nervously, she approached Charlie at the beginning of December and asked if she could purchase a pair of china figures for her mother, and a boxed set of model cars that she knew Innes would love.

He squinted up at her from his desk. 'This is an auction room, lass, not a shop.'

'I know that, but I thought that if I paid the reserve price . . .'

He tutted and shook his head. 'They might go for more than the reserve price if they're auctioned, and if I sold to you instead, I could be depriving my clients of money – and myself of commission. If you want 'em, lass, you must go into the auction room at the right time and bid for 'em.'

Her mouth went dry at the prospect, and a gleam of amusement came into the eyes surveying her. 'Scared, are you? No need to be – I'll not let you buy a wardrobe by mistake. Go on and bid for 'em – it'll be good experience for you. When it's your turn to run an auction you'll know what the other folk in the room feel like.'

'When I—? I'm not going to be an auctioneer. I'm office staff.'

'Think so?' Charlie Blayne tilted his chair back, openly grinning now. 'Everyone turns their hands to everything here, and I think ye'd do well as an auction-eer, once ye learn the ropes.'

The thought of Catherine McAdam's reaction if her daughter was ever to run an auction made Ainslie feel faint. 'I'll maybe just have a look round the shops.'

'That's the coward's way out, and ye never struck me as a coward, Ainslie McAdam. Go on,' Charlie urged, 'I'll be auctioning the items ye want later this week, and the office can look after itself for an hour. I'll expect ye to be there – and that's an order, young lady.'

Ainslie scarcely slept on the night before the auction. She told herself a dozen times that she couldn't go through with it, and her stomach started churning when, looking down from the interior office windows the next day, she saw the public surging in through the street doors. Still unsure as to her final decision, she finished the work she was doing, blotted and closed the big ledger, then took a deep sustaining breath and went down the outer stairs, into the street, and into the auc-tion room via the public door.

She had watched a few sales from the safety of the gallery, and had been aware of the surge of excitement wafting up from the floor below, but being in among it all was quite different. There was a tingle in the air, a sense of anticipation. Some people stood about in groups, heads together, arguing, dissenting, sometimes agreeing, all the time eyeing each other slyly, measuring up the opposition. Others drifted in ones and twos around the room, examining the stacked furniture and rolled carpets, running their fingers over the china or through drawers of cutlery, making notes on scraps of paper. Ainslie, too, walked about, studying items she had no intention of buying, carefully ignoring the pieces she was interested in, trying to look as though she was an old hand when it came to attending auctions.

There was a buzz of excitement as Charlie swept down the stairs from the gallery, dressed in his usual auction-day clothes, a smart lounge suit with a bow-tie at the collar of his crisply starched shirt. Leonard, his clerk, was in close attendance, his arms filled with ledgers and lists.

Some people moved to the rows of chairs below the platform, but Ainslie remained on her feet at the rear of the room, ready to slip out through the street door if her nerve failed her. To her horror, Charlie, after casting a quick glance round the room, saw her lurking in the background and rapped his gavel on the lectern, booming, 'Order now, ladies and gentlemen – and make way for the young lady at the back there. Come forward, madam, and take a seat. Don't worry, we won't expect ye to bid for it.'

A ripple of appreciative laughter ran through the crowd, and there were hearty guffaws from the furniture movers as they recognised Ainslie. The bidders standing in front of her looked over their shoulders, then stepped aside. Blushing, she had no option but to walk through their midst like Moses moving between the parted waves, to take a seat. Charlie gave her the ghost of a wink, then rapped again on the lectern, and the auction began.

He was good at his profession, taking his audience neatly through the lots, occasionally tossing out a joke to set them at their ease. His eyes seemed to be everywhere, and no bid, no matter how unobtrusive, went unnoticed. Beside him, Leonard scribbled furiously, keeping pace with each and every bid and the names of the successful bidders, while the aproned men responsible for putting each lot on view without any time-wasting worked smoothly and efficiently.

Ainslie's terror ebbed away as she watched the proceedings, fascinated, then her mouth went dry when Charlie, giving her a meaningful look, announced, 'Lot twenty-six, ladies and gentlemen – a handsomely boxed set of model cars, every detail correct. An excellent buy for the car enthusiast. What am I bid?'

Ainslie put a hand up and called out an amount that she knew to be well below the reserve. Charlie's eyebrows rose.

'The young lady knows a good bargain when she sees one,' he told his audience smoothly. 'Any other bids?'

Somebody at the back of the room put in a bid. Ainslie topped it, then had to top it again, and again. They were over the reserve price and approaching her limit when, to her astonishment, the other bidder dropped out, and Charlie slammed the gavel down once, twice, and said, 'Sold to the young lady in the front row.'

The unexpected success boosted her confidence, and when the china figures she wanted for her mother were brought out half an hour later, she bid with more confidence, again starting below the reserve price. This time, though, the bidding was rapid, quickly going beyond her limit, and she had to concede the figures to a plump woman further down the row. During her look around before the auction, she had noticed a set of china wall plates, so she waited, and managed to buy them when their turn came. Then, flushed with success, she escaped back to the office.

'That was a dirty trick to play on me – starting the bidding below the reserve price,' Charlie said when he came up to the office later. Ainslie shot him a quick sidelong glance, and was relieved to see that though the words were grim, he was smiling.

'I thought that that was what bidding was all about, Mr Blayne,' she told him demurely. 'If I'd started at the reserve price, I might not have got the cars.'

He laughed. 'Ye're quite right. Well done, lassie, ye got a bargain both times, and my clients still got a price they'll be happy with. D'ye see now what I meant about not selling at the reserve price?'

Ainslie nodded. 'I didn't know an auction could be such a challenge.'

'It can be enjoyable, but it can be like gambling, too. It's amazing the folk who come in and buy stuff they don't need, just for the fun of bidding.'

'And the folk who bid, then can't pay,' chipped in Leonard, a small, elderly man who, with his large hooked nose and sharp eyes, looked like the picture of Punch in one of Ainslie's childhood books. He put the plates and the box of model cars down on a table, and gave her a broad wink as Charlie continued on into his own office. 'Ye did all right, hen,' he whispered. 'Good for you!'

Ainslie and Innes attended the midnight church service on Christmas Eve, debating over the following day's routine as they walked home. It had always been the family custom to take their presents downstairs and put them on the dining-room sideboard to be opened after breakfast, but this year everything was different.

'I think we should,' Ainslie said firmly.

'But if Mother stays in bed we can't open the presents.'

'Then we'll leave them there until dinner. She'll be at the dinner table.'

'But that means that I'll have to wait all day to open them!' Innes's voice was anguished.

'That can't be helped. We should do as we've always done.'

To their surprise, Catherine was already seated at the breakfast table when they went into the dining-room in the morning, and there were two wrapped parcels on the sideboard. Ainslie and Innes, who had met on the stairs and entered the room together, exchanged glances.

'Merry Christmas, Mother.' Ainslie kissed Catherine's cheek. 'It's good to see you downstairs at this time of day.'

'One must make an effort, I suppose, on special occasions.'

When they had finished eating and the dishes – Catherine's scarcely touched – had been cleared away, the servants were summoned to the dining-room to receive a sealed envelope each from their mistress. They curtsied and scurried out, then it was the family's turn. Innes tore at his parcels and exclaimed with delight over the model cars and the *Boys' Own Annual* he received from his mother. Catherine unwrapped the parcel he had given her to reveal a wooden teapot stand.

'I made it in school,' Innes said proudly. 'Yours too,

Ainslie, but I didn't have time to finish the other one. I should have it done by February.'

Ainslie put the book-end down and went round to his side of the table to give him a hug. 'Thank you, Innes, it's beautiful.'

He wriggled out of her embrace. 'Aren't you going to open your other presents?'

Catherine had given Ainslie a pair of leather gloves. She herself glanced at the decorated plates and said vaguely, 'They're very pretty,' then put them aside, and excused herself, saying that she had a headache and must go upstairs to lie down.

Unlike the English, the Scots worked through Christmas and holidayed on New Year's Day, their own special celebration. There was an air of excitement about the auction rooms when Ainslie went in that day, a holiday feeling. Charlie Blayne presented a small box of chocolates to each of the women on his staff, and a miniature bottle of whisky to each of the men, and as the day drew to a close he summoned them all together in the auction room, where a table covered with a white cloth held trays bearing small glasses of whisky and ginger wine, and plates filled with thick slices of dark fruit-cake.

When they had all taken a glass, Charlie raised his. 'A good year it's been, and a better one to come. My thanks to all of ye,' he said, beaming round at them. 'Drink up, now, and eat up too. My missus made the cake and she'll have something to say if I take any of it back home.'

Going home at the end of the day, Ainslie could still

taste the sharp tang of the ginger wine on her tongue, and feel its fire in her stomach. Her spirits sank as she let herself into the house and breathed in the usual funereal atmosphere. It was as though Christmas had been shut out, left on the doormat.

As soon as she went into the dining-room she saw that Innes's teapot stand had gone, but the plates she had given her mother still stood untouched on the sideboard. They ate in the usual silence, broken only by Innes as the dessert was cleared away.

'Mother, may I go to the matinee in the Glen Cinema on New Year's Eve?'

'Certainly not,' Catherine said at once. 'Cinemas are dirty, unhygienic places. You don't know who you'll be sitting next to.'

His face fell. 'But it's Tom Mix! You let me go last year, and I'm a whole year older now.'

'I said no, Innes.'

'But Douglas is going, his parents said he could.'

'Douglas isn't in mourning,' Catherine snapped, and he flushed scarlet and said no more, excusing himself a few minutes later and going up to his room.

'He's still a little boy, Mother,' Ainslie ventured when they were alone. 'It's hard on him, keeping a whole year of mourning.'

Catherine gave her an icy look. 'It's hard on us all, and it has been much harder on me than it should have been. When are you going to stop this foolish nonsense?'

Ainslie kept her eyes on the table-cloth. She had made herself apologise abjectly to her mother after their bitter quarrel on the day of the tennis party; Catherine had acknowledged the apology stiffly, but ever since then the wall that had always stood between them had been noticeably stronger. 'I'm not going to tie myself to marriage for the sake of living a comfortable life, Mother,' she said doggedly, for what seemed like the hundredth time.

'It's what you were raised to do!'

'It's what you were raised to do as well, and it's brought you nothing but grief. Why try to make me follow in your footsteps?'

As soon as the words were out she regretted them. Catherine's face went bone-white. She got to her feet so abruptly that for a moment Ainslie thought her mother was going to come round the table and strike her. Instead, Catherine walked to the sideboard, reaching out to clutch at its dark solidity for support.

'That,' she said in a low voice, 'was a cruel thing to say.'

'Yes, it was. I'm sorry.' Was she going to spend the rest of her life apologising for speaking her own mind? Ainslie wondered wearily. 'But we've already been over it all, Mother, and we'll never agree.' She heard the pleading in her own voice. 'Even if I did change my mind, Colin has his pride. He wouldn't marry me now.'

'There are other eligible young men, but none of them will want you either, if you don't pull yourself together soon.' Catherine's voice was tight with anger. 'Do you want to become an old maid? Do you want to lose what looks you have and skivvy away in that stupid auction house until they decide they don't want you any more? And you needn't think I'll support you then, for Innes and I will have better things to do!'

Her hand swept out in a strange groping motion, catching the three plates Ainslie had bought for her, sweeping them on to the floor. One bounced on the thick carpet, but the other two crashed against the chair Catherine had just vacated, and fell to the floor in a shower of fragments. For the space of a breath mother and daughter stared at each other, then Ainslie got up and walked out of the room, brushing past the maid, who had come running at the sound of breaking china.

After the maid had swept up the pieces of china Catherine McAdam sent both servants to bed and sat huddled in the drawing-room, staring into the fire while the house settled around her for the night.

Through no fault of her own, everything in her life had gone wrong. Catherine had been raised to be a good wife, and was quite certain that she had fulfilled her purpose in life admirably. She had never enjoyed Kenneth's attentions in the privacy of their marriage bed – it had always been her belief that no well-bred woman could ever go through such a business without feeling disgust and repugnance – but the thought of him sharing a bed with another woman while she herself wore his ring was more than she could bear. He had dealt her the final humiliation by killing himself, making her the object of vulgar gossip in the town and among her neighbours.

And as if that wasn't enough, she was now cursed with a daughter who might as well have been born into a working-class family for all the gratitude she ever showed. An ungrateful, uncaring girl with no sense of duty, no feeling for anyone else but herself.

She took the brandy decanter from the cupboard and poured a generous measure into a glass. The doctor had prescribed brandy with a raw egg whipped into it to keep her strength up, but in recent months Catherine had found that she preferred the brandy on its own. It soothed the bitterness and dulled the memories of Kenneth's and Ainslie's faults. She refilled the glass, and by the time she had emptied it again the fire was a silver-rose glow in the grate, and the room was chilly. Stiffly, she got to her feet and went into the hall and went up the stairs, holding tightly to the banisters, halting as she neared the top to study her father-in-law's portrait.

It, like the brandy, always soothed and calmed her. The landing light had been left on, and its glow brought his painted face to life, picking out the twinkle in his blue eyes, the crispness of his snowy hair, the firm planes of his face. Catherine stood motionless for some time, drinking in each detail, then went up another few carpeted stairs and reached out to the cool glass, running the tips of her fingers over the outline of his mouth, then up to touch his cheek.

Innes McAdam had been able to transform a room simply by walking into it, she thought, her stiff, ageing limbs becoming fluid at the memory, just as they had each time she saw him, all those years ago, when she was sixteen and he twenty-five years her senior. Her father's friend, quite unaware of her, other than as one of Kenneth's friends; unaware that she only came to his home whenever she could in the hope of seeing him. Even if he was away from the house she was content just to be there, touching door-knobs he had touched, books his hands had held.

His wife, Kenneth's mother, had never been worthy of him in Catherine's opinion. She was generally acknowledged to be a woman of strong character, an intellectual who sat on committees, raised funds, and was known for her work among the poor. Catherine had merely seen her as a bad wife, content to spend her time with others instead of devoting it to her husband's comforts, and spoiling her only son when she should have encouraged him to grow up to be as strong and as noble as his father.

Catherine's smile faded, and her hand stilled on the glass. Marrying Kenneth had been the closest she could get to marrying Innes McAdam himself. At least it gave her his name, made her part of his family. But he had died just over a year after the marriage, shortly after Ainslie's birth. And tragically, Ainslie had inherited her grandmother's nature rather than her grandfather's. Her mother-in-law, Catherine thought bitterly, would probably have approved of the girl's stubborn foolishness.

But at least there was another Innes, young and now hers alone, who would be raised to be a worthy successor to his grandfather. At the thought, Catherine's smile returned. Her Innes would carry on the family name and make it mean something in Paisley again. He would atone for all the mistakes his father had made.

Soothed, she let her hand fall away from the portrait and continued on to the upper landing. As long as she had Innes, nothing else mattered.

13

In the weeks before Christmas, Isla went along to Flora Currie's house every day to work on the little dolls' house. She had decided to turn it into a country cottage, painting the roof to resemble thatch and giving the exterior walls the look of rough white-washed stonework.

She added mock timbering, and climbing roses all round the walls. Then, using scraps of wallpaper and linoleum and carpet that Flora provided, she papered the interior and covered the floors.

Digging about in the box, she found furniture that could be adapted, cutting out rockers for the chairs from strong cardboard then glueing them on and painting them, making tiny cushions, curtains that tied back with ribbon, frills for dressing-tables and stools.

Flora was overcome with admiration. 'Where did you learn to do all that?'

Isla, making a cradle from a matchbox, cardboard, and glue, smiled up at her. 'I enjoy finding ways of making things.'

Flora raked through drawers and cupboards, finding broken necklaces, bits of ribbon, scraps of material for

Isla to use. She insisted on contributing a family of little china dolls, and Isla dressed them – a dress and apron for the mother, smocks for the two little girls, overalls and a work shirt for the 'daddy doll' she knew Barbara would insist on. Strands from an old summer hat of Flora's were deftly woven into straw hats for the family, and in the cradle lay a tiny baby wearing a white lacy gown.

The work took time, and Magret soon wanted to know where she got to in the mornings. Isla, knowing instinctively that it was best to keep her two lives apart, said that she had managed to find some cleaning work in one of the houses at Castlehead.

Barbara, too, was fully occupied. With Christmas approaching, her class was rehearsing for its part in the school Christmas concert, and Barbara, who had always loved singing, was in her element, warbling carols in her clear, sweet little voice all the time she was at home. Ross, not to be outdone, sang along with her, much to her annoyance.

'He keeps getting it wrong,' she protested.

'But he's learning the words quite well. Aren't you, my clever lad?'

Ross beamed up at his mother from where he sat on the fireside rug. 'Oil city,' he agreed.

'It's Royal – David's – City, not oil city,' his exasperated sister snapped, and flounced out to practise her carols with Greta in the wash-house.

Isla finished the little doll's house in good time, and was able to spend the last few days before Christmas studying the Victorian house and planning the renovation work. She was nervous about undertaking it, but Flora Currie was adamant. 'You said you would do it, and I have every faith in your ability. In fact, I insist!'

On the last day of the school term, Isla and Magret, dressed in their best, attended the concert, which was staged in the large gym hall. They went alone, because Tommy was on the late shift at the mill.

'Not that he'd have gone anyway,' Magret said as they walked to the school. 'The men always leave that sort of thing tae their womenfolk. Ye'll mebbe get some grandads, though.'

Sure enough, the few men among the crowd flocking into the large hall tended to be older – retired men, bored and looking for any diversion that might brighten the monotonous days. A lot of the women had brought small children with them, for there was nobody to look after them at home. Ross clung to Isla's hand while Magret carried Daisy, bound snugly to her by a shawl, as usual.

The large echoing hall was decorated for the occasion: Ross stared about, enchanted, while Daisy reached grasping fingers up towards the brightly coloured paper streamers criss-crossing over the ceiling and walls. A small decorated Christmas tree stood at one side of the stage, and there was a vase of paper flowers on the piano at the opposite side. As the hands on the clock above the stage reached the time announced for the beginning of the concert a self-conscious young teacher in a low-waisted wool stockinette grey dress, her hair plaited into braids curling like shells around her ears, crept out of the wings to take her seat on the piano stool and flutter through the sheets of music before her.

'That's Miss Wilson,' a hoarse voice said from behind Isla. 'She taught our Myra last year. Awful nice lassie, but awful shy.'

'She looks as if she's wearing her mother's dress,' Magret whispered loudly into Isla's ear just then. 'She'd be pretty if she just wore something more modern.'

Miss Wilson, uncomfortably aware that the entire audience was staring at her, cast an imploring look into the wings, and then, at a hidden signal, raised her hands high and crashed them down on to the piano. Daisy, now slumbering contentedly against her mother's soft pillowy breasts, jerked violently, while Ross, on Isla's lap, clutched at her sleeve for reassurance. A small child somewhere near the front of the hall let out a wail of fright. The hall lights went out, the curtain opened to reveal a row of carol singers clutching paper candles with scarlet crayoned flames, and the concert was under way.

When the 'babies' ' turn came, Greta lurked shyly in the back row, while Barbara was right at the front, singing lustily and beaming down at the audience, her cheeks pink with excitement. Ignoring her teacher's frowns, she waved happily at her mother and brother when she spotted them, and her voice soared above the others as they launched into, 'Once in Royal David's City'. Ross, kicking his heels painfully against Isla's shins, joined in with great enthusiasm.

'I told you not to sing, it was just the schoolchildren that were supposed to sing,' Barbara nagged huffily when she joined her mother and brother later for tea and mince-pies in one of the classrooms which, like the hall, was decorated with paper streamers. Ross bit into a mince pie, ignoring her.

'Nobody could hear him,' Isla said in his defence.

'I could, all the way up on the stage,' said Barbara, then, hopefully, 'Could you hear me? Was I good? Was I the best?'

Filled with mince-pies, they walked home in the dark, the lights going off one by one in the school behind them. It was long past the children's bedtime, and Ross grizzled to be carried. He fell asleep almost at once, his sticky little face nuzzling into Isla's neck, and his breath, sweet with mincemeat, puffing warmly against her chin. Barbara and Greta ran hand in hand ahead of their mothers, singing snatches of carols, shrieking with laughter, then suddenly falling silent as a drunk man lurched out of a pub and towered over them, telling them in a slurred voice that they were bonny wee lassies, so they were.

Isla felt her stomach tighten. She often heard intoxicated men lurching home past her window at night, sometimes singing, sometimes quarrelling, their voices loud and their words ugly and menacing. She had seen them in the street now and then during the day, but she had never before had to confront one.

Magret had no such qualms. 'Now you leave the lassies be,' she ordered sharply as the man reached out a hand towards Barbara's bright hair.

He jerked round towards her voice. 'Who d'ye think ye're . . .' he started to say, then the tone of his voice changed. 'Is it yersel', Maggie? How are ye, hen?'

The light from the pub window caught his face, gaunt and stubbly. Hair stuck in tufts from under a peaked cap, and he stank of drink.

'I'm fine, Willie, and so will you be, when ye've slept

it off. Away home, now, for I've got more tae dae at this time of night than stand in the cold talking tae ye.'

'Aye, right ye are, pet. Nae harm done, eh?' the man said, and lurched off along the road. Barbara, subdued now, came hurrying back to Isla's side and took a firm grip on her coat.

'I didn't like that man.'

'Ach, there's no harm in him, pet,' Magret assured her. 'But it's as well no' tae talk tae men that smell of drink, eh?' To Isla she added, as they hurried towards their own close, 'Poor soul – he was a gaffer in the mills when I worked there. A good, sober man he was too, then his wee boy died of the diphtheria and his wife went off with someone else. Look at him now. It's a shame, so it is.'

'Drunk men scare me,' Isla admitted.

'Ach, they're all right, most of them. They drink for comfort, but the pity of it is that some of them don't have the sense tae settle for one or two glasses. My own father was drunk more often than he was sober, and my poor mother had a time of it tryin' tae keep us from starvin' tae death.' Magret huffed air angrily out of her nostrils. 'The publicans never have that worry, though! They're happy tae line their pockets with other folks' hard-earned money. I'm fortunate that my own man knows how tae take a sociable drink then call it a day.'

The dolls' house was smuggled into the George Street flat on Christmas Eve and hidden beneath the bed. On Christmas Day, Barbara's astonishment and delight made Isla feel that her hard work had been well worth while.

Greta was summoned at once to admire it. 'You can

have my other house,' Barbara announced graciously, and Greta's thin little face lit up.

'She must be a real nice lady ye're workin' for, Isla, tae give ye a house like that for the wean,' Magret marvelled. Then, as Ross charged across the space between them, towing his Christmas present, a brightly painted, jointed wooden dog that nodded its head and moved its legs when pulled along on a string, 'He'll wear your oilcloth out by New Year.'

'It's already worn out. I doubt if it'll last another six months,' Isla said in despair. Small though the room was, there always seemed to be something that needed replacing.

Daisy, allowed down on to the floor more often now that she was two months from her first birthday, squirmed after the wooden dog on her stomach, with no hope of catching it. Magret scooped her up and planted a loud kiss on her head, now covered with fine downy brown hair, then sniffed the air appreciatively. 'That smells good.'

'It's a boiling fowl I put on to simmer on the stove for our Christmas dinner. I made a dumpling, too.'

'We always have our special dinner at New Year.' Magret's bright little eyes twinkled with anticipation. 'Wait till the New Year, Isla – that's a grand occasion here. Everyone gets the day off work, an' there's parties in just about every house, with dancing and singing – out in the street tae, if the weather's no' too bad.' Her twinkle broadened into a grin. 'Ye'll not get much sleep on Hogmanay, for the noise.'

Kenneth had always claimed to prefer celebrating Christmas, and Isla was keeping the custom alive for his children, although now she realised that Kenneth must have established the custom because his other family had naturally expected him to be with them for New Year – a time, he had told her, when his office was at its busiest. Staring absently at the two little girls down on their knees by the dolls' houses, she wondered why she had always believed every word he said, never questioned him about those busy times when he had to be away from home for days and occasionally weeks. She supposed that it was because she had loved him too deeply to do otherwise.

'Magret, why don't you and the children have your dinner with us today?' she suggested, anxious for company on a day that held so many memories for her.

'That'd be grand – if ye're sure there's enough for us all.'

'Of course there is. That's what Christmas is about – sharing.'

Even with Magret's cheerful company to dull the edge of her memories, Isla was glad to see Christmas Day past and eager to get to work on Flora Currie's Victorian dolls' house on Boxing Day. She felt a tingle of anticipation as she unhooked the catch and the front of the house swung open like double doors, to expose the rooms within.

Ross, used to Miss Currie's house by now, went happily to the kitchen with Annie, who shrugged Isla's protests aside with, 'Ach, I'd plenty wee brothers and sisters when I was a lassie. I can surely manage tae see tae just the one.'

Fired by enthusiasm after the school concert, Barbara

had decided to organise her own carol concert, and was too busy coaxing some of the street children to form a choir to accompany her mother to Castlehead. Magret had agreed to keep a watchful eye on her.

'She's got quite bossy since she started school,' Isla told Flora as her fingers worked confidently at glueing a length of fringing round the canopy of a double bed for the master bedroom. The original canopy had come unstuck in several places, and it was easier to renew it than replace it. 'To think that I was worried when we first moved to George Street in case the other children ostracised her and broke her heart! But it was never easy to keep Barbara down. I can't think where she gets her determination from.'

Flora, a willing assistant, was sifting through a box of old costume jewellery, sorting beads into sizes and laying aside lengths of chain. Isla had earlier discovered part of a necklace which included tiny crystal drops, and had decided to try her hand at making a chandelier, if she could find enough fine chain.

'She gets it from you, my dear. It takes determination and courage to face life with no money to speak of, and two small children to care for.'

Isla arranged fringing on a sheet of paper and brushed glue carefully along its length. 'That's not courage, it's necessity. I was such a timid child – nothing like Barbara. I'm sure she's got her strength of mind from her fath—'

She stopped abruptly, and Flora Currie flicked a sidelong glance at her, then said casually, 'I wonder what the thirties will bring. It seems no time at all since we were approaching 1920. I used to think when I was young that time would slow down as I got older, but it doesn't. It gets faster and faster.'

'I've found the years rushing by since the children were born,' Isla said, relieved that they had moved on to a safer subject. 'A few years ago they didn't even exist, yet in no time at all they'll be into their teens, and thinking of what they want to make of their own lives. What's that wee box you've got there?'

Flora held it up. 'I remember keeping bits and pieces in it as a child. I can't think where it came from – my father may well have brought it back from one of his trips.'

Isla wiped her fingers on a cloth, then took the little box from her and studied it. 'You know that nice laquered chest you've got in your front hall? I could paint this up to look just like it for the dolls' house hall. And I could make a nice vase to put on it, with a spray of flowers . . .'

In return for the shared Christmas dinner, Magret had invited Isla and the children to eat their New Year's Day dinner with her and Tommy and their children.

'It'll be steak pie, same as we always have, with tatties and carrots. That's what we like best,' she said, her eyes bright with happy anticipation. 'There'll probably be some folks comin' in after – my mam and my sister, and her lot. I love New Year, so I dae, we always have such a good time!'

New Year's Eve was always a busy day for Scottish housewives, for tradition demanded that every house had to be rid of the old year's dirt and dust, ready to start a new year afresh.

As well as cleaning out every nook and cranny, the womenfolk also had to make sure that there was food for the flood of visitors they might expect. The children, roped in to help, were sent to the shops with long lists wrapped round the money to pay the shopkeepers, or set to minding smaller brothers and sisters or beating carpets and rugs in the backyards and helping their mothers to shift furniture so that every corner of every room could be cleaned thoroughly.

Wash-houses were in great demand for the final few days of the old year, and the clothes-lines in every yard were crammed, as were clothes-horses indoors. Smaller items of clothing bubbled and steamed in metal pails and tubs on top of stoves and ranges, cheek by jowl with 'clootie' dumplings, tied in clean dish-cloths or pillow-cases, simmering in pans of water. Flat irons were fitted in among the pots and tubs wherever room could be found for them, so that they would be hot enough for use once the clothes were dry. There was scarcely an oven in the town that didn't hold at least one steak pie in the making.

It was the men's task to see that there was enough drink available in the house for all who might call in after the bells rang to welcome the new year. Those men with dark hair were expected to 'first foot' other houses, arriving as soon as possible after the bells rang, armed with a bottle of whisky, a large wedge of black bun – a rich cake crammed with fruit – and a lump of coal to bring plenty and good fortune to the household for the coming year.

The Hogmanay cleaning usually brought a rich harvest to the children, as empty bottles and jam-jars that had lain forgotten in cupboards came to light, some to be borne off to the nearest shop and exchanged for halfpennies and farthings, some carefully set aside for the penny matinee at the Glen Cinema, down at the Cross, a welcome haven from parental tyranny on Saturday afternoons, and every Hogmanay.

By early afternoon on that final day of 1929, many of the mothers were beginning to lose patience with their offspring, and deciding that they could probably manage to get on with the work faster on their own. Gradually, the children returned to their play, banished to the street with thick wads of bread and jam and instructed not to come in again until summoned for the obligatory bath, hair-washing, and change into clean clothes. The lucky ones were despatched to the cinema, some of the older girls carrying the baby of the family, a dummy stuck in his or her mouth.

One of Greta's older cousins, an eight-year-old girl, called to take her to the cinema, and Barbara, who had heard of the delights of the moving pictures from the older children in the street, begged to be allowed to go too. When Isla refused permission, Barbara flew into a tantrum and, on being smacked, climbed on to the box bed, drew the curtains shut, and sulked. Isla left her to it, wondering if she was being over-protective, yet uneasy about letting the little girl go.

'Mebbe next year, when you're six,' she opened the curtains to tell Barbara, who flounced round in the bed so that her back was to her mother. Sighing, Isla got on with her work.

She was on her knees by the cooker, trying to reach right under it with a brush to coax every bit of fluff out of hiding, when Magret burst into the room, her face white and strained, Daisy in her arms.

'Take the bairn for me,' she gasped, 'There's somethin' happened at the Glen – I'm away tae look for our Greta!'

Isla scrambled to her feet. 'What do you mean—?' she began, but Magret bundled the baby into her arms, and with a wail of, 'Oh God – my wee lassie!' she was out of the house, through the close and out into George Street, running as fast as her curved legs and stocky body would allow.

14

Ross, who had been put into his cot to play and had fallen asleep, woke in fright. With her free arm Isla scooped him out on to the floor, and he staggered drowsily after her, still grizzling, as she carried Daisy outside.

Women had come to the close-mouths all up and down the street, and some had started running in the direction of the Cross, still carrying dusters or floor brushes. Others hung out of windows, loudly demanding to know what had happened.

'It's the Glen!' The news was passed from mouth to mouth along the street. 'It's on fire!'

A woman who had appeared at the next close dropped her metal bucket with a clatter as the words reached her, giving a cry of pure anguish. She started to run, kicking off shabby down-at-heel slippers and running on in her bare feet, lurching clumsily from side to side, sawing her clenched fists through the air. 'My bairns!' she screamed as she went. 'My bairns are in there!'

'Mummy, what is it? What's happened?' Barbara arrived on the pavement. Just as Isla opened her mouth to reassure her, a boy came hurtling past, yelling, 'The Glen's burnin'! The bairns is all killed!'

'Greta?' Barbara's eyes filled with tears. 'Where's Greta? I want to see her . . .' Her voice was an anguished wail that set Ross to crying again and started Daisy off. Up and down the street people were weeping, and more and more of them were taking to their heels. Mrs Leach and her thin, pale daughter joined Isla on the pavement, along with Mrs Brown and Granny Thomson. Drew Brown was there too, clutching a carpet beater. His mother put a hand on his arm when she heard the news.

'Thank God you didnae go this year, son. These poor, poor bairns!'

'Greta was there – Magret's gone to look for her.'

'Mebbe they all got out in time,' young Mrs Kelly ventured, and her mother sniffed.

'That's no' likely, is it? Now ye know,' she nagged at the young woman, 'why I would never let ye go. If it's no' fleas, it's fire!'

Men began to appear round the corner of Maxwellton Street, earlier than usual, come from the mill as word of the fire spread. One or two stopped to question the women at the close-mouths before hurrying on to the Cross in search of their children, or to see if they could help.

Numbly, Isla shepherded her three tearful charges back into the tenement. There was no sense in standing out on the pavement, and Daisy was heavier than she looked. She sat the little girl down on the rug, and Daisy promptly fell over and lay there, breaking her heart. Isla picked her up and sat down so that she could hold Ross as well. Barbara insisted on burrowing into her arms too, and the four of them huddled together, cramped in the small armchair, waiting for news.

An hour dragged by before Magret came back, her husband Tommy with her, carrying Greta, her face streaked with dirt and dried tears, a bruise purpling one cheekbone. At sight of her, Barbara burst into tears, setting off Greta and Ross and Daisy.

'If ye'd seen it, Isla,' Magret choked against the background of wailing children. 'All the folk screamin' and shoutin' for their bairns, an' the firemen an' the polismen carryin' these poor wee souls out, some of them just lyin' there and not movin'. Not even cryin' . . .'

Tommy clumsily patted her shoulder with his free hand. They were both ashen.

'Was the whole place on fire?'

Tommy shook his head. 'We never seen any flames. They'd stopped the trams, an' we found her on one of them.'

'A polisman wanted tae take her tae the Infirmary, but she's all right – not like some of those other poor wee pets. She just needs tae be safe with her mammy and daddy, don't ye, my wee hen?' Magret reached up and stroked her daughter's face gently.

'What about Greta's cousin?'

'She's – she's all right.' Tommy's voice was husky, and choked on the first word. 'They was both lucky. Come on, pet, we'd best get her tae her bed,' he urged, and Magret nodded and held out her arms for Daisy.

'I'll see ye later, Isla.'

'You're wet, Mummy,' Barbara said when they had

gone. She sniffed tears back and pointed to the large damp patch on Isla's skirt, then looked down at her own skirt. 'I'm wet too – so's Ross.'

For the first time Isla noticed the sharp smell of urine hanging in the air. 'Poor wee Daisy, I never thought to change her.'

More washing to do if she wanted everything to be clean for the new year, she thought. But at least Greta was safe, and so were her own two. She knelt and gathered them both into her arms. If she had let Barbara go – if she had lost her in the same year she had lost Kenneth –

The thought was more than she could bear.

Contrary to rumour, the cinema had not caught fire. A reel had started to smoulder in the projection room and the smell of burning celluloid had permeated the packed cinema. Before anything could be done to reassure them, the children had panicked, rushing to the exits only to find that they couldn't open the doors. Those who reached them first were the victims – crushed and smothered as the frantic children behind them struggled to escape from the building forcing them to the ground, clambering over them in search of safety.

Sixty-nine children died needlessly, and at midnight the bells that rang in 1930 tolled, too, for the lost children, and a town in mourning.

Magret insisted on her Ne'erday dinner going ahead as planned. 'We've still got tae eat,' she said, and so Isla and Barbara and Ross, together with Granny Thomson, who had no relatives of her own, crowded into the small one-roomed flat. With the resilience found only in children, Greta had recovered from the previous day's ordeal, though it would be at least a week before the bruising on her face disappeared. The children ate heartily, while the adults picked at their food, still numbed by what had happened.

'It's a terrible way tae start a new year, losin' a bairn,' Magret voiced all their thoughts as she carefully mashed potatoes for Granny Thomson then ladled gravy over them. 'More than one for some folk – I heard that four were lost from the one family, an' one of them a bairn just about the same age as your Ross, Isla.' Her voice shook on the last few words, and Isla noticed that she and Tommy kept glancing at Greta, as though reassuring themselves that she was still with them.

'There ye are, Granny,' Magret went on with determined cheerfulness, 'you eat that up. The poor soul's no' got a tooth left in her jaw,' she mouthed to Isla across the old woman's head. 'Cannae manage the meat.' Aloud, she said, 'I did custard an' stewed apple for after, ye'll enjoy that, won't ye?'

Granny Thomson nodded, loudly sucking the purée of potatoes and gravy from a spoon, her face almost touching her plate, her back hunched and the bones of her spine pushing against the material of her dress. She left not long after the meal was finished, her thin colourless lips stretched in a toothless smile of gratitude, and Isla made her own excuses a little later, when members of Magret's and Tommy's families began to arrive. The small room was becoming unbearably crowded, and the talk was all about the cinema disaster. Isla felt that she couldn't bear to hear about it any more.

Not that it could be avoided. Everywhere she went, people were talking about the tragedy. Early in January the pavements were thronged to see the small coffins go by on their way to Hawkhead Cemetery for burial in a communal grave, some of them children who had been in Barbara's class at school. Many of those who had survived were still receiving treatment in Paisley Alexandra Infirmary. Funds were set up to help the bereaved families and the victims, and the cinema manager was arrested in connection with the closed exits that denied safety and life to so many small victims.

Even Flora Currie talked about the tragedy when Isla went back to her house to work on the Victorian dolls' house.

'I heard that there were riots outside the Infirmary, with people wanting to get in to see what had happened to their children, and the police trying to hold them back. Those poor, poor souls. In my childhood a little girl we played with was killed in the street when a cart ran over her – I can still remember the shock of hearing the news. I'd been so sure until then that only old people died. It was dreadful – and it still is – to realise that it can happen to little children too. I recall my mama trying to write to that child's parents and saying to my papa, what comfort can one give to people who have lost a child?' She sighed. 'And now I must find the right words myself.'

'You knew one of the children?'

Flora nodded. 'Innes McAdam, the son of people I used to know.'

They were taking tea in the parlour. Isla, about to sip from her cup, set it back in the saucer with a faint clash of china. For a moment the room seemed to shift around her, then to her relief it steadied. Flora Currie didn't notice.

'I only knew the boy slightly. Such a nice child, and so polite, even as a little tot. His father was very friendly with one of my brothers at one time. They grew apart after they left school, long before Arnold left Paisley. Arnold was a bit of a perfectionist, and I believe that eventually Kenneth McAdam just didn't match up to his standards, though I thought him a very pleasant youth. As it turned out, my brother's judgement may have been correct.'

Her voice rattled on and Isla, quite unable to stop her, had no option but to listen.

'Kenneth's problem was that he grew up in his father's shadow. His father was a fine man, very well thought of in the town, but I always pity children who have to follow perfection. After all, we're all as God made us, for better or worse. Unfortunately, Kenneth didn't inherit his father's strength of character as well as his father's business. I remember Arnold saying that Kenneth tended to take the easy way out of a dilemma instead of facing up to it.'

She paused, and Isla frantically sought for some way of changing the subject. Before anything came to mind, Flora went on, every word a spear plunging into Isla. 'Poor man, I'm not so sure that he did take the easy way out in the end. Apparently his business began to fail, and he speculated foolishly with clients' money in a bid to save it. Instead, inevitably, he lost good money after bad, then took his own life. It was a terrible blow to his wife. She's a very proud woman.'

'Miss Currie—'

But the old lady was well into her subject now, her eyes cloudy as she looked into the past. 'As if she didn't have enough to bear, she discovered that he had set up a second wife somewhere else, a woman much younger than himself, and had two children by her. So poor Kenneth ruined the lives of another three people when he decided to put an end to it all. Such a tragedy, and now his own son's gone as well. He looked like his father, too. Kenneth was a handsome young man, with vivid blue eyes and red hair that seemed to light up any room he was in. I can see it yet – like autumn leaves on a sunny—'

Ross was playing on the carpet, in a patch of January sunlight that made his downbent head glow. Flora's eyes had been resting absently on the little boy as she spoke. Now her voice stopped abruptly, her eyes clearing and widening, flying up to meet Isla's frightened gaze.

'Oh, my dear,' she said on a breath of sound. 'What a very stupid old woman I am, talking about Kenneth's other wife and two children, never stopping to wonder where they might be, or what they might be doing . . .'

'It's—' Isla choked and tried again. 'I—' But the words wouldn't come. She put down the cup and saucer, blundered to her feet, and ran from the room.

The dolls'-house room was comforting and familiar, a haven where nothing bad could happen. Isla picked up the four-poster bed she had been working on before the New Year, blinking hard to clear the mist from her eyes. The new canopy was firm and straight now; she found the curtains that had been hemmed for it, then began to glue each one into place so that it could be gathered back later and tied to the bedposts. Her mind was numb and she left it in peace, concentrating on her fingers, shutting the rest of the world out.

Half an hour passed before Flora Currie tapped on the door and came in, cup and saucer in hand.

'I made some fresh tea. Annie's taken the children out for a walk. I hope you don't mind.'

Isla stared at her, startled. For once, she had forgotten about her children. 'I'm sorry, I shouldn't have just walked out and left them like that.'

'You needed time on your own – and Annie loves being with them,' Flora said timidly, then, 'Oh, Isla! Oh, my dear, I wish someone had broken into the house and cut my tongue out while I was asleep last night. My mama always said that I spoke before I thought, but the things I said today were quite inexcusable!'

'You weren't to know.'

'But I should have guessed!'

'I was hoping that nobody would guess. A lot of Scots have red hair, and you wouldn't have expected to find us right here, in Paisley.'

Now that her secret was out and she had got over the first shock of it, it was a relief to tell someone about it all. Once she started, though, she couldn't stop; the words poured out, and Flora Currie had the sense to let her talk without interruption.

'My dear child, what a hard time you've been having – and nobody to turn to,' she said when Isla had at last come to a stop.

'I'm managing, and the children are thriving. And I've good memories of the time I had with Kenneth.'

'You don't resent what he did to you?'

'Resentment doesn't come into it. I loved him.'

'I really didn't think I'd missed out on anything, staying single,' Flora said after a moment. 'Now I'm beginning to wonder.' Then her tentative smile faded. 'Now that I know, I hope that you'll continue to come here, and go on working on my little house.'

'Are you so sure that you want me to? It could be embarrassing for you, having me around,' Isla explained, when the older woman looked puzzled. 'After all, you know the McAdams.'

'Scarcely at all, now, and anyway, why should I let the past hinder a good friendship? Annie and I would miss you and the little ones sorely if you stopped coming, so I hope we'll hear nothing more about that,' Flora said firmly. 'And I give you my word that nobody, not even Annie, shall know what you've just told me.'

She beamed at Isla, who summoned a wavering smile in return. Then Flora rubbed her bony hands together vigorously.

'I do hate sentiment,' she announced. 'It embarrasses me. Now then – what plans do you have for today's work?'

Charlie Blayne called at the McAdam house on New Year's Day to tell Ainslie to take as much time off as she wanted. Standing on the step, twisting his cap round and round in his big hands, he said, 'We'll manage fine till you get back, lass. Your poor ma'll be needin' you.'

She stared at him through the cotton-wool haze that

had wrapped itself around her since Innes's death. 'I'm sorry I can't ask you in,' she heard herself saying.

'I'd not expect it – not at a time like this.' He stumbled backwards down the steps to the gravel drive. 'I just wanted you to know – for as long as your ma needs you.'

But Catherine McAdam didn't need anyone but Innes. She didn't want anyone but Innes. Time after time, as she served tea to the few people allowed into the house, or tried to coax Catherine to eat, Ainslie caught her mother looking at her with eyes that told her, clearly and coldly, that the wrong one had died.

'She could have borne my death better than his,' she said through frozen lips to Colin when he called at the house. Her mother, who couldn't sleep at night, had fallen into one of her sudden, exhausted dozes on the drawing-room sofa, and the two of them sat in the dining-room, at either side of the polished table.

'Don't say that.' He reached across the table and covered her hand with his. His fingers were warm and real; Ainslie, who had had the eerie feeling since Innes's death that she wasn't really there, and that her own flesh had become transparent, half expected his hand to sink through hers on to the surface of the table, but it didn't.

'It's the truth. She never cared for me, it was always Innes – and I didn't blame her, because he was such a – such a nice little boy, wasn't he?' She hadn't cried before, not even when she saw her brother in the Infirmary, pale and calm, looking as though he was asleep, the only sign of the violence that had ended his life a large bruise at his temple, flaring up into the red hair that someone had carefully combed. But now the tears spilled down her face, and Colin came round the table and held her, not as a would-be lover, but as a friend, someone she could lean against, a support and a comfort.

'Why did he do it?' she wept into his jacket. 'Why did he defy Mother and go to that beastly cinema?'

'Because he was young, and restless, and because he'd had enough mourning.' His hand was gentle on her hair. 'Ainslie, kids always do impetuous things. Innes wasn't to know what was going to happen any more than anyone else.'

By the time he left, she felt as though she had been completely emptied of tears. She looked in on her mother, who still slept, then went quietly into Innes's room, feeling a need to sit among his possessions for a while.

Catherine McAdam's eyelids fluttered and lifted, and she was wide awake. Since Innes's death, she only knew that she had been sleeping when she woke, for there was no drifting, no drowsiness or sense of letting the day go and slipping into rest. She was either asleep in a deep black pit filled with nothing, or awake with unbearable anguish tearing at her, sharp-toothed and bloody-clawed.

She sat up slowly and lowered her feet to the floor, then stood up carefully, holding on to a nearby occasional table, feeling very old and very frail.

'You must eat, Catherine,' Phemie Forbes had coaxed that morning. 'You must keep your strength up.' She had visited every day since the cinema disaster, bringing beef tea and calves' foot jelly and urging the red-eyed servants to make nourishing broths that Catherine could scarcely touch. 'You have to keep going, dear, for Ainslie's sake.'

She was like an irritating housefly, buzzing and droning and refusing to go away. She didn't understand, Catherine thought impatiently as she made her way across the room, moving from one piece of furniture to another, testing the carpet with each step as though it was a marsh. None of them understood. The pain she felt had nothing to do with lack of food. In any case, why keep going for Ainslie's sake, when Ainslie had done nothing for her?

She groped across the precarious, furniture-free desert of the hall, finally clamping a hand tightly on the newel post with a grunt of relief. After a pause to gather her strength, she started to climb the stairs one step at a time, the beast inside her snapping at her heart as she recalled Innes going upstairs in exactly the same way when he was learning to walk, his nurse by his side. She remembered the way he swatted the woman's protective hand aside and insisted on climbing on his own. So determined, so like his grandfather!

She paused for breath, clinging to the banister, misery washing over her in fresh waves as she looked up at the portrait. Now there would be no McAdam to carry on the name and make amends for Kenneth's sins.

As she opened the door of Innes's room Ainslie looked up, startled, from where she sat on the bed, her eyes swollen. The two women stared at each other, then Catherine said harshly, 'How dare you come into his room!'

'Mother—'

'Get out!' She stepped aside, holding the door open, and the girl went without another word. Closing the door behind her, Catherine erased her presence from the bedcover with swift, angry movements of her hands, muttering angrily to herself as she worked.

When she was satisfied that the covering was free of Ainslie's presence, she moved about the room, touching Innes's possessions to calm herself. The model cars Ainslie had given him at Christmas annoyed her, so she swept them off the top of the bookcase and into the waste-paper basket. Finally she settled in an armchair and closed her eyes, soaking in the atmosphere of the place.

Innes was still very much a part of this room. It didn't know that he was dead, and while it waited for his return, he was still alive.

15

Most of the small victims of the New Year tragedy were buried together in Hawkhead Cemetery, but Innes McAdam was laid to rest beside his father in Woodside Cemetery. Catherine refused to attend the funeral service, and it was left to Ainslie to travel with her young brother on his last journey, Gilchrist Forbes and his son by her side.

There was a great throng of people around the open grave, some of them friends of the McAdam family, many of them strangers from all over the town, united in their sorrow. As the minister's voice droned on, Ainslie remembered the last time she had stood by this grave. Then, she had been filled with shock and bitterness, but now there was only a deep, aching grief.

Glancing up, she saw Charlie Blayne among the throng, unusually sombre and serious in black. The sight of him brought a little warmth to her heart. He was a reminder that although her past had been shattered beyond repair, she still had some sort of future.

A small reception was held for close friends in the McAdam house after the funeral. Catherine, with Phemie Forbes hovering protectively by her side, received her guests in the drawing-room, a bleak-eyed ghost of the gracious hostess she had once been. They stood around in uncomfortable groups, eating sandwiches, drinking tea, trying to make conversation in hushed voices. The funeral of a child was so much more harrowing than that of an adult. Ainslie, moving among them, trying to make sure that everyone present was thanked for their attendance, bent over her mother's chair.

'Can I get you anything, Mother?'

Catherine shook her head without looking at her.

'At least, dear,' Ainslie heard someone say to her mother as she moved on, 'you still have Ainslie. She must be such a comfort.'

'So one would have thought.' Catherine's voice, strengthened with bitterness and contempt, rang out. 'But it seems that my daughter cares far more for her place of employment than her home, or her family.'

There was a sudden, uncomfortable silence. Heads turned, and all eyes fixed on Catherine, who gazed back at them arrogantly, then on Ainslie, who looked as though she had just been slapped hard in the face. Colin Forbes stepped forward to put a hand on her arm, his fingers tightening; she looked up at the mingled anger and pity in his gaze, forcing her lips into a smile, then moved on, away from him, saying something banal to one of the staring faces. The woman blinked, answered, and the soft hum of voices started up again, with an undertone of relief.

Ainslie went back to the auction rooms two days later. There was no sense in staying at home. It was clear that her mother had no need of her presence.

*

Isla had become so involved in working on the Victorian house that even when the snow came she made a point of struggling along to Castlehead, wrestling Ross's push-chair over frozen, slippery humps of snow, glad of its support as her shoes skidded on the ice. He was almost two years old now, and well able to walk, but not for long distances.

She had been working hard since Christmas and the dolls' house was almost finished. A cook in a volumi-nous white apron ruled over a little scullery maid in the well-stocked kitchen, the master sat in his armchair in the library, while his wife, in plum-coloured silk, occu-pied the drawing-room, busy with her embroidery, which was stretched over a curtain ring Isla had found in one of Flora's boxes of odds and ends. There were two children and a baby in a lacy cradle in the nursery, under their nurse's watchful eye.

In the hall stood the small wooden box Isla had noticed several months before, painted to make a pass-able copy of the inlaid chest in Flora's hall. She was still working on the chandelier, which was proving to be a long-drawn-out, difficult task.

'We could hang it in the dining-room,' she suggested one Monday afternoon. She had come on to Castlehead after collecting Barbara from school; Greta was at home nursing toothache, so Isla had taken advantage of her absence to spend some extra time on the dolls' house. Both children were in the kitchen with Annie, who had become a firm favourite.

'You'll have finished that house in a few more weeks.'

'Yes.' Isla had enjoyed every minute of the task. It

had given purpose to her days, and the thought of being without it saddened her. They were having tea in the drawing-room; glancing at the window, she saw that the snow had stopped falling.

'We'd better go, before it comes on again.'

Someone tugged at the bell-pull just then, and they heard Annie bustling along the hall, then after a moment the parlour door opened and Ainslie McAdam walked into the room. She stopped in her tracks as she recognised Isla, the rosy glow that the cold weather had brought to her face deepening.

Isla, as horrified as the other girl by this unexpected encounter, struggled to her feet as Flora said, 'Ainslie, my dear, how good of you to call. This is my friend, Isla Moffatt; Isla, this is Ainslie McAdam.'

'How do you do?' Ainslie came further into the room reluctantly, unable to do anything else, short of turning on her heel and leaving the house she had just entered. She pulled her glove off and held a hand out. Isla took it and they exchanged a brief clasp of fingers, Isla's warm, Ainslie's icy.

'You'll have some tea?'

'I – I think not, Miss Currie, I must get home. I just called to thank you for sending the basket of fruit to my mother.'

'My dear girl, of course you must have tea – I'll not have you going back out into that snow without something warm to drink.' Flora put her hand to the bell-pull just as Annie came in with fresh tea and an extra cup.

'Sit down, both of you,' Flora instructed, pouring tea. Watching her, admiring the calm, unhurried way in which she guided the conversation, bringing first one of her guests in, then the other, making it seem that they were conversing with each other when, in fact, she herself was acting as go-between all the time, Isla admired her fluent ability, recognising the years of training Flora had undergone while growing up in her mother's house. She would have made a grand wife for some ambitious businessman.

But not even Flora's skill could bridge the gap between herself and Ainslie McAdam; unable to bear the tension in the room a moment longer, Isla shook her head when Flora went to fill her cup, and stood up.

'I must go, Miss Currie – please, stay where you are,' she added as Flora began to get up. 'I'll collect the children and Annie can see me to the door.'

'Very well, my dear. I'll see you soon.'

'I came at a bad time,' Ainslie said when the door closed.

'Not at all, Isla was about to go home anyway. She brings the children to visit me often.'

'Really?' Ainslie couldn't hide her surprise.

'Oh yes. She saved my life one day – helped me home when I'd gone out too soon after a bout of illness, and wasn't able to get back under my own steam. She's a considerate young woman, and I admire her very much,' Flora said calmly, giving her visitor a swift sidelong glance. 'Life's extremely difficult for her, poor girl. It can't be easy for a young widow, raising two wee ones on her own like that, with hardly any money, but she never complains.'

Ainslie remained silent, staring at her fingers, which

were crumbling a piece of Annie's excellent fruit loaf. Flora took pity on her.

'How is your mother, my dear? I thought of calling, then I decided that it might be best to leave it for a while. She probably has more visitors than she can cope with.'

Ainslie looked up, her face shadowed. 'She's started eating again, though scarcely enough to feed a bird.'

'It's a terrible thing, losing a child,' Flora agreed.

Ainslie nodded, then said, as though unable to stop herself, 'I'm worried about her, Miss Currie. She sits in Innes's room for hours at a time, and she insists on making the servants lay a place for him at the table at every meal. She keeps looking at his chair all the time we're at the table, as if she's listening to something he's saying.' Her lower lip trembled, and was brought under control. 'The housemaid's given notice – when I asked her to reconsider, she said that my mother frightens her.'

'Have you spoken to her doctor?'

'I tried, but he just says it's her way of dealing with her loss, and she'll come out of it in time. I'm not so sure.'

'We can only hope that he's right. It must be a terrible thing, losing a son.' Flora paused, then went on gently, 'Losing a brother's a terrible thing, too, though sometimes other folk forget that. But once the edge of the grieving dulls, my dear, you'll have all the years of knowing him to sustain and comfort you.' After letting silence hang between them for just the right amount of time, she asked briskly, 'Would you like to have a look at my collection of dolls' houses?'

'Dolls' houses?' Astonishment swept away the tears that threatened to spill from Ainslie's eyes.

'It's a daft hobby for an old woman like me, I know, but I like to show them off now and again – when I meet someone I think will understand. This way . . .'

The girl's amazement turned to admiration when Flora unlatched the front of the big Victorian house.

'This is perfect!'

'You should have seen it before Isla started on it.'

'Isla?'

'Oh yes indeed, she's been working very hard. She's making a chandelier just now, and look at the family portraits she cut out of magazines. She made the frames herself, and this rocking chair,' Flora told her proudly. 'The thing is – what do I do with it when it's finished?'

'Oh, you must keep it and enjoy it.'

'Nothing's enjoyable, my dear, when there's nobody to share it with. Besides, I have so many.'

'Not like this one. It's a collector's item.'

'Then perhaps some collector should have it. I feel that all Isla's hard work should be seen, and admired.'

'If you ever think of selling it, let me know,' Ainslie said earnestly. 'I'm sure my employer would like to have a look at it – he's a good valuator.'

'Really?' A light came into Flora's eyes. 'Ainslie, I've just had an idea – what about asking your employer to auction it for me, then the amount raised can be handed over to the Glen Cinema fund?'

'You mean that you'd give away that beautiful wee house?'

'Why not? I've had my pleasure in watching it come to life again, and I intended to make a donation to the fund in any case. This seems to be a fitting way to do it.'

'If you're quite sure . . .'

'Oh I am,' said Flora. 'Quite sure. The more I think of the idea, the more I like it. Would you ask your employer to call? And come with him – I'd like to see you again, my dear.'

Later, when she had seen her guest out, Flora returned to the back room to study the Victorian house.

'A very fitting contribution,' she said to herself, well satisfied.

Isla finished the Victorian house a few weeks later, but refused to be present when Ainslie brought Charlie Blayne to see it.

'But, Isla, you must be here! After all, you've made such a wonderful job of renovating it, and I'm sure Mr Blayne'll want to meet you.'

'It's your house, and your idea. I think it's a very generous idea, but I'd as soon not be involved,' Isla insisted, and wouldn't be swayed. She did, however, agree to go along the day after the auctioneer's visit to find out what had happened.

Flora met her at the door, glowing with excitement. 'My dear, Mr Blayne was very impressed indeed, and most disappointed not to meet you. He came back this morning in person to pack the house up and take it away. It's to be auctioned next week, and I've been invited to attend.' She drew Isla and Ross into the hall, talking all the time. 'Apparently they fix what's called a reserve price on things that are auctioned, and they won't sell below it—'

When she named the reserve price Isla gasped, then said faintly, 'Well, it is an old house, and very well made.'

Flora brushed the words aside with a wave of the hand. 'It was the work you put into restoring it that's brought the value up.'

Annie brought a tea-tray into the drawing-room, heavy-footed as usual. 'I don't know,' she grumbled as she set it down. 'Strangers tramping in and out the place, auctioneers carrying things out to a van – the neighbours'll think you're having to sell everything you own to make ends meet.'

'Away with you,' Flora retorted. 'You're enjoying the excitement as much as I am. We've been a pair of old fogies for too long – we need a bit of a stir in our lives.'

'We don't need footprints all over my newly scrubbed doorstep,' Annie shot back, and held a hand out to Ross. 'Come on with me, son – there's still some sanity in my kitchen, thank goodness.'

'I'm going to miss the pleasure of bringing that wee house back to life,' Isla said later as they gazed at the gap left by the Victorian house.

'I haven't had such a good time for years,' Flora admitted. 'Of course, there are the other houses.'

'Miss Currie, I doubt if Annie could stand any more of our nonsense.'

'Och, away with you, lassie, she's had the time of her life. There's nothing she likes more than a reason to grumble. Besides, she's taken to your wee ones. She'd miss them as much as I would.'

'And I'll miss coming here. I've enjoyed having

something to do apart from housework, and looking after the children.'

'We all need some sort of interest in life. I feel ten years younger myself, and you look better. When you first came here you were worn down by worries. Now there's colour in your face, and a sparkle to your eye. You've filled out a bit, too.'

'It's all Annie's home baking.'

'I think it's a sense of fulfilment. And it's not all one-sided, you know. Look at me – not a sniffle or an ache have I had since that day you had to half carry me home. We're good for each other – we mustn't give up now.'

Flora looked around the room, then pointed to a modest little house. 'That one could do with a bit of cheering up.'

'D'you know what that one always reminds me of?' Isla asked. 'Have you read *Little Women*?'

'Many times.' The older woman looked puzzled, then understanding dawned. 'Are you talking about the house that Jo and Beth and their sisters lived in? An American dolls' house? Could you do that?'

A tingle of excited anticipation ran through Isla. 'I'd like to try.'

Flora beamed at her. 'I've got the book somewhere – come and help me to look for it.'

The Victorian house fetched a very good price at the auction rooms, and resulted in considerable publicity for Flora Currie. She came straight from the auction to George Street, throwing Isla into a panic when she arrived on the doorstep. Flora swept into the small room and beamed at Magret, who was sitting by the fire.

'How d'you do?'

'This is Miss Currie, Magret, my . . .' Isla swallowed hard, then said, 'My employer, the one I've told you about. This is my neighbour, Mrs McDougall.'

With the merest hint of a raised eyebrow in Isla's direction, Flora shook Magret's hand while with her free hand she patted Ross's head when he came to throw his arms affectionately about her knees.

'I'll be going, then.' Magret gathered Daisy up and edged towards the door, and Isla, completely thrown by Flora Currie's arrival, nodded.

'I'll see you later. I'm sorry,' she added as soon as the door had closed. 'I had to tell her that I was working for someone at Castlehead. She was wondering where I got to every day, and I didn't want to say about the dolls' houses.'

Flora, more interested in the room than in Isla's dealings with her neighbours, was at the orange-box cupboard, fingering the curtain across it. 'What a sensible idea. Isla, I just had to come and tell you . . .' She launched into a description of the auction, and the interest the Victorian dolls' house had attracted before finally going to a collector who had paid an amazingly large sum of money for it.

'Everyone wanted to know who had restored it, but I didn't give them your name,' she said reassuringly. 'I merely said that it had been done by a very talented young friend. A young man from the Paisley *Daily Express* spoke to me, he's going to put something in the newspaper about it.' Her eyes were shining and her voice rattled on; Isla had never seen her so animated.

Almost as soon as she had gone, Magret returned, her face concerned. 'She didnae come tae turn ye off, did she?'

'No, nothing like that.'

'That's all right, then. She seems tae be a decent woman, for all her posh talk,' Magret said. 'It's good tae be appreciated, isn't it?'

16

In March, Barbara and her friends presented their concert in the wash-house to an invited audience of mothers and little brothers and sisters. Heedless of the fact that Christmas was long over, the gathering of little girls, many with dirty faces and bare feet and runny noses, bawled their way through a selection of Christmas carols, followed by some Great War songs, most of them sung by Barbara herself.

The women enjoyed every minute of it, clapping loudly at the end, while the little girls curtsied low, the smallest falling over and being hauled to her feet by those on either side.

'That Barbara's a right clever wee lassie,' Magret enthused afterwards. 'She'll mebbe go on the music halls when she's old enough.'

Barbara had wanted to invite Flora Currie, but Isla managed to dissuade her. Instead, Barbara ran through the entire repertoire on her own before Flora and Annie in the drawing-room at Low Road. Drunk on their praise, she then danced along the pavement all the way home, clutching a silver sixpence and a bag of sweets she had been given as a reward for her hard work.

Flora Currie's donation of the entire amount raised by the auction of the Victorian house to the Glen Cinema fund had created quite a stir in the town. Both local newspapers, the *Express* and the *Gazette*, had written articles about it, and Mr Leckie, owner of a big toyshop in New Street, had called.

'He did all he could to get your name out of me, but he didn't succeed,' Flora told Isla later. 'However, I did tell him about your plans to make a *Little Women* house, and he's shown an interest in buying it when it's finished. If he does, you must overcome your shyness and start charging for your work. In fact, I could advance some of the money to you now.'

'No! If he buys it you can pay me part of the money – but not until it's finished and paid for,' Isla said warily. She could have done with some extra money, but she couldn't take payment for work that hadn't been done. Secretly, she didn't believe that the sale to Mr Leckie would ever go through. The man would have lost interest, surely, long before the house was finished.

In April, when work was under way on the *Little Women* dolls' house, Ross had his second birthday. Isla bought him a toy delivery van, and baked a cake for the occasion, inviting Magret and her daughters in for tea.

A few days after the little birthday party, Isla lost the rent money. There were few hiding places in the single-roomed flat, and she felt safer with the little money she had tucked into her bag. On that particular Friday, she had spent an hour or two window-shopping along the High Street and through the Cross, the busiest area of the town, returning home via St Mirrin Brae and Causeyside Street. Barbara and Greta were old enough now to make their own way home from school, so they didn't have to be fetched.

When they got back to George Street Ross ran ahead of her into the close and out into the backyard. Isla fetched the old hoe that Flora Currie had given her and went to work on her little garden, where the first potato shoots were beginning to show. When Barbara arrived home, she put the hoe away and went into the house to make tea. It was then, going into her bag to get the packet of tea she had bought on her outing, she realised that her shabby purse had gone.

Panic blossomed as she checked her coat pockets, then the pocket of the pinny she wore in the house, then looked under the cushion on the chair and even, futile though it was, in the cot that was getting too small for Ross, and on and under the wall-bed.

'My purse – it's not here—'

'Have we been burgled?' Barbara asked, wide-eyed.

'No, pet, but your mummy's been very careless.' Isla fought back panic. 'Run and ask Mrs McDougall if she'll keep an eye on you and Ross while I go out to look for my purse.'

Barbara did as she was told, and returned with Magret, whose expression mirrored Isla's sick fear. Nobody in George Street could afford to lose money, that scarcest of commodities. 'How much was in yer purse?'

'Everything I had. I'll need to go back along the

street – mebbe I left it in the shop where I bought some tea.'

Isla ran all the way back to St Mirren Brae, but the grocer and his assistant shook their heads when she asked breathlessly if a purse had been handed in.

'I mind ye comin' in earlier, hen,' the grocer said, 'but I never saw what ye did with yer purse after ye paid me.'

Isla retraced her steps along the High Street and down Castle Street, peering into the gutter and along the foot of the house walls, returning to George Street empty handed.

'I'll just have to tell the rent man I'll pay him next week,' she told Magret, who retorted, 'He'll not like that.'

'He'll just have to like it. I've never been behind with the rent before.'

'Can ye not ask that woman ye work for tae pay ye next week's wages in advance?'

Isla shook her head, appalled at the thought of asking anyone, particularly Miss Currie, for financial help.

'I couldn't do that.'

Magret sniffed. 'See these rich buggers? They'd not give a crust tae a dyin' dog, most of them. I wish I could help ye, Isla, but we've not got much more than our own rent.'

'Don't worry about it, I'm sure Mr Reid'll be willing to wait for one week.' It would be hard to make up two weeks' rent next Friday, but she would do it somehow. The thought of explaining the situation to Gilchrist Forbes and asking him to have a word with the rent collector came to her, and was dismissed. For one thing, she couldn't rid herself of the feeling that it was wrong to be treated differently from the other people in the tenement, and for another, the older Forbes might not be in the office, and she couldn't, wouldn't, ask for favours from that cold-eyed son of his.

The children were both asleep when the rent collector arrived that night. He scowled and pushed his lower lip out when Isla explained the situation, taking a step into the room so that she had no option but to retreat before him.

'My employers'll no' like that.'

'I told you, I'll make it up next week.'

He continued to move forward until he was in the middle of the room. 'An' how dae I know that? How dae I know ye'll no' do a moonlight flit and be out of here by next week?'

'I've no intention of leaving.'

'Have ye got nothin' ye could pay on account? Somethin's better than nothin'.'

'Every penny I had was in my purse.'

His eyes travelled over her, then he said, 'I could mebbe put it in the book that ye'd paid somethin'.'

'I'm not asking you to lie for me, Mr Reid, or to use your own money. I'm just asking you to wait for a week.'

The man blinked rapidly, then said, 'That'd be fine with me, hen, but ye see, it's the man that owns this place that's not very patient. He likes tae get his rent in time, and it's me that'll get intae trouble if it's not. So . . .' his tongue moistened his lower lip and he noted something in his book, ignoring her protest.

'That's the entry made, all nice and tidy like,' he

announced, stuffing the book into his pocket. 'The thing is, hen, what can ye dae for me in return?'

'I didn't ask you to lie, Mr Reid. I don't owe you anything.'

'Aye ye dae . . .' He stepped towards her again and Isla, suddenly realising what he meant, retreated behind the fireside chair.

'I've said I'll pay you double next week.'

'Mebbe so, hen, but it seems tae me that there's still that wee bit on account tae be settled.'

'Mr Reid, if you don't get out of here, I'll—'

'Ye'll what?' The chair was scooped aside, then the man was crowding Isla against the wall, his hand on her arm, the stubby fingers squeezing into the soft flesh. 'There's always another way for lassies tae pay their debts. It suits them – an' it suits me.'

Isla tried to drag back on the grip that was drawing her towards him. The smell of the man was thick in her nostrils, a mixture of tobacco and spirits and hair-oil and clothes in sore need of washing. 'Let go of me!'

'I will, hen – in my own time.'

'I'll scream,' she warned, knowing even as she said it that she couldn't shout for help, couldn't waken the children.

He laughed, moving in on her, confident of himself now. 'Go ahead, hen, scream all ye want. Folk round here know how tae mind their own business.'

Isla, caught between his body and the wall, tried to bring her knee up sharply, but he was too close. Instead, she managed to stamp hard on his instep, causing just enough pain to make him step back for a moment. He swung in towards her almost immediately, but she had

gained enough time to slide sideways along the wall
and reach the poker, which she had propped up against
the fireplace before going to answer his knock at the
door. She gripped it between both hands, forcing it up
towards his face. 'If you don't get out of my house, I'll
use this on you. I mean it!'

He stepped back, his gaze flicking between her face
and the poker. 'There's no need to be like—' A whine
came into his voice as Isla took the advantage and followed him, still clutching the poker. 'I only wanted tae
help ye.'

'And to help yourself,' she said between her teeth. At
that moment, she would have swung the heavy poker
without hesitation, would have done anything she had to
do in order to rid herself of him. 'Get out of my house,
Mr Reid.'

'It's you that'll be gettin' out, ye wee bitch. I'll see
tae that. I'll see you and yer brats out on the street!'

She pulled her arm back as though to swing the
poker, and he ducked instinctively, then ran for the
door, his nerve broken. Isla slammed it shut behind him
and leaned on the panels, her heart pounding so hard
that she thought it would burst out through her ribs.

'Mummy?' Barbara, startled awake by the slamming
door, sat up in bed, knuckling her eyes. Ross, a heavy
sleeper, didn't stir.

'It's all right, pet, I – I opened the door to shoo a fly
out and the wind slammed it.'

'Did the fly get hurt?' Barbara asked drowsily. The
thought of her daughter's concern for a fly after what
had almost happened brought a sudden spurt of laughter to Isla's throat.

'No,' she said on a giggle. 'The fly's fine.'

'Good.' Barbara slid back into sleep as Isla groped her way to the chair by the fire and sank into it, the poker still clutched tightly in her hand.

'He'll complain about ye. Ye'll mebbe be put out,' Magret fretted the next morning.

'Put out for refusing to let him molest me? It's me that'll be complaining about him.'

Magret's eyes darkened with alarm. 'Don't go makin' trouble, Isla, they'll no' listen tae ye. They always believe their own.' She twisted the dish towel between her hands into a rope. 'I was that worried about ye last night. I'd've asked Tommy tae sit with ye till the man had gone, but . . .' She stopped, and looked away, embarrassed. Isla understood. Magret couldn't risk losing her own home, even for a friend.

'Has this happened before?'

'Of course. It happens all the time.'

'Has it happened to you?'

Again, Magret's eyes slid away. 'There was one time, when he was laid off and there wasnae enough money.' She shivered, then said, 'I made sure after that that the rent was paid, even if it meant us goin' without.'

'Does Tommy know?'

'Of course not!' Magret was shocked at the very idea. 'Men have their pride, the shame of it would've near killed him. Either that or he'd've killed Geordie Reid, then we'd've lost the room for sure.'

'I wish now that I'd hit him with the poker, instead of just threatening him,' Isla said between her teeth. 'A

man like that shouldn't be allowed to go round bullying
women and – using them.'

'Ach, it's just life, hen. Plenty women have tae face
worse than that, day in and day out.'

'Your envelope's not ready yet. You'll have to wait, or
come back later,' the receptionist told Isla when she presented herself at the offices in Moss Street first thing on
Monday morning.

'I'm not here for the envelope, I'm here to speak to
Mr Gilchrist Forbes.'

'Mr Forbes isn't in the office this morning.'

'What about his son?'

'He's here, but—'

'Then I'll see him,' Isla said. Since the father wasn't
available, the son would have to do. She wasn't going to
leave the office until she had had her say.

The woman hesitated, then shrugged and went away.

A few minutes later she reappeared, and Isla,
clutching Ross by the hand, followed her into an
office smaller than Gilchrist Forbes', but just as cluttered.

Colin Forbes' expression showed it clear that he, too,
deplored this meeting. 'Mrs – Moffatt. Won't you sit
down?' He made no move to shake hands, but stayed on
his feet until she was seated.

Isla drew Ross to her side, taking some comfort in his
nearness, and instructed him in a whisper to be a good
boy. Then over his red curls she told Colin Forbes,
clearly and calmly, exactly what had happened on the
previous Friday evening. The event was burned into her
mind – she had thought of little else all weekend – and

she repeated everything George Reid had said, every move he had made, in detail.

Colin Forbes listened with growing distaste. 'I find it hard to believe that one of our employees . . .' he began when she had finished.

'I'm sure you do. I'm also aware that you're more concerned with protecting your employee's interest than mine.'

Colour rose beneath his fair skin. 'I assure you—'

'And I assure you, Mr Forbes, that every word I've told you is the truth. Not only that – I've been making enquiries over the weekend, and it seems that I'm not the only woman in the street to have had this experience.'

'Nobody has ever complained to us before about Mr Reid.'

Isla gave a short laugh. 'Tell me, Mr Forbes, would you complain if it meant being thrown out of your home? I've heard of one poor young woman who was left with three children to feed after her husband had to go into the Infirmary. She didn't pay any money at all to Mr Reid for a few weeks, but I'm quite sure that his book says differently. Mr Reid puts in the money himself, then claims his reward for keeping a roof over their heads. When – or if – the tenants can afford to pay back-rent he makes them repay to the last penny. That way, he gets his enjoyment without having to pay for it.'

The young man was almost crimson now, one hand fiddling with a pencil. 'Mrs Moffatt, all you had to do was to let my father or me know that you were unable to pay the rent this week, and we would have had a word with Reid.'

'Why should I seek favours that my own tenants can't have? I believe that every landlord should try living in their own property now and again, Mr Forbes. They may well learn something to their own disadvantage.'

They glared at each other across the desk, openly hostile now, then he asked, 'You realise that this may well mean that George Reid will lose his job?'

'In my opinion, he deserves to.'

'Very well. My father will be in the office this afternoon,' he said stiffly. 'I'll tell him about your visit.'

'Please do.' Isla got to her feet. 'And you can also tell him that if Mr Reid should call for the rent in future, I'll not be opening my door to him. Nor will my neighbours, if I have my way of it.'

17

In spite of her brave words, Isla grew more and more nervous as the week passed, and on Friday evening she kept the poker close at hand.

She was breaking stale bread into a bowl for the children's supper when someone knocked at the door, and Barbara, washed and in her nightdress, scampered to open it before Isla could stop her.

'Come in,' she said hospitably, and stepped back. Isla's fingers, reaching frantically for the poker, fell to her side as Colin Forbes walked in.

'Good evening, Mrs Moffatt. I came to assure you that Reid won't be troubling you again.'

Relief flooded over her, but, stubbornly, she didn't want to reveal it to young Forbes and let him think that she was being pathetically grateful. So she went on with her work, picking up the kettle and pouring warm water from it into the bowl. 'You mean he'll be troubling the poor souls in another area?'

His voice sharpened. 'My father and I looked into your complaint very thoroughly, and as a result of our investigations the man no longer works for us. Until we find someone more trustworthy, I'll collect the rents.'

Isla added milk to the bowl, then divided the mixture between two smaller bowls and put them on to the table. 'Barbara, stir these for me – carefully, mind, no splashing.' As the little girl scrambled importantly on to a chair, she bent to lift the tin bath to the side.

'Let me do that for you.' The young man put the rent book on the table and hoisted the bathtub up, moving towards the sink.

'Not there,' Barbara told him sharply. 'Mummy empties it in the backyard, over the potatoes, 'cos it's not been raining and they need water.'

He put the tub down by the sink then straightened.

'You're growing potatoes?'

'It's cheaper than buying them,' Isla said dryly, fetching her purse.

'Mummy's mixed a lot of dung into the earth,' Barbara told him blithely as she stirred at the bread and milk. 'It smells, but it's good for the potatoes. Would you give me the sugar, please?' She indicated the paper bag on a shelf by the cooker, and he handed it to her.

'Thank you. Dung comes out of horses,' Barbara explained as she dipped a dry spoon into the bag.

'So I've heard,' he agreed solemnly.

'Here you are.' Isla tipped coins on to the table and sorted them out, pushing most of them over towards him.

'There's too much here.'

'I wasn't able to pay last week's rent,' she reminded him, 'so I must pay it this week.'

He coloured. 'Aren't you being unnecessarily exact, Mrs Moffatt? How much have you left yourself to live on?'

'We'll manage.' She had had to pawn Kenneth's last Christmas gift to her, a bracelet that she had been hoping to keep. Even so, the next week was going to be difficult, but she had no intention of admitting it to this well-dressed man who had never in his life known what it was like to have to do without.

He glanced at Barbara, dribbling sugar, grain by grain, into one of the bowls, then at Ross, who stood by her side, craning up to watch the procedure, his blue eyes bright with anticipation, and said, low-voiced, 'D'you think you're being fair to your children?'

Isla fisted her hands on the table.

'We'll manage,' she repeated. Overhead, someone walked across the floor, and the ceiling gave out a series of creaks. Colin Forbes glanced up involuntarily, then looked round the room. Isla bridled as she saw that, unlike Miss Currie, who had noted only the attempts to improve it, all he saw was the shabbiness, the cracks in the ceiling, the damp patch in the corner.

'It's not much of a place, is it?' Isla asked, watching his face. 'It doesn't seem fair to me to take rent from the folk that have to live here.'

'People must pay their way.'

'Did my – did Kenneth McAdam own many other properties like this one?'

He had opened the rent book and was noting the amount she had paid. His hand faltered, then moved on. 'A few.'

'D'you think he ever visited them, and looked at the leaking windows and the draughts and the water running down from the backyard and into the close when it's been raining?'

'I'm sure my father could find something better for you.'

'I doubt if I could afford it. And as you just said yourself, Mr Forbes, people must pay their way.'

'Good night, Mrs Moffatt.' He snapped the book shut and swept the coins up, then turned on his heel.

As he opened the door, Barbara said cheerfully, 'Bye!'

'Bye,' Ross sounded like an echo.

Colin Forbes's face softened into a smile. 'Bye,' he said, and left.

She followed him into the close, closing the door behind her so that the children couldn't hear. She must have been left to the last, for he was on his way out of the close. 'Mr Forbes, why do you dislike me so much?' she asked his departing back bluntly.

He swung round. 'I beg your pardon?'

'I asked why you dislike me so much. I think I have a right to know.'

The close was only dimly illuminated by a gas lamp in the street, and Colin Forbes was a vast black shadow blocking out most of the feeble light. 'I get the distinct impression that the feeling's mutual, Mrs Moffatt.'

'Only because you made it very plain that you disliked me intensely from the first moment you saw me, at your father's office. If you have a reason, I can't think what it is.'

There was a pause, then he said bitterly, 'Ainslie McAdam and I were engaged to be married.'

'So your father told me. I understand that she ended the engagement.'

'She did – because she was ashamed over the way her father had betrayed his family with you.'

Isla stared, then began to laugh. She was shocked by her own reaction, but the laughter bubbled up of its own accord, filling the space between them, before she could stop it.

'I'm glad someone's amused,' she heard Colin Forbes say coldly above her mirth. 'At least the whole sorry business hasn't been wasted entirely.'

'I'm – I'm sorry.' Isla pressed her fingertips against her mouth to quell further laughter. She swallowed hard, then said, 'It's just that I've never been held responsible for so many crimes in my life. All I did was marry the man I loved in the belief that he was free to marry me. Yet Ainslie's convinced that I plotted to tear Kenneth from his family, you're certain that somehow I forced her to end your engagement – and now Mr Reid's lost his job because of me. I'm beginning to wonder if I started the Great War without realising it.'

'You're being ridiculous, Mrs Moffatt,' the shadow looming against the street light told her coldly. 'Ridiculous and childish.'

'Possibly, but I'm not the only one, Mr Forbes. From what I know of Ainslie McAdam, I'd say that she's an intelligent young woman, with a mind of her own. You make her sound like a lassie with a powder puff for a brain, someone who could be easily pushed into ending her engagement.' Anger began to replace the amusement. 'If she gave your ring back to you, Mr Forbes, it wasn't just because of me. She must have had her own reasons, and perhaps it's time you began to ask yourself what they might be.'

She heard him draw his breath in sharply, then

without another word he strode out of the close and along the street.

Isla sagged against the clammy, peeling wall for a moment, then pulled herself clear and stood upright. She had been cruel – but he had asked for it. 'Him and his disapproval!' she said aloud, the words echoing through the dim close, then with a quick, decisive gesture she spun round and went back into the house.

'For goodness' sake, Barbara!'

'What?' Barbara asked blankly, looking up from her bowl. Ross had clambered up on to a chair and the two of them were relishing their bread and milk. No wonder, Isla thought, peering into the sugar bag as she put it away. In her absence, Barbara had used up almost the entire week's supply.

'Did you have to talk like that to Mr Forbes?'

'I said please when I asked for the sugar, and thank-you when he gave it to me.'

Isla wiped milk from Ross's chin. 'I meant, did you have to chatter on about dung?'

Barbara, unperturbed, dug her spoon into her bowl and scraped up the last of the mush. 'Oh, that. I thought he might want to know about how to grow potatoes,' she said.

On the first anniversary of Kenneth McAdam's death, Isla didn't go to Flora Currie's house. Instead, she stayed at home, cleaning the room from top to bottom, throwing herself into hard work in a bid to keep her memories at bay. When the children were asleep that night and the tenement had creaked into silence, she wept into her pillow. The edges of her grief had dulled, but she still missed and wanted him.

The next morning Barbara, visiting the privy before going off to school, came hurrying back. 'Mummy, someone's dug your garden up!'

It was Mrs Leach's turn for the wash-house, and her washing was already on the line. Isla ducked beneath it and went to the far corner, where the tumbled earth was draped with stripped plants; when she picked one up it lay limply across her fingers, already dead. The thief must have struck the night before, after dark. Looking up at the building, she glimpsed Drew at a window, watching her, and a moment later he came hurrying out in shirt and trousers, thumbing his braces over his shoulders. Mrs Brown and Magret arrived at his back, with Greta and Daisy in tow.

'After all your hard work – it's a shame, so it is.' It was the first time Mrs Brown had directly addressed Isla.

'And after your Drew's digging, too.'

'I hope they were all bad,' Barbara announced. 'I hope that whoever ate them got a sore tummy.'

'Barbara! What's done's done, so we might as well hope that whoever took them was in real need of them.'

'The shaws were still small,' Drew mourned. 'The potatoes must have been like wee marbles.'

Isla nodded. 'I know. Could they not at least have left them until they could steal a decent meal?'

'Ach, most of the folks round here would never think of that.' Magret glanced up at the surrounding windows. 'It could have been anyb'dy.'

Mrs Leach came out of the wash-house with another basket of washing, her daughter at her back. 'I knew it wouldnae be worth the bother,' she said without sympathy as she began to peg out the clothes. 'Ye were askin' for trouble.'

'It was nice to see things growing, though,' Mrs Kelly ventured, and her mother gave a snort.

'It was a waste of time, that's what it was.'

Isla pounced on Ross, who had scampered into the yard dressed only in vest and trousers, and, Daisy at his heels, was approaching the looted bed with the clear intention of plunging his bare feet into the soft earth. As she pulled him away, struggling and protesting, she heard Mrs Leach say, 'Catch me workin' my fingers tae the bone just tae give some thief a meal!'

A few weeks later Isla was putting a batch of scones into the oven when the door, on the latch, was pushed open and Ross, now old enough to play outside with the other children, came hurrying in and made straight for her. His free hand locked on to her apron and his fiery head butted at her thigh as he attempted to get as close to her as possible.

She dusted flour off her hands. 'What's wrong, pet?' Ross was still learning to cope with the rough and tumble of street life, and often came running to her for comfort when things got too much for him.

'Lady . . .' he whined as someone rapped on the door. Isla moved to open it, but the little boy was like an anchor, holding her back, and she had to gather him into her arms before she could get to the door.

Despite the mildness of the day, the woman who stood in the close wore a heavy black coat reaching almost to her ankles. As soon as the door opened she moved forward imperiously, so that Isla had no option but to step back and let her into the room.

'What d'you want?'

The newcomer's head tilted back slightly, the brim of her hat lifting to reveal a pale, haggard face dominated by cold grey eyes.

'I am Mrs McAdam – Mrs Kenneth McAdam. And this' – the grey gaze moved to Ross – 'must be Kenneth's son. I saw him out on the pavement.' She was well spoken, but her voice was harsh, the words falling like stones from her thin mouth.

Icy water seemed to trickle down Isla's spine. 'What do you want?'

'The boy, of course.'

'The—?'

'I've come for the boy,' Catherine McAdam said slowly and clearly, as though talking to an idiot. 'He's my husband's son—'

'He's my son!'

'—and naturally, he must be raised in my husband's house,' the woman went on as though Isla had not spoken. 'Not in this' – she looked round the room, her lip curling in disgust – 'this hovel.'

'Mrs McAdam.' It was strange, addressing another woman by the name she had once thought to be hers. 'This is my son, mine! And you and I have nothing to discuss.'

Catherine McAdam surveyed her dispassionately, then dismissed her, looking back at Ross. The pale lips shaped a slight smile. 'He's a true McAdam. He's going to grow up to look just like his grandfather.'

Isla began to have the eerie feeling that the woman

who had invaded her home wasn't even aware of her as a human being, only some sort of mechanism that had produced Kenneth's son. His second son, she thought, and knew why Catherine McAdam was there. She had lost her own child, and she was looking for a replacement.

'Nobody's going to take my bairn away from me.' As Ross tightened his grip on her neck she put a hand up to his curly head, over one ear, wondering if he understood what was being said.

Catherine looked surprised. 'But he's a McAdam, with the McAdam blood in his veins. I can give him everything – a comfortable home, a good education. His room's waiting for him, with toys and books in it. I can teach him to follow in his grandfather's footsteps.'

'No!'

'Would you deny him all that, when you yourself can give him nothing?'

'Mrs McAdam,' Isla fought to keep the growing fear from her voice, 'I have every sympathy with you in the loss of your own son, but you can't walk into my home and demand mine to take his place.'

In answer Catherine took an impatient step towards her, coming close enough for Isla to catch the faint scent of brandy on her breath. She held her arms out towards Ross, and Isla backed away. This woman represented a threat far more terrifying than the blundering, lustful rent collector had. She could scarcely take a poker to her supposed husband's legal wife, she thought wildly.

'You're – you're not yourself, Mrs McAdam. You should be at home.'

Ross began to whimper and struggle; his weight was

almost too much, but she daren't even shift his position lest Catherine McAdam took the opportunity to lunge at her while she was off balance, and snatch him from her arms.

The woman's hands fell back to her sides. 'If it's money you want, you can have it,' her harsh voice said. 'I have no objection to paying you for the time you've spent caring for him.'

'I don't want a penny of your money, I just want you to get out of my house!'

'My dear, your sort of woman always needs money,' Catherine told her with sweeping contempt. 'I shall instruct my lawyer to have a legal agreement drawn up and delivered to you tomorrow. As for now . . .' she held her thin arms out again. 'Give him to me.'

'No!' Isla's voice rose above the little boy's frightened wails. 'Don't you touch him!'

For the first time, Catherine McAdam looked puzzled. 'If you didn't want me to have him, why did you bring him to Paisley? It was meant to be – don't you see that? You were sent here to help me in my time of need.'

'Please – go away!'

Again, Catherine's reaching arms fell away. 'I must have him, and I will have him, though not today, since you've seen fit to upset him.' She turned and walked unhurriedly to the door, opening it with only the tips of her fingers as though afraid that the wooden timbers might contaminate her. Then she turned.

'My lawyer will contact you tomorrow. He will pay you an adequate sum, and you may hand the child over to him.'

18

When Catherine McAdam had gone, closing the door quietly behind her, Isla dropped into her fireside chair, still clutching Ross, murmuring reassurance. His sobs gradually died down; he was hot, and sticky with sweat and tears, but Isla, almost out of her mind with terror, couldn't bring herself to ease her grip on him.

Just when everything seemed to be working out for her, her world had begun to shatter. Losing the rent money, having to fight the rent collector off, then being robbed of the potatoes she and Drew had so carefully tended. And now this, the most frightening threat of all. She should never have come to this town. Ainslie McAdam was quite right, she should have found somewhere else for herself and the children. They would have to leave at once, go where nobody knew them and where Ainslie's terrifying mother would never find them.

Her mind raced like a mouse caught in a cage, hurling itself from side to side but unable to find a way through the bars that held it captive. She couldn't just leave Paisley, much as she wanted to. For the children's sake, she must first have somewhere to go. She thought fleetingly of asking Flora Currie for help and shelter, then dismissed the idea. Flora had been kind, but her family and the McAdams had known each other socially, and Isla herself owed Flora too much to drag her into the dreadful situation. She suddenly remembered Aunt Lally in Edinburgh. She could go there, but first she would have to find money to pay for the journey.

She and Ross both jumped as Magret came barging in from the close. 'Isla? Somethin's burnin', can ye no' smell it?' Then, after one swift look at Isla, 'God, lassie, what's happened? Ye look as if ye've seen a ghost!'

Snatching a towel from the nail by the stove, she opened the oven door, then gave a wail. 'Look at them, they're all spoiled – did ye no' smell them?' She put the tray of blackened scones on top of the cooker and flapped the towel to waft the smoke away. For the first time Isla became aware of the acrid stink of burning.

At the sight of Daisy, standing in the middle of the kitchen, her fine hair wispy round her small skull and one index finger stuck firmly into a nostril, Ross reverted to his normal self and struggled to get down. Isla resisted, but finally gave in when he began to kick and pummel at her.

'Never mind the scones.'

'Never mind? Since when did any of us have money tae throw away like that?'

Isla got to her feet stiffly, feeling as though she had aged years in the past half hour. She had to do something before Catherine McAdam changed her mind and came back for Ross. She took the towel from Magret and wet one corner under the tap, then wiped her son's sticky, protesting face.

'I have to go out. Could you fetch Barbara from school, and keep her with you until I get back?'

'But the weans is old enough to find their own way home—'

'I don't want her left to come along the street by herself,' Isla interrupted sharply, snatching her coat from the nail on the door. 'I'll be back as soon as I can – just keep an eye on her till I get home.'

Ross was getting too big for his go-chair now, and he had begun to hate it. There was no time to struggle with him, so Isla scooped him up into her arms and hurried out, regardless of her friend's baffled face. By the time she reached Moss Street and turned in at the close that bore Gilchrist Forbes' gleaming brass plate, she was staggering beneath the little boy's weight.

The receptionist, seated in her small office behind its sheltering glass window, was speaking on the telephone. She flicked a cool glance in Isla's general direction, then her eyes widened and she began to scramble from her chair as Isla, ignoring her, marched round the corner into the open waiting area outside the offices.

Sunlight poured in through the windows of Gilchrist Forbes' large office. He and his son, bending over papers on the large desk, looked up as Isla burst into the room.

'Nobody's going to take my child away from me – nobody!'

Colin's exasperated, 'For goodness' sake, not again!'

clashed with the receptionist's, 'I couldn't stop her, Mr Forbes, she just—'

Gilchrist Forbes held up a hand for silence, looking at the distraught young woman who had just invaded his office, realising that she was on the verge of hysteria. 'Sit down, Mrs Moffatt. Miss Lang, could we have some tea? And perhaps you could take the little boy into your own office and keep him amu—'

'No!' Isla glared at him over Ross's head. 'He's staying with me!'

'Very well.' Forbes nodded at the receptionist, who withdrew with an offended sniff, then he picked up some blank sheets of paper and a pencil from the desk, and held them out to Ross.

'Would you like to draw pictures, young man? Over here, where your mother can keep an eye on you.' He took a stool from a corner and placed it in a puddle of sunlight. Isla hesitated, then released the little boy, who went at once to the stool and knelt down on the carpet, reaching for the pencil the lawyer held out to him. The sunlight turned his downbent head into a mass of dancing flames and the sight of the nape of his neck, soft and innocent, wrenched at Isla's heart. She couldn't bear the thought of losing him.

'Mr Forbes, you're not going to take my son away from me. I won't let you!'

Father and son exchanged puzzled looks. 'Why should we want to do that?' the older man said mildly.

'Mrs McAdam . . .' Then, seeing that both men were bewildered, Isla said, slowly and carefully, 'Mrs McAdam came to my house this afternoon. She w-wants . . .' The horror of the meeting swept over her again and her voice began to waver. 'She wants Ross.'

'You mean that she offered to adopt your child?' Colin asked.

'She just wanted him! She said that he was a McAdam, he had Kenneth's blood in him and she could give him things that I couldn't. She said that you'd – you'd come for him tomorrow, with an agreement for me to sign. She wants to b-buy . . .' Despite the warmth of the room Isla had begun to shiver.

The door opened and Colin Forbes hurried forward to take the tray from the receptionist. He poured tea then put a cup into Isla's hand and said, in the gentlest voice she had ever heard from him, 'Drink this, Mrs Moffatt.'

The hot sweet tea began to revive her and the shivering eased. She looked up to see Ross sinking his small white teeth into a biscuit, the crumbs glittering in the sunlight as they sprayed towards the carpet.

'Ross, look at the mess you're making . . .' she began automatically, but Gilchrist Forbes put a hand up to stop her.

'Never mind the mess, m'dear, just tell us exactly what Mrs McAdam said to you.'

Isla forced her mind back to the confrontation, speaking haltingly at first, then faster as she relived the scene. By the time she had finished she had begun to shake again.

'Nobody can make me give up my children. I won't let them!'

'You've got nothing to fear, Mrs Moffatt,' Gilchrist assured her. 'Nobody can take your children from you without your permission.'

'I've heard of folk in George Street who've had their bairns taken from them.'

'Only if they were unable to care for the children, or if they ill treated them. Only if it was in the children's interests, surely?' He spoke gently, but to Isla's ears the words were condescending, easily voiced by a man who had never known the insecurity caused by hardship or the gnawing worry over where his next meal was to come from.

'It's not as simple as that, Mr Forbes,' she told him sharply. 'Not if you've got no money behind you and the folk with the power decide otherwise. Mrs McAdam, for instance – she's right when she says that she can give Ross more than I can, but that doesn't mean that she can love him more than I do.'

Ross, his cheeks bulging with biscuit, came over to lean against her. She put her arm about him and hugged his small body to her. The thought of him, ill or alone in a strange big house, calling in vain for her, was more than she could bear. 'She doesn't look to me like a woman who could love a wee bairn properly,' she said to the two men, the tears beginning to flow again. 'She doesn't look to me like a woman who could love anyone.'

At his father's request, Colin Forbes drove Isla back to George Street in his smart car with its smell of leather seats. The children playing in the street and the women leaning against the close-mouths, arms folded, gaped as first Ross then Isla got out.

'Are you all right?' Colin Forbes asked from the car's interior. 'Do you want me to come into the house with you?'

'We're fine, thank you.' He had been kind to Ross, courteous towards Isla, but the irritation was still there, every time he looked at her or spoke to her. The last thing she wanted was to spend more time in his company.

'My father will be in touch with you tomorrow,' he said, and drove off as soon as she closed the door.

Barbara sped out of the close, Greta at her heels. 'Mummy, where've you been?'

'I goed in a motor car,' Ross bragged to her, pulling back on Isla's hand to watch the car disappearing along the road as she hurried him into the close, away from prying eyes.

'Phemie,' Gilchrist Forbes asked as soon as he got home, 'did you tell Catherine McAdam where Kenneth's other – other wife lives?'

'Of course not – as if I'd do a cruel thing like that!'

'But she knows?'

His wife, setting the table for the evening meal, paused in her work. 'She told me that she'd heard about the woman, though I can't think how, since she never goes out.'

'What else did she say?'

'Nothing.' Her eyes brightened with curiosity. 'Why? Has something happened?'

'Nothing of any great importance.'

Phemie almost stamped a plump foot on the carpet. 'It has – it must have. Gilchrist, are you going to give me that nonsense about lawyers' confidences again?'

'No, my dear—'

'Because if you are, mebbe it's time I started think-

ing about lawyers' wives' confidences too. I don't
know,' Phemie said, thumping knives and forks down
on the table, 'it's one thing when you want to know
something from me, and quite another when I ask you
anything—'

'Dinner smells good, mother,' Colin said from the
doorway.

'It'll be ready in twenty minutes. Colin, what's your
father hiding from me now?'

'Hiding?' her son asked, his face expressionless.

'Men!' She glared, then shooed them out of the
room. 'If you're not going to tell me what's going on,
you might at least have the decency to get out from
under my feet when I'm busy!'

They went willingly to the small library, where Colin
said as soon as he closed the door, 'You surely don't
believe what that woman told us today?'

Gilchrist was already pouring whisky into two
glasses. 'Mrs Moffatt is a client of ours, Colin, and she
has a name.'

'She had another name before that – but it turned
out to belong to someone else.'

'That's enough,' Gilchrist said sharply, handing a
glass to his son. 'I don't know why you have to be so
disapproving. If an old fogey like me can accept the idea
of a bigamous marriage without blinking, I don't see
why a modern young man like yourself should make
such a song and dance about it.'

Colin, suddenly reminded of Isla Moffatt's laughter
in the dark, smelly close, her voice pointing out that
Ainslie must have other reasons for ending their
engagement, swallowed down a mouthful of fine malt

whisky. 'Being modern has nothing to do with it. She should never have come to Paisley.'

'But she did come to Paisley, and she's our client, and we must do our best by her. Whatever his faults, I believe that McAdam cared for her, and as his friend as well as his lawyer, it's my place to do the best I can for the girl. She's got nobody else.'

'Being the mother of his children doesn't give her the right to make accusations against his lawful widow.'

The older man walked to the window and looked out on the side drive where a red brick wall was covered with yellow climbing roses. After a long moment he said, 'Colin, Catherine McAdam telephoned just after you and Mrs Moffatt left the office. She told Miss Lang that she wanted me to call on her tomorrow morning at eleven o'clock.' He emptied his glass and turned to look at his son. 'To deal with an urgent and very important personal matter on her behalf.'

Colin stared for a moment, then asked, 'What are you going to do?'

Gilchrist Forbes sighed, and moved to his favourite chair, suddenly feeling very weary.

'I think that I must have a talk with Ainslie first,' he said. 'Tomorrow, at her place of work, so that Catherine knows nothing about it.'

Isla took both children into the wall-bed with her that night and lay sleeplessly staring into the darkness. It was a warm night, and the little room was stiflingly hot; the children tossed and mumbled in their sleep, faces and hair damp with sweat, throwing their arms and legs wide, digging sharp little knees and elbows into her.

Every time footsteps approached the close-mouth, or a car or cart came along the road, she sat upright, convinced that Catherine McAdam had sent someone to steal Ross away from her.

She walked to school with Barbara and Greta in the morning, then went along to Castlehead, where Flora immediately whisked her into the dolls'-house room to show her some bits and pieces she had found that might be of use for the *Little Women* house, which was already coming along well.

'She's been ferretin' in every cupboard and every drawer,' Annie said gloomily from the doorway. 'I'm at my wit's end, following her round and tidying up after her.'

'Nobody asked you to,' Flora snapped. 'I'm not in my dotage yet – I can do my own tidying.' She laid ribbons and buttons and costume jewellery and cardboard before Isla, who looked on listlessly, reacting only when Annie tried to take Ross into the kitchen.

'He's fine here, with me.' She put an arm about the little boy and drew him to her, lying to the two puzzled faces, 'He was a bit crabbit this morning. I think he might be coming down with a chill.'

Annie and Flora looked at Ross's clear eyes and happy grin, then at each other.

'Whatever you think best, dear – Annie can bring his drink of milk in here, then.' Flora signalled to the servant, who withdrew, a hurt expression on her round face. 'Is there something worrying you?' Flora ventured when the maid had gone.

'No, nothing,' Isla told her, and Flora said no more. When she took him back to George Street, Isla couldn't bear to let Ross play outside with the other children. He stormed and stamped, then bawled when she smacked him, and she gathered him up in her arms and cried along with him, rocking and kissing and soothing him until he fell asleep.

'What's amiss with ye?' Magret wanted to know when she came in and found the two of them huddled in the chair.

'I'm fine.'

'Ye've been out of sorts since ye burned those scones yesterday.' She waited, then when no explanation was forthcoming said, 'I'll make us a nice cup of tea.'

'Where's Daisy?'

'She's fallen sound asleep on the rug by the fire, bless her. She was up half the night with her teeth. She'll be fine on her own for a minute,' Magret said comfortably. Watching her as she gathered the cups together and took the muslin cover off the milk jug, Isla envied the other woman her placid assumption that Daisy, alone, was safe from harm.

Ross woke just then, and again demanded to be allowed out to play. 'Ach, let him go,' Magret advised. 'He needs the fresh air, don't ye, pet?'

'I'll go outside too. It's a nice afternoon . . .' Isla picked up one of the chairs standing by the table.

'Aye, all right, on ye go. I'll bring the tea out, and fetch Daisy.'

The afternoon was pleasantly warm and there were quite a few women enjoying the sun, some sitting on the close steps, some on chairs and stools they had brought out, others 'windae-hingin' ', leaning out of open windows, their forearms supported by cushions or blankets laid on the window-sills. While they gossiped and laughed and lifted their faces to the sun and yelled at their children, Isla kept her gaze fixed on Ross.

Catherine McAdam had spoken the truth when she said that she could give the little boy much more than Isla could. Was she being unfair to him, she wondered, craning her neck round the bulk of a woman who happened to move between them, afraid to lose sight of him for a minute. Should she put her own selfish need of him aside and let him have the chance of growing up in a big house and getting a fine education? What would Kenneth have wanted for his son? She had a terrible suspicion that he would have wanted Ross to have all the things that his legal wife was offering.

'It's all right, hen, yer wean'll no' catch somethin' nasty just 'cause he's mixin' with the likes of our bairns,' the woman who had blocked her view said sharply, and Isla drew back, flushing.

'I just – Ross, come back here,' she called as he ventured a few yards further along the pavement. Magret and the other women exchanged looks, and exchanged them again when the time for the schoolchildren to be let out drew near and Isla got up and announced that she was going to fetch Barbara.

'Ye don't want tae go runnin' after yer weans all the time, hen,' someone advised. 'They'll only get spoiled.'

'I feel like the walk. Come on, Ross.'

'Ach, let him play,' Magret said comfortably, from her seat on the hollowed stone step leading to the close. 'I'll keep an eye on him.'

'No, he's to come with me. Ross, did you hear me? And stop dragging your feet like that, you'll ruin your shoes!' Isla ordered as the little boy left his friends reluctantly and went to her, his bottom lip sticking out and his toes scuffing along the pavement. She took his hand, pulling him along behind her as she hurried towards the corner of Maxwellton Street, where the West School stood.

'Yew'll ruin yewr shoes,' she heard someone mimic as she went, and there was a ripple of laughter from the women at the close-mouth. Most of their children played barefoot in the summer, and a few went barefoot through the winter too.

'Hoity-toity!' someone else said loudly. The tears that were never far from the surface now burned Isla's eyes as she walked on. It had been hard enough to win the friendship and trust of those women. If it hadn't been for the peg dolls she had made for their daughters, some of them would still be ignoring her. She was aware that her sudden possessiveness towards her children would only remind them that she was indeed an outsider, but what else, she wondered in despair, could she do? Gilchrist Forbes had been reassuring on the previous day, but his wife was a friend of Catherine McAdam's. He might be put under pressure to help Catherine rather than Isla. His son would have no difficulty in deciding between herself and Ainslie's mother, Isla thought bitterly.

By this time even the most possessive of mothers had stopped coming to fetch their children home, so she and Ross waited alone outside the school railings. Isla fidgeted, looking up and down the road every few seconds, half expecting to see Catherine McAdam, all in black, bearing down on them.

At last, a handbell clanged within the school, and a few seconds later one or two children came running out of the main door. More and more followed, until the playground was seething with them. Isla, clutching Ross with one hand and the railings with the other, strained for a glimpse of Barbara's tawny head, waving and shouting when she finally saw it.

Barbara, like Ross, came to her reluctantly, not at all pleased to see her mother waiting for her. 'What're you doing here?' she wanted to know, brows drawn down between hostile brown eyes. Greta trailed at her back, as usual.

'We thought it would be nice to walk back with you.'

Barbara gave her mother a withering look. 'Nobody's mummy comes to fetch them home! Come on, Greta,' she ordered, and ran ahead, heels flying and her curly hair, now quite long, bouncing on her shoulders. Ross, who had dragged behind Isla all the way to the school, made a futile attempt to break free of her imprisoning hand, then, unable to get away, tried to pull Isla along in an effort to catch up with his sister and Greta.

As they went, Isla turned her tired mind to Magret. It wasn't possible to keep secrets from her neighbour, she knew from experience. The safest course was to tell her something, though not necessarily everything. Isla began to put together the story of a nameless woman who had lost her son in the Glen Cinema tragedy, and after seeing Ross playing out in the street, had recognised a similarity to her own dead child and offered to raise him in the other boy's place. Isla knew that by telling that story she could enlist Magret's support in her struggle to keep Ross safe.

Her life, she thought wryly as Ross hauled her round the corner and into George Street, was beginning to sound like a novelette.

Gilchrist Forbes himself arrived not long after Isla got home, stepping out of his car, tipping his hat courteously to the staring women still gathered round the close-mouth.

Isla, in the middle of making the evening meal, motioned him to a chair, wiping her hands nervously on her pinny. He put his hat and cane on the table and smiled at her. 'I've come to put your mind at rest.'

She sank into a chair. 'You mean she can't take Ross away from me?'

'There was never any question of that, my dear. Mrs McAdam is – unwell. None of us realised just how unwell she was, until now. She got it into her head that you had been sent to Paisley by some higher agency, so that she could adopt your son in place of her own. I've explained to her that she cannot possibly do this.'

'But did she listen to you? She might try again—'

He held up a reassuring hand. 'I've already made arrangements for a nurse-companion to care for Mrs McAdam until such time as she recovers from her illness.'

He looked strained, Isla thought with compassion. 'Can I make you some tea, Mr Forbes?'

'It's a kind thought, but my wife expects me home. Besides . . .' he smiled down at Barbara and Ross, 'You've got your hands full. The companion I mentioned will take up her duties tomorrow, and in the meantime Ainslie will stay with her mother.' He got to his feet, saying as he reached for his hat and stick, 'She's asked me to tell you that she's extremely upset over the worry you've had.'

'Ainslie?' Isla was scarcely able to keep the disbelief from her voice.

'I can assure you, Mrs Moffatt, that she was very upset when I spoke to her this morning. Like the rest of us, she had no idea that her brother's death had had such an effect on her mother. I feel very sorry for Ainslie,' he said thoughtfully, as he left. 'She's not had an easy life lately.'

19

A few nights later, when the children were in bed and asleep, someone knocked at the door. Isla, who hadn't recovered from the fright Catherine McAdam had given her, felt her heart turn over beneath her ribs with a painful wrench.

The trousers she had been darning for Ross fell from her limp fingers to her knee, then to the floor as she pressed her body back into the chair, hoping that whoever waited outside would go away and leave her in peace.

The knock came again, more insistently. Afraid that the children would be wakened, she got up and opened the door an inch, peering through the small space, ready to slam it shut again if need be.

'Who is it?'

'Ainslie McAdam.'

'Go away,' Isla said against the crack. 'I want nothing to do with you or your family. Leave us in peace!'

'I've not come to cause trouble. I have to talk to you.'

Reluctantly, Isla opened the door, and the girl came into the room, pulling her close-fitting hat off to let her red hair fall loosely about her face.

'Are your children asleep?'

Isla nodded, watching her warily. The arrogance had gone out of Ainslie McAdam's face; as she stepped into the pool of light shed by the gas mantles above the fireplace Isla saw that her eyes were shadowed, and the skin beneath them was shaded a delicate violet, as though she too had been enduring sleepless nights.

The official year of mourning for Kenneth McAdam was over, and Isla had discarded her black armband. She would have thought that Ainslie would now be in mourning for her brother, but the girl wore a slim skirt in a deep violet shade, with a silky tailored jacket patterned with small violet and white squares. On any other redhead, violet might have been garish, but on Ainslie, it looked stylish.

The two young women eyed each other warily for a moment, then Ainslie lifted her hands away from her sides, palms out, in a helpless gesture. 'I'm sorry. I'm so sorry. I had no idea of what was in my mother's mind, none at all, until Mr Forbes told me.' Then, as Isla said nothing, 'I don't blame you for not believing me, but it's the truth. She's been in a bad way since my brother's death, but she seemed to be coming out of it. I thought that she was improving. Instead she was thinking up this – this nonsense about replacing him with your wee boy. You'll hear no more about it, I promise you.'

'How can I believe you? How can I be sure?'

'I don't blame you for mistrusting me. You've had a bad time at the hands of the McAdams, haven't you?'

'You needn't presume to speak for your father. I don't regret a moment of the time I shared with him.'

Ainslie's eyes flared with surprise – just as Kenneth's did, Isla thought, as she had thought the first time she and Ainslie set eyes on each other. Her lips tightened, and for a moment she was the Ainslie that Isla knew, arrogant and bitter. Then the look was gone. She dipped a hand into her jacket pocket, then laid a small paper-wrapped package on the table.

'This is for the children,' she said, then went past Isla towards the door, leaving the faint scent of floral perfume in her wake. At the door, she paused. 'May I call again, when things have settled down?'

'I don't see that—'

'Please,' Ainslie said. 'I need to talk to you. I need to talk about my father.'

'If you want to,' Isla said, against her own instincts.

As the click of Ainslie's smart shoes faded away along the pavement, she hoped that that might be the end of the matter. She didn't believe that the girl would come back. She herself would prefer it if Ainslie stayed away, for she had had more than enough of Kenneth's other family. They might hold her to blame for their own troubles, but they themselves had caused her more heartbreak than she wanted in one lifetime.

She picked up the small packet from the table. It smelled faintly of moth-balls and the light scent Ainslie had worn. When she pulled at the ribbon tied around it, the wrapping paper fell away to reveal two books. The first was a sturdy, brightly coloured picture book, designed for a child of Ross's age, depicting balls and kittens, kites and building bricks. The second had imaginative, well-drawn pictures and a simple story that Barbara could read for herself.

Opening it, Isla caught her breath as her eyes fell on a few words in a firm, familiar handwriting that she would have known anywhere. The few short, treasured notes Kenneth had written to her in that same hand during their brief courtship were still in her possession.

'To Ainslie Isobel McAdam,' the words said. '12th October, 1912, from her father, Kenneth Innes McAdam.'

A gift from Kenneth to his daughter. A gift that had clearly been cherished and cared for over the years, and had now been handed over as a peace offering to his other, secret daughter.

The promises made by both Ainslie and the lawyer held. Catherine McAdam didn't come back to George Street, but Isla had had such a fright that it was several weeks before she allowed herself to believe that the threat no longer existed, and Ross could safely play with his friends without her constant supervision. By then the damage had been done; although Magret remained loyal to her, the other women in the street had decided amongst themselves that Isla Moffatt thought herself better than they were, and they took to turning away when she walked down the street, or making loud asides to each other in her presence about folk who thought they were something they weren't.

'Ach, it's just the way they are,' Magret said. 'Pay no heed.'

Fortunately, the antagonism towards Isla didn't extend to the children, who continued to be accepted by their friends. The school summer holidays began and Barbara, at home all day, passed the time by organising another back-court concert.

Lena McNab, the handsome woman who lived across the close and owned the little bakery down the road, went regularly with her young husband to the Paisley Theatre in Smithhills, and took great pleasure in teaching Barbara the songs she heard at the music hall, even coming round the counter, if the shop was quiet, to dance a few steps. Barbara often came back from the bakery with another song.

'Hello, hello,' she would warble, setting down the loaf she had been sent to buy and dancing across the floor, Ross jigging up and down in her wake. 'Who's your lady friend? Who's the little girlie by your side?' Or, linking her arm with some difficulty through his, she would break into, 'Roamin' in the gloamin'.'

Unfortunately, willing though Ross was, he had none of his sister's sense of rhythm, and when he was involved, the songs usually ended with the two of them falling over because Ross had moved the wrong way, or Barbara being put off the melody by his enthusiastic, noisy off-key renderings.

'She's a natural wee music-hall turn, that lassie of yours,' Mrs McNab told Isla when she went into the bakery. 'She should go on to the halls herself one of these days.'

Isla smiled, and nodded, and wondered what Kenneth would have made of it all.

To her surprise, Ainslie came back again, and as the summer went on, her visits took on a weekly pattern. At first they talked about Paisley, Barbara and Ross, books, the auction rooms, Flora Currie's dolls' houses, circling round each other warily, keeping well away from any subject that affected them deeply.

Noticing how relaxed and animated the girl became when she talked about her work at the auction rooms, Isla suspected that life wasn't easy, had perhaps never been entirely easy, for Kenneth's elder daughter. She couldn't understand why this should be, because Kenneth had been a loving and demonstrative father to Barbara and Ross. She had often asked him teasingly what his business colleagues would say if they saw him playing with the children, or cuddling them both on his lap while he read to them.

Now that she thought of it, he had never really responded to those questions, fobbing them off with a smile, or changing the subject.

The sight of Ainslie walking down the road and into the close, smartly dressed and clearly from a different world, only added to the other women's suspicions that Isla was a 'neb in the air'. She explained her new visitor to Magret by saying that Ainslie was the daughter of the household where she worked, and then had to admit the lie to Ainslie herself.

'Just in case the two of you meet, and she says something. I sometimes feel as though I'm living two separate lives, but if the people round here knew that I owned this building they'd never accept me, and there's nowhere else for us to go just now.' She looked round the shabby room. 'It's still up for sale, but who would want it?'

'My father would be turning in his grave if he knew that his flesh and blood were living in a place like this.'

'It's not his fault.' Isla immediately went on the defensive. 'He signed the building over to me so that I'd have some income coming in – he didn't dream that we'd have to live in it.'

'He should have taken the trouble to think things through.' There was suddenly more than a hint of Ainslie's former arrogance in her voice. 'Because of him you're having to struggle along on hardly any money and tell your neighbours all sorts of untruths.'

Isla was ironing, using the table in place of an ironing board, with an old blanket folded on it to protect it from the heat. Now she set the flat-iron on its end with a thump. 'If you're going to insult your father's memory, this isn't the place to do it,' she said quietly. 'I'll not allow anyone to speak ill of him in my hearing, especially his own daughter.'

'You're beginning to sound like all the rest. Just because he was my father it doesn't mean that I have to idolise his memory. Folk should earn respect, not take it for granted.'

'Earn it? The man educated you, clothed you, fed you – and provided a nice home into the bargain. If that's not earning respect, I don't know what is!'

Ainslie's fair skin flushed crimson at the criticism. 'Are you saying that having money makes everything all right?'

'I'm saying that you should be grateful for what Kenneth did for you, and give some thought to what he must have gone through in the last weeks of his life.'

'He brought it on himself. If he hadn't been trying to support two families—' Ainslie stopped, a hand flying to her mouth, then said, 'I'm sorry, I shouldn't have said such a thing, not to you.'

Isla pushed a straggle of black hair back from her forehead. Now the truth was coming to the surface. 'Yes, you should. It's why you came here, isn't it? To try to understand your father?' The words that had gone through her mind again and again in the past thirteen months came easily to her lips. 'If only he'd told me about his worries, I'd have done all I could to help.'

'How could he tell you, of all people?'

'That's what makes it worse – thinking for five years that everything was open and honest between us, then discovering that it was all—'

'All lies?'

Isla shook her head and sat down at the table, the ironing forgotten. 'He didn't lie. He made up a story in his own mind about the way he wanted things to be, and then he tried to live it, with me.'

Ainslie, in the fireside chair, looked down at the hands clasped round her knees. 'And my mother and Innes and I were left outside, in the real life that he didn't want.'

'I didn't mean that. You were his daughter.'

'But that doesn't mean that he loved me! Oh, he liked Innes well enough, but that was because he was a boy.'

'What about the lovely books you gave the children? They were his gifts to you.'

'Where we live, everyone has nicely bound books on show. My father wanted me to have the right books, that was all.'

'You're wrong, Ainslie. Kenneth loved his children. I

mind the patience he had with Barbara, spending hours with her on his knee, reading stories to her—'

'How nice for Barbara.' The girl jumped up and reached blindly for her bag and her gloves. 'At least he cared for one of his daughters—'

'Ainslie, I didn't mean – Ainslie!'

But the door had opened and closed, and Isla was alone.

'Tell me about Kenneth McAdam.'

Flora Currie blinked at Isla, then said, 'You surely know more about him than I did.'

They were working on the *Little Women* dolls' house, Flora, with glue and cardboard and narrow strips of beading, making a frame for a tiny sampler that Isla had drawn with coloured crayons, Isla brushing pieces of wall-paper with flour and water paste and pressing them into place on the parlour walls.

She told Flora, briefly, about her conversation with Ainslie on the previous day, ending with, 'I'm not asking you to gossip, or tell tales. I just think it's time I knew more about the man I thought I was married to for five years.'

'We all present different faces to different people, my dear.'

'I know that – goodness knows I do it myself all the time these days,' Isla said wryly, 'what with paying myself rent for a building I own, and changing my name. But for my own sake – and the children's – I have to understand him better. For instance, *my* Kenneth wouldn't have made money out of renting rooms in tired old buildings to folk who have no choice but to live there. But the Kenneth that Ainslie knew did that.'

'A lot of folk make money out of owning homes they'd not live in themselves. It's the way of the world,' Flora said evasively.

Isla, realising that the older woman heartily disliked talking to her about Kenneth, changed tack. 'Tell me about his – about Ainslie's mother, then.'

'Catherine? Her people were well off, and I mind that everyone thought it a very suitable match, though my brother Arnold – you mind I said he and Kenneth had been friends – was surprised at Catherine choosing Kenneth. He said that she'd not had much time for him before. I saw her on her wedding day, and she looked radiant. The next time I saw her was at her father-in-law's funeral, and then she looked quite ill. She wasn't long past Ainslie's birth at the time, as I remember.'

She paused to collect her thoughts, then said, 'When Catherine's parents died, I heard that she wanted to move into their big house, but Kenneth would have none of it. I don't think he could have afforded the upkeep. Catherine could – she inherited quite a lot from them – but he'd not have wanted to live on his wife's money. Come to think of it, that might have been what finished his own business, trying to show Catherine that he could make a lot of money. I always felt a bit sorry for Kenneth – I don't think he ever felt comfortable with the life he led.'

Flora Currie's words fitted in with what Isla herself had said to Ainslie about Kenneth inventing a world, and sharing it with her. Waiting for sleep to come that night, she mulled over them. He seemed to have been so many things – a husband who wasn't a husband at all, a loving father who hadn't, it seemed, shown much love towards his older children, a caring man who charged rent for sub-standard housing he had made no effort to improve.

Ross muttered, and she got up and looked into the cot. He was sound asleep, twisted in the sheet, the pillow wedged alongside him. Lifting his head and slipping the pillow beneath it, she wondered if she had ever really known Kenneth at all.

20

Mr Leckie, the toyshop owner who had spoken to Flora at the auction sale, called on her unexpectedly one day to see the half-completed *Little Women* house, and met Isla.

'You have an interesting talent, Mrs Moffatt. I wonder – would you be interested in decorating another little house for me when you've finished this one? Something simple and straightforward, that I can put on show to advertise the furniture and houses I sell.'

'Surely you could do that yourself.'

The man shook his head. 'I'm not talking about just putting furniture into a doll's house, Mrs Moffatt. Anyone can do that, but you have the ability to create a home in miniature.'

'I quite agree,' said Flora. 'Of course you must do it, Isla.'

'I'll supply the house,' the shopkeeper added as Isla hesitated. 'And the furniture, though I'd leave the choice of furnishings entirely to you, and pay for any other materials you may need.'

'But I haven't got anywhere to work on it.'

'Yes, you have,' Flora said firmly. 'You'll work here. She'll do it, Mr Leckie.'

'I can't use your home as a workplace,' Isla protested when the man had gone.

'Nonsense, I enjoy seeing you and the children, and so does Annie, though she'd rather die than admit it. And now you'll be earning some money – you can do with that, surely.'

'At least it means that I can afford to pay you for the use of your premises.'

Flora looked shocked at the very idea. 'My dear girl, it's me who should be paying you for the interest you've brought into my life. Your visits are the only thing that have kept me going, since poor Agnes passed away.'

Flora's neighbour, a woman she had known for many years, had died after a long illness, and now the house next door lay silent and empty, waiting for the next-of-kin to decide what was to be done with it.

'It reminds me of my own mortality every time I see the closed door and the curtains pulled across the windows,' Flora Currie had told Isla with a shiver not long after the funeral. 'Poor Agnes was such a lively woman before her illness, always popping in.'

Young Mr Kelly upstairs lost his job again and couldn't get another. He and his little wife began to look more and more desperate, and Mrs Leach looked more and more like a dragon.

Going into the wash-house one day, Isla hesitated as she heard the woman's voice from inside, nagging and complaining. She turned and went quietly back into the close. 'She was going on at poor Mrs Kelly about how she should never have married him,' she told Magret later.

'She's a right bitch, so she is. I'm heart-sorry for that

lassie. It's bad enough havin' yer man out of work without yer ma going on and on about it. It's not her fault, poor soul – or his.'

The Kellys fell behind with their rent, and Isla refused to let Colin Forbes, who was still collecting the rents, threaten them with eviction. 'He's doing his best to find work – where's the sense in making their lives more difficult by making threats, or putting them out?' she asked.

'People have to pay their way, Mrs Moffatt.'

'The Kellys have every intention of paying their way. They're not deliberately trying to cheat – they're not committing a crime, so why punish them?'

Colin Forbes glared. 'Mrs Moffatt, you keep asking me about repairs – when can the roof be fixed, when can the close be lit. D'you not understand that nothing can be done unless you yourself have the money to do it? And you'll not get the money while you protect tenants who don't pay!'

'In that case, wouldn't it make more sense to try to find work for Mr Kelly than to put him out of his home?' she shot back at him. 'The man's an office worker, and from what I know of him I'm quite sure very conscientious. Is there any chance of finding him a place with Forbes and Son?'

'Not at the moment. And even if there was, would it be wise to put him where he might learn who owns this building?'

She hadn't thought of that. She stuttered for a moment, confused, then rallied as she saw the cold smile on his lips. 'There are other offices. You might be able to place him elsewhere.'

'I'm a lawyer, Mrs Moffatt, not a nursemaid,' he said, and slapped the rentbook shut.

Without Gilchrist Forbes' help, Ainslie would never have been able to persuade her mother to let the nurse-companion into the house. Gilchrist, under the guise of bringing papers for Catherine to sign, talked of a respectable woman of his acquaintance, fallen on hard times through no fault of her own, searching for a position as a useful companion to some lady, and by the time he set down his empty teacup, Catherine herself had suggested that, with Ainslie busy about her own affairs, it would be pleasant for her to have someone else in the house, other than the servants.

Ann Dove, a woman of about Catherine's own age, calmly and with just the right amount of meekness, submitted to being ordered about, but Ainslie was acutely embarrassed by her mother's high-handed attitude.

'You're a nurse, not a servant,' she protested to the woman when Catherine was out of earshot.

'Your mother doesn't know that, does she? She's a very sad woman, Miss McAdam, and a lonely one – through no fault of yours,' Miss Dove added swiftly as she saw the stricken look on Ainslie's face. 'It's just part of being the sort of person she is. She needs someone to order around, and it's better that it's me and not you. And don't worry,' she added with a faint smile, 'if things get too bad, I can look after myself.'

Her presence in the house eased Ainslie's life a great deal, giving her freedom to concentrate on her work. She hadn't gone back to Isla's house since leaving it in a rage a few weeks earlier. She wanted to, but at the same time, she was wary at what she might find out if she and Isla really talked to each other.

Colin called, and found her in the front garden, weeding a flower bed. Walking up the drive, he looked beyond her kneeling figure and saw that the curtains were looped back from the windows. Daylight had at last been permitted back into the house.

At the sound of footsteps on the gravel Ainslie looked up, then scrambled to her feet, smiling. Her hair was escaping from the green ribbon that tied it back, to curl round her face like little flames.

'Are you here on business?'

'Strictly for pleasure, to see you.'

'Would you like to come in? Or we could sit in the summer-house.'

He opted for the summer-house, and as they walked round the side of the house together she dusted the soil from her hands then took off the heavy apron she had been wearing.

'Mother isn't pleased,' she said as she saw him glance at her white and green dress. 'She thinks I should be in mourning black for Innes, but I've had enough of mourning. In any case, I don't think Innes would have wanted us to dress in black for him.'

'How is your mother?' he asked as they stepped into the summer-house's cool shade.

'The nurse is very good with her. I'm grateful to your father for finding her.' She flicked a sidelong glance at him, then asked, 'Did you know that Mother had been drinking?'

'What?' He stared at her in disbelief.

'I knew that she was taking rather a lot of the tonic wine the doctor recommended to get her strength up, and that she had a glass of brandy sometimes. But I didn't think that . . .' She stopped, then said, 'It was Miss Dove – the nurse – who told me. Apparently the servants knew, because they were the ones who bought the bottles for her, and disposed of them. But they couldn't bring themselves to tell me, poor souls. I thought your father might have said something to you.'

Colin was appalled at the thought of Mrs McAdam, always the lady, turning to drink. 'Not a word. He probably wanted to protect your mother, but I wish I'd known, for your sake. You've been through hell over the past year or so, haven't you?'

'If it hadn't been for the auction rooms and the people there, I would probably be fighting Mother for the brandy bottle,' Ainslie agreed, with a faint laugh. She picked a leaf from her skirt and smoothed it between her fingers, staring intently down at it. 'Isla Moffatt says that my father loved her children,' she said suddenly. 'He played with them.' She began to shred the leaf, tearing tiny neat strips from it. 'It wasn't that he didn't have any love to give, Colin. He'd just chosen to give it to another wife and other children.'

'Everything comes back to Isla Moffatt, doesn't it?' Colin rose abruptly and paced to the door. After the shadows, the sun was almost like a blow against his face and arm. 'If she hadn't come to Paisley—'

'That's what I thought at first. But now,' Ainslie said, 'I'm not so sure. It hurts to learn the truth, but it's the only way forward. And that's the way I'm going from now on, Colin. Forwards.'

In the shade of the summer-house, her face swam like a water-lily within the glow of her hair. Looking down on her, Colin Forbes accepted, at last, that there was no chance now of Ainslie marrying him.

The day after Colin's visit, Ainslie went back to George Street, stepping round groups of children squatting on cracked paving stones warmed by the sun, forging her way through the huddle of women snatching what fresh air they could at the close-mouth. She stood at Isla's door, fists thrust into the pockets of the sleeveless jacket she wore, and said, 'No matter how it hurts, I want to know the truth about my father.'

Isla had been washing clothes at the sink, and her face was flushed with heat, her hair wisping across her cheeks. She stepped back, drying her hands on her crossover pinny. 'Come in,' she said.

'I wanted him to love me,' Ainslie told Isla an hour later, getting the words out at last. 'All my life I tried so hard to earn his love. That's why it hurt when I realised he'd given it freely to your daughter. Now, I'm beginning to think that my mother stood between us, for reasons of her own. She tried to stand between me and Innes, even after he died. She's always wanted to possess people, and she's always been afraid of them loving each other, because she thought that that would shut her out.'

'Poor soul. It must be terrible to be afraid all the time.'

Ainslie shot Isla a startled glance, then said, 'They should probably never have married. Mother was disappointed in my father, and perhaps he withdrew because he knew it. So she turned all her ambition on Innes instead.'

Isla, wringing out the last of the small clothes she had been washing, shivered inside at the thought of the misery Ross might have suffered in Catherine's hands. 'People aren't made of Plasticine. Try to shape them against their natures, and you'll only end up misshaping them.'

Ainslie ran a hand over the back of her neck, lifting her hair to let what little air there was cool her. It had been a long afternoon and she felt bone-weary, but also as though she was on the road to recovery after a serious illness.

She and Isla had been ruthlessly honest with each other; Ainslie had heard about the human side of her father, a side she had never been privileged to see in all the twenty-one years she had known him, while Isla had discovered the darker side of his nature, the cold, reserved husband and father, the ruthless businessman.

'That's probably why he wanted another marriage, with you,' Ainslie said now. 'You knew nothing of his background or his family. You accepted him as he was, without criticism. What are you doing?' she added as Isla opened out the ungainly wooden clothes-horse and began to hang the wet clothes on it. 'It's a lovely day, they'd dry in half an hour if you put them outside.'

'You've never lived in a tenement, have you? This is Mrs Kelly's day for the washlines.'

'She might not be using all the line.'

'Even so, this is her day, not mine,' Isla said, and went on with her work.

Ainslie watched for a moment, then asked, 'D'you feel any differently towards my father now that you know more about him?'

Isla took time to consider. It had been hard to face the fact that her Kenneth had been so different, so uncaring, in his other life. But she still had her own memories of him to offset these pictures.

'He was a human being,' she said at last, 'and no human being's perfect.' She glanced up at the cracked, stained ceiling then at the warped window frame and the dripping sink, and the corners of her mouth turned down. 'I'm a fine one to talk – this place is mine now, and I haven't done any more to improve it than he did.'

'That's another responsibility he put on your shoulders – looking after this place. We're all what he made us, when you think of it,' Ainslie said thoughtfully. 'You and me, and Mother too. All McAdam's women. And there's your Barbara as well.'

'I doubt if anyone could influence Barbara,' Isla told her dryly. 'She's got a mind of her own.'

'Are you going to tell the children the truth about Father?'

'Mebbe one day, when they're grown up, if I think they can take it and understand. But not for a long time.'

As though on cue, the children arrived at that moment, hot and grimy from play, in search of food, but hanging back a little at the sight of Ainslie.

'I haven't had time to make anything yet,' Isla told them, fetching a loaf and a half-full jar of jam.

'I'm thirsty,' Barbara whined, and Ross, his eyes fixed on Ainslie, joined in.

'Make up your minds.' Isla paused, about to cut

slices from the loaf. 'I can't do both things at once.'

Ainslie got to her feet and took the breadknife from her. 'You get them something to drink,' she said. 'I'll see to the bread and jam. After that, I wouldn't mind a cup of tea. I think we've both earned one.'

In September, the *Little Women* house was finished and borne off by Mr Leckie, who brought with him another house for Isla to work on, and a box of furniture. He gave her a fair price for the finished house, and Flora insisted on Isla taking all the money.

'All I contributed was bits and pieces that were already here,' she said when Isla protested. 'The Victorian house was a gift, and I can't even remember where the other one came from. You did all the work.'

Isla, who badly needed the money, finally gave in, and they started to sift through the box of furniture from the toyshop.

'It's awful plain,' Isla said when they had finished.

'Make your own furniture, then, the way you did for the others. Mr Leckie said you could alter it if you wanted.'

'The other houses were just for show, but this one's supposed to be played with, so it needs good solid furniture. But I'd like something better than this. Something – different.' She frowned down at the sturdy little table she was holding.

'Mebbe we could find someone who's good with his hands,' Flora suggested. And suddenly Isla remembered Drew Brown, sitting on the steps in the back court, using the point of his penknife to shape a proper face for Barbara's peg doll.

She took the table back to George Street with her, and went up to his flat that evening, while the children were playing with Greta and Daisy in Magret's flat. It was raining, and too wet for them to be outside.

Isla had never gone to the upper floor before. The stone steps were hollowed in the centre, and she had to feel her way up, her outstretched hands pressed against the chill, damp walls. Drew himself opened the door, peering into the gloom. 'Mam, it's Mrs Moffatt,' he called, and his mother appeared at once, looking anxious.

'Come in,' she said, then, as Drew moved back to let Isla in, 'is there something wrong?'

'No, it's Drew I really came to see.' Isla stepped into the little flat, and instantly recognised the smell of damp. A metal bucket stood on newspapers, yellowed with age, against the outside wall near the sink, water dripping into it with a continuous, steady tinny little beat.

'You've got a bad leak there.'

'Only when it rains,' Drew said with a bleak grin, while his mother explained, 'The roof's rotten.'

'Have you not complained about it?'

Mrs Brown shrugged. 'Early on I did, but it wasnae any use. Now I just don't bother.'

'When did it start?'

'Och, three or four years ago,' the woman told her vaguely. 'We're used tae it. Ye'll have a cup of tea, Mrs Moffatt?'

'I can't stay, the children'll be looking for me soon.' Isla remembered why she had called, and held out the little table she had brought. 'Drew, could you do something with this for me? Mebbe carve the legs into a

247

better shape, full at the top here, then tapering down, with the feet curved.'

'You mean like a bandy-legged woman with nice neat ankles? I've seen that sort somewhere. Table, not woman,' he added hurriedly as his mother, shocked, said, 'Drew!'

'Could you do it?'

He studied the little table, running his thumb down over the legs. 'I think so.'

'I'll pay you for it.'

'Wait till we see if I can do it first,' the boy said, but his face was alight with interest as he studied the tiny table, and she could see that he was longing to start work.

'I think you should have another word with the factor,' she said as she left.

'I don't want to be a nuisance . . .' Mrs Brown began.

'I keep tellin' her that the man that owns this place'll be living in a grand house that doesn't leak when the rain comes,' Drew said.

The contempt in his words rang in Isla's ears as she felt her way back down the dark stairs. When the roof first started leaking, Kenneth had had the money to repair it, she thought. But there was no sense in dwelling on the faults of a man who was dead and no longer able to defend himself. She was the landlord now, and it was up to her to do what she could.

21

After careful calculation Isla divided the money Mr Leckie had given her into three lots. One was for Drew, if he managed to alter the table for her, another for herself and the children. She took the third sum with her when she went on the following Monday to collect the rent money. When she asked if she could see Mr Forbes, the receptionist shook her head.

'He's not in the office just now. Mr Colin's here, though.'

'I'd better see him, then,' Isla said without enthusiasm.

Colin Forbes stared at the coins she put on his desk. 'What's this?'

'Mrs Brown's ceiling's been leaking since I first moved here. The roof badly needs repairing.'

He frowned. 'Mrs Brown's not complained to us.'

'If she had, what would you have done?'

'I suppose we'd have had to pass the matter on to you.'

'The poor soul's scared that if she makes too much fuss she'll mebbe be put out. It's easier for her to keep emptying a bucket, and do without the use of that part of her living-room. Her son sleeps in the other room, and I've a suspicion that the rain gets in there too.'

He pushed the coins around with a forefinger. 'There's not nearly enough here to get the work done.'

'I know, but you can keep that safe for me until I can afford to give you the rest.'

'Mrs Moffatt,' he said, the familiar exasperation in his voice, 'your money would be better spent on your children.'

'I can assure you that my children are well cared for, Mr Forbes.' Isla indicated Ross, who had climbed on to a chair and was looking out of the window. 'Does he look under-nourished and neglected?'

'No,' he admitted, then, leaning forward and eyeing her, 'but you don't look as well as you might be.'

'There's nothing wrong with me!'

'A few days by the sea might do you good. You could use the money for that.'

'I'm too busy earning the rest of the money for the roof repairs.'

He looked as though he was going to go on arguing, then shrugged. 'Very well, if that's what you want, I'll see that it's put away safely, and recorded.' As she rose to go, he added, 'By the way, a friend of my father's with an office in Incle Street has an opening for a clerk. I've passed Mr Kelly's name to him.'

To Isla's delight, Drew managed to carve the plain little table into something graceful and delicate, even varnishing it before handing it over. More and more dissatisfied with the solid, unimaginative furniture Mr Leckie had given her, she asked the boy if he could make a chaise longue for one of the rooms. Together, they pored over a book he had brought from the library, then, using scraps of wood from the workshop where he was employed, Drew managed to provide just what she wanted.

Isla padded and covered the little piece of furniture, working at nights after the children were asleep. She had to work standing at the mantel on most nights, for the gas light above the mantelshelf was poor, and the work she was doing was very fine. By the time she fell into bed her legs and ankles were sore and stiff. But the chaise longue was perfect, and Flora's admiration the next day made all the work worthwhile.

Spurred on by the need to get the roof repaired before the winter came, Isla gave Drew more furniture to work on, and spent as much time as she could on the new doll's house. Her eyes felt sore and tired, and she began to suffer from headaches caused by the amount of time she spent on the detailed work of stitching tiny cushions and curtains.

'Ye'll make yersel' ill,' Annie said bluntly, leaning against the frame of the dolls'-house room door, arms folded, and Flora nodded.

'She's right, my dear, you look pale. You need to take a day off now and again. Why not take the children up to Brodie Park for some fresh air?'

'They're outside most of the time, and I get plenty of fresh air walking round here and home again,' Isla told them. Now that the little house represented much-needed money, she lay awake at nights, planning the next day's work, and hurried round to Castlehead as soon as she could in the mornings.

Magret nagged at her about not eating properly.

'It's too hot to eat,' Isla told her shortly. The early autumn was unusually warm and dry, and although the continual smell from the drains didn't seem to affect the children as badly as it affected Isla herself, she fretted in case they caught some disease from the poor sewerage. It seemed to her, sometimes, that she worried about everything. She finished the little house for Mr Leckie, and the toyshop owner, delighted with it, had promised to put more work her way. Even so, Isla fretted. Earning some money of her own, even a little, had made all the difference, and there was no jewellery left to pawn. If Mr Leckie didn't give her more work, she didn't know what she would do.

It was because her mind was full of such concerns that she didn't see the tram bearing down on her as she crossed the High Street on her way to collect the rent money one Monday morning. Alerted by a sudden jangling of bells, and shouting from the driver, frantically leaning on his brake, she finally looked up, too late.

Colin Forbes had just arrived in his office and was opening the window to let some air into the stuffy room when he glanced down in time to see the cowcatcher in front of the tram hit a young woman. Her body was tossed through the air like a discarded rag doll, and as it landed in the gutter her head glanced off the kerb.

'My God!' He ran from the office, almost knocking the receptionist over as she came through the door, a pile of envelopes in her hand.

'Telephone for the ambulance wagon,' he shouted into her startled face, and ran on, through the door and down the stairs and across the road to where a policeman was pushing his way through the gathering crowd. The officer knelt down beside the woman in the road, slipping an arm under her shoulders.

Her head lolled against his sleeve and Colin, breaking through the people who had gathered, recognised Isla Moffatt, her eyes closed and her face as white as paper, apart from a ribbon of shining crimson blood that crawled, slowly but steadily, down her face from the wound in her forehead.

'Slight concussion,' the ward sister said briskly. 'Nothing to worry about, but the doctor wants you to stay with us for a few days.' Her professional smile faded when Isla, dazed and confused, struggled to get up. 'Now don't be silly, dear.'

'My children – I have to see to my children!'

'They're fine.' The sister tucked Isla back into bed, pulling the blankets tightly over her. 'A Miss McAdam came to visit you earlier, while you were sleeping. She says you're not to worry, the children are being well looked after.'

'Better do as she says, hen, they're a bossy lot in here,' a voice said from the next bed as the sister moved away on silent feet. Isla began to turn her head, but stopped as pain washed through it. Putting a hand up to the source of the pain, she felt a padded bandage across her forehead, then sleep came, and she drifted away from the big, high-ceilinged room into nowhere.

Pictures came to her as she floated in and out of sleep – uniformed nurses crossing and re-crossing her line of vision like ships in sail, a balding man in a neat suit with a gold chain strung across his waistcoat bending over her, a woman with an elaborate feathered hat perched on her head marching past, carrying a bunch of flowers – they had come and gone before she could register them. It reminded her of her childhood, and rides on the merry-go-round's painted horses when the shows came. Up and down and round and round, clutching tightly to the pole that grew out of the back of the horse she rode, daringly freeing one hand to wave to her parents as they came into sight then fell away again.

'I must take the children to the shows,' she said aloud, and was startled when a familiar voice replied, 'That's a good idea.'

Isla's lids lifted and she looked up into Flora Currie's green eyes. 'What are you doing here?' she asked, confused and still thinking of the merry-go-round.

'I'm visiting you. You had a nasty accident crossing the road, but you're fine now, and so are the children. They're staying at my house – you'll see them in a day or so, when you're better. Annie sent some home-made scones, they're on your locker. And Ainslie will be in to visit you tomorrow.'

When she had gone, Isla slept again, wakening once or twice during the night to the sound of snoring and an occasional groan or mumbled sentence from the beds around her. A voice called a man's name plaintively further up the long ward and a nurse went past, a silent ghost in the dimly lit ward. The voice stopped, and Isla slept again, until she was wakened to face the day.

Her head still ached, but the confusion had left her, and when the doctor made his rounds she begged to be allowed home.

'You had a nasty crack on the head, and we want to

be quite sure that you're over it. Besides,' a frown crossed his face, 'you're in sore need of rest and nourishment. You've not been feeding yourself properly, have you?'

She started to protest, but he cut in with, 'It won't hurt you to be cosseted for a day or two,' and turned back to the group deferentially waiting for him at the foot of the bed. As they moved off, Isla heard him murmur something about women who allowed themselves to become rundown.

The woman in the next bed heard it too. 'It's all right for the likes of them to criticise,' she said with a sniff, then lowered her voice slightly, as the ward sister turned and looked sharply at her before hurrying after the doctor. 'They don't know what it's like, do they? What sort of mother would feed herself and leave her kids hungry?' Then, settling herself comfortably, 'But what can't be cured must be endured, eh? Make the most of it, hen – that's my advice.'

The long narrow ward, with its double row of beds and its uniformed nurses, brought back memories of Isla's training in Edinburgh. All she had wanted then was to become a nurse, perhaps rising to the post of ward sister or even matron, one day. But Kenneth McAdam had been brought into her ward from the operating theatre when she was halfway through the course, after being struck down with appendicitis during a business trip to Edinburgh. And from that moment, her life had changed.

Ainslie came in that afternoon, turning patients' and visitors' heads as she walked up the long ward. She was dressed in a blue knee-length skirt with knife pleats at the front, and a long V-necked blouse in the same colour, with a geometric pattern in gold, and a gold leather belt around her waist. Her vivid hair was tied back at the nape of her neck with a blue ribbon, and a beret dipped rakishly over one ear. She had developed new confidence, Isla thought, watching her approach the bed. Ainslie was coming to terms with herself.

She put a small basket of fruit on top of the locker. 'I'd have brought flowers, but you're not going to be here long enough to enjoy them.' Her eyes swept over Isla and she said bluntly, 'I hadn't realised that you'd got so thin.'

Isla hurriedly tucked her arms beneath the sheet. 'I'm not thin!'

'The ward sister told Miss Currie that you were under-nourished.'

'It's just this hot weather. Nobody feels like eating when it's hot. How are the children?' Isla asked anxiously. 'Have you seen them?'

'I saw them last night, and this morning too. Your neighbour told me what had happened when I called on you, and where the children were, so I went round to Castlehead. They're very well. Missing you, of course, but they know you'll be back soon. Isla, we've been talking – me and Miss Currie and Annie – and we all think that you should have a wee holiday when you come out of hospital.'

'How could I afford that?'

'Colin told me about you giving him money to have the roof repaired. You'd be better spending it on yourself.'

'But the work needs to be done. And it needs to be done before the winter comes.'

Ainslie fidgeted, then said, almost guiltily, 'Miss Currie's written to your aunt to tell her what's happened.'

'She hasn't!'

'She found the address in your house when she was getting the children's things. It's all right,' she added hurriedly, 'she just said you'd been widowed, and that you're living in Paisley now. And you'd had a wee accident, but you're fine.'

Isla stared at her in dismay. She didn't want Aunt Lally to know the truth about Kenneth, or about the struggle she had had since his death.

Ainslie and Colin Forbes took her home on the following day. Barbara, waiting on the pavement, jigging from one foot to the other in a frenzy of impatience, threw herself at Isla as soon as she got out of the car, but Ross hung back for a moment, finger in mouth, unsure of this white-faced mother with a sticking plaster on her forehead.

'We've been staying in Miss Currie's house,' Barbara said in a rush of words. 'We had a bedroom all to ourselves and a big bed, where's your bandage, Miss Currie said you'd have a bandage . . .'

'I don't need it any more. Ross?' Isla held her hand out to the little boy, just as Magret arrived at the close-mouth, her round face wreathed in smiles. Ross ducked his head and whirled round to bury himself in Magret's apron. Daisy, not to be outdone, followed suit.

'Ross!'

'Ach, they forget quick at his age,' Magret soothed. 'Come on in, hen, and sit down. I've got the kettle on. There's enough for everyb'dy,' she added, looking beyond Isla to where Ainslie and Colin stood.

'On you go, Isla. Barbara, carry your mother's case.' Ainslie handed the small cardboard case to the little girl. 'I'll come and see you this evening, when you've had time to settle in,' she said, and turned back to the car as Isla went into the close, Barbara clutching her hand and chattering like a little monkey. As she went, she was aware of the women at every window and every close-mouth up and down the street.

Ross released Magret's apron and shot across the room to climb on to his mother's lap as soon as they got into Magret's flat, while Magret herself, reaching for the condensed milk tin, confessed, 'It's just as well they couldnae stay, for there's no' enough cups. I didnae like tae say, though. Mind yer mammy's poor sore head, Ross,' she cautioned, but Isla hugged the little boy tightly.

'My head's all better. I'm all better,' she said, smiling at her children's anxious faces.

Even so, she was glad to go to bed early that night, and she felt so listless the next day that the thought of walking round to Castlehead was too much. Instead, Flora called on her, her face wrinkled with concern.

'I'll be fine tomorrow,' Isla assured her, but she wasn't. It was as though she had come up against a brick wall that refused to allow her to get on with her life. She recalled that the ward sister had warned her about this just before she left the Infirmary.

'It'll take some time before you get back to your old self, Mrs Moffatt. The accident wasn't serious, but you've worn yourself out, and you need a longer rest than you've had here.'

'I've not been doing nearly as much as most women,' Isla had argued. It was true – some of her neighbours had large families to cope with, some had sick parents or in-laws staying with them, others went out to work or took in laundry or sewing in addition to caring for their husbands and children.

'Mebbe not, but there are other ways of exhausting yourself, and continual worry's one of them. You'll have to be kind to yourself for a while,' the woman had advised.

Isla felt that the kindest thing she could do for herself was to get on with her life, but the harder she tried to spur herself on, the more difficult it became.

When a letter arrived from Edinburgh, informing her that Aunt Lally would like to see her again, and to meet the children if she cared to bring them to Edinburgh for a short visit, both Ainslie and Flora Currie urged her to accept.

'But what about Barbara's schooling?'

'She could stay with me,' Flora suggested, but Isla had got such a fright over almost losing Ross that she refused to go to Edinburgh without Barbara.

She thought that that was the end of the matter, but Ainslie went with her to the school, where the head-mistress agreed, under the circumstances, to let Barbara take two weeks off.

'She's a quick learner. If you take her school books with you, Mrs Moffatt, and undertake to see that she does some work while she's away, that would be acceptable.'

Colin Forbes called to hand back the money Isla had given him for the roof repairs, and suggest that Forbes and Son should advance the money needed to cover the most essential repairs, recovering it from the proceeds when a buyer came forward for the building.

'But it's been over a year now, and nobody's put in an offer,' Isla pointed out, adding suspiciously, 'has Ainslie put you up to this? Or Miss Currie?'

He had been pleasant to her on the day he drove her home from the hospital, but now the usual edge came into his voice and the usual irritated gleam darkened his hazel eyes. 'It's often done in business, Mrs Moffatt. You'll get more for the place if it's seen that some work's being carried out on it, and it's in our interest to try to sell at a good price because of our commission. Since you're determined to get the roof repairs done soon, my father and I feel that we should do what we can to help. But only insofar as the essential work is concerned,' he added hastily. 'It would cost more than the whole building's worth to have all the roof repairs carried out.'

'As long as Mrs Brown and her son can escape the worst of the rain when it comes,' Isla said, and couldn't help adding, 'at least you'll get a bit of peace while I'm in Edinburgh.'

He flushed. 'I don't know what you mean, Mrs Moffatt.'

That night Isla wrote to Aunt Lally to let her know that she and the children would arrive the following week.

'You're no sooner back home than you're gone again,' Magret lamented.

'That's what I think too, but so many folk are nagging at me to go to Edinburgh that I might as well give in. Anyway, Aunt Lally seems to be eager to see the children. Mebbe she's mellowed in her old age.'

Magret offered to lend a battered old suitcase for the journey. 'It's only used to keep the bairns' winter jerseys in below the bed,' she explained, 'and they'll not come to any harm wrapped up in paper for a wee while.'

22

Barbara and Ross gaped in amazement as their great-aunt Lally Moffatt came sailing towards them in Edinburgh's Waverley Station. She had scarcely changed in the six years since Isla had last seen her. She was still tall and commanding, straight of back and large of bosom, and she still favoured startlingly bright colours and floating, wispy scarves.

On this occasion, she was dressed in a scarlet calf-length dress topped by a pale-grey overtunic splashed with embroidered roses. Crimson feathers drifted from her grey hat, and a red feather boa rustled round her throat and floated in her wake.

'Isla, my dear!' Isla was enveloped in a perfumed embrace, her face briefly smothered against the boa, then released, to be held back at arms' length and studied through narrowed blue eyes. 'Your friend was right when she wrote to say that you needed a holiday. You look like something the cat dragged in,' Lally announced in ringing tones that had once reached to the back of theatre galleries with ease. Heads turned all up and down the platform.

'And these are your little ones! Darlings, come to your auntie!' Lally stooped with an ominous creaking of stays and swept a child into each arm. When she released them, Ross sneezed.

'It's the feathers,' Barbara explained, bright-eyed. 'They got up his nose. Mine too.'

'How sweet!' her great-aunt trumpeted, and spun round, her eyes searching the platform. 'Porter!'

More heads turned. 'We only have two small cases,' Isla protested, embarrassed by the attention they were attracting. 'I can carry them.'

'Nonsense, a lady should never carry her own luggage – remember that, little girl,' Lally added to Barbara, who nodded eagerly, standing on one leg and bending the other back to catch her foot in one hand.

'I can hop. I can hop all down the platform.'

A porter was already scuttling eagerly up to them. 'Kangaroos hop, young ladies walk, head up and shoulders back,' said Lally. 'Come along!' And she set off down the platform, Barbara forging along by her side, and the porter trotting behind her.

Following, Ross's hand clutched in hers, Isla began to wonder if she had the strength to spend two weeks in Aunt Lally's company.

Lally Moffatt had lived in the same first-floor flat in a handsome tenement building ever since Isla could remember. Climbing the stairs, she recalled her aunt's claim that the flat had been bought for her by a wealthy admirer during her days in the music hall chorus, and wondered again if it was true.

The flat hadn't changed much, and the children's

mouths rounded, as well as their eyes, when they went inside. The living-room walls were covered with framed paintings, photographs, decorative plates, bows, bunches of dried flowers, fans, and programmes. Every piece of furniture held more photographs, albums, books, vases filled with more dried flowers, gloves, more decorative plates, and fancy little boxes. Even the mirror over the cluttered fireplace had its share of cards and programmes pushed into the frame. Footwear – shoes and slippers in patent leather, kid, suede, satin, velvet, buckskin, lizardskin, and snakeskin – stood in rows along the skirting board.

'Nothing's changed,' Isla said in wonder.

'I believe I've collected a few more mementoes.' Lally unpinned her hat and tossed it carelessly on to a chair already overflowing with hats, gloves, and long scarves. Her hair, which Isla remembered as daffodil yellow, was now pure white, still cut short, level with her ears. Her mouth was a bright pink cupid's bow, and her eyebrows had been plucked out and replaced by delicate arches, pencilled in. 'Now then' – she clapped her hands briskly together – 'let's have some tea!'

'Yes!' said Ross, and trotted after her as she marched off to the small kitchen. Barbara stayed where she was, still turning round slowly to take everything in.

'Look, Mummy, a piano!' She pointed to a corner of the high-ceilinged room where a small piano was almost hidden by the shawl that had been tossed over it. Barbara drew in a deep breath and let it out in a sigh, her eyes bright.

'I'm going to like staying here!' she said.

*

'I don't remember you making a fuss over me when I was small,' Isla said that night when the children had been put to bed and she and her aunt were sipping sherry on either side of the fireplace. Lally's raised eyebrows disappeared under her fringe.

'Don't tell me you're jealous of your own children!'

'Of course not, just making an observation.'

'For one thing I'm much older, and old age tends to yearn towards youth. For another, your two are really quite beautiful, whereas I remember you as a quiet, dark, sallow little girl. Such a pity you didn't take after me and your father, instead of your mother.'

'Mother was lovely.'

'She was, wasn't she, bless her,' Lally remembered, her face softening. 'But she was of Italian parentage, my dear. She still had the Mediterranean sun on her cheeks, like the bloom on black grapes. You never had that at all. You still don't.'

'We don't get a lot of sun in Paisley,' Isla said dryly.

'Your hair doesn't help – all that dark stuff round that wee pale face. You should get it bobbed.' Then, seeing Isla's involuntary glance at her own uncompromising short cut, Lally said, 'Don't worry, it'll not look like a chopped field the way mine does. You've got nice soft hair, it would lie in well round your face.'

'Mebbe so, but I've got more to do with my money than spend it on myself.'

'There's a friend of mine . . .' Lally had always had friends who could turn their hands to everything, Isla remembered. 'A dresser she was, but she could cut hair very well. She once trimmed Marie Lloyd's hair in an emergency, and there was never a complaint. She'd do it for nothing.'

'I'll think about it.'

'Your little ones, now – what wonderful hair! Their father was a very handsome man, as I remember from our two brief meetings. What happened?' Lally asked so abruptly that Isla was disconcerted for a moment.

'He – he died. If you remember, he was older than I was.'

'Why take up your own name again?'

'I just wanted to,' Isla said shortly.

Lally gave her a long shrewd look from beneath darkened eyelashes, then shrugged, and sipped at her sherry. 'You always were secretive – now that, you got from your mother. D'you have plans to marry again?'

'Who would want a penniless widow with two children to support?'

'You'd be surprised.' The blue eyes studied her face. 'Whatever's happened to you, you've had to walk a hard road. But you're still young enough to attract men.'

'I've no wish to attract men.'

'Nonsense, there isn't a woman alive who doesn't want to look her best,' Lally said briskly. 'You need fattening up – and some stimulating company.'

'What I need is some peace and quiet.'

'Away you go, lassie,' said Lally Moffatt. 'At your age?'

Later, in the small, crowded spare bedroom, Isla tucked the blankets round Ross, who slept on a small truckle bed, then turned out the gas mantle and climbed into bed beside Barbara, who murmured sleepily and turned over. Gradually her eyes became accustomed to the dark, and the silhouette of a macabre headless body, the tailor's dummy Lally had used in the old days to make her stage costumes on, outlined against the window.

Outside, she could dimly hear the hum of traffic passing along the main road two blocks further down, and the occasional motor car chugging its way along below the windows. With surprise, she realised that she felt homesick for the single room in George Street.

The bracing winds of Scotland's east coast seemed to blow Isla's cobwebs away. During the day she and Lally took the children to visit Edinburgh Castle and the Palace of Holyrood House, strolling down the narrow cobbled Royal Mile and along Princes Street to look in the shop windows, exploring Princes Street gardens and the warren of streets and closes in the Old Town.

Almost every night some of Lally's friends dropped in, for she loved company, and had always been famed for holding open house. Dressed in crêpe de Chine frocks with bold patterns and loose sleeves and floating sashes and scarves, a cigarette in a holder and a headdress thick with paste jewellery clamped on to her short white hair, Lally held court.

Most of her friends had been on the stage, or connected with the theatre, and almost every sentence began with 'D'you remember?' They laughed a lot and talked over each other, and spoiled the children outrageously.

Sometimes during the day Barbara and Ross went off with Lally and some of her friends, leaving Isla to enjoy some time to herself, and sometimes their great-aunt kept them amused in the house, teaching them songs and letting them dress up in the trunkfuls of stage clothes she had kept, so that Isla could wander round the streets and through the shops without worrying about them.

She never knew what would meet her when she came back from those trips. It could be a dramatic play, with the children tottering about in Lally's shoes, with dresses and jackets far too big for them falling off their shoulders and threatening to trip them up at every step. It could be a music hall turn, with Lally thumping out a song on the piano and the children strutting around the room with canes, Ross with his head tipped back so that he could see from under a top hat stuffed with newspaper, Barbara with her top hat wedged on by her hair, which had been bundled up for the occasion.

Once or twice Lally took the children to an afternoon matinee. Ross tended to fall asleep, but Barbara came back with eyes like saucers, able to recite most of the show, with some prompting from her great-aunt.

'She's got a marvellous memory, darling,' Lally enthused, 'And such style! She must have inherited it from me.'

Watching her daughter, a sailor hat tipped saucily over one eye, strutting across the living-room and bellowing out 'All the Nice Girls Love a Sailor', Isla had to agree with her. Barbara certainly hadn't inherited her outgoing personality from either of her parents.

Egged on by the children, Isla finally gave in to her aunt's insistence, and had her hair bobbed. She sat with her eyes closed, listening to the crunch of the scissors and the soft regretful sighing sound her hair made as it fell in clumps to the floor, where Barbara gathered it up. She thought, as Lally's friend worked, of how Kenneth had loved to loosen her hair at night and brush it for her, stopping now and again to bury his face in its softness, or lift it aside so that he could kiss the nape of her neck. A shiver ran through her at the memory, and the woman said at once, 'Did I hurt you?'

'No.' No sense in living in the past, Isla told herself. Lally was right, her hair would be easier to care for now, and that was all that mattered.

Even so, she was reluctant to open her eyes when the cutting was finished, despite the two women's assurances that she looked lovely. Barbara finally climbed on to her knee and said, her nose bumping Isla's, her breath tickling Isla's top lip, 'Look, Mummy, you're beautiful!'

Isla opened her eyes and found herself staring into her daughter's face. 'You're not made of glass, Barbara. I can't see through you.'

The little girl giggled, and squirmed round until she was sitting on Isla's lap. Looking into the mirror, Isla saw a neat, wide-eyed face, framed with dark wings that curved softly round on to her cheeks, staring back at her in astonishment.

'I look like a different person!'

Lally's friend, standing behind her, nodded her satisfaction, while Lally herself said, 'It's about time!'

In their second week in Edinburgh, Lally, who loved parties, held one to mark their visit, inviting all her theatrical friends. Barbara provided the entertainment all on her own, glowing at the applause that greeted each song.

Halfway through the evening, watching her children, particularly her daughter, being fussed over by all the adults, Isla knew that it was time to go back to Paisley, back to their usual life. Lally pouted when she announced the next day that it was time to start making plans for their return.

'But you've only just got here!'

'We've been here for almost two weeks, Aunt Lally, and that was the arrangement. Besides, Barbara has to get back to school.'

'Talking of Barbara,' Lally said slowly, flashing a quick look at her niece from beneath her lashes, 'she's a very talented little girl, Isla. Bertie was just saying the other day that she'd be a natural on the stage.'

'That depends on what she wants to do when she grows up.'

'But she ought to start as soon as possible. I was at elocution and dancing by the time I was her age.'

'Aunt Lally, I can't afford to pay for these things for Barbara, and even if I could, it would only set her apart from her friends. She's managed to make a place for herself in Paisley, and it wouldn't be fair to her to change things now.'

'Paisley! What chance will she have there? There are some excellent classes here in Edinburgh, and you can't deny that we have good schools – look at your own education.'

Isla put a hand up to the nape of her neck, and was astonished, as always, to touch skin instead of a heavy mass of hair. 'I've no intention of uprooting myself and the children again.'

'I'm not talking about the entire family being uprooted. Why don't you leave Barbara here with me, just for a year, until we see how things work out? I'll bear the cost of her education and her dance classes and singing classes. And for elocution too, she'll need that,' Lally went on as Isla stared at her. 'I still have some influence, you know. It could all be done on very little, and she deserves—'

'No!' The cold terror Isla had known when Catherine McAdam tried to take Ross away from her returned. The older woman looked at her in astonishment.

'My dear child, I'm not suggesting kidnap! I've no intention of coming between you and your daughter, I'm only asking you to give her one little year, to see how she does. I can guarantee that with the proper training now, she'll be a star in ten years – we'll be so proud of her—'

'No!' Isla, aware of the children in the next room, trying on Lally's clothes, fought to keep her voice calm. 'We've been through enough as it is, and all I want for Barbara is an ordinary upbringing.'

'But—'

'She's only a little girl, Aunt Lally. She has years ahead of her to make up her own mind. But not now, not yet – and don't try to persuade her,' she added swiftly as she saw her aunt's eyes narrowing. 'I'll not have it, no matter how much she pleads.'

'Do you realise what you're denying that child? She may well grow up to resent you for it.'

'That's a chance I have to take. I want her to grow up like any other child, and I know that that's what her father would have wanted, too.'

They eyed each other, then, 'Oh, very well,' Lally said at last, huffily. 'But I warn you, Isla, you're being most unfair!'

Barbara sulked when she was told that they were going home. 'But I like it here! Why can't we stay with Aunt Lally?'

'Because holidays don't go on forever,' Isla told her sharply, aware of her aunt's hurt looks.

The old fear of losing one of her children had been re-awakened, and she didn't feel entirely safe until the train was pulling out of Waverley Station, leaving Lally alone on the platform. Sinking back into her seat, Isla struggled to justify her decision to take Barbara back to Paisley. Lally was getting older, she couldn't possibly be expected to care for an active little girl, she told herself. Besides, she had had difficulty in getting Barbara to do her lessons every day. Barbara had objected, and Lally had supported her. If she left the child in Edinburgh for a whole year, she told herself as the train moved westwards, the child would be quite illiterate.

But she knew that the truth was that the children were all she had in the world, all that was left of her life with Kenneth. And that, quite apart from the deep love she had for both of them, was very important to her.

'Ye'll never guess,' Magret said almost as soon as Isla got home. 'They've repaired the roof above the Browns' flat! Ye could have knocked the lot of us down with a feather when the men arrived and began to put up ladders.' She handed Isla a cup of her strong, sweet tinned-milk tea. 'I don't mind anyone doing any repairs on this place in all the time we've been here. Mrs Brown's fair thrilled about it.'

That evening, Drew came down to show Isla a small wardrobe that he had made. The interior was hollow, and the double doors opened. 'I minded you sayin' that you didnae like that solid wardrobe you had for the wee house, so I thought I'd see what I could do,' he explained, glowing with pride in his success and her pleasure. 'The hinges came from a box my mam had. And I've found another book in the library, and bought myself an exercise book so's I can copy the pictures down.'

'Look, it's even got a rail! Now I can make some clothes, and some cardboard hangers to put them on. You're clever, Drew!'

When she took some coins from her purse and insisted on paying for the wardrobe, Drew protested.

'Och no, you didnae ask me tae make this for you. You can just keep it.'

'I'm buying it,' she told him firmly. 'You deserve payment, and anyway, it means that I can feel free to ask you to do more, if I get another order for a house.'

'I enjoyed it,' he said as he gave in and took the money, then, 'did you hear that there's been some work done on the roof?'

'Mrs McDougall told me.'

'My mam's fair pleased,' Drew said happily. 'She cannae wait for the rain tae come, so that she can enjoy being dry.'

23

Annie beamed – a rare event – when she saw Isla on the doorstep. 'It's grand tae see ye back. She'll be fair pleased.' She nodded at the parlour door. 'She's in by.'

'Isla!' Flora Currie came forward with hands out-stretched. 'My, your holiday's done you good – I've never seen you look so well. Your hair's very smart!'

Isla put a hand to her short hair. 'It was my aunt's idea, not mine. It still feels . . .' Her voice trailed away as a man got up from the chair by the window, his long body seeming to unfold in sections.

'Come and meet Philip Hannigan,' Flora said briskly. He towered over both women as she made the intro-ductions, his teeth flashing white in a tanned face.

'My friends call me Phil. I'm very pleased to meet you.' He spoke in a soft, attractive drawl and her hand seemed to disappear into his.

'Phil comes from Canada,' Flora said proudly, as though she had made him all by herself. 'His great-aunt was my dear friend Agnes from next door. He's inher-ited her house.'

'You're going to settle here?'

'No, ma'am, I've got a timber business back home in

274

Ontario, and that's where I belong.' Philip Hannigan smiled down on his hostess. 'Miss Flora's been my guardian angel ever since I got here.'

'Och, away with you, man!' Flora flushed like a young girl. 'I just did what Agnes would have done for my kin if things had been the other way round. He's insisted on staying in that house on his own,' she explained to Isla. 'So of course I said he must have his meals with us. Ainslie McAdam's been a great help with sorting out the house – she's arranged for her employer to have a look at the furniture to see what should go for auction.'

'I'd like some of the furniture to be sold along with the house,' Phil put in. 'They sort of belong together, but Ainslie – Miss McAdam – thinks there's too much of it, and some of it should be disposed of separately.'

'Where are the children, Isla? I was looking forward to seeing them again.'

'Barbara's back at school, and Ross wanted to stay and play with Daisy. Barbara's learned a lot of new songs from Aunt Lally,' Isla said, half-ruefully. 'She's planning another back-court concert.'

'I told you that Isla's little girl was musically gifted, didn't I?' Flora asked Philip Hannigan.

The Canadian dipped his head in agreement. 'I'm looking forward to meeting both of them.'

'Isla, Mr Leckie's got a special order in for a dolls' house, from a customer who wants you to furnish it.'

'That's wonderful!'

'I said I was sure you'd want to do it, so he brought it the other day. His customer wants it for Christmas, and you can decide on the style.'

'I've heard all about your talent, Mrs Moffatt,' Phil Hannigan put in. 'It sounds to me as though you've got yourself quite a business there.'

'It's just a hobby.'

He shook his head. 'Don't you believe it. Finding out what folk want, then supplying it – that's how businesses begin.'

It would have been very easy to sit back and drown in that soft drawl, but Isla was longing to see the new house. When she excused herself Philip unwound himself from his chair, reaching the door before she did and holding it open for her.

'I look forward to meeting you again, Mrs Moffatt.'

'Isla.'

'Isla,' he agreed. 'It's a very pretty name.'

As she crossed the hall Isla glanced in the mirror and saw that she, too, was blushing. The man had that sort of effect on women, she decided, as she opened the door of the doll's-house room.

On the following Saturday, when Isla and the children arrived at Castlehead, Philip Hannigan and Ainslie were both in Flora's drawing-room, Ainslie equipped with a notebook and pencil.

'We're going to start making a list of the furniture that's going to auction. Come and have a look around,' the Canadian suggested. Isla hesitated. She had planned to spend her time at Castlehead making a mirror by glueing some tiny jet beads from an old necklace round silver paper stuck on to cardboard.

'I'm not going, because the house holds too many memories for me. But you should, Isla, you'd enjoy seeing round it,' Flora urged and she gave in.

Outside, Phil lifted the children over the hedge then swung his long legs over without any difficulty. Isla and Ainslie declined his offer of help, and took the longer route through Miss Currie's gate and along the pavement.

'He's a good-looking man, isn't he?' Ainslie murmured.

'Probably married.'

'Actually, no. Your holiday's done you good.'

'I ate far too much in Edinburgh.'

'You suit a little more weight.' Ainslie herself looked more relaxed. She wore a summer dress in pale blue, the same colour as her eyes, with an open jacket in navy to match the braiding at the dress's neck and hem.

'How is your mother?' Isla asked, formally, and a shadow passed over Ainslie's face.

'Her health has improved, but her mind . . .' She stopped, her hand on the gate leading to the neighbouring garden, then said, 'She seems to live in a world of her own making. She talks of nobody but Innes and my grandfather. She doesn't seem to be aware of my existence.'

'I'm sorry.'

For a moment Isla saw hurt in the other girl's gaze, then it was gone, hidden behind a mask of indifference as Ainslie opened the gate, then closed it behind them.

'It's that nurse I'm sorry for. Mother's become very arrogant, and she orders poor Miss Dove about all the time. Fortunately Miss Dove doesn't seem to mind, she treats Mother with just the right mixture of deference and firmness.'

'Come on, you two,' Phil called from the porch. As she went up the steps Ainslie tripped and Phil put out a hand to steady her.

'I'm all right,' she said hurriedly, pulling herself away. He raised an eyebrow.

'Do all Scottish girls hate being touched?'

She coloured. 'I don't hate it. I mean . . .'

'Only teasing. Come on in.' He stood back to let them pass, winking at Isla.

The house smelled musty, as though it hadn't been lived in for some time. The children were already on their way upstairs, Ross puffing in Barbara's wake.

'Let them go where they want,' Phil said easily when Isla called them back. 'Kids like to explore. I understand that Great-Aunt Agnes more or less lived in the drawing-room,' he went on, opening the door.

Isla, fascinated, moved about the stuffy room, edging round occasional tables, plant-pot stands, chairs and cabinets. She studied the massive sideboard, laden down with ornaments, then tipped her head back to look up at the ceiling and the cornices. The room was similar to Flora Currie's drawing-room, but not as square. There were alcoves on either side of the fireplace, and the window had more of a bay.

'It's a very graceful room, isn't it?' she said thoughtfully. 'This' – she put a hand on a small cabinet – 'suits it, and so does that corner cupboard, while this sideboard's out of place.'

'The room's big enough to take it,' Phil said.

'Yes, but the piece itself's far too big and clumsy for the lines of this room,' Isla told him, moving around, rejecting and selecting, while the other two watched.

'Try to imagine it with only a third of the furniture in it and most of the ornaments gone,' she said at last. 'Think how light and airy it would look then.'

'I quite agree,' said Colin Forbes from the doorway. She turned, and saw his eyes widen as he recognised her. 'Mrs Moffatt! I thought it was – you've done something to your hair,' he said feebly, and Ainslie laughed.

'Did you think we'd brought in an expert? I believe we have, at that. I didn't know you knew about interior design, Isla.'

'I don't, it's just that I . . .' Isla stopped on the verge of saying 'I learned a lot when Kenneth and I were furnishing our house', and changed it to, 'I like houses, and furniture.'

'I never did have any imagination,' Phil Hannigan admitted. 'I can only see what I see.'

'I understand what Isla means,' Ainslie said. 'You should shift most of this furniture out, Phil, but keep the pieces she mentioned. That'll make the house look more attractive, and easier to view as well. If the buyer doesn't want them, they can be auctioned off later.'

Forbes and Son were handling the sale of the house, and Colin, like Ainslie, had come on business, bringing notebook and pencil with him. They moved upstairs, and after taking a quick look round Isla left them there, Ainslie listing the furniture, Colin thumping walls and jumping on the floors, with the children's enthusiastic help, to test the joists. She slipped back down to the kitchen, where she washed the few dishes Phil had left in the sink. She was rinsing the dishcloth when Ainslie arrived.

'Here you are. Colin and I are going to drive Phil down to the Clyde coast this afternoon. Come with us.'

'I couldn't possibly . . .'

'The children too, they can sit on our laps, and I'm sure they'd love to see the sea,' Ainslie coaxed. Isla was shaking her head firmly when Barbara and Ross burst in, shouting, 'Mummy, we're going to the seaside!'

'Ainslie! You told them without asking me first!'

'I must have let it slip out,' Ainslie said guiltily, then brightened. 'You'll have to say yes now, won't you?'

They went to Barassie, where the car could be driven right on to a wide stretch of firm sand and the children could shed their socks and shoes and paddle in the shallow water. Ainslie went with them, while the two young men stayed by the car with Isla. They were from different worlds, she thought, looking at them. Colin Forbes, formal in a blue suit, with shirt and tie, stood staring out at the glittering water, while Phil, dressed casually in cream-coloured trousers and an open-necked checked shirt beneath a sleeveless tan pullover, sprawled bonelessly on the sand, completely at his ease.

'Look at the way the light catches their hair – they've all got the same colouring,' he marvelled, watching the three figures at the water's edge. 'They look more like Ainslie's kids than yours, Isla.'

There was an awkward silence, broken by Colin saying easily, 'Red hair's common among the Scots. By the way, Mrs Moffatt . . .'

'Is stuffiness common too? Calling Isla Mrs Moffatt,' Phil explained when Colin looked puzzled.

'Mrs Moffatt is a client.'

'So am I, but you call me Phil. What's the matter, don't you like each other?' The Canadian looked from one to the other, then grinned. 'Personally, I can't imagine anyone not liking Isla.'

If Isla hadn't been just as embarrassed as he was, she would have laughed at the mixture of expressions that chased each other across Colin Forbes' reddening face. Finally he said stiffly, 'As I was saying – Isla – I think we may have found a buyer for the tenement building.'

'Really?'

'I should be able to give you further details when you come to the office on Monday, but I need to be able to tell the prospective buyer whether the building's fully tenanted or not. Will you be moving out if you sell?'

'I don't see how I can.'

'Surely you'll be able to buy another place with the money you make from the sale?' Phil asked. His interest was so sincere that it didn't occur to Isla to feel annoyed at the question.

'I've already spent some of the money I'd get from a sale, paying for essential repairs. It would probably be wise to stay where I am, and invest the rest.'

'Why not make an offer for my great-aunt's house? It would be a great place to raise kids, with that backyard and all. And you'd have room to develop that dolls'-house business of yours.'

'I couldn't begin to afford a house like that!'

'Make me an offer,' he invited, and when she laughed, he persisted. 'Go on – I've not had any offers yet. You might as well be the first.'

'Five shillings is as much as I could afford.'

'Five shillings. There you go, Colin – the first bid's in.'

Colin Forbes grunted, and ran a finger round his constricting collar. He stooped and picked up a stick, flicking at the sand with it as he wandered down to the water's edge, where Ainslie and the children were playing.

'What's troubling Ainslie?' Phil asked when Colin was out of earshot. 'She flinched away like a startled deer when I tried to steady her back at the house. Made me feel she'd rather have been left to fall flat on her face.'

'She's – not had an easy time lately.'

'Uh-huh?' He settled his back more comfortably against the car wheel. 'I can't imagine why anyone would want to cause problems for a girl like that.'

The offer made for the tenement was lower than Isla had hoped.

'It's not a good time to be selling,' Colin Forbes explained. 'Ordinarily, we'd advise waiting in the hope of the market improving, but . . .'

'I can't afford to wait.' The repair bill for the roof was still haunting her. 'I'll have to take it.'

'And remain as a tenant?'

'I've no option. At least I can stop feeling guilty about the state of the place if I don't own it.'

'Then I'll get the papers drawn up, and let you know when they're ready for signature.'

Phil always seemed to be around when Isla went to Castlehead, and Ainslie was there often too, helping him to clear out cupboards and get the house ready for sale.

The lanky Canadian took a liking to Barbara and Ross, who both adored him, and somehow, without Isla knowing how it happened, the three of them – Phil, Ainslie and Isla, had fallen into the habit of taking the children on outings. Colin often accompanied them – so that he could be near Ainslie, Isla assumed.

To her consternation, Phil even turned up at Barbara's back-court concert with Ainslie, causing more than a ripple of excitement. The women were far more interested in him than in their children's talents, nudging each other and whispering amongst themselves. Phil, unabashed, tipped his hat and beamed at them all, then settled down to enjoy the concert, applauding each song loudly, and handing out coins afterwards to all the performers, who immediately ran off to the corner shop to buy sweeties.

'Ye've got some strange friends, Isla,' said Magret after he had gone, adding with a coy giggle, 'mind you, he's a fine-looking man, is he no'?'

'I think he's the nicest person in the whole world,' Barbara, flushed with the success of her concert, said indistinctly round a large peppermint ball.

One windy day, they all drove up to the top of the braes flanking Paisley to fly Colin's old kite.

'Phil likes your company,' Ainslie said as the two of them sat on the springy grass, watching the children jump about with excitement as the kite soared.

'He likes everyone, he's got that sort of nature. And if you're trying to matchmake you're wasting your time. I've become used to my independence, and I like it fine.'

'But think of it, Isla – life in Canada! The children would love it. Phil's got his own business, and a fine house, with beautiful countryside around it, and Lake Erie not far away.'

'He's been telling you a lot about himself, hasn't he?'

'I'm not the marrying kind,' Ainslie said at once.

'Neither am I, now.'

'Hey, look at this – it's going up to the sun!' Phil called as the two men skimmed past, Colin controlling the kite while Ross, on Phil's shoulders, reached up towards the dancing, colourful kite with one hand, and clutched Phil's thick hair with the other. Barbara raced alongside, her ribbon long since lost and her red hair streaming in the wind.

Following Isla's advice, Phil had the surplus furniture removed from his great-aunt's house and sold at auction. Left with only the smaller furniture, the house looked just as Isla had visualised it – spacious and elegant, despite the clean patches on the wallpaper where the furniture had stood for many years.

Phil, in plus-fours and a casual jacket, attended the sale, lounging at the back of the large auction room. Whenever Ainslie, who was assisting the clerk, found a moment to glance up from the lists she had to follow meticulously, he caught her eye and winked. Afterwards, he stayed behind and gave the men a hand to clear the room, carrying lots outside to pack on to carts and lorries, putting unsold goods back into storage. Then he joined them for a mug of strong tea.

'You did all right,' Charlie told him, and Phil shrugged. He was leaning against a wall, mug in hand, looking, as he always did, as though he belonged.

'It wasn't bad. To tell the truth, it goes against the grain, making money out of someone else's possessions. I prefer to know that what I've got was earned by my own efforts.'

Ainslie, eyeing the rangy Canadian, was taken by his relaxed self-confidence, his ease with his surroundings. Compared to him, the Scots seemed to be confined in invisible boxes, limited by self-imposed rules of behaviour.

'How do you get home?' he asked as they left the auction rooms together.

'By bus from the Cross.' Then she said impulsively, 'But today, I think I'd like to walk.'

'To the other side of the town? Won't your mother wonder where you've got to?'

'She won't notice,' Ainslie said, then, as they stepped out briskly together, she found herself telling him about her mother and about Innes. He was a good listener, and it seemed natural to go on to talk about her father, about giving Colin back his ring, about Isla, and her own guilt at having treated the other woman so badly when she first came to the town. She spoke freely of her need to make amends, to her half-brother and sister as well as to their mother. As she talked, the pavement seemed to skim past beneath their feet, and suddenly they were standing at her gate. She felt tired after the long walk, but it was a good, healthy tiredness, as though all the talking had cleansed and eased her.

'I wish I could invite you in for tea, Phil, but . . .'

'I understand.' He looked beyond her, to the garden and the house, then back at her face. 'This doesn't look like the right sort of place for you. It's too closed in.'

She turned to study the house where she had been born and raised. 'I feel that way too, whenever I'm in it.'

'Tell me, d'you feel bad about breaking off your engagement to Colin?'

'Yes, but I still think that it was the right thing to do.' She held her hand out. 'Thank you for being such a good listener, Phil.'

His hand was reassuring as it clasped hers. 'Any time,' he said, then released her, flipped a finger at the brim of his soft hat, and swung round, walking away with that long, unhurried step she had found easy to adopt.

For once, there was no feeling of apprehension as Ainslie went through the front door. She felt warm and at ease – and safe.

24

⬥

Isla handed the pen over, and watched as Colin Forbes scribbled his own name as witness to her signature. Over the past week or two, thrown into his company more than before, she had discovered that he could be much nicer than she had thought possible.

She had seen him glancing at Ainslie when he thought he was unobserved, and had recognised the look on his face. It was clear, in those brief, private glances, that he knew that he had lost Ainslie McAdam for ever, and was still coming to terms with the truth. Isla knew what that was like. By selling the tenement she herself had broken another of the few, delicate strands that still linked her to Kenneth.

'When the money comes through, we can discuss what you want to do with it.' His voice broke through her thoughts.

'I'm hoping that we'll be able to live on it for at least two more years. Once Ross goes to school, I'll be free to look for paid employment.'

The little boy, standing by the window where he could look down on the passing tramcars, turned at the sound of his name and came to her. She smiled down at him, smoothing back his hair.

'You'll not make much from the sale.'

'I've learned a lot about managing on very little money,' she said wryly, getting to her feet. 'Most of the folk in George Street are experts at that.'

It was ironic that just as Isla had sold the tenement, Mrs Leach discovered that she had owned it.

The woman came storming down the street, battered shopping bag in hand, just as Isla and Magret, on their way back from the bakery, reached the close.

'So – what's like tae be a landlord, then?' she shouted from several yards away. Mrs Kelly, her daughter, trotted just behind her, pale and anxious. 'You – I'm talkin' tae ye!' A hand caught Isla's shoulder, pulling her back as she was about to step into the close. Ross, who had been running ahead with Daisy, came back to his mother, his small face tight with concern.

'Let go of me!'

'Did ye know?' Mrs Leach swung round on Magret. 'Did ye know that it's her that owns this building? It's her we pay our rents tae—'

'Ach, away wi' ye,' Magret scoffed. 'Don't be so daft. Isla's in the same boat as the rest of us – she's tryin' tae raise two weans on her own.'

'Mam—' Mrs Kelly plucked at her mother's sleeve. Mrs Leach threw her off with a twitch of the arm.

'Her that's let the place fall down about our ears while she lives on our money!'

'Ye're haverin'!' Magret was getting angry. 'Look at the lassie. Does she look like a landlord?'

'She looks like a sly wee besom, that's what she looks like,' Mrs Leach roared back. By now there wasn't a window without a face framed in it, not a close-mouth without its group of staring women.

'I don't own anything!'

Mrs Leach sniffed. 'Not now ye don't. But ye did, didn't ye? Oh, ye thought ye were so clever, pretendin' tae be a poor wee widow. But I've found ye out – I've got yer measure now, milady. There's no' much can be kept hidden from me!'

'Tell her she's haverin', Isla,' Magret said contemptuously.

'Haverin', am I?' Mrs Leach caught her daughter's arm and pulled the distraught girl forward. 'And what about her man, was he haverin' tae, when he heard in the very office where he works that she's the one that owns this building?'

'Mam, I told ye that in confidence,' Mrs Kelly whimpered, but her mother wasn't interested.

'Tell the truth and shame the devil,' she shouted to the gathering audience. 'That's the way I was brought up.'

Magret began to waver. 'It's no' true, is it?' she asked Isla. 'It cannae be true!'

Ross, clinging to Isla's legs, started to wail, and she put a hand on his head. 'It's all right, pet.'

'See? She'll not answer ye,' Mrs Leach told Magret. 'She's scared tae answer ye!'

'But she pays her rent, the same as the rest of us.'

'Aye – and then she goes tae the factor's every week an' gets it back, along wi' our hard-earned money!' Mrs Leach's hard finger rammed into Isla's shoulder, forcing her to retreat. Her ankles collided painfully with the step, and she almost fell, but managed to stay upright, stumbling on to the step. Ross was almost hysterical now, and she scooped him up in her arms, retreating to the safety of her own room. Mrs Leach followed her along the close, her bulk shutting out the light, her voice hounding and nagging.

'We don't want the likes o' you livin' here,' she brayed, her voice rolling like thunder round the narrow close. 'The folks that live here's decent! We've no time for liars. Ye can just get out of this building – you an' yer weans!'

Even when Isla reached the safety of the room and slammed the door in the woman's face, her fist pounded on the panels and her voice kept bellowing on, magnified by the enclosed passageway.

Trembling on the other side of the door, hugging Ross to her and trying to hush him, as though afraid that his weeping would somehow give them both away, Isla heard Magret arguing, and Mrs Kelly pleading with her mother to come away. At last, Mrs Leach allowed herself to be led upstairs, after one final thump at the door. After a moment, there was another, gentle tap at the door.

'Isla?'

She put Ross down and opened the door. Magret came in, Daisy gawping at her side. 'She's bletherin'. The woman's gone clean off her head – I knew it would happen one day.'

'It's true, Magret.'

Magret's mouth opened and shut. Finally she said feebly, 'The landlord? You?'

'I did own the place, but I've sold it now. I didn't want to say anything because—'

Magret looked dazed. 'I'll have to see what he thinks about all this business,' she said, then caught Daisy by the hand as the little girl made a move towards Ross. 'I'd – I'd best be gettin' his tea ready. I'll see ye later,' and she almost ran out of the room.

Isla turned away from the door, just in time to see faces at the window, peering into the room. She managed, for Ross's sake, to swallow back her involuntary yelp of fright, then went across to pull the curtain shut. As she did so, something thumped against the glass, but didn't break it. Ross jumped at the sound and ran to her.

'It's all right, pet, it's all right,' she soothed him, but she didn't dare to venture out, or to draw back the curtain. They sat in the gloom, listening to the sound of voices outside as the news was relayed from one person to another, until Barbara came home from school, tears in her eyes, wanting to know why the women in the street had pointed at her and shouted nasty things about her mummy.

From that day, life in George Street became impossible. None of the other children were allowed to play with Ross, and Barbara, bewildered, wanted to know why the children at school had turned against her.

'Have you been bad?' she asked suspiciously.

'No, love, it's just that – this tenement belonged to your daddy, and he gave it to us when he – had to go away. But the neighbours didn't know that, and they're angry with me for not telling them.'

Barbara's eyes were like saucers. 'The whole building? Did they think he should have given it to them instead?'

Isla tried to explain, but Barbara got it into her head

that the neighbours had somehow taken the tenement away from her mother, and arrived home next day with her snub nose bloody and her blouse torn after a fight in the playground over the issue.

Isla couldn't stay in the house all the time. When she went out, people stared and pointed and made loud asides to each other about rich folk slumming, and poor folk unable to trust their neighbours. The curtains stayed closed, because every time she opened them, people stared in. The owner of the corner shop, a friendly man who had previously been willing to put Isla's purchases on the slate until the beginning of each week, refused to sell her anything until she had cleared her debts.

'But you give credit to most of the folk round here.'

'Aye, missus, because I want tae keep my customers,' the man said. 'If I serve you, most of them'll go elsewhere. I cannae afford tae let that happen.'

The other women in the shop stepped aside ostentatiously to let Isla out, muttering amongst themselves. She had no option but to go to the lawyer's office to ask Colin Forbes if she could take some money out at once.

'Is there something wrong?' His gaze moved from her to Ross, unusually silent and clinging.

'No.' She was too ashamed to tell him about what had happened. It was her problem, and she must cope with it. She was sure that if she and the children could just wait out the storm, it would die down. Once the George Street folk realised that, like them, she was struggling to support her family and worrying about where the next meal was coming from, they would surely come round.

She arrived home to find a pile of horse manure out-

side her door. She fetched the shovel from the back
court and cleared it, then scrubbed the close out. After
sluicing the water away down the street drain she came
back into the close to find Magret lurking there.

'Oh, Isla, it's a rotten shame, so it is. I'd have cleaned
it up for ye, but Tommy says I've no' tae talk tae ye,
and the bairns cannae play together. I'm sorry . . .'

'It's all right, I can understand why he's so angry.'

Magret held back Daisy, who was trying to reach
Ross. 'Why did ye keep it a secret, Isla?'

'Because I knew that if the folk round here knew the
truth, they'd do just what they're doing now,' Isla told
her, and went into the house.

Drew tapped on the door that night; when she was
certain he was alone, she opened the door, closing it
quickly behind him.

'I've finished that wee sideboard.' He handed it over
and she ran her fingers over it.

'It's lovely, Drew.'

He reached into his pocket and brought out a small
parcel, fragrant-smelling and still warm. 'My mam's
just baked these scones. She thought you and the
bairns'd like them. And here's a wee pot of raspberry
jam to go with them.'

Tears of gratitude stung Isla's eyes. 'Thank you –
and thank your mother for me.'

'It was you that got the roof fixed, wasn't it? If
there's anythin' we can dae for ye, mam an' me, ye just
have tae let us know. It's no' right, the way folks is
treatin' ye,' the youth said hotly. 'It's that old Leach
that's got the rest of them stirred up against ye. It'll be
forgotten in a week.'

As he stepped out into the close again, she heard him say, with a boldness that she never would have believed of Drew, 'Evenin', Mrs Leach. Is there somethin' wrong wi' yer eyes? They look awful stary.'

The old woman's scandalised sniff reverberated through the close as Isla closed the door.

Drew was wrong – Isla's betrayal, as Mrs Leach and her cronies saw it, wasn't forgotten in a week. Instead, the persecution became increasingly worse, until finally one night, someone threw a stone through the window, shouting, 'See how long ye take tae repair that, landlady! Nob'dy wants your sort here!'

The children, who had just been put to bed, screamed with fright, and Isla, working at the sink, jumped back as shards of glass flew into the washing-up water. She caught Ross up out of his cot and jumped with him into the wall-bed, where the three of them crouched together.

'Look, Mummy,' Ross said suddenly, wide-eyed, pointing at the back of her hand, which was bleeding freely. There was blood on the blanket, and on Ross's clothes.

Isla put her hand to her mouth, tasting the saltiness of her own blood. Round it she said reassuringly, 'It's just a wee cut,' to the two frightened little faces peering up at her in the wall-bed's gloom. She wound her handkerchief around the cut to stop the bleeding. They all stayed in the wall-bed that night, for Isla was afraid to put Ross into his cot. The children went to sleep quickly, but Isla lay awake, jumping at the slightest noise from outside, her mind conjuring up alarming pictures of people smashing the door down, robbing her, harming the children. Her hand throbbed all through the night.

Isla had been going to Flora Currie's house in Castlehead every morning as usual, and had managed to persuade Ross to say nothing about the trouble in George Street.

The day after the window was smashed was a Saturday, and after boarding the broken window up with cardboard, Isla took the children to Flora's, braving the walk along George Street, under hostile eyes. It was a relief to turn the corner into Maxwellton Street.

Barbara had been safely tucked away in her classroom during the week. Now, as they passed the West Station and made for the gate in the wall, Isla did her best to tactfully suggest to her daughter that nothing should be said about what had happened in George Street. Barbara, looking forward to being cosseted by Annie and as glad as Isla was to get away from the unfriendliness in George Street for a little while, agreed cheerfully.

Ainslie, who had become a regular caller at Castlehead, was already in the house when Isla arrived, and so was Phil. His sharp eyes fell on the bandaged hand at once. 'Been in the wars?' he asked, and before she could say a word, Barbara, completely forgetting all that she had promised, launched into a dramatic story about the broken window.

Flora tutted. 'Those children that throw stones! Do their mothers never think to teach them how dangerous it is?'

'It was a man,' Barbara chirruped. 'I heard him

shouting, "Nobody wants your sort here!"' Her clear little voice dropped to mimic the harsh taunt she had heard the day before.

'A man?' Flora asked. 'Why would a man do a thing like that?'

'It's because my daddy didn't give them the tenement,' Barbara explained, ignoring her mother's glare. 'The folk are all angry with us, and nobody'll . . .' She stopped and gave a gulp, then went on, her voice wobbling slightly, 'Nobody'll play with me and Ross—'

She stopped as Phil jumped to his feet, staggered, clutched at a chair, then limped theatrically towards the door, opening it then clutching at it for support.

'Oh, my leg – it's gone again,' he said dramatically. 'Barbara, would you and Ross go to the kitchen and ask Miss Annie if she knows what I did with my spare wooden leg?'

'You haven't got a wooden leg,' Barbara said, the threatening tears vanishing.

'Sure I have. I've got two, and this one's giving out on me. Tell Miss Annie that I think I might have left it in the biscuit tin,' he called after them as they scampered out, giggling.

'You'll drive Annie daft with your silliness,' Flora told him as he closed the door.

'Not her, she loves a bit of fun. Now . . .' Phil came back into the room, his face suddenly grim. 'What's going on, Isla?'

'It's nothing important.'

'Sounds pretty important to me.'

'She's not been herself for the past week,' Flora fretted, 'but I didn't want to pry.'

'I think you should pry,' Phil told her. 'I think it's time we all pried.'

'It's not your worry.'

'Nonsense. Anything that harms you and your bairns is my worry. Out with it.'

'Better do as the lady says,' Phil drawled. 'She can be mean when she puts her mind to it.'

'I wish Agnes could have met you, Philip. She'd have loved you! Come on, now,' Flora added with a change of tone, and Isla shrugged helplessly and started to talk.

'They can't treat you like that,' Phil exploded when she finished. 'Who do they think they are?'

'You should go to the police,' Ainslie chimed in, and Flora nodded.

'I certainly will not. They're hurt because I deceived them, and I can't say that I blame them.'

Phil's eyes were blazing with suppressed fury. 'You don't blame someone for smashing your window and terrorising your kids?'

'No – I mean yes – I mean,' Isla said helplessly, looking at her friends' tense faces. 'The trouble is that now they think I'm wealthy, when I'm not. I'm no better off than they are. It'll blow over.'

'You think so? And how many broken windows d'you think it'll take?' Phil made for the door, but Ainslie's voice stopped him in his tracks.

'Going to George Street and making a fuss won't help matters, nor will reporting it to the police. It'll only make things worse for Isla and the children. They'll have to move out.'

'I can't afford to move!'

'Colin's father owns property in Paisley. He might have a flat you could rent.'

'It'd have to be the same rent as the place I'm in now. I didn't make much money from the sale of the tenement, and part of that went to pay for the repairs. We'll have to live on the rest until Ross goes to school and I'm free to look for a job.'

'You've already got a job, doing up those dolls' houses.'

'That doesn't bring in much, Phil,' Ainslie said absently, staring into space, her neat brows drawn together in thought.

'Why don't you move in here? There's enough room.'

Isla reached out to pat Flora Currie's hand. 'It's kind of you, but I'm not going to impose two active children on you.'

'I love the bairns!'

'I know you do, but they're more lovable in small doses, believe me.'

'What are we all fretting about?' Phil said. 'There's my aunt's house, lying empty right next door.'

'I couldn't afford to pay rent on a house that size!'

'Who said anything about rent? I need to sell it and get back home. I'm not interested in renting.'

'Then it's out of the question.'

'You already made an offer for it a few weeks ago.'

'Phil, that was just a bit of fun!'

'What was it again?'

'Five shillings, and that's still as much as I could—'

'Done.' The Canadian strode over to take Isla's hand and shake it firmly. 'You've got yourself a deal, Mrs Moffatt.'

'But—'

'Don't tease the lassie, Philip,' Flora snapped, but Ainslie, her eyes bright, touched the older woman's arm.

'Wait a minute, Miss Currie, I don't believe he's teasing her at all. You mean it, don't you, Phil?'

'We shook hands on it. I've never in my life gone back on a handshake.'

'But . . .' Isla said again, feeling as though the world had been turned upside down like a snow scene in a glass ball. 'You can't sell a house for five shillings!'

'Sure I can. I can do anything I want, as long as it's not breaking the law. Listen, I've got everything I want back home – well, almost everything,' Phil added, with a swift sidelong glance at Ainslie, who coloured slightly and looked away. 'I didn't come over here to make money out of my great-aunt's death, I came to try to make up in some way for not having come over earlier, while she was still alive. I reckon that having folks like you and your redheads living in her house, and you working in it at those dolls' houses, is as good a way as any of making amends.'

'Isla, you could put a room aside for your dolls'-house work,' Ainslie said excitedly.

'Great, I've got an ally!' Phil put an arm about her shoulders. Even in her confusion, Isla noticed that Ainslie didn't break the contact as before, but stayed within his casual embrace.

'Well now, Isla,' said Flora Currie, sounding as dazed as Isla felt, 'it looks as though you've just bought yourself somewhere else to live.'

25

Isla had fully expected Colin Forbes and his father to show Phil Hannigan the error of his ways, and explain to him how ridiculous his scheme was. But to her surprise, both men were willing to let the five-shilling sale go through, though Colin was tight-lipped.

'Mr Hannigan has quite made up his mind that this is what he wants, and therefore it stands as a proper business arrangement,' Gilchrist Forbes said. 'For your part, it's clearly advantageous, and the papers will be drawn up as soon as possible. I understand that Mr Hannigan wants them to be signed as soon as possible, and the matter brought to a conclusion.'

'But I can't just buy a house that size for five shillings!'

'Normally, I would agree with you, but this is not a normal transaction. For five shillings, the house is yours. And from what Ainslie and Colin tell me,' the lawyer added, 'the sooner you move out of George Street and into Castlehead, the better.'

The George Street folk gathered to watch the 'flitting' in sullen silence. Both Phil and Colin were there to help carry Isla's few pieces of furniture out to the van that had been hired for the occasion, and their presence acted as a deterrent to those who might have made something of the occasion.

As the van drew away from the kerb and Phil helped Isla and the children into Colin's car, Mrs Leach, who had been standing by the close watching every move, said loudly, 'Good riddance tae bad rubbish!'

The tall Canadian immediately turned, cupping a hand behind his ear. 'I didn't quite catch that, ma'am, you've got such a quiet voice,' he said politely. 'Can you speak a little louder?'

Mrs Leach went crimson as some of the onlookers tittered, and flounced back into the close with a loud sniff. The titters strengthened into a laugh as she disappeared. The George Street folk had united against someone they saw as an outsider, but on the other hand, Mrs Leach herself wasn't popular, and many of them relished the sight of her being bested.

Phil had insisted on including the furniture still in the house in the deal, pointing out that Isla herself had said that it belonged there, and Flora donated two small beds from her attic for the children. Ross was overcome with excitement at having a real bed, instead of a cot that had become too short for him.

Isla, who was living in a daze, had thought of turning the small room beside the kitchen into her workroom, but Ainslie talked her into taking one of the two big front rooms instead.

'You may well end up with quite a lot of work, and if so, you'll need the space,' she pointed out. Isla, seeing the sense of her argument, decided that one front room should be the living-room while the other, formerly the dining-room, became a workroom. She would have no need for a separate room to eat in, the kitchen was as large as the room she and the children had lived in at George Street. She took one of the three bedrooms upstairs, and put both children into another room. It was too soon for Ross to be on his own. Once he was old enough, he could move into the smallest bedroom.

'As far as they're concerned, the most exciting place in the house is the bathroom,' she said wryly to Ainslie, who had insisted on helping her to get the workroom ready. Annie was making up beds upstairs, with the children hindering more than helping. 'I can see that I'm going to have trouble keeping Ross away from that running water.'

Ainslie, whisking a handbrush along the skirting board, sat back on her heels and looked round the room. 'This place has so much space. I never noticed until recently how dark and crowded our house is.' She hesitated, then said slowly, 'My aunt's here from the Border on a visit. She's suggested finding a small place there for Mother, so that they can see more of each other.'

'D'you think she'll agree?'

'I think she feels the same way I do – that that house has too many memories. She and her sister always got on well. I believe Mother would be the better for a move.'

'What will you do? Go with her, or stay in Paisley?'

'Mother and I both know that we can't share a house. As to staying in Paisley . . .' Ainslie hesitated again, fidgeting with the brush in her hands.

A sudden thought struck Isla, but it was so delicate that she daren't put it into words, in case she blundered. Instead she kept her voice light when she said, 'Phil's going to see what Mr Blayne has in the way of long tables and a good chest of drawers for this room. I shall miss him when he goes back to Canada.' She sneaked a glance at Ainslie. 'He's very good at knowing just how to make people happy, isn't he?'

'Yes, he is.' Ainslie looked up, her lips curved into a determined, but wavering, smile, her eyes sparkling. 'Isla . . .'

Isla decided that she wouldn't be blundering after all. 'He's asked you to go to Canada with him. He's asked you to marry him!' Then, as Ainslie nodded and burst into tears, Isla dropped to the floor beside her and hugged her. 'That's wonderful!'

Ainslie caught and held her so tightly that she felt her ribs creak.

'No it's not, it's ridiculous!' she wept into Isla's neck. 'I said – I swore – that I'd never marry. And I meant it! I scarcely know him – I might hate living with him in Canada!'

'That's not what you said when you were trying to persuade me to consider it.'

'Yes, but you're you and I'm . . .' Ainslie gave a huge sniff and sat back, scrubbing a wrist across her face just like a child. She was so like Barbara, Isla thought. Even when they cried, they both looked beautiful. 'I'm such a difficult person, Isla, such a mixture. I'd probably be a terrible wife!'

'Phil doesn't seem to think so.'

'I might not even l-like Canada!'

'You're quite right. It's all ridiculous, and you'd both be very unhappy, and Canada will probably turn out to be the most dreadful place on earth.'

'Isla!'

'Ainslie! If you love the man, marry the man!'

Ainslie burst into tears again and, this time, Isla joined her. They sat on the floor, in each other's arms, and cried their eyes out.

Ainslie McAdam and Philip Hannigan were married quietly in Oakshawhill Church on a crisp, sunny December day, just before Christmas, with Isla and Colin as their witnesses. The date of their wedding had been carefully planned to ensure that eight days later, on the anniversary of Innes's death, Catherine and Ainslie would both have left Paisley, one moving to the borders, the other on her way to Canada with her new husband.

Colin watched impassively as Ainslie, beautiful in a suit of deep green with a huge sable collar and sable at the cuffs of her jacket and round the hem of her skirt, became Phil Hannigan's wife, and even managed a cheerful smile and a kiss for the bride as they left the church. Isla, watching, felt heart-sorry for the young man.

At Catherine's insistence, a small reception was held in the house. Isla, given her own way, would have gone back to Castlehead, where Annie was looking after the children, when the ceremony was over, but Ainslie and Flora both persuaded her to see the occasion through to the end. 'The children'll be fine with Annie, and I'm going to be at the reception,' Flora said. 'We'll be company for each other.'

Even so, Isla faltered at the front door, and might not have managed to step over the lintel if Colin Forbes hadn't taken her arm and drawn her into the long rectangular hall by his side, murmuring, 'If I can go through with the wedding, Isla, you can go through with the reception.'

It was the first time he had spontaneously used her given name, and Isla was so taken aback by the sound of it on his tongue that she was inside the house and being greeted by Flora, striking in a yellow and black dress beneath a black coat, before she knew it.

Catherine McAdam sat in state in the drawing-room, graciously receiving her daughter's guests. She proffered her cheek formally for Ainslie's kiss, then Phil's, only coming to life when Colin's turn came to greet her.

'My dear boy!' She took his hands in hers, smiling warmly up at him.

'This must be a very happy occasion for you, Mrs McAdam.' He bent to kiss her, then drew Isla forward. 'I'd like you to meet Mrs Isla Moffatt.'

Kenneth's first, legal wife and his second, unlawful wife looked into each other's faces, and Catherine's gaze swept over Isla without recognition. 'How d'you do.' She touched Isla's hand briefly, then turned back to Colin. 'Unfortunately, my daughter's chosen a Colonial,' she told him, her voice ringing out. 'She never does the right thing. But at least he's wealthy.'

There was an audible, collective gasp, as everyone within earshot swivelled towards the bridal couple, avid to record their reaction. The colour drained from Ainslie's face, and Isla sensed Colin tensing beside her, ready to jump to his former fiancée's defence. Then Philip Hannigan, an arm about Ainslie's shoulders, drawled in a voice just as clear and carrying as

Catherine's, 'Well I'll be darned. I thought that I was the one marrying money!'

Ainslie laughed, a peal of genuine, unselfconscious amusement, while Catherine stared coldly at her upstart new son-in-law and the cream of Paisley society blinked and murmured and bridled, sensing that it had just been mocked, and not sure what should be done about it.

'Phil's done that girl the world of good already,' Flora approved, arriving beside Isla. 'She's learning that cattiness doesn't matter, even when it comes from her own mother.'

Later, someone came and swept Flora away to meet someone else. Isla, on her own, sipped at the glass of champagne offered by one of the maids, looking around the drawing-room, trying to imagine the Kenneth she had known at home in it. It was impossible. There had been so many Kenneth McAdams.

'Mrs – Moffatt, isn't it?' Two stylishly dressed women bore down on her. 'The Mrs Moffatt who made that delightful *Little Women* house?'

'Yes, that's right.'

'Dolly McNair bought it from Leckie's toyshop,' the speaker informed her friend. 'It's really quite sweet. I wonder if you would do one for me?'

'I'd be happy to. If you let Mr Leckie know what you want, he'll pass the information on to me.'

'I'll do that,' the woman gushed, then, eyes sharpening, 'I understand that you bought Agnes McFall's house in Castlehead. For five shillings, someone told me, but of course they must have got it wrong.'

'Five shillings? Surely not,' her friend chimed in.

'My dear, I can assure you – the five-shilling mansion, people are calling it.'

'But nobody sells a house for that price – are we getting confused with your dolls' houses?'

Their eyes were bright, greedy with the desire for some lucrative gossip. Isla, taken aback by what she now realised had been a planned attack, stammered, her mouth going dry. She was looking from one face to the other, searching wildly for something to say when a hand closed on her arm and Colin Forbes said smoothly above her head, 'Pardon me, I couldn't help overhearing. Mrs Moffatt and Mr Hannigan came to a private agreement regarding the sale of his great-aunt's house, and as Mrs Moffatt's solicitor, I can assure you that everything was in order.' Then, turning his back on the two women, who had begun to quack out protests, 'Isla, my mother is anxious to meet you.'

Gilchrist Forbes stood by the window with a plump, maternal-looking woman.

'Mother,' Colin said, 'this is Isla Moffatt. I've just rescued her from that pair of nebby old crows.'

He jerked his head towards the women who had been talking to Isla, and Phemie Forbes, followed the movement, gave an outraged gasp. 'You're talking about two friends of mine. Gilchrist, speak to him!'

'Colin's too old to be spoken to, Phemie,' her husband said calmly. 'In any case, I'm more likely to agree with him than disagree. Mrs Moffatt, this is my wife.'

'Tchah!' Phemie glared at her menfolk, then turned her attention to Isla, her gaze swiftly evaluating the sage skirt and long tailored jacket with dark green trimmings that Ainslie had insisted on buying Isla for the wedding. She held out a ringed hand. 'How do you do, my dear. I hope you've settled into your new home?'

'We have. I think we're going to be very happy there.'

'I must say, though, that it's a very strange situation. Did you really only pay five—'

'Phemie!' her husband cut in hurriedly, while Colin said, 'I'd wondered where these old biddies got their information from.'

'Are you suggesting that . . .?'

'What, Mother?' Colin smiled down on the woman, who glared back at him. It was clear to Isla that there was affection between the three members of the Forbes family; it reminded her, achingly, of the bond there had always been between herself and her own parents.

'Men can be quite impossible, can't they?' Phemie turned to Isla to include her in the general conspiracy of womanhood, then her still-pretty features blurred and her eyes widened. 'I mean – that is . . .'

Suddenly, Isla knew that for all the older woman's apparent friendliness, in Phemie Forbes' eyes, she herself was outside the conspiracy, a woman apart, wife yet not wife, widow yet not widow.

It was a relief when Ainslie and Philip marked the end of the reception by leaving. They had decided to spend a few days on honeymoon before sailing to Canada. Catherine McAdam stayed in her chair, announcing that she was too tired to accompany her daughter and son-in-law to the gate. Once again, she accepted Ainslie's kiss without any show of emotion, and Phil's arm went protectively about his new wife as she turned to leave her home for the last time. She pressed her head briefly against his shoulder in recognition of his gesture, while Isla, watching, swore to herself that she would never allow anything to destroy her own small family as the McAdams had been destroyed.

As the couple made their farewells out on the driveway in a flurry of kisses and handshakes, the last of the day's sunlight struck rich copper glints from Ainslie's hair. At the gate, she left Phil's side to hug Isla.

'Write to me – long letters telling me every single thing that happens. And I'll write back, I promise. Kiss the children for me.'

She released Isla and turned to hug Colin as Phil caught Isla up in a brief embrace. 'Be happy in greataunt Agnes's house,' he said.

As the car moved off, and Ainslie's hand fluttered from the window, the final rays of the sun sparkled on the gold wedding ring. Isla, hanging back from the press of people crowded at the gate and spilling on to the pavement, saw that Colin was beside her, his face expressionless.

'It must have been hard for you, today.'

He blinked down at her as though he had never seen her before, then his eyes cleared. Today, she saw, they were the green of deep water. 'I think she's married the right man. She's never looked at me the way she looks at him.'

The guests had started to move back towards the house. An involuntary shiver ran through Isla at the thought of going back inside.

'I think I'll just go home.'

'D'you mind if I walk with you?' Colin asked. 'I'd welcome a change of scene.'

26

'I don't expect to be long, Robert,' Phemie Forbes told her chauffeur as he opened the garden gate for her.

Walking up the flagged path between small neat lawns, each with its circular rosebed, she forced back the fluttery feeling that invaded her stomach and told herself that she was doing nothing wrong. She was merely safeguarding her son's interests; any good mother would do the same. She gave the bell-pull a smart tug, and almost at once saw movement through the stained-glass upper half of the door.

When it opened, Phemie, fully expecting a maidservant, was taken aback to see the lady of the house herself. Isla Moffatt, for her part, looked just as astonished to find Phemie on her doorstep, but quickly produced a welcoming smile.

'Mrs Forbes, what a pleasant surprise. I haven't seen you for some time. Please,' she stepped back, 'come in.'

'I've only dropped in for a moment,' Phemie said as she stepped inside and followed Isla into a room to the right of the hall, noting the young woman's blue crêpe de Chine blouse with a large bow at the throat, and the navy skirt that fitted snugly over slender hips, then flared out.

'You'll have some tea, of course.' As protocol dictated in the west of Scotland, the phrase was more of a statement than a question. It was a standard joke in the west that in the Edinburgh area, where the people were reputed to be more formal, the greeting to a casual caller was, 'You'll have had your tea?'

'I only called in for a few minutes . . .'

'But I was about to have one myself, and I'd welcome the company.'

'Well, perhaps a quick cup.' Phemie allowed her hostess to relieve her of her sealskin wrap.

'I'll not be a moment,' Isla promised, and hurried out.

Taking advantage of her absence, Phemie set about a close scrutiny of the room as she drew the gloves from her plump little hands. In the five years since moving to Castlehead, Isla Moffatt had done very well for herself. It had become the fashion in Paisley and further afield to have one of her dolls' houses on show in one's home. Many of Phemie's friends had bought them, and she herself had two, both presented to her by Colin. One was based on Haworth Hall, the home of the Brontë sisters, while each room in the other house depicted a scene from *Alice in Wonderland*.

Isla's home reflected her financial success. The room Phemie stood in was furnished in modern style, with walls of pale rose, not papered, but painted, and bearing only two paintings, whereas Phemie's drawing-room walls were crowded with pictures. Long curtains in a deeper shade of rose hung at the bay windows, and the carpet was patterned in rose and pale green against a creamy background. The wooden surrounds were highly polished, and the rest of the woodwork was cream. The soft, inviting sofa and chairs were covered with a rose and pale green patterned material, with small cream and gold cushions scattered over them.

The room was fragrant with the smell of roses from a large bowl on a table by the window. Their rich colours reflected in the table's gleaming surface, and they also filled another bowl set on the hearth, in front of the empty grate. Phemie recalled noticing more flowers in a tall vase in the hall, by a telephone.

The few pieces of furniture in the room were made of polished walnut, and the overall effect was one of space, light, colour and comfort.

The door opened. Caught in the act of studying the high ceiling, which, like the walls, was painted soft rose, Phemie jerked her chin down so sharply that pain shot through the back of her neck. 'Won't you sit down?' Isla put the tray down on a small table before the fireplace as Phemie sank into one of the chairs. It was extremely comfortable, and she wondered, a trifle grimly, how often her son had sat in this very same chair.

The tea service was patterned with geometrical shapes filled in with bold colours. It looked very like a dinner set that a friend of Phemie's had recently shown to her, boasting that it was designed by Clarice Cliffe, one of the leading designers of the day.

Isla talked about her garden as they drank their tea, apparently unaware of her guest's silence. Phemie, sneaking little glances over the rim of the cup that she was now quite certain must be Clarice Cliffe, recalled how sorry she had felt for the girl at Ainslie's wedding, with her pinched, sallow face. Feeling sorry for her, she had invited Isla and her children to her home several times, and had even begun to like the little family. But gradually, as she noted the growing friendship between Colin and Isla and began to sense problems ahead, the invitations had ceased, and for the past three years the two women had only encountered each other occasionally in the town, exchanging brief greetings and moving on.

Now, five years after their first meeting at the wedding, Isla's face was nicely rounded, her skin like smooth ivory, with just a touch of dusky rose over each cheekbone. Her brown eyes, once anxious and apprehensive, sparkled with life, and her dark hair fell sleekly to her jawline, curling inwards slightly at the bottom. She looked positively pretty, Phemie thought, with a pang that gave her the courage to introduce her reason for calling.

'I understand that your little houses are doing very well, Mrs Moffatt.'

If the younger woman had noticed the deliberate condescension in 'little houses', she gave no sign of it. 'I'm continually surprised by the number of orders that keep coming in,' she confessed with a smile. 'I fully expected interest to have fallen away quite early on.'

'My son tells me that they're even selling in England, and abroad.'

Isla picked up the teapot, then put it down again when Phemie gave a decisive shake of the head. 'Ainslie took some leaflets and photographs back to Canada with her the last time she and Phil were over here, and

313

managed to obtain several orders for me, for both decorative and practical houses.'

'By practical, you mean houses that are to be played with, rather than to be put on show?' When Isla nodded, Phemie forged on. 'Several of my friends have bought your practical houses for their little granddaughters.' She smiled, a smile that didn't touch her eyes. 'I'm hopeful that one day soon I'll be able to give you a similar order.'

'Really?' Isla looked up, interested. 'Is Colin planning to marry?'

The time had come. Phemie drew in a deep breath and dusted an imaginary crumb from the lap of her tan woollen skirt. 'I thought you might know more about that than I do, Mrs Moffatt. He seems to spend a great deal of his time in this house. I expect he confides in you – since you're an older woman.'

The barb went home; she saw the colour in Isla Moffatt's cheeks deepen. 'He does call in frequently, but he's said nothing to me. And I'm quite sure that he doesn't keep secrets from you.'

Phemie's hand again whisked across her skirt. 'The fact is, Mrs Moffatt, my husband and I would both like to see our son settling down, instead of gallivanting around with this girl and that. He never used to be so – so flighty.'

Amusement danced into her hostess's eyes, and was suppressed. 'I never thought of Colin as being flighty,' she observed mildly.

'Nor I, until recently. I take it he talks to you about his thoughts, his hopes for the future?'

'From time to time, as friends do.'

Phemie pounced. 'Friends?'

Isla Moffatt regarded her for a moment, then said, 'You might as well speak your mind, Mrs Forbes, rather than dancing around your reason for calling.'

Phemie, who had been raised to believe that 'dancing around', as the younger woman put it, was the correct thing to do, blinked, then rallied. 'Very well, if you prefer it. It seems to us, Mrs Moffatt,' she stated, invoking Gilchrist's support, confident that if she had told him what was on her mind, he would have agreed with her, 'that Colin spends altogether too much time in this house. Folk are beginning to talk.'

'I'd have thought that with all the troubles in the world just now folk would have more to gossip about than friendships.'

'There's bound to be talk when one of the friends is a respectable young bachelor of good family, and the other an older woman with—'

'With a past?'

'With two growing children!' Phemie snapped. 'It's time Colin was settling down.'

Colour surged into Isla's face, and her hands, bare except for Kenneth McAdam's gold band on one finger – a ring he had had no right to put there, Phemie reminded herself – gripped the arms of her chair. 'I can assure you, Mrs Forbes, that there has been no talk of marriage between your son and myself. We've never even considered such a thing.'

'It's time Colin did consider it, and there are plenty of young women in Paisley who are eminently suitable.' Over the past five years Colin had brought some of them home – pretty girls of good family, just the right age to start bearing his children, and in many cases clearly willing to walk down the aisle of Paisley Abbey by his side. But one by one they had drifted away, married other women's sons, presented other women with grandchildren. 'You must tell him to stop calling and look elsewhere for his – friends,' Phemie said flatly, and Isla Moffatt put her cup down and got to her feet.

'Now that you've said what you came to say, Mrs Forbes, I think you should go.'

'I intend to.' Phemie began to struggle out of the chair, which showed a tendency to want to keep her within its soft depths. Eventually, she had to suffer the indignity of taking her hostess's proffered hand, and being helped to her feet.

In the hall, accepting her wrap, she said with as much dignity as she could muster, 'I hope that you'll pay heed to what I've had to say.'

'I can assure you of that,' said Isla Moffatt, opening the door.

Comfortable living had piled weight on Phemie Forbes as the years went by. As a result, her self-righteous, straight-backed march down the path to the waiting car appeared, from where Isla stood on the porch, more like the waddling of an elderly, contented bear; a bear with short legs and only a patch of gleaming fur left across the shoulders.

But Isla was in no mood to be amused by the thought. She was embarrassed, confused, and very angry, although she wouldn't for the world have let Colin's mother know that. As the car drove off with Phemie, in the back seat, resolutely staring ahead,

Barbara arrived at the gate, her schoolbag dangling from one hand, her skirt swirling round legs that seemed to be growing longer by the month. Ross was immediately behind her, and as Barbara opened the gate he tried to squeeze past. The two of them, jammed in the narrow gap, squabbled briefly before breaking free and scurrying up the garden path, both starting to talk about their day at school as soon as they saw their mother standing on the porch.

They were unmistakably Kenneth McAdam's children, Isla thought as she watched them come towards her. Although twelve-year-old Barbara's eyes were brown, like her own, her expressions were Kenneth's. She also had his enthusiasm for life, and the same swinging, easy stride that had caused the breath to catch in Isla's throat the first time she saw Ainslie walking towards her. Isla's dark hair had tempered Kenneth's red-gold head to produce, in their daughter, a rich, striking auburn.

Ross had Kenneth's blazing red hair and pale skin and light blue eyes, and he also had the more serious side of his father's nature. There were times, when he pulled at his lower lip and drew his brows down in thought, when strong memories of the man she still thought of as her husband flooded back to Isla.

'That was Colin's mother, wasn't it?' Barbara asked as she reached the porch. 'I remember seeing him with her in the town.' Her gaze was direct, just like Kenneth's. 'What did she want?'

'She was just visiting.'

'Why?' asked Ross. 'She's never visited you bef—'

'Upstairs, the two of you, and change out of your

school clothes.' Isla scooped them before her into the house. 'I've got work to do.'

'I'm too weak with hunger to climb the stairs,' announced Barbara, who possessed an excellent appetite, yet never seemed to put on any weight. Her brother was already on his way to the kitchen, where Nan, who had moved in as housekeeper when Isla's work had begun to take up most of her time, would be putting out milk and scones. The children always came home from school hungry.

'Five minutes – then upstairs and get some work done before teatime,' Isla called after them, then went into her favourite room, the dolls'-house workshop opposite the living-room.

Its cream-painted walls were lined with counters holding a variety of miniature houses, boxes of materials, small pots of paint or glue, and books on furniture and fashions. In the window recess Mabel Torrance, the seamstress who had worked full-time for Isla for the past eighteen months, sat at one of the two sewing machines. She smiled at her employer, then went back to her work. Isla sat down at the desk in one corner, where she had been planning a new house when Colin's mother had interrupted her.

She picked up her pencil, put it down, and started riffling through one of the books, staring blankly at the pages without seeing them. Instead, Phemie Forbes' visit played itself over and over again in her mind, like one of the films she occasionally took the children to see.

The whole episode had been just like a film, she thought – unreal, the sort of thing that didn't really happen. Only it had happened. She gave up all pretence of looking for something, and let the book in front of her lie where it had fallen open. After Ainslie's departure for Canada, Colin, in the double role of Isla's lawyer and Ainslie's friend, had helped Isla to settle in the Castlehead house. He had advised her on business matters as the demand for her work grew, suggesting and drawing up a contract between her and Mr Leckie, the toyshop owner.

It was Colin who had suggested having leaflets advertising her work printed and distributed to attract more clients, Colin who had taught her how to cope with the paperwork as orders started to come direct to her home. He had somehow drifted into the habit of calling in once or twice a week, occasionally taking them out in his car, even helping now and again with homework. As Ross grew from toddler to schoolboy, Colin had become, in some ways, the father-figure Ross had never known.

But nothing more than a friend. In the years following Ainslie's departure for Canada, he had plunged into the local social life and, to his mother's delight, had become one of the town's most eligible bachelors, often bringing the latest conquest to visit Isla and see the dolls' houses.

'It's more comfortable here,' he had said when she pointed out that his mother might prefer to play hostess to his friends. 'Mother would pry and simper, and probably start planning wedding outfits. Anyway, I need someone like you to tell me who should be taken to meet her, and who should be kept well away from her.'

After each introduction, he inevitably asked for Isla's

opinion of the latest girl. She enjoyed meeting them all, and became genuinely fond of one or two, but stead-fastly refused to criticise any of them, insisting that he must make his own judgements. After a few weeks, or, at most, a few months, the current girl would disappear, to be replaced by someone else.

'She was too possessive,' Colin would say vaguely, sprawling at his ease in Isla's comfortable living-room. Or, 'She giggled too much,' or perhaps, 'She began to get that engagement-ring gleam in her eyes.'

'You must stop comparing them all with Ainslie,' Isla told him one day, and he stared at her, astonished.

'You think I do that?'

'Of course you do. It's not fair to them, Colin. People deserve to be judged on their own merits.'

'Mmmm,' Colin said, and gradually, fewer girl-friends had been brought to Castlehead for Isla's inspection. She hadn't even realised that, until now.

'People are bound to talk – a respectable young bach-elor of good family – an older woman . . .' Phrases the older woman had used came back to her as she stared down at the open book, taking on new meaning, turning an easy, happy friendship into something suspect and distasteful.

'I'll see you tomorrow morning, Mrs Moffatt.' Isla came back to the present with a jerk. Mabel was cover-ing the sewing machine, which meant that it was five o'clock.

'Yes, Mabel, thanks.' She rubbed a hand over her eyes, then panic flared through her as she heard a man's voice in the hall, talking to Mabel. Colin sometimes looked in on his way home from the office.

Isla stood up, almost knocking the book to the ground. She couldn't face him now – she needed time to think things through—

But when the door opened it was Drew Brown who came in, pulling his jacket on over his overalls. 'That's me away home. I've varnished the table, it'll be dry by tomorrow.' He looked down at the open book and gave a low whistle. 'That'll take some work. Still, I reckon I could manage it.'

Isla, glancing down, saw that the book had fallen open at the picture of an elaborate three-seated chair in green velvet.

'I've not decided, Drew, so don't worry your head about it yet.' She closed the book. 'You go off and enjoy your evening at the theatre with Mary.'

'I will. G'night, then.' He went off, whistling cheerfully.

Only days after Isla had left George Street, Drew had come shyly to Castlehead to offer to go on making furniture for her.

'I'd not want to get you into trouble with your neighbours, Drew.'

'Ach, what happened was just a storm in a teacup. My mam and me both think it's only right for me tae go on helping ye, seeing as it was you that got our roof fixed,' he had said, standing in the hall, twisting his cap round and round in his hands. 'Anyway, I like making the wee furniture.'

For three years he had worked for Isla in the evenings and weekends. As the orders began to flow in she had become increasingly dependent on the young man's talents, and when he was dismissed from the joinery shop after finishing his apprenticeship, Colin had suggested that she employ Drew herself.

He had scribbled figures on paper, convincing her that she could afford to pay Drew, suggesting that the carriage-house, still packed with its former owner's rubbish, could be pressed into service.

Between them, Drew and Colin had turned the carriage-house into a decent workshop, and Drew had settled in happily. Now, two years later, he had become an essential part of Isla's life, thanks to Colin.

Isla bit her lip realising that, unbidden, Colin had managed to steal back into her thoughts. He would have to go, not just from her mind, but from her life. It would be hard to turn her back on him, for although she knew a lot of people now – neighbours, clients, acquaintances – her only close friends were Colin, Ainslie, far away in Canada with her husband and twin sons, and Flora Currie, who had become frighteningly frail during the past year. But if, as his mother had said, folk were gossiping, a break had to be made. Since Kenneth's death, Isla had developed a dislike, almost a fear, of being talked about.

She heard the children leaping down the staircase on their way to the kitchen for tea, and was grateful beyond measure for their existence, their casual conviction that life would never change. As long as Ross and Barbara were in her world, she would never be alone, or lonely.

Cheered by that thought, Isla squared her shoulders and went out to meet her children in the hall.

27

With relief, Isla remembered during tea that that evening Colin, who had joined the Territorial Army as Britain uneasily watched the steady growth of strength and power in Germany, would be attending the weekly meeting in their headquarters, and wouldn't come to Low Road.

Too restless to sit and read after the evening meal, she went into the garden with the intention of tiring herself out with some brisk weeding. Ross was playing with several other boys in a garden further along the road, and as she worked, Isla could hear their voices on the soft evening air, while the beautiful, sad strains of 'Ol' Man River', floated from the open window of Barbara's room. A steady stream of girls, like a line of ants, had begun to converge on the house immediately after tea, trotting up the stairs to Barbara's room to rehearse yet another of her concerts.

Aunt Lally had died in 1934, leaving everything she had to Barbara and Ross. Isla had put the proceeds of the sale of the flat and the furniture, together with the little money her aunt had left, into trust for the children, but Barbara had insisted on keeping all Lally's scrapbooks and sheet music. A cupboard had had to be bought specially to house it all in her room. She used the music for her concerts, which had already raised considerable sums of money for various charities.

After her sudden, enforced move to Low Road, Isla had decided – largely on Colin's and Flora's advice – to keep Barbara at the West School, rather than unsettle the child by moving her elsewhere. Once they were away from George Street, the animosity Barbara had begun to experience in the school playground had ebbed away, and in no time at all she was bringing her former friends from the street home to play at the end of each school day.

Greta and, once she began to go to school, Daisy, were among the group. Only weeks after the 'flitting', Isla had encountered Magret in a shop, and her former neighbour had greeted her as though nothing had happened.

'Ach, life's too short tae bear a grudge,' she had declared, her face wreathed in smiles. 'It's only sour-faces like that Mrs Leach that never forget. Mrs Leach, and elephants, eh?'

Since then, Magret had called in at Low Road now and again, refusing to sit anywhere but in the kitchen, where she and Isla and, eventually, Nan, enjoyed many a cosy gossip over a cup of tea. With Daisy at school, Magret had gone back to work in the mills, only five minutes' walk from Low Road. She was saving hard in the hope of moving to a better house. There was a good chance, being overcrowded, that the McDougalls would get a house in the new scheme at Ferguslie Park, but Magret wanted to stay near the mills and near her friends and neighbours. She had her eye on a rented flat further along George Street, on the other side of Maxwellton Street.

In June, Barbara's stint at the West School had come to an end, and now, in early September, she and Greta had just started attending Camphill Secondary School. Most of the Low Road children were attending the John Neilston Institution or the Grammar School, both fee-paying, but Barbara insisted on staying with her former classmates, and Isla, who would have found it difficult to pay school fees as well as wages for Drew and Mabel, had been content to go along with her daughter's wishes.

All Barbara asked of her friends was that they were willing to take part in her back-court concerts, now back-garden concerts. As a result, the children who marched up the path most evenings and weekends were a mixture from the Paisley schools, and at each of Barbara's concerts, held in the garden in fine weather and the living-room in bad weather, mothers from comfortable homes and cramped tenements gossiped and laughed and applauded side by side.

Isla straightened up, rubbing at her back. It was almost dark now, and the house-lights looked inviting. There was just a touch of autumn in the air, the slightest hint of approaching winter. As she gathered up her trowel and fork and locked them in the little shed, then walked down the path towards the house, the turmoil Phemie Forbes had caused began to fade away.

'I don't know, Drew,' Isla said the next day, studying the sketches Drew had made of the three-seater chair he had seen in the furniture book the day before. 'It looks very complicated to me.'

Glancing up at Drew, she could tell by the gleam in his eyes that he had already made up his mind. Drew loved a challenge.

'Not when you think of it piece by piece. It'd look bonny in that fancy house you're doing for – oh hullo, Mr Forbes.'

Isla, taken off guard, spun round to see Colin leaning against the frame of the open carriage-house door, grinning at her. 'What are you doing here at this time of day?' she asked sharply, and his eyebrows rose.

'I'm running the old man home for some lunch because his own car's having some work done on it. I thought I'd look in and ask if you and the kids want to go to the Regal tonight.'

'John Gilbert,' Drew said enthusiastically. 'I've seen it, it's good.'

'No, I don't think so.'

'It's Friday – no school tomorrow.'

'We're already going out.'

'Where?'

'Just out.' She bustled Colin out of the workshop, blinking in the sunshine. 'Look, I'm really busy, and your father's waiting . . .'

'Is there something up?'

'Of course not.'

'Then come to the cinema. The kids'll enjoy it—'

'I told you, I'm busy, we're going out.' She had managed to get him as far as the gate, but as she moved to open it, Colin put his hand on the top rail, preventing her.

'There *is* something wrong.'

'It's nothing – just . . .' she wavered, then said in a

rush of words, 'you spend too much time with us, Colin.'

This time his eyebrows soared. 'I enjoy your company, and Barbara's, and Ross's.'

'But we've all got our own lives to lead. We can't be in each other's pockets all the time.' She glanced up at him, and saw the smile die out of his eyes.

'In other words, I've outstayed my welcome.'

'Colin, I'm very grateful for all you've done for me – for us – but—'

'But you'd prefer not to be – pestered.'

'I didn't say . . .' Isla began, then, realising that he had offered her a way out of her dilemma, and she must take it, she said lamely, 'well, yes.'

'You should have said something.'

'I just have,' she said to a spot just beyond his right shoulder.

'So you have.' His voice was cold now. She risked a swift glance at him, and saw that he was looking at her just as he had at their very first meeting. Then, she hadn't understood why. Now, she did.

'Colin, I really am very grateful for—'

'Good day, Isla,' he said, and turned away, striding out of the garden and along the road towards the gate that led to the main road and his car and his father and his real life.

It was over, just like that. She had expected an argument, perhaps even a quarrel, but now she realised that that wasn't Colin's way. He had his pride, and if he felt that he wasn't wanted, that was that. It had happened swiftly and easily, and as she turned back to the carriage-house and Drew, she told herself that she should be glad of that, at least.

Before she reached the carriage-house, the sun had gone in behind a cloud.

A week dragged by. The invigorating tingle that had been in the air as summer's dying blended with winter's approach vanished, washed away by drizzling, constant rain. Barbara and Ross came home from school each day soaked to the skin, and squabbled a lot because Ross hated to be indoors all the time. Drew was depressed because the little Victorian loveseat had proved to be too difficult for him after all, and a very particular customer made a fuss over a dolls' house that wasn't ready on the agreed date. It seemed to Isla that everything was going wrong, and the low cloud and persistent rain made her feel tired and despondent.

The previous winter had laid both Flora and Annie low with 'flu; Flora had battled her way through it, but despite all that Isla and the doctor could do, Annie had developed pneumonia and died.

Isla had found another housekeeper, kindly and efficient, but although the woman did everything she could to make Flora comfortable and content, it wasn't the same, and a lot of Flora's old fire and drive had evaporated.

'It's the fighting I miss,' she confided in Isla when she paid her usual daily visit. 'Whenever I snap at Betty her lip trembles and she almost turns cartwheels trying to please me. Annie knew how to give as good as she got.' Her green eyes, still lovely although the sparkle had gone from them, were wistful. 'You know you're still alive when you're having a good quarrel.'

Then she leaned forward in her chair and fixed her

gaze on Isla. 'You've heard my grouse against life, now tell me yours.'

'I don't have any, other than being tired of this wet weather.'

'Something's been troubling you for the past week, lassie, and it's not the rain. Anyone living in this part of the world should be used to that. Come on now, what is it?'

'It's nothing.'

'Fiddlesticks! But if you won't say, you won't. Go ahead and treat me like a stranger, see if I care,' Flora said with an echo of the little girl she had once been.

'You do so care,' Isla mimicked the childish note in the old woman's voice, and Flora grinned at her.

'Of course I do, you daft lassie. Is that not what friends are for?'

'I'm just being silly. Colin's mother called on me last week and she's got some daft notion in her head that I'm getting in the way of him finding himself a suitable wife. It upset me a bit.'

Flora snorted. 'Phemie Forbes was always kind-hearted, I'll give her that, but as thick as a plank, even as a young woman. You're surely not going to take any heed of what she says?'

'Flora, she said that folk have started to talk. I don't want to be the subject of gossip, I've had my share of that.'

'Gossip should always be ignored, even if it's telling the truth,' Flora said blithely. 'Have you talked to Colin about this?'

'I've spoken to him, but I couldn't bring myself to tell him what his mother had said. I just said that I didn't want him to come to the house so often.'

'That's a fine thing to say to a man whose got his pride. So he's not been back since?'

'No.'

'I'm not surprised. So that's why you've been going about with a face like a wet washing. You're missing him.'

'I'm not – but I enjoy his company, and the children like him. They've been asking about him, and I don't know what to tell them. I didn't mean that he shouldn't come at all, just that he shouldn't come so often.' Under the steady green gaze, Isla floundered, then said feebly, 'Mebbe I didn't make myself clear.'

'And mebbe you don't even know what you want yourself,' Flora said dryly.

'I just want to live my life in peace, without folk talking about me.' Isla got to her feet and roamed about Flora's drawing-room restlessly. 'Oh, I wish his mother had never come near me!'

'Poor Phemie.'

'Why? She's got what she wanted. She must be really pleased with herself.'

'For the moment, mebbe. But she'd have been well advised to tend to her own business and let Colin tend to his. He's old enough. Sometimes,' said Flora, 'if you throw a stone in the wrong place, it comes bouncing back and hits you. Phemie should have thought about that before opening her mouth.'

Mercifully, the rain stopped on the following day and the weather brightened. Over the next two days the sun, together with a fresh, drying wind, made it possible for the once-a-week gardener Isla employed to gather up the fallen leaves and old vegetation and burn them at the bottom of the garden. The bonfire smouldered all afternoon, scenting the air with its smoke, and after the children had gone to bed Isla went out to make sure that it had died down.

Dawdling back up towards the house, she stopped halfway to sink down on to the swing that Colin had put up for the children years earlier, resting her heels on the grass and letting the swing drift to and fro, trying to slough off the lethargy that was still troubling her.

She was just beginning to feel the tension easing from her body when a voice from the darkness said, 'Isla Moffatt, just what the hell are you playing at?'

Her startled reaction sent the swing spinning, and she might have hit her shoulder against the wooden supports if Colin hadn't caught at the ropes and steadied her. Still holding them, standing so close that she could smell the familiar, comforting smell of soap and tobacco from him, he said again, 'What are you playing at?'

'What are you talking about?'

'Don't pretend. Did Ross not tell you I met him this afternoon?'

'No.' Trapped by his body, she had to crane her head back painfully to look up at him.

'He stopped to watch me playing cricket on his way home from school. I went over to talk to him and he happened to mention that my mother had called on you last week – the day before you decided that you didn't want me hanging around any more.'

His head was a dark mass, surrounded, from her viewpoint, by stars. 'I did not say—'

He gave the ropes a little shake, and the swing jiggled. Their knees were pressed together, and she could feel the warmth of his legs against hers. 'That's what it sounded like. I thought . . .' he stopped, then said, 'I thought you must have met someone, some man.'

'It was nothing to do with another man! You've been very good to us, Colin, but you've got your own life to live, and your own friends and interests—'

'And my own right to choose my friends?'

'Yes, but . . .'

'Thank you for that concession, at least.' At last he released the ropes and took a turn away from her, towards the edge of the lawn.

'Poor Mother,' Colin said out of the darkness as Isla got up from the swing, rubbing at the back of her neck, 'she never could understand that actions must have consequences.'

A breeze rustled the bushes and Isla shivered. 'I'm going indoors. D'you want some tea?' she asked automatically.

'I want you to hear me out first. You listened to my mother, so it's only fair that you listen to me.' Colin took her place on the swing. 'It wasn't until Ross told me about Mother's visit that I realised how wise she had been.'

'Wise?'

He edged the swing seat back until he was almost upright, supported by his feet on the ground. 'Very wise. She'd sensed something that I hadn't, fully. That I'm in love with you.'

'You – what?' Isla couldn't have been more astonished if the stars had suddenly swooped down to turn the garden into a circus ring.

'Think about it, Isla. Would I have kept coming here all those years if I didn't love you?'

'That's nonsense,' she said briskly, sounding, to her own ears, just like Flora. 'You think of me as a – an older sister. Why else would you bring all your girlfriends to this house and ask for my opinion about them?'

'Exactly. I put that very question to myself, and the answer was so obvious that I can't think why neither of us saw it before. You once accused me of looking for another Ainslie, remember?'

'Yes,' Isla said cautiously.

'Yet none of the girls I brought here were redheads, were they? They were all dark, like you. I suppose,' Colin mused, 'that I must have been making comparisons, and each time I found the others lacking, and stopped seeing them. The only woman I kept on seeing was you, Isla Moffatt, because the only woman I wanted to see was you – and my clever little mother was the first to see it.'

'Have you been drinking?'

'Not a drop. Oh, I thought about it, after you sent me away and I thought that perhaps you'd found someone else. But I didn't get around to it, thank God. Nor did I realise why I felt so miserable until I met up with young Ross. Talk about babes and sucklings,' said Colin with sudden jubilation. 'I'm going to take that lad out on Saturday and buy him a Knickerbocker Glory, whether you approve or not.'

'You have been drinking! And I'm going indoors n—'

Colin lifted both feet and the swing, released, soared through the air. As it reached the end of its curve, he let the ropes go and landed lightly in front of Isla, who

333

was turning towards the house. Before she had time to utter more than a faint squeak, she had been spun round and into his arms.

Her first thought was that it was all wrong to be kissed by a man who was almost like a brother. Her second thought, arriving almost immediately on the heels of the first, was how wonderful it was to be kissed passionately after all those years of abstinence, and to want to dissolve in the kiss and return it fourfold.

'It's all wrong,' she said shakily when he finally released her.

'No it isn't, it's all very right,' Colin whispered, and kissed her again.

'You're younger than I am,' she protested a few minutes later.

'Only by a couple of years. And before you think of any more objections, let me say that I like your children, and I'd enjoy being their stepfather. Think about young Ross, surrounded by women,' he urged, his mouth moving against her ear, sending ripples of desire through her awakening body. 'It's your duty to bring a man into his life, and I'm recommending myself for the position. Officially, on Forbes and Son headed office notepaper, if you insist.'

'Your father—'

'Who cares?' Colin kissed her again, and again she melted into his arms, her mouth softening and opening beneath his. The past week's depression had vanished, to be replaced by joy that seemed to bubble up from the depths of her body to fill her with golden fire.

'Your mother,' she protested weakly, 'will be dreadfully upset.'

'I'll buy her a Knickerbocker Glory too,' Colin promised. 'If it wasn't for her, heaven knows how long it would have taken us to realise how much we needed each other.'

'You can't be serious,' Phemie Forbes whimpered the next morning, a piece of toast falling from her fingers.

Colin beamed at her. 'I've never been more serious in my life, Mother.'

'But – an older woman, with two children! A woman who's—'

'Who's what? Who's struggled against incredible odds to raise her family with no help from anyone? A woman who's built up a business and earned respect from the community?'

'She's tricked you into this!'

'I'm thirty-two years old, Mother. If I was as easily led as you seem to think, I'd have been married to some scheming minx years ago. As for being tricked, it took me some time to talk Isla into accepting me.'

'Gilchrist,' Phemie appealed frantically, 'make him come to his senses before it's too late!'

'You've already done that yourself, Mother,' Colin told her, then, as she stared blankly, 'because of your visit, she sent me packing, and that was when I realised how much I wanted to be with her. I'll never be able to thank you enough for that.'

'Gilchrist!' Phemie almost screamed through the lacy handkerchief clutched to her mouth. 'I demand that you speak to your son!'

'My dear, Colin's old enough to make his own decisions,' Gilchrist Forbes pointed out, then, as the door slammed behind his wife, he laid down his fork and sighed. 'God knows if she'll ever get over this.'

'She'll have to. I meant what I said, Father, I won't give Isla up.'

The older man's brow was furrowed. 'Colin, you'll be taking on all the responsibilities of a ready-made family. Are you quite sure that Isla Moffatt means that much to you?'

'I've no doubt of it. I'd like you both to be happy for me, but if needs be, I can do without your approval. I'm going to marry Isla, as soon as possible.'

Gilchrist pushed back his chair, eyeing his half-eaten breakfast with regret. 'In that case,' he said, 'the sooner I can bring Phemie round to the idea, the better.'

28

Isla opened her eyes to darkness and the soft murmuring of the River Clyde breaking against the shore across the road from the Helensburgh hotel where she and Colin had spent their three-day honeymoon. In a few hours they would be on their way back to Paisley, back to Low Road and the children and their new life together.

Although their bodies weren't touching in the large bed she could feel his warmth lapping against her just as the broad river outside lapped the shore. Isla smiled drowsily and wriggled across the mattress until she could feel his body against hers. In spite of the chill November weather they had had three wonderful days, walking and driving together, talking, laughing, getting to know each other in an entirely new way. And there had been three wonderful nights, too, rediscovering the joy of lying in a man's arms, of loving and being desirable and loved, a luxury that she had thought would never be hers again.

They had been married quietly in the vestry of Oakshaw West Church, the church Colin's parents worshipped in, with Barbara and Ross present, and Mabel and a friend of Colin's standing as witnesses. They would have liked Ainslie and Phil to be their witnesses, but the Hannigans' twin sons had just started school, and Ainslie was reluctant to leave them with Phil's sister at such a time.

The reception had been held at Low Road. Phemie Forbes, who had no option but to accept the marriage once she realised that her son wasn't going to change his mind, had wanted to hold the reception in her home, but Colin refused.

'Miss Currie isn't strong enough to go to Stanley Drive, and we both want her to be there, so it has to be in Low Road,' he said firmly, and Phemie had no option but to give in, and be a guest at the home of her new daughter-in-law.

'You look very – pretty, my dear,' she said graciously, eyeing the pale blue wool and angora dress that Barbara had helped Isla to choose. Barbara had insisted on the hat to go with it – a slouched felt decorated with a jaunty curve of dark blue feathers. Isla had settled it at an angle on her dark head with foreboding, but when she saw the look in Colin's eyes when she stepped from the hired car at the church, she knew that Barbara had been right.

Phemie presented a powdered cheek, and Isla dutifully kissed it, knowing that Colin's mother would never fully accept her as a member of the Forbes family.

Flora, on the other hand, had regained all her former animation for the wedding reception, her cheeks flushed and her green eyes sparkling. 'I knew you two were right for each other,' she said smugly, surveying the couple before her. Colin, laughing, put an arm about his wife's shoulders.

'I wish you'd told me, then, instead of letting me waste all those years blundering about in the dark.'

'Och, I knew you'd find out for yourself eventually. Best to let things work out naturally. Anyway, you've got the rest of your lives together.'

Isla, recalling the words in the dark hotel room, smiled drowsily and brushed her lips against her husband's warm, naked shoulder. He wakened at once, turning over to scoop her into his arms. His face, already scratchy with the night's growth, snuggled against her neck.

'What time is it?'

'Go to sleep,' she whispered. 'It's not morning yet.'

'Good.' His hands slid over the silky nightdress she wore, rousing her body to an instant response. As they met and merged in the bed's warm nest, Isla felt that nothing could ever hurt her again.

In the summer of 1938, Catherine McAdam took a bad stroke and Ainslie, summoned to Scotland, arrived too late to see her mother. After the funeral she and Phil, together with their twin sons, came to Paisley.

'If I'm honest, the only emotion I have is pity,' Ainslie told Isla during one of their long talks together. 'She wouldn't let me love her, but she couldn't stop me from feeling sorry for her. She didn't really have much of a life, did she?'

'By her own choice. She could have got some pleasure out of seeing Mike and Jamie.' Isla had been appalled to hear that when Ainslie offered to bring her sons on a visit while they were still small, Catherine had refused. Ainslie had never made the offer again.

Now, she shrugged. Over the past seven years, she had absorbed much of Phil's easy-going nature. She was more relaxed than Isla had ever seen her, happy in her marriage, and delighted with her active sons. 'That was just Mother. I never could understand her, any more than she could understand me.' She stretched luxuriously. 'Isn't the house lovely and quiet?'

'For once,' Isla agreed. Phil had taken all four children down to the seaside for the day, and Colin was at work. The two women were in the kitchen, Ainslie sitting at the table, Isla icing a cake for the twins, who were to celebrate their sixth birthday in Scotland.

'What affected me most, after the funeral, was realising that I'm the only one left. There we were, the four of us, Mother and Father and me and poor little Innes – I thought that we were there for ever, and now there's only me.'

'And Phil, and Jamie, and Mike,' Isla reminded her. The boys were clearly Phil's sons, wiry and cheerful, but they both had their mother's blue eyes, and Jamie, the younger and slightly smaller twin, had red glints in his thick brown hair.

'And Barbara, and Ross,' Ainslie said. 'I'm their half-sister, remember?' She hesitated, then said carefully, 'They don't know about their father yet, do they?'

'Only that he died when they were both very small. They get on so well with Colin, and I don't want to throw any stones into the pond.'

'But isn't it time they knew the truth? Barbara at least is old enough to understand. She'll be fourteen soon.'

Isla put the icing knife down and wiped her sticky

fingers on a towel. 'I want to be sure that it's the right time – and I want to tell them myself, in my own way.'

Ainslie gave her a long look, then had the sense to change the subject. 'You and Colin are perfect together. I've never seen a couple who looked so right together. You're like—'

'A set of book-ends?'

'What I'm trying to say is that you fit each other. Colin wouldn't have been nearly as happy if he'd married me. I can be prickly at times, but Phil copes so well when I'm being difficult. He knows when to steer clear, and when to tell me to shut up and calm down.'

'He's wonderful. I just wish he would let us pay the proper price for this place.' After their marriage, Colin had tried to persuade Phil to take the market price for Isla's house, but the Canadian refused point-blank.

'We made a deal, and we shook hands on it. If I went back on it now I'd never live it down,' he drawled.

'But when you made the deal Isla was on her own, with very little money. Things have changed now. We can afford to pay the proper price.'

'No way,' Phil said flatly, then added, a gleam in his eye, ' 'Sides, at the time I got a real kick out of telling the folks at home that I'd sold a house for a few dollars. I don't want to ruin my reputation.'

'He's got no intention of taking a penny more for the house,' Ainslie said now. 'As far as Phil's concerned, the deal was fair. Do people still call it the five-shilling mansion?'

'Some, sometimes. It used to bother me, but not any more.'

'Good.' Again, Ainslie stretched her arms catlike over

341

her head, then gave a lazy laugh. 'If anyone had told me eight years ago that I'd move to Canada and settle happily into marriage, I'd have called them a liar. Isn't life strange?'

'Mmmm. But it's good, too.'

Ainslie used a finger to scoop up some icing that had fallen from the knife.

'Very good,' she said indistinctly, but enthusiastically, round the fingertip in her mouth.

The Hannigans tried to persuade Isla and Colin to return to Canada with them for a visit, but Gilchrist Forbes had retired shortly after his son's marriage, and it was difficult for Colin to leave the business just then. Instead it was agreed that the family would spend the following summer in Canada.

But while Isla was enjoying the happiest phase of her life for many years, clouds had begun to gather over Europe. German soldiers had marched into Czechoslovakia; Jews in Germany were being systematically terrorised and stripped of all rights, and by the summer of 1939 it looked as though war was becoming inevitable. The Territorial Army was being strengthened, and as well as finding the task of running the office without his father's presence demanding, Colin found himself spending more time than ever before at Army headquarters as 1939 progressed. Isla, too, was flooded with orders from clients, and before the school holidays arrived it became clear to them both that the planned Canadian holiday would have to be cancelled.

Barbara and Ross, who had been looking forward to

the trip, were heart-broken at the news. 'You promised!' Ross said accusingly, a tremor in his voice.

'I know, but that was before we realised how busy we were going to be,' Isla tried to explain, while Colin chimed in with, 'We'll go next year.'

'That's what you said last year,' Barbara pointed out, tossing her long red hair back over her shoulders.

It was pleated into pigtails for school, and combed out when she came home. Colin reached for a handful and tugged it gently.

'We'll go to North Berwick for two weeks instead. You like it there, don't you?'

'Not as much as we'd like Canada,' she told him sharply, twitching away and jerking her hair free.

'You promised!' Ross said again, his voice breaking and the gathering tears spilling over, despite all his attempts to hold them back. He scrambled to his feet and ran out of the room, banging the door.

Colin put out a restraining hand as Isla began to get to her feet. 'Leave it, love. Let him have a good bawl without being fussed over.'

'Why can't we go on our own?' Barbara persisted. 'I'm old enough to look after the two of us.'

Isla's temper began to rise. She was as disappointed as the children about their cancelled plans. Like them, she had been looking forward to seeing another country, and visiting Ainslie's home. 'For goodness' sake, Barbara, don't be so silly,' she snapped. 'We couldn't possibly do that!'

Barbara scowled, her lower lip pushing itself forward. 'I think it's very unfair!' she said hotly, and flung herself out of the room.

Listening to the sound of her daughter bounding up the stairs, Isla sighed. 'At times like this, you must regret marrying me.'

Colin reached out and raised her hand from the arm of her chair, squeezing it hard. 'Not me. They're disappointed, and who can blame them? But they'll get over it.'

But the children refused to get over it. They moped to school in the mornings and moped back again in the afternoons, long-faced and sulky. They squabbled with each other almost all the time, and refused to become interested in any plans Isla and Colin tried to make for the summer.

Isla had already written to Ainslie to explain the situation, and her reply arrived while both children were still sunk in gloom. 'We're really disappointed about your change of plans, particularly the twins. Phil and I have talked it over, and we think that you should let Barbara and Ross come for the summer anyway. You needn't worry about them travelling alone, it would give me a marvellous excuse to come to Scotland, to bring them back with me. You and Colin could surely take a little while off at the end of August to come over and take them home. It would be better than nothing. Please say yes.'

Luckily, Barbara and Ross were at school when the letter arrived. Isla kept it in her pocket, out of sight, and showed it to Colin that night when the children were in bed.

'I think we should agree,' he said when he had read it.

Isla gaped at him. 'Of course we can't agree! For one

thing, we can't have Ainslie coming all the way here just to fetch them, and for another, it would mean them being far away from us for at least six weeks.'

'I'd rather be apart for six weeks and know they're happy than have them sulking around all summer because we ruined their holiday,' Colin said reasonably. 'It's Ainslie's own idea to come for them, so we're not imposing on her. It sounds as though she'd like the chance to make the trip, and it would be good for them – and for us – to spend a little time apart. You know they'd be safe as houses with her and Phil, and they'd have a wonderful time.'

'But what if the war comes while they're away?'

'I don't think it'll happen all that quickly. We'll have time to fetch them back. I think I should be free by the end of August – it only means asking their schools to let them start the autumn term two weeks later than usual. They'll probably agree to it under the circumstances.'

'But they've never been away from me before,' Isla argued in growing panic. Colin put the letter aside and came to kneel by her chair, his hand warm against her cheek.

'Darling, I know how much they mean to you, and I've not forgotten that time Ainslie's mother tried to take Ross away from you, but that was a long time ago. Barbara's going to be fifteen in August, and Ross is eleven. You can't tie them to your apron-strings for ever.'

'I don't!' she said at once, vehemently. Then, as he said nothing, 'Do I?'

'Not exactly, but you do have a tendency to worry over them like a mother hen.' Colin's voice was light, but with a serious undertone. 'It's understandable, but at the same time, it's not good for them to be over-protected, Isla.'

'I'm going to bed.' She got up quickly, the movement knocking his hand away from her face. Alone in their bedroom, brushing her hair, she stared into her own eyes in the dressing-table mirror. Colin's words had hurt, but they had to be faced.

For years, between the time of Kenneth's death and her marriage to Colin, the children had been her sole responsibility, all that she had. Every meal they ate, each day they survived, had been the result of her efforts. She could still recall, as though it had happened only the day before, the terror of almost losing Ross to Catherine McAdam, and the lesser, but still frightening, threat of losing Barbara to Aunt Lally. But as Colin had pointed out, these fears belonged to the past, to a time of deep insecurity and uncertainty. The children were growing up now, Colin was part of their lives, and Ainslie was nothing like her mother. There was no threat as far as she and Phil were concerned.

The brush slowed, and stopped. When Colin came into the room some time later Isla was still at the dressing-table, gazing into her own reflected eyes. She jumped slightly at the light touch of his hands on her shoulders, looking up to meet his gaze in the glass.

'You're right, I do tend to fret about them too much,' she said slowly, reaching her fingers up to cover his. 'It's time to start letting go.'

The cloud that had been hanging over the household lifted as soon as Barbara and Ross were told that they could spend summer in Canada after all. They immediately began to shower Isla with assurances of their very best behaviour during the visit to Ainslie and Phil.

'If they keep their vows, you'll find yourself playing hostess to a pair of saints,' Isla said wryly to Ainslie when she arrived in Scotland a few days before Barbara and Ross were due to finish school.

'I hope not, I couldn't take the strain. Try to come over before the end of August,' Ainslie coaxed. 'If you wait until then you'll have very little time with us, and I've been so looking forward to introducing you to all our friends.'

'We'll try. But Colin's really busy, and for some strange reason everyone wants to buy dolls' houses – I've never had so many orders all at once.'

'Mebbe they're trying to hold on to the good things of life while they can.'

'You sense it too?'

Ainslie was curled up in an armchair in Isla's living-room, her feet tucked beneath her. She was still lithe, though motherhood and maturity had softened and rounded her body. Her curly red hair had been cut short, framing a tanned face with freckles sprinkled like a drift of gold dust across nose and cheekbones. The twins were also freckled, but much more heavily. 'With more freckle than face,' Barbara had teased them the previous summer.

'It's hard to ignore the atmosphere in this country at the moment. People don't actually come out and talk about the possibility of a war, but I can see it in their eyes, hear it in their voices.' She gave a sudden, involuntary shiver. 'We talk about it in Canada, too, but the threat of it seems to feel closer here. Britain's such a small country, and everything's more concentrated in a place that's surrounded by water.' She shivered again, then, said briskly, 'Listen to me – all gloom and doom. It probably won't come to anything, and the children'll have a wonderful time with us, I promise.'

Upstairs, a door opened and shut loudly several times. Voices clamoured shrilly above the noise of feet thundering down the stairs and across the hall. The front door opened, then closed, and the voices rocketed past the window, fading as the group of boys, led by eleven-year-old Ross, ran round the house to the back garden.

'Are you quite sure you want to take on the responsibility of my two?' Isla asked as the noise died away. 'Ross never seems to tire, and Barbara can be quite an insufferable little madam at times.'

'It'll be fine, don't worry. There's lots of space at home to run wild in, and Phil's great with kids. He knows when to put his foot down without stamping on anyone. As for Barbara – I'll enjoy getting to know my kid sister,' Ainslie said.

She and the children sailed from Greenock a week later. Ross, who hadn't quite shaken off the little-boy look, and was chubbily cherubic in grey shorts and a grey jacket over shirt and tie, couldn't wait to start the great adventure that lay before him. He gave Isla then Colin a strangling hug, then raced up the gangplank of the steamer waiting to take the passengers out to the Tail of the Bank, where the liner lay. One sock, Isla noticed as she watched him go, was already coming down, and his ginger hair had broken free of the cold-water combing she had given it not much more than an hour earlier.

Barbara, already a stranger in her first grown-up costume, hugged her mother, then Colin, more sedately, but with warmth.

'I'll write every week – I'll tell you everything that happens,' she promised.

'And I'll make sure she does – that they both do,' Ainslie said. 'Don't fret. And take good care of yourself, and each other.' She hugged them both, then said in a choked voice, 'Come on, Barbara, let's go and get it over with. I hate goodbyes. They make me cry, and I hate crying even more than I hate goodbyes!'

As the two of them went towards the gangplank, Barbara's flared skirt swung round slim, sleekly stockinged legs and the sun sparked red lights from her hair, peeping out from beneath the green beret set stylishly to one side. Isla had never felt so desolate in her life. She clung to Colin's arm, convinced that if she didn't restrain herself she would run up the gangplank and snatch her children back.

'They change so quickly,' she said tearfully as she and Colin drove home after watching the liner move regally down-river towards the open sea, tugs fussing round her. 'They'll be entirely different by the time we see them again!'

'It won't be all that long. We'll be joining them in a matter of weeks,' Colin reassured her. 'In the meantime, just think about the fun we're going to have, with some time to ourselves for a change. It'll be like being newly-weds. We'll start tonight – I'll take you out for dinner in a restaurant, somewhere special, with candles on the table.'

That summer seemed to pass more swiftly than any other. In August, Barbara celebrated her fifteenth birthday in Canada, and Ainslie and Phil gave her a big party. Judging by the letters they wrote every week, both children were having a wonderful time.

But the news from Europe grew more ominous, with the Germans poised to march into Poland. Towards the end of August it became clear that Colin wouldn't be able to get away from the office after all, and Isla would have to go to Canada on her own. But when she tried to book a passage, she discovered that all the shipping lines were busy because of a flood of bookings from Canadians returning home, and parents sending their children away from Britain to the safety of another country.

Reluctantly, because she had never flown before, she tried the airlines, only to find that they were in the same situation.

'If it comes to it, you could go on a one-way ticket,' Colin suggested. 'I'd rather have the three of you safe in Canada if we do go to war.'

'I don't like the idea of leaving you here on your own for goodness knows how long,' she said, then tried to make light of the situation. 'Your mother would probably start introducing you to eligible young women as soon as my back was turned.'

'Oh, I think she's realised by now that I'm a very married man.'

'I'm not so sure,' Isla said dryly. Since the wedding,

she and Phemie Forbes had only met each other when they had to, and on those few occasions there was still a coolness in the air. It was clear that Phemie could not get over her disappointment at her son's choice of wife.

'Isla, I may not be here for long.'

'But you're thirty-four, Colin. They'll be calling up younger men, surely.'

'I'm not exactly Methuselah,' he protested, then, his smile fading, 'I'm in the Territorials, love. I've been trained, and if they want me, I'm willing to go.'

'What about the business?'

'My father's going to come out of retirement, so that he can take over when the time comes. We've already discussed it and I think he's quite excited at the thought of being in the office again. So you see, you might be left here alone. At least in Canada you'd be with the children.'

'If it comes to war, the children will be fine with Ainslie. And if you do go away, I'd want to be here for you when you have leave. Anyway, there's Flora to consider – I'd not leave her now, after all she's done for me.'

Ainslie phoned, her voice crackly and distant, coming and going as though the telephone cable was being swung to and fro on waves, to say that she had investigated the possibility of bringing Barbara and Ross back to Scotland herself, only to find, as Isla had, that liners and aeroplanes alike were fully booked. Ross and Barbara both spoke to their mother, sounding excited at the prospect of staying on in Canada for longer than planned. Ainslie had taken the first step towards

351

enrolling them in local schools, just in case, and Ross was looking forward to that.

'It won't be like being in school at home, because of them sounding different because they're Canadians,' he explained.

Barbara at least had the tact to say, just before the call ended, 'We miss you both, Mum, but everything's fine here, and it won't be for long, will it?'

'Not long,' Isla agreed, praying that she was telling the truth.

Colin, struck to the heart by the look on her face as she put down the phone, redoubled his efforts to get her to Canada, and almost managed to get her a berth on the liner *Athenia*. But even as Isla was packing for the trip the booking fell through, and the liner sailed without her.

Two days later, the German army marched into Poland, and Britain declared war.

'There's still the chance of getting the children back,' Isla said hopefully as Colin switched off the wireless, Neville Chamberlain's war announcement still ringing in their ears. 'Surely nothing will happen for a little while. I'll keep trying.'

On the following evening Colin came into the kitchen where Isla and Nan were getting the evening meal ready, his face like stone.

'Look . . .' He held his newspaper out and Isla took it, sinking into a chair as she read the headlines. The *Athenia*, packed with passengers, had been torpedoed on the previous day, only hours after Britain had declared war on Germany. More than a hundred people had died, including children on their way to safety in Canada.

'That's that,' Colin said flatly. 'You stay here, and Barbara and Ross stay with Ainslie, until this business is over.'

Later, in the privacy of their bedroom, he said wretchedly, 'Isla, I'm so sorry. I should never have talked you into letting them go. If it hadn't been for me, they'd be here, with us. I should have known better!'

'You weren't to know that things were going to happen so quickly. And you were right – it was time they learned to spend time away from me.' She summoned up a smile. 'We're more fortunate than some of those poor souls that are having to send their children away from the cities without knowing who they're going to. Barbara and Ross will be fine with Ainslie and Phil – they'll look on the whole thing as an adventure.'

But behind the smile was the icy realisation that the die was cast, and her children thousands of miles away from her, perhaps for years. There was no chance, now, of getting them back until the matter was resolved. Isla kept on smiling reassuringly into Colin's worried, guilty face, but inside, she felt as though her heart was breaking.

Paisley, like every other town in Britain, seethed with preparations for war. Policemen were to be seen on the streets with gasmasks hanging at their sides and tin helmets slung over their shoulders, and Isla stood in long queues to obtain heavy black curtaining for the windows, and sticky netting which she and Nan and Colin, with Drew's help, put over every window to prevent shards of glass flying into the rooms in the event of the windows being smashed during air-raids. As there was no basement to shelter in if a raid came, she bought a large solid table from Charlie Blayne's auction room and had it placed against the back wall of the living-room.

'It's hideous,' Colin said flatly when he saw it.

'But it's solid. If there's a raid, Nan and I can pull the couch across in front of it and even if the whole window comes in we'll be safe.'

'And if the house collapses about your ears?'

She banged on the table with her knuckles. 'It won't, but even if it does, Nan and I and Flora, if we can get her under it, will be quite safe beneath that table until we're dug out.'

'For God's sake, woman, don't say things like that!' Colin pulled her into his arms and held her tightly. She clung to him, knowing, though she would never admit it to him, that the thought of his going away from her, possibly being badly hurt or killed, was far more frightening than the fear of anything happening to her. For the time being, at least, she had lost her children; she couldn't bear the thought of losing Colin, too.

First Aid posts were set up, one of them in the West School, and Drew came back from registering for the services and proposed to his girlfriend, who accepted him.

'We're not going to get married before I go,' he explained to Isla, shyly but proudly. 'But when I'm away from Paisley it'll be good to know that she's mine. It'll give me something to stay alive for.'

'I hope you both have a very long and happy life together.' On an impulse Isla reached up and kissed Drew, who went crimson and escaped to his workshop

354

as soon as he was released. He was twenty-five now, but, to her, he was still the shy teenager who had helped her to dig the potato patch in George Street. Isla watched him hurry from the room, and hoped that the war might be over soon, before too many young lads like Drew were dragged into it.

A blackout was imposed at once, and by the end of the year a number of local people were among the first victims of the war, some of them knocked down in the darkened night streets by cars and buses and tramcars, others killed or injured by tumbles down narrow stone stairs in unlit tenement buildings. Gas masks were issued and after trying hers on, Isla hurriedly tore herself free of the constricting straps, dragging in gulps of air.

'I'd rather take my chances with the gas!'

'You'll wear that mask if you're told to, for as long as you must,' Colin told her grimly.

'But I couldn't breathe!'

He caught her by the shoulders and shook her. 'Listen, Isla, I've been through a gas tank in training, and believe me, you're much better off with the mask. So wear it!'

Magret, too, hated the gas masks. 'It doesn't seem to bother the lassies,' she said mournfully on a visit to Isla's kitchen. 'They go off every day with their masks over their shoulders in wee cardboard boxes, and not a care in the world, and there's me worried sick, wondering what would be worst – me choking in that nasty smelly thing, or them coming home to find me gassed on the floor,'

'I'll be wearing mine,' Nan said firmly. 'I'm all for

staying alive.' Nan had already volunteered for duty in one of the town's first-aid posts, and was an avid collector of silver paper and waste paper and cardboard for the war effort.

Shy little Mrs Kelly, Mrs Leach's daughter, had given birth to a son almost a year earlier, and to George Street's astonishment, Mrs Leach, the dragon who had been the bane of the street children's lives for many years, had become a doting grandmother. When 'baby helmets', the small compartments intended to hold the entire child and protect it against gas attacks, were made available, Magret's account of helping to fit little Boyd Kelly into his helmet had Isla and Nan in tears of laughter.

'Honest tae God, ye'd need at least a week's warnin' tae get that wean ready,' Magret insisted, elbows on the kitchen table. 'As fast as we got an arm in, a leg popped out. It was like trying tae fit a chicken back intae its egg three days later. What with the wee soul roaring his head off, and Mrs Leach giving orders, the place was in an uproar. Finally she pushes the lot of us out of the road and says she'll dae it herself – you know what she's like, Isla, aye has tae be in charge. Then she lifts the bairn up and starts tellin' him that Gran wants him tae be a good boy and let her tuck him intae the contraption.' She beamed at her listeners. 'That was when his nappy fell off and he peed all down the front of her good blouse.'

Despite all the haste of the war preparations, a strange lethargy fell on the town as 1939 gave way to 1940. Men who had registered for call-up continued to work, and for a while life went on as before. Orders still came in for dolls' houses, and in the little spare time he had, Colin, following exhortations to dig for victory, helped the elderly gardener who came once a week to dig up most of the back lawn and plant vegetables for future consumption. It was like waiting for the starter's gun to start the race, Isla thought, and being unable to move until it was fired.

Canada, too, had declared war on Germany, but to his chagrin, Phil was unable to sign up because of a knee injury he had sustained shortly after the twins' birth, when he had been caught in the path of some timber that had broken loose in his yard.

'He's needed here in any case, because the yard's important to war work,' Ainslie wrote. 'Several of his friends are going, and I've given them all your address in case they ever find themselves in Scotland. Barbara and Ross have settled in very well at school. Barbara's keeping her piano lessons going, as well as studying dancing. She wanted to take singing lessons, too, but Phil and I thought that that might be too much for her to cope with on top of everything else. A music teacher I know heard her sing, and says that she has a natural talent that shouldn't be suppressed, so thankfully Barbara's given up on that idea.'

For their part, Ross and Barbara's letters were filled with enthusiasm and excitement.

'It's all a big adventure to them,' Isla told Magret bleakly. 'They're having a wonderful time.'

'Bairns is like men and pet dogs, hen,' her friend said knowledgeably. 'As long as there's someone around tae keep their bellies filled and give them a fireside tae sit by and a roof over their heads, they're happy enough.

But that doesnae mean they're no' missing ye. They will be, but they'll no' want tae say too much about that, because they know that it'd worry ye. Everything'll turn out fine, you'll see.'

Busy though Colin was with the garden and further training with the Territorials, and with organising the office so that his father could run it in his absence, Isla sensed a growing restlessness about him.

'You can't wait to go, can you?' she asked one evening as they stumbled home arm in arm through the pitch-black night, with only a pencil-thin line of light from a hooded torch to guide them. At Colin's suggestion, they had been to the Regal Cinema to see the Ritz Brothers in *The Three Musketeers*, but even during the film, with people laughing all around them, she had been aware of his tension.

'In one way I don't want to go at all, but in another – well, I've got this daft notion that if I can just get away and do something, the whole rotten business might be over and done with and we can all get on with our lives. I hate all this waiting!'

Isla, who had put her name down with the Nursing Reserve and was waiting to hear from them, understood how he felt. But they had no option but to wait.

Greta reached her fifteenth birthday and went to work in a shop in the High Street. Not long after that, Magret achieved her greatest ambition when she and her family moved into a two-bedroomed flat in a more modern tenement further along George Street. There was a tiny scullery, only large enough for one person at a time, and a bathroom.

With three of the family working, Magret achieved another long-term ambition, and got Tommy's auntie's clock out of the pawnshop. It sat on her new mantelshelf in pride of place – a huge and hideous black marble creation like a Greek temple, complete with a roof and pillars. Magret was in her element.

Isla and Colin celebrated Christmas quietly with Nan and Flora Currie, and early in 1940 the dolls'-house business was put into mothballs when Drew was called up and Mabel went into the Women's Auxiliary Air Force.

In April, Hitler's army invaded Denmark and Norway. Colin was summoned to Aldershot for further orders and Isla started nursing in the Craw Road Sanatorium, about ten minutes' walk away from Low Road.

Suddenly, the starter had fired his pistol, and the grim race to win the war was on.

29

All the sanatorium patients who were well enough to be sent home had gone by the time Isla started work there, and the remainder were put into two small wards. The other wards dealt with a mixture of patients, so that the Royal Alexandra Infirmary, Paisley's largest hospital, could be freed for incoming wounded, or people injured in the air-raids that were already hitting southern England.

As a partially trained nurse, Isla was given the more mundane tasks, fetching and carrying, emptying bedpans, helping to clean the wards and serve meals and bathe patients. But despite that, and despite an aching back and feet that were so sore at the end of a shift that they could scarcely carry her home, she enjoyed being back in a hospital routine. For one thing, it kept her occupied, easing the helpless frustration of missing Colin and the children and worrying about them continuously.

Colin was sent to France, and had scarcely landed there when the German tanks broke through and the British Expeditionary Forces found themselves outnumbered and in retreat. He came home only a month after leaving for Aldershot, with one arm in a sling after being hit by flying shrapnel at Dunkirk, embarrassed at being wounded before he had had a chance to do any fighting, and bitter with memories of the nightmare on the French beaches, where men under fire from the enemy clawed their way desperately through the shallows, trying to scramble aboard the mongrel flotilla of ships and boats that had come to snatch them to safety. Two short weeks later he returned to his regiment, fit for action again.

Letters arrived regularly from Ainslie, Barbara and Ross. Ainslie sent photographs, and parcels of tinned meat and fruit that were gratefully received, for rationing was already biting deep into civilian life. Isla shared the food with Flora Currie, and with Magret and, through Magret, the residents of the old tenement. Although she no longer lived there, Magret still took a keen interest in the place. She had even persuaded young Mrs Kelly, whose husband had been called up, to secure a job in the mills, and now the two of them worked beside each other.

Only Mrs Leach, who looked after her grandson while his mother was at work, declined to take anything from Isla. She did her best to make her daughter follow suit, but Mrs Kelly, with a growing son to feed, defied her mother and accepted her share of the tins gratefully, as did the others.

'Is that no' what life's all about?' Magret asked. 'War or no war, if we don't help each other we deserve all we get. Never mind that Mrs Leach, there's no understanding her at all, but the lassie's really nice, when ye get her away from the old woman. She must take after her da, rest his soul.'

Phemie Forbes threw herself into war work with enthusiasm. She joined the Women's Voluntary Service, and in her spare time she knitted for the troops. She was hardly ever to be seen these days without knitting needles in her hands and a half-finished garment in khaki wool on her lap. Isla, who for Colin's sake made a point of calling on Phemie at least once every week, sitting on the edge of a chair in the Forbeses' drawing-room and making small talk to the background of clicking needles, often thought that her mother-in-law looked like a fly perched in the middle of a khaki web.

Gilchrist, guiltily revelling in the luxury of having the reins of the business in his own hands again, referred to his wife's continual industry as knitting for victory, or stitching up the war. He and Isla got on well together and he often called in on her on his way back from the office, sitting in the living-room with his feet sprawled over the carpet, just as his son had once done.

Colin, in England for the remainder of 1940, was able to come home on leave fairly regularly, but at the end of the year his regiment was sent overseas and Isla was forced to settle down to a life bereft of husband and children. Throughout 1940, radio broadcasts had conveyed reports of the horror of the interminable raids on London and Coventry and Liverpool; once 1941 arrived, Paisley's sirens started sounding more frequently, and Isla and Nan, both busy with their war work, saw little of each other.

Clydebank, a shipbuilding town not far from Paisley, was almost destroyed by a devastating two-night air raid in March. Isla was on duty both nights, and as most of the patients were kept awake by the unnerving wail of the sirens, the sound of wave after wave of German planes rumbling through the sky, and the distant thump of anti-aircraft guns, all the staff on duty had a hard time of it. Hurrying from one building to the other on the first night of the raid, Isla saw the searchlights weaving back and forth across the sky. A faint rosy glow on the horizon, almost like the early promise of a beautiful sunrise, marked Clydebank's agony by fire.

Some of the 'Bankers' who had been bombed and burned out of their homes came to Paisley, and a family of four, a dazed young mother and her three children, spent a few weeks in Isla's home. It was like the old days, when Barbara and Ross were home. Both Isla and Nan revelled in the luxury of having children around, and Nan, the most efficient person that Isla had ever known, worked wonders when it came to finding enough food to keep ever-hungry little stomachs content. They were both sorry when the family moved on, to stay with relatives in Stranraer.

Early in May it was the turn of Greenock, another Clydeside town famed for its large shipyards. It, too, was bombarded for two nights, and again, the enemy bombers flew over Paisley, but this time they didn't pass by harmlessly. On the first night, an incendiary bomb landed not far from Low Road, on the railway embankment close to Ferguslie Mills.

On the following night, Isla, who was off duty, was wakened by the mournful wail of the sirens. Nan was on duty that night, and Isla was alone. She dressed hurriedly and ran through the dark to Flora's house, blundering into bushes, fumbling impatiently with the stiff catch on Flora's gate.

Betty, the housekeeper, opened the door to Isla. 'Thank goodness you're here, Mrs Forbes. She refuses to let me help her to get dressed. She'll not leave her bed!'

'I'll see to her.' Isla hurried across the hall to the little room that had once housed Flora's dolls' houses. Not long before the war began, they had been moved upstairs so that the ground-floor room could be turned into a bedroom for the old lady, who was finding it increasingly difficult to cope with stairs. Colin had supervised the installation of a small ground-floor bathroom adjacent to the kitchen.

In spite of all Isla's pleading and coaxing and threatening, Flora refused to leave the comfort of her bed. 'After all those years, I see no sense in trying to prolong my life by making it a misery,' she announced. 'Squatting beneath a table isn't dignified. I decided the last time you got me to do that that I'd never do it again. I'm fine where I am.'

She could scarcely be heard over the noise of the planes passing overhead. The sky must be thick with them, Isla thought, glancing fearfully up at the ceiling. It was hard to credit that so many could crowd into such a small patch of sky. The mind-picture of big heavy machines colliding with each other and falling on the houses beneath came to her, and refused to leave. 'Flora, you might get hurt if you stay here. You're right beside the window. It's far safer in the living-room.'

'If my end's coming, it'll come no matter whether I'm cowering on the carpet or lying comfortably in my bed.'

'What about Betty? And me? If you insist on staying here, we'll have to stay with you.'

'No you don't.' All that could be seen of Flora were bright eyes, grass-green in the lamplight, peering over the edge of the quilt gripped in her two hands. Her voice was muffled, but determined. 'I don't want your deaths on my conscience, but I'm not stirring one step. I'm too old to be bothered by all this palaver!'

'Flora Currie, if you don't let us help you up right now, we'll just have to drag you out of your bed and carry you into the living-room.'

There was no reply. Isla and Betty looked helplessly at each other, knowing that they couldn't leave her, or risk a heart attack by forcing her into safety.

Isla thought wistfully of the big solid table in the living-room next door, then said slowly, 'There's that old folding screen we found in the attic and put in the drawing-room.'

After a struggle, the two women managed to fit the large, ungainly screen between the window and the bed, then settled down in the dim light of a torch to wait the raid out. Flora dozed, and was still asleep when there was a great blast of sound from somewhere and their empty teacups, placed on the bedside table, jangled together with the vibration. The entire house shook, and Isla threw herself across the bed to protect the old woman against breaking glass. Betty screamed, then went scrambling after the torch, which had rolled from the bedside table to the floor, as Flora, waking with a start, hit out with her fists at the sudden weight across her.

'In the name of God, lassie, I thought I'd been attacked,' she said reproachfully when the torch was found and order restored.

'I was trying to keep you from getting killed.'

Flora tutted. 'It's you that needs saving, not me. Didn't I say that if my time's come, it's come? There's a man and two bonny children that'll be wanting to see you safe and well when this nonsense is over.'

'D'you think it landed in Low Road?' Betty whispered when Flora had drifted back into sleep.

'It wasn't that close. Maybe the mills – or George Street.' The day before, the railway embankment close to the mills had been set alight by incendiary bombs. Some thought that the mills had been the real target.

'Whatever it was, it was close,' Betty said. 'And it was big.' They stared at each other, wondering what the dawn would bring.

They finally slept, huddled in armchairs by the bed, sleeping right through the All Clear and waking to blessed silence, broken only by the birds' dawn chorus.

Leaving Betty to snatch an hour's sleep in her own bed, Isla went back home. It was early yet to expect Nan home; if the night's explosion had meant death and injury to some poor souls, she might be later than usual, kept busy at her first-aid post.

Isla went to bed, but couldn't sleep. Finally she got up again, dressed, and made breakfast, expecting to hear Nan's key in the lock at any moment.

She was drinking her second cup of tea when Mr Smith from further up the road came to the door, wearing his official ARP tin helmet and armband. He looked as though he hadn't slept for a week.

'Mrs Forbes, I'm afraid I've got bad news,' he began. 'Colin—'

'No, no, it's got nothing to do with your husband,'

he said hurriedly, then, 'that explosion last night – a landmine scored a direct hit on the first-aid post at Woodside . . .'

The church at the foot of New Street had been set aside as a temporary mortuary. Isla walked to it down George Street, her feet crunching on broken glass, and waited in line to go in to identify Nan. War meant queuing for everything, she thought drearily. Buying food, buying clothes, identifying the dead. She caught snatches of talk from the others waiting with her. The landmine had been clearly seen, drifting down through the searchlights, swinging from its parachute. If the wind had only carried it a hundred yards further on, it would have landed on the cemetery where Kenneth and his son lay. Almost immediately after the landmine had hit the first-aid post, killing doctors, nurses, ambulance drivers, and helpers like Nan, another bomb had landed on the east wing of the West School, used as an auxiliary fire station, killing several firefighters. Again, the general belief was that the mills, so close to both explosions that most of their windows had been blown in, had been the target.

When her turn came, and the corner of the blanket was lifted aside, she looked down at Nan, eyes closed, mouth slack, her greying brown hair, always in such a neat roll, untidy and darkly clotted at one side. 'Yes, that's Nan – Mrs Agnes Urquhart,' she corrected herself.

'Is she from Paisley?'

'Her sisters live in Stirling. She's been widowed for years. I'll write to her family,' Isla said. Her guide nodded and dropped the blanket.

'Ninety-two killed in all,' he said as he escorted her from the church, 'and every last one of 'em decent folk doing their duty. When's this terrible business going to stop?'

Isla left the building, passing the people who still waited outside, to claim their own dead, and walked home, heedless now of the broken glass under her feet. At that moment, she was glad that Barbara and Ross were safe in Canada, where the bombs couldn't reach them.

The house seemed very empty when she let herself in. Once there had been Colin and Drew and Mabel and the children – and Nan, who had, in her own way, been the very heart of the house. Now there was only Isla. She paused at the foot of the stairs, the newel post solid beneath her hand, and looked up towards the landing, remembering all the times she had stood there in the past, calling to the children to make less noise.

For a moment she knew blind, suffocating panic, wondering how she was going to be able to keep going on her own, then, quite unexpectedly, the tears came. She clung to the polished post, letting all the grief come out, crying noisily like a child, because now there was nobody there to be disturbed by her misery. When the tears finally ebbed then stopped, she went into the kitchen – Nan's kitchen – and sluiced her face with cold water, then made herself a cup of tea before going to tell Flora about Nan.

At the end of the year, the Japanese bombed Pearl Harbor, and America came into the war. And the terrible business continued.

*

'Here, let me give you a hand.'

Isla, who had assumed that she was alone in the garden, jumped and almost sliced off the toe of her wellington boot when she heard the voice. For a moment she thought that the easy drawl was Phil's, then as she spun round she saw a stranger advancing towards her from the corner of the house.

'Sorry, did I startle you?' He took the spade from her and eyed the rows of green shoots. 'They're too small to be dug up.'

'I know, but I wanted to give my neighbour some new potatoes.'

'Okay.' Effortlessly, he buried the spade to its shaft in the earth. Isla stepped aside and left him to it. She had no idea who he was, but she was glad of the chance to straighten her aching back.

The man bent to the spade, then heaved it up with a soft grunt. The potato shaw keeled over and small pale potatoes gleamed through the crumbling earth. He put the spade aside and knelt to run his hands through the soil, gathering the frugal harvest.

'There aren't many.'

'There's enough.' Isla held out her basket and he put the potatoes into it, then dusted his hands together as he stood up.

'Are you Isla? Isla Forbes? Phil and Ainslie told me to look you up if I was in the area.'

'You're Canadian?'

A grin split his thin face. 'Most folks can tell that the minute I open my mouth,' he said, then thrust his hand out. 'Gregg Marshall.'

A sudden April shower began to fall, and Isla, who

hadn't slept well earlier in the day despite being exhausted by her busy night on duty, smothered a yawn and collected her wits. 'I was just going to make myself a cup of tea. Would you like one?'

'That'd be fine, if it's not too much trouble.'

She led him into the house through the back door and put the basket of potatoes down on the dresser, then began to ease her first wellington off.

'Sit down.' He knelt before her, taking her muddy foot in his hands, levering the tight boot off skilfully. 'There we are – now the other one.'

'That one's always hard to get off.'

'I've never yet met the boot that could get the better of me. Tod, my eldest, has the darnedest knack of getting his socks wedged down inside his boots, so I learned at a hard school.'

Sitting on a wooden chair, clinging to the seat to avoid being pulled off by the final tug on the boot, Isla looked down on a mass of curly light brown hair. The boot came off and he tipped his head back to smile triumphantly at her before setting it to one side with its companion, then washing his hands at the sink. Isla, padding barefoot across the kitchen in search of her slippers, was uncomfortably aware that she didn't look her best in one of Colin's jerseys and an old skirt. She hadn't been expecting anyone to call.

'D'you mind if I get these potatoes ready for Flora?' She eyed the clock. 'We'll be eating in an hour, because she likes to get to bed early and I'm going on duty.'

'Not at all. Can I help?'

When she declined the offer, he peeled off his leather jacket then sat down at the table. 'I'm stationed down at

Prestwick Aerodrome, and Ainslie said that if I found myself in Scotland I had to call and say hello from the Hannigans, and from Barbara and Ross.'

Isla, washing the tiny potatoes, turned from the sink, heedless of the water dripping from her hands. 'You know the children? How are they? Are they happy?'

'I know them well. We live pretty close to Phil and Ainslie. You've got a couple of nice kids, Mrs Forbes – and they're doing fine, believe me. Barbara has a wonderful voice. She sang in a concert for the troops just before we left for Europe. She's doing a lot of singing, helping to raise money for the war effort as well as singing for the troops.'

'She's always loved music.'

As she put the potatoes on to cook and made the tea Isla told Gregg Marshall about the back-court concerts Barbara used to run, and he listened with genuine interest, then said, 'You know she's been on radio a few times?'

'Oh yes, she wrote to tell me all about it.'

'Pat – my wife – envies you, you know. She always wanted a girl, just like your Barbara, but after three boys she's given up hope. Maybe when this is all over . . .' He paused, lost for a moment in his own thoughts, then said, 'You must miss them a lot.'

'I do. I miss them dreadfully,' Isla said, fussing over the potatoes in order to hide the tears that had gathered in her eyes.

Luckily, she had managed to make some buns the day before. She put them out on a plate, together with a precious pot of raspberry jam Nan had made a year earlier from Flora's raspberry bushes, and watched with carefully hidden concern as Gregg Marshall spooned precious sugar into his cup. She herself had learned, like most civilians, to get used to drinking tea without sugar.

'Ainslie told me your husband's in the Army.'

'The artillery. He's with the Fifty-first Highland Division now, in Egypt as far as I know.'

'I thought most of the Fifty-first were captured in France?'

'They were, after Dunkirk. They were cut off, trying to get to the beaches. But the regiment's been rebuilt with men seconded from other regiments. That's how Colin came to be with them.'

Gregg put the sugar bowl down and started stirring his tea, then stopped suddenly. 'Oh heck!' He looked across the table at Isla, his eyes, very clear blue, concerned. 'I've just realised – is this all the sugar you're allowed?'

'It's all right, I don't use much.'

His thin, rugged face flushed. 'I should have thought – we're not used to this rationing you folks have to deal with. I'll bring you some from the base.'

'You don't need to do that, I can manage very well.'

'You live alone?'

'Our housekeeper, Nan, used to share the house with me, but she was killed last year by a landmine.'

'I'm sorry.'

'So am I.' Isla felt the tears threatening again, and blinked hard. 'I still miss her very much.'

'You must get very lonely, with your husband and kids away.'

'Not really. Most of the time, I'm working at the sanatorium, or with my neighbour. Life's so frantic at times that on the few occasions I'm on my own here, I've learned to quite enjoy the solitude.'

'Pat would hate it. She could never stand her own company, not that she gets the chance now, with three boys to raise on her own.' Gregg reached for his jacket and brought a handful of photographs out of an inner pocket, proudly showing off his pretty blonde wife and his three sandy-haired sons. To Isla's delight, Ross was in a few of the photographs, squinting into the camera as he always did, and seventeen-year-old Barbara was in one, long-legged and mature in trousers and a blouse, perched on a wall, laughing into the camera, her mane of curly hair blowing about her face.

Isla studied the children she hadn't been able to touch for almost three years, hungry for every detail. Ross, who had lost the last trace of infant plumpness, was only a week away from another birthday. She had posted a long letter to him, and a book inscribed on the flyleaf, 'To Ross on his fourteenth birthday, with much love from Mum and Dad. April 1942.'

When she relinquished the photographs to Gregg he separated those with Ross and Barbara in them and gave them back. 'They're for you.'

'But your own boys are in them, and Ainslie's been very good about sending letters and photographs. I'm filling my third album now.'

'Keep them anyway, I've got plenty of snapshots of the boys.' He looked at his watch. 'I'd better be going.'

'Come next door and meet my neighbour first. She doesn't get out now and she loves company. Stay and have a meal with us,' Isla urged.

'If you're sure—'

'I'm quite sure. It won't be much, but we'd both be glad of the company.'

The rain had stopped when they left the house, but enough had fallen to give the earth a fresh, cool smell. As they walked out of her gate, then along the pavement for a few yards and in at Flora's gate, Isla tried to work out how to stretch the meal to cover another person. She had made some vegetable soup, and had handed her meat ration over to Betty so that she could make a stew for the three of them. They often pooled their resources.

Flora, looking almost like a faded photograph of the woman Isla had first met outside the West School, was in her usual chair in the front room, a blanket that Isla, Barbara and Nan had knitted for her tucked over her knees. Her white hair covered her skull in soft wisps and her face was gaunt, but her green eyes were still able to sparkle up at the tall airman when Isla introduced him.

'It's just like having Phil here again. So you're at Prestwick? A pilot?'

'Nothing as grand, ma'am. I'm ground crew – a mechanic to trade.'

'You'll have some whisky,' Flora stated. 'The bottle's in the sideboard, Isla, and the glasses. No need to worry, young man, we'll not send you back to the aerodrome drunk. There's not that much whisky left, so you'll only get enough to make you thirst for more.'

Gregg took the tiny glass from Isla and looked at its spoonful of amber whisky. 'I see what you mean, Miss Currie.'

'It's the thought that counts – and I can assure you

that the thought's worth half a tumblerful of Scotland's finest malt,' Flora told him. His laughter followed Isla out of the room as she went in search of Betty to tell her that there would be a guest for dinner.

'But, Mrs Forbes, there's scarce enough to feed us, let alone a man!'

'We'll manage. We'll have to – I thought it would be good for Flora to have some new company for a change, and anyway, it was good of the man to come and visit.' Isla lifted pot lids and peered inside. 'We can use small plates for the soup, and with Flora eating the wee new potatoes, there'll be enough of the others to go round. If I'd known he was coming I could mebbe have got a rabbit,' she fretted, studying the stew that would be hard put to it to stretch to four helpings. 'D'you have any corned beef left?'

'Just a slice, but I was keeping it for Miss Currie's lunch tomorrow.'

'I can let you have some of mine for her lunch,' Isla said rashly. 'Break the slice up and mix it into the stew, and beat a slice of bread in as well, to make it look more. Add some water to the gravy, too. I brought the rest of the buns, so we can fill up with them afterwards, with a cup of tea. He's heavy on the sugar, but we'll get by.'

Even though she and Betty served the meal on the smallest plates they could find, it didn't amount to much. Gregg Marshall made no comment, but Isla noticed that he took only one spoonful of sugar with his tea.

'She's a wonderful old lady,' he said when the two of them left Flora's home.

'She enjoyed your company. You must visit us again.'

'I surely will – and I'll bring you some sugar.'

'There's no need for that.'

'I feel bad about taking your supply. Can I give you a lift to your hospital?' he asked as they stepped on to the pavement. Isla eyed the motor-cycle propped on its stand outside her gate, and explained that the sanatorium was just a step away, and she would walk there. When the machine had roared off up the road, bringing one or two neighbours to their windows, she went into the house to get ready for work.

Flora was in bed, her eyes still bright, when Isla looked in, as she always did on her way to and from the sanatorium.

'It was nice to see a new face, wasn't it? He was just like Phil – these Canadians seem to get such enjoyment out of life. Not like the dour Scots at all. I hope some of that rubs off on your bairns, Isla. It'd be good for them.'

30

◆

Gregg came back often, roaring up to the gate on his motor-cycle, bringing delicacies such as sugar or a small packet of butter, and occasionally some delicious crunchy doughnuts from the canteen. These gifts, like Ainslie's food parcels, were shared with Flora and Magret and the people in the tenement in George Street. Tommy McDougall had been called up now, and was stationed in England.

Isla's gardener had had to give up work because of ill-health, and she hadn't bothered to find anyone else. Gregg willingly helped her in the garden when he called, or sat for hours in the kitchen talking about his home and his family, frequently introducing Barbara and Ross into his reminiscing until Isla felt as though she had been present with her children at the sledging parties in the winter, the picnics, the visits between the Hannigan and Marshall houses to view new kittens or puppies. These word-pictures of her children in Canada made the temporary separation more bearable for her, and went a long way to easing the pain of being without them. Gregg also spent a lot of time with Flora, who had developed a new interest in life since his unexpected arrival.

'You've done her so much good,' Isla told him gratefully. 'She needs company, and I can't spend as much time as I'd like with her these days.'

The Canadian tipped the kitchen chair back and stretched his legs across the linoleum floor. 'I'm the one who's getting all the favours. You and Miss Currie have been like family to me, and it's great to be able to visit a real home.'

Isla looked around the kitchen, which had grown noticeably shabbier since Nan's death. 'I'd scarcely call this place a real home nowadays. The house used to be full of people coming and going, and now I almost live in this room. I hate to see the place so – alone.'

'You're like my Pat – wherever she happens to be is home to me. I get that same feeling when I'm around you.' Gregg smiled at her, then asked, almost shyly, 'Could I have a look at those dolls' houses I kept hearing about from Ainslie and Phil and the kids?'

Isla rarely visited the dolls'-house room now. Walking into it with Gregg, she felt for a moment as though time had looped back. As far as this room was concerned, the war had never happened, her family hadn't been scattered far and wide, and Nan was still alive, bustling round the kitchen pouring out milk and putting fresh-baked scones on a plate, ready for the children's return from school.

Gregg, unaware of the memories she was experiencing, was moving carefully round the tables, fascinated by the little houses and the miniature furniture. 'I wish more than ever now that I had a daughter. It would have been great to give her something like this.' He stopped in front of one with a murmur of delight. 'Hey, this is just like the place my grandparents used to have!'

'It's supposed to be from *Anne of Green Gables*. I'm hoping to complete it one day, but at the moment my furniture maker's in the Navy.'

'He certainly loved his work,' Gregg marvelled, his fingers gently caressing a tiny rocking chair in pale gold wood. 'Listen, would you make me a house just like this, to give to Pat?'

'Of course, but you'll have to wait until after the war. Even if I had the time, I can't get the materials just now. Anyway, I couldn't do it without Drew to make the furniture.'

Gregg was still admiring the little chair. 'I can't get over how perfect this is. I can almost see my grandma sitting in it!' He held the miniature piece gently, lovingly, just as Drew would, Isla thought, and on an impulse she took him out to see the workshop.

Despite being locked up, the place still smelled of fresh wood and paint and glue and textiles. 'Your carpenter certainly cares about his trade. These tools have been well looked after.' Gregg turned his head and smiled at her, and suddenly she was looking at Drew, hearing her long-ago voice saying, 'How are things coming along?' and his voice replying, 'Fine. I'll have time to finish this before I go home for my tea, and it'll be dry in the morning, ready for the handles to be put on.'

Drew was thin, whereas Gregg was as lean and strong as a whip. Drew had serious grey eyes, Gregg's were blue and full of a love of life. Both had light brown hair, but Gregg's was fairer, and curly, whereas Drew's was straight and often flopped over his eyes. The two men were unlike each other in many ways, yet their shared love of fine craftsmanship, and the way Gregg had just turned and smiled absently at her, reminded her so strongly of Drew that to her horror, she burst into tears.

At once he was beside her. 'Isla? What is it? Did I say the wrong thing?'

She shook her head and tried to explain, then gave up and rested her head on his shoulder, letting the tears have their own way. Gregg said nothing more, just stood and held her while she sobbed out her grief over Nan's violent and unnecessary death, her longing to see Barbara and Ross again, her fears for Colin's safety, her exhaustion and loneliness, and her continuous, strength-sapping fear.

When at last the weeping had slowed to sniffs and hiccups, he mopped her face dry with his handkerchief, then locked the workshop door and led her into the house, where he sat her down at the kitchen table and made some tea.

'I shouldn't have asked to see your workplace. It brought back too many hurtful memories.'

'It wasn't that – I'm just being daft.'

'You're not daft,' Gregg told her, the Scottish word sounding so different on his lips. 'You're worn out with work and worry and not getting enough to eat.'

Isla flopped in her chair like a rag doll, completely drained, shaken by an occasional involuntary shudder. When he put the cup into her hands she sipped at it, then wrinkled her nose.

'It's t-terrible!'

'I'm not used to making tea,' Gregg said matter-of-factly, taking a seat at the other side of the table. Eyes closed, he inhaled the steam rising from his cup, then sipped. 'It tastes fine to me.'

'It's too strong, and too sweet, and . . .' She sipped again, then it was her turn to sniff at the brew. 'You've put something in it.'

He dipped into the pocket of his leather jacket, hanging from the back of his chair, and held up a small silver flask. 'A few drops of brandy, that's all.'

'No wonder it tastes terrible!'

'Don't look a gift horse in the mouth, that's what my grandma used to say. Drink·it up, it'll do you good.'

Although she grimaced at every mouthful, she had to admit that she did feel better when she had drained the cup. She got up to put it in the sink, then gave a gasp of horror as her gaze fell on the small mirror hanging nearby. Her face was stained, her eyes and mouth swollen with weeping. 'I look awful!'

'Everyone looks awful when they've been crying as hard as you were. Splash cold water on your face.'

She did, and looked marginally better, though her eyelids were still puffy. Gregg rinsed the cups and set them on the draining board while she was still peering into the mirror and making small sounds of horror. 'Take a couple of aspirin and go to bed with a hot-water bottle. You'll feel fine after a sleep.'

'But I said I'd call in on Flora this afternoon. She'll know at once that I've been crying, and it'll upset her.'

Gregg dried his hands and reached for his jacket, moving about the kitchen comfortably, as though in his own home. 'I'll go. I'll tell her you've got a headache and you've had to go to bed.'

'Gregg,' she said as he opened the back door. 'I've never in my life made such a fool of myself. You've been very kind.'

'What are friends for? Listen, Isla, nobody can be strong for ever, not even you. Don't be so hard on yourself – you needed a good bawl, and today just happened to be the day for it,' he said, and went out, closing the door.

In July, Colin came home on leave. Isla had been living for that day, but as he stepped off the train at the West Station and came towards her, his nutbrown face almost split in two by his grin, she suddenly felt ridiculously shy. He was like a stranger, bronzed and more muscular than when he had first been called up, his teeth astonishingly large and white against his tan. Then she was swept up into his arms and despite the rough khaki uniform and the bronzed skin, she knew that he was still the man she had married.

She had worked hard in preparation for his return, putting in extra hours at the sanatorium in order to win some time off, cleaning the house from top to bottom with Betty's help, saving her coupons and the extras Gregg had brought so that she could feed him well.

He paused for a moment in the hall. 'The house hasn't changed a bit. I've dreamed of the smell of that furniture polish you always use.'

'Is that all you thought about while you were thousands of miles away? Furniture polish?'

He caught at her hand as she started to move towards

the kitchen, spinning her round and into his arms. 'Oh, I've thought of other things as well,' he murmured against her mouth, then scooped her into his arms.

'Colin, your parents are coming round in a little while!'

'And we'll be the perfect host and hostess when they arrive,' said Colin, marching up the stairs as though his wife weighed nothing at all. 'First, there's a little matter I've been dreaming about since the last time I was with you.'

'I've missed you,' he whispered later as they lay together in bed. 'Looking up at all those beautiful stars in the sky at night, and wishing that you were there to see them with me.'

Isla trailed her fingers down the side of his face and he caught at her hand and nibbled on her fingertips, then stretched and yawned. 'I suppose we'd better get ready to entertain our guests.'

She lay for a moment, watching him dress. His body had been tanned all over by a sun much more fierce than the sun that shone over Scotland.

'D'you think we'll ever get back to the way we were?'

He grinned down at her, his fingers moving nimbly down the front of his shirt, popping buttons into buttonholes with practised speed. 'Back together as a family? Of course we will, there's no doubt about it.' The grin faded. 'Though we're all going to miss Nan such a lot.'

'Yes, we are.'

'I felt even worse about persuading you to let Ross and Barbara go away when I heard about Nan,' Colin said sombrely. 'Now you're all alone and I can't do a damned thing about it. I often wish I could turn the clock back.'

'I'm managing – and they're fine where they are.

Mebbe it was for the best after all. At least I don't have to worry about a bomb mebbe falling on them at school. It's helped to hear so much about them from Gregg Marshall.'

'When am I going to meet him?'

'At the weekend. He offered to stay away and let us have time to ourselves while you were home, but I said you'd want to meet him. You'll like him, Colin, he's a very nice man.'

'I'm sure I will.' Then, stooping to kiss her nose, he added, 'But if you don't stop lying there, Mrs Forbes, looking so desirable and so tempting, I'll not be in a fit state to meet him, let alone my parents in about ten minutes.'

As Isla had expected, Gregg and Colin got on well together, and the Canadian paid several visits before Colin had to report back. When the time came, Isla found it hard to let him go, to step back and watch the train carry him away, knowing that his regiment was being sent to North Africa, where the fighting had been fierce and the Eighth Army forced back almost to Alexandria by Rommel's troops.

She missed him even more this time. The big bed was an island of loneliness, and she often lay awake, despite being exhausted by her work at the hospital, yearning for Colin. She knew, from the talk she heard from the rest of the staff at the sanatorium, that she wasn't the only woman to have such feelings. One or two of the nurses confessed, sometimes defiantly, sometimes tearfully, that they had found comfort with some other man.

For her part, there were times, particularly in the

first weeks after Colin's leave, when Isla found herself glancing at Gregg as they worked together in the garden, or sat on opposite sides of the kitchen table. She found herself wondering what it would be like to be held in his arms, caressed by those large, well-shaped, sure hands. She thrust the thoughts away as soon as they arrived, embarrassed and angry with herself. Once or twice she considered asking him not to come back, but he got such pleasure out of the visits that she couldn't bring herself to be so cruel.

Drew came home, no longer a gawky lad but a man in his naval uniform with the cap tilted jauntily over his eyes. He came to tell Isla that his sweetheart Mary had agreed that on his next leave they would marry.

'Our mums are going tae save their coupons, and their clothes coupons too, tae give us a smashing wedding,' he said happily, 'I can't wait to see my Mary as a bride. She's a lovely dresser – makes all her own now. She even knows how to paint her legs to look as if she's wearing stockings – the seam down the back and all!'

In the workshop, he ran his hands lovingly, just as Gregg had done, over the tools awaiting his return. 'It'll be good to get back to work again.'

'I'm not going to lose you to the Navy after the war?' Isla asked, and he looked round and grinned – again, just as Gregg had done.

'Not a chance. I'm enjoying the life, but I'm looking forward to coming home, too, and settling down. I've been sketching furniture in my spare time. I've got all sorts of plans – just you wait and see.'

For her part, Isla was afraid to look too far ahead. All her thoughts these days were with Colin, in North

Africa. His letters home made no mention of the life and death struggle for supremacy that they both knew couldn't be far away now. Instead, he wrote about everyday life in the desert.

'I suppose the flies were here before we were, but you'd think they'd be willing to have discussions with us about what should be theirs and what should be ours. They're even more obstinate than Rommel, and insist on being my food tasters, often getting eaten themselves if they don't get out of the way in time – and if I don't spot them in time. As to the sand, I wonder if eating and drinking sand with everything means that my teeth will benefit? They're constantly being scoured with the stuff. You'll be heading into winter now. It's cooler here, thank goodness, but still hot compared to home. I wish I was an artist, and able to capture the sunsets on paper and send them to you, my darling. They're beautiful, but they'd be even more beautiful if we could only be watching them together. Perhaps one day, when this war's over, I'll take you to Africa and show you those sunsets.'

The inevitable battle came in October, a fight that, once started, had to be fought to the bitter end. Even after the news came through that the Eighth Army had succeeded, at El Alamein, in forcing the enemy back and winning a massive victory, Isla couldn't rest until Colin's letter arrived, telling her that he had come through without injury. Then, and only then, she allowed herself to weep with relief.

Early in December, while Gregg and Isla were playing cards with Flora in her drawing-room, Gregg asked Isla to go with him to the Christmas dance at Prestwick Aerodrome.

'It'll be fun,' he coaxed when Isla refused. 'It's time you had some fun in your life, and you'd be doing me a big favour.'

'I'm not a dancer.'

'That doesn't matter, it's just a case of moving with the music.'

'On you go, Isla,' Flora urged. 'Everyone needs time off, and if you're not at the sanatorium you're dancing attendance on me. It's time you enjoyed yourself. It's Christmas!'

Isla finally gave in and agreed, then wished she hadn't when she surveyed her wardrobe in search of something to wear. The two evening dresses she possessed were rejected as being too formal, and all she could find was a pale pink silk blouse, and a dark blue evening skirt. They still fitted, but a glance in the mirror showed that they looked dated and uninteresting.

Magret called in at least once every week after her shift at the mills, since there was no longer any need to have 'his' dinner ready on time each evening, so Isla put on the blouse and skirt and paraded round the bedroom for her friend's benefit.

'I see what you mean,' Magret said. 'They've no' got much life tae them, have they?'

Isla lifted a handful of skirt, then released it. It fell limply against her thigh. 'I haven't time to make anything, and I'm not going to waste coupons on something I'll probably never wear again. Besides, I told Drew that I'd save some clothing coupons to help towards his wedding. I'll have to tell Gregg that I've changed my mind.' Peering in the mirror again, this time at her face, she added, 'Anyway, I'm thirty-nine, not nineteen. Far too old to go gallivanting off to dances.'

'Ach, ye're only as old as ye feel.'

'All right – forty-nine.'

'If that's the truth, it's probably time ye had a good night out. I tell ye what, I'll bring our Greta over tonight tae have a look at them. She's awful clever at making things over.'

'She'll have to be a miracle worker to make anything of this outfit.'

'Don't give up hope yet, hen,' Magret advised, and later that evening, she arrived on the doorstep with Greta.

Isla hadn't seen the girl since Barbara had gone to Canada, though she frequently heard from Magret about Greta's job in a draper's shop, and about her boyfriend, who was on important war work in the India Tyre factory at nearby Inchinnan. To her astonishment, the thin, plain little girl who had always been in Barbara's shadow had blossomed into a self-possessed young woman, casually smart in a red woollen jersey that showed off her full breasts and slim waist to advantage, worn over a snug-fitting tweed skirt. Greta's hair, once nondescript brown, had a chestnut glow to it, and was swept up to form a halo round her skilfully made-up face.

'How's Barbara?' she asked.

'She's fine – she's singing with a band now.' Isla produced some photographs that had just arrived from Canada, and Magret went through them, exclaiming over each one.

'My, wee Ross's nearly a man now, isn't he? Oh, Greta, look, isn't Barbara just beautiful?' She handed her daughter a photograph that Isla had looked at again and again, unable to believe that the lovely young woman standing at the microphone in a tight-bodiced, long-skirted dress with a sweetheart neck and short puffed sleeves, her long hair curling on her shoulders, could be the schoolgirl who had gone off with Ainslie.

'I like the frock,' Greta said. Later, in the bedroom, she eyed the pink blouse and navy skirt critically. 'I see what ye mean.'

'I haven't got anything else.'

'Mind if I have a look?' Greta riffled through the wardrobe and drew out a summer dress in navy, with large white spots, navy buttons down the bodice, and a cluster of artificial navy and white flowers pinned to the collar.

'The buttons are pretty, I could use them, and mebbe the flowers, but it'd mean spoiling yer dress. The skirt hangs well, though, ye could still use it, with a new waistband.'

'I doubt if I'd be wearing that dress again anyway. Do what you want with it – keep the skirt for yourself, if you can use it.'

'Oh, great!' For the first time, Greta looked animated. 'That Peter Pan collar on the blouse'll have tae go. All right if I change it about a bit?'

She took the clothes home with her, and returned them the day before the dance. When Isla put on the blouse and skirt she was stunned by the difference. The blouse now had a plain round neck, enlivened by a row of navy blue flowers from the bunch on the dress, alternating with pink flowers that Greta had made from the discarded collar. The plain pink buttons down the front of the blouse had been replaced by decorative navy buttons from the dress, and the starched skirt and underskirt swirled and rustled as Isla moved around the bedroom.

'Ye look bonny, Isla,' Magret marvelled, adding with justified pride, 'I told ye our Greta was clever with a needle, didn't I? Have ye noticed her skirt?'

Greta gave a twirl. She wore the same red jersey as before, but tonight her skirt, snug-fitting over the hips then full to the hem, was navy with white spots.

'Nothin' tae it, I just made up a waistband from the bodice,' she said casually. 'Sit down and I'll cut yer hair.'

She was as good with scissors as she was with a needle. Isla's dark hair was neatly trimmed, then washed. Then, using a poker heated in the kitchen range, Greta curled the ends under.

'Ye're gettin' a bit grey at the temples,' she said matter-of-factly. 'Wearing yer hair like this'll help tae hide that.'

She tore up some newspaper into strips and used it to put Isla's hair into curlers before she left.

'It'll be uncomfortable in bed tonight, but it'll be worth it.' Then, delving in the large shoulder-bag she had brought to produce bottles and boxes, 'Now I'll show ye how tae do yer face.'

31

Greta was right – the newspaper curlers meant that Isla spent an uncomfortable night, but on the following evening, when she went over to show Flora her outfit, she had to admit that her suffering had been worthwhile. Her hair had brushed out into a soft bell about her face, and the blouse and skirt looked as though they had been made for each other.

For once Gregg had left his beloved motor-cycle in Prestwick and borrowed a car. When he arrived at Flora's, as arranged, to collect her, he stopped in the drawing-room doorway, staring. It was the first time Isla had seen him in uniform; they gaped at each other for a long moment, then caught each other's eyes and laughed.

'Stand side by side, and let me take a look at you,' the old woman commanded, nodding her satisfaction when, self-consciously, they obeyed. 'Very nice indeed. You make a smart couple. Now mind and give her a really good evening, she deserves it,' she commanded Gregg as he helped Isla into her everyday navy serge coat.

'I surely will, ma'am,' he promised solemnly.

In peace-time, Isla and Colin had often taken the children for summer holidays to Troon, close by to Prestwick. It was a pleasant part of the Clyde Firth, with great stretches of sand, and shallow water just right for paddling. She hadn't been back there since the war began, but had heard that the sandy beaches were covered with rolls of barbed wire to defend the Clydeside towns against invasion, and most of the hotels and gift shops and tearooms and ice-cream kiosks were closed and shuttered.

They drove down in the dark, so Isla had no chance to see the changes for herself. The dance was held in the canteen, which Gregg called the PX. It was a long wooden hut, with paper chains looped over the ceiling and walls, and a Christmas tree on either side of the stage where the band sat. They stepped through the dark entrance into a dazzle of light and a clamour of music and voices, and for a moment Isla hesitated. Gregg put an arm about her and steered her confidently round the edge of the dance floor, crowded with men in uniform and women, some uniformed, others in their best dresses, to a table where they were clearly expected. Chairs were hauled out for them, and Isla was introduced to more people than she could possibly remember.

'Now before she sits down, I'm taking her off to give her a few words of advice on how to handle you lot. Get her a drink, Gregg, we'll be back in a minute.' A young woman with blond hair swept up into a mass of curls at the top of her head took Isla by the hand and led her to the ladies powder room, where she leaned against a wash hand basin and took out a cigarette packet, lighting one for herself when Isla shook her head.

'I'm Doris, you're staying at my house tonight.' She blew a smoke-ring and studied Isla with bright blue eyes. 'I know they're a bit much when you're not used to them, but they're all nice lads. Far from home, and desperate to have as good a Christmas as they can, bless 'em.'

'You've been here before?' Isla combed her hair, then studied herself in the mirror.

'Here . . .' Doris took the comb from her and deftly flicked a stray wisp of hair into place. 'I work here, so I know them all. Gregg's one of the nicest. He's talked about you a lot – I'm glad you agreed to come to the dance, he didn't think you would.'

'Neither did I. I'm not used to socialising any more, it terrifies me.'

'There's no need, none of us bite. He really wanted to give you a good night out, in return for all the kindness you've shown him.'

'He's done more than enough, bringing us things, and helping in the garden.'

'But you've provided a home he can feel comfortable in, and that means a lot to all those lads out there. He's a real family man, is Gregg. It's a shame, what this war's done to his sort. Ready to go out and face them now?' Doris paused at the door and winked reassuringly. 'Just give yourself time to get used to us all, and make up your mind to have a good time.'

She was right. As Isla began to concentrate on the people around her, her nervousness faded. It returned when Gregg drew her on to the dance-floor, but he was a good dancer, and in his blue-uniformed arms she learned how to relax and follow the music. During the evening she danced with several of the men, but discovered that she was most comfortable with Gregg. They danced well together, moving in easy unison, and it came as quite a shock when the band struck up 'Auld Lang Syne' and she was whisked on to the floor to squeeze into a great circle, arms crossed, one hand in Gregg's, the other in the grip of Doris's partner, a navigator called Mike, to mark the end of the evening.

Gregg and Mike drove the two women to Doris's house in Prestwick, but didn't come in, because Doris's parents were asleep, and her father, a baker, had to get up early the next morning to start work in the bakehouse.

Declining Doris's whispered offer of a cup of tea, Isla followed the girl upstairs on tiptoe, carrying the small case she had brought with her. There were two beds in Doris's room, one of them the property of her sister, who was in the WAAC.

'I hope it didn't spoil your evening, having to come back here with me,' Isla said into the darkness when the two of them were in bed.

'No goodnight kiss from Mike, you mean?' Doris chuckled softly. 'Don't worry about that, we're just mates. My boyfriend's in a German PoW camp.'

'I'm sorry.'

'So am I.' For the first time Doris's voice was bleak, devoid of laughter. Then she said firmly, 'But he'll be home soon, you wait and see. Winnie says we've reached the beginning of the end, and I think he's right. G'night.'

Gregg drove Isla home on the following morning and they had lunch with Flora, who was waiting to hear all about the dance. Gregg, who had to go on duty that evening and would remain on duty over Christmas, presented Flora and Betty with their Christmas presents, a soft woolly bed-jacket for Flora, two pairs of stockings for Betty, and enthused over the hand-knitted scarf and the bottle of whisky he received in return.

'I'll savour this drop by drop,' he said, eyeing the whisky, but Flora snorted.

'Nonsense, man – half a tumblerful at a time, and don't forget to drink a toast to me.'

'Miss Currie, I'll be doing that for the rest of my life, believe me,' Gregg said sincerely. Later, in Isla's kitchen, he took a wrapped packet out of his pocket. For her, too, there were stockings, as well as a small box containing a butterfly brooch. She gave him a tie-pin, with matching cufflinks.

'Thank you for a lovely evening,' she said as he reluctantly got up to go.

'It's me who should be thanking you. You looked beautiful.' Then, as she began to move past him to open the door, he stopped her with a hand on her arm, and bent to kiss her, his mouth warm and hard on hers. In a reflex action, Isla's arms went round him, and his own embrace tightened. Suddenly overwhelmed by the need to be close to someone after all the months of abstinence, she clung to him, and he responded. When they finally stood back from each other, she saw her own hunger, her own need, mirrored in his rugged, normally laughing face.

As they stared at each other, their faces only inches apart, thoughts spun giddily through Isla's head. She wanted him to go away and never come back. She wanted him to kiss her again, to stay with her. She wanted to be able to turn the clock back, only five minutes, to the time before the kiss and the turmoil it had caused.

Finally, 'I have to go,' Gregg said, his voice husky, unsure of itself. 'Have a happy Christmas.'

'You too,' she said, and stood looking at the door long after he had gone through it.

'The man's a fool!' Flora glared at the wireless, where the Radio Doctor's fatherly voice was giving Boxing-Day advice on how to deal with the discomforts of overeating on Christmas Day. 'Overeating indeed – it seems to me that a fragment of chicken and a spoonful of potatoes followed by mashed parsnips with banana flavouring's not that far away from bread and water. How can anyone overeat on the rations we get? Switch him off, Isla, for goodness' sake!'

Isla obeyed, and silence fell on the room. Flora seemed to be dozing, as she often did these days, and Isla was startled when the old woman said abruptly, 'I've a feeling I did you a wrong when I persuaded you to go to that dance.'

'What?'

'Isla, we've known each other long enough to be honest. You've not been the same since you went to Prestwick.'

'There was nothing wrong with Prestwick, the folk there were very nice. I just miss the children, and Colin. Christmas is a bad time to be apart from your family,' Isla said shortly, burying her nose in the magazine she had been pretending to read.

She had been in a panic all through Christmas Day. Gregg's kiss had altered their relationship for ever. The memory of his mouth on hers, his arms about her, had haunted her ever since. Everything had changed, and suddenly he was no longer the friendly, likeable Canadian she had grown to depend on. He was a man, a very attractive man, who had succeeded in stirring up emotions that had lain dormant since Colin's last leave.

'It's more than just Christmas,' Flora said. 'I'd no worries about coaxing you to go to the dance with Gregg, for he could never be anything but a gentleman. But now I've a suspicion that that very thing might be the trouble.'

'Are you sure you didn't overeat? You're talking a lot of nonsense.'

'Am I? You're two decent people, and you've both been away too long from those you love. I should have thought of that, instead of just telling myself how nice it would be for the two of you to have a break from all this war business.' Flora's fingers twisted restlessly at the blanket about her knees.

'Flora, you've got nothing to reproach yourself about. Nothing happened!'

'No? There was a glow about the two of you when he brought you back the next day. I thought it was just the pleasure of the dance, but you've been ill at ease ever since, lassie, worried about something.'

'Who wouldn't be worried with her man . . .' Isla's voice wavered and she got up and made a business of stacking the used tea things so that Flora couldn't see her face. 'Her man away fighting?' she finished, gaining control over herself.

'One man away fighting, another nearer at hand, and both of them good caring souls,' Flora said from behind her. 'I nearly married once, you know.'

'You?'

Flora nodded. 'The marriage was all but settled, then a friend of my family's who'd been away from Paisley for years came back, and suddenly everything was changed. I swithered from one to the other, and I swithered too long. They both lost patience and looked elsewhere.' Flora gave a soft chuckle. 'It's as well for them that they did, for if they'd had the patience to wait, they'd be waiting still. To this day, I don't know myself which I wanted the most. But one thing I do know to my cost, Isla – it's possible for a woman to love two men.'

'In all the years I've known you, you've never said a word about this before,' Isla said suspiciously.

Flora's eyes, normally heavy-lidded now, flashed emerald fire at her. 'That's because I've never had need to,' she said.

Letters arrived early in January from North Africa, where Colin expected to remain for some time, and from Canada. Barbara, who at eighteen had left school and was singing with the band every week, wrote excitedly about their regular slot on radio. Ross, still at school, working for Phil at weekends and holidays, wrote about the timber-yard. Colin wrote about the flies and the sand and the other men. Isla had little to tell them in her replies, other than that she had been moved from nightshift to dayshift. Her days off were always the same, filled up with gardening, queuing outside food shops, visits next door, the petty annoyances of rationing and queues and having to do without, and the endless longing for peace and a return to normality.

She had dreaded meeting Gregg again, but when he roared up on his motor-cycle a few days after Christmas he was his usual relaxed self, and his visits continued as usual, though Isla noticed that, like her, he tended to avoid any physical contact with her, no matter how small or how innocent. By mutual, unspoken consent, they spent most of his time in Paisley with Flora.

Returning on a pleasant April afternoon from a dutiful visit to Colin's mother to find Gregg's motor-cycle on its rest at the front gate and Gregg himself working in the back garden, his jacket slung over the clothesline, Isla stood for a moment at the corner of the house, unnoticed, watching him. She knew that his father had been a farmer, and that Gregg had expected to follow in his footsteps. But a growing interest in machinery had led him to leave the farm in his late teens and set up his own business, supplying farm machinery. He still had a deep love of the land and enjoyed working it, no matter how small the scale. He was digging now to an easy rhythm, his lean body bending and swinging, his arms tensing then relaxing as he worked. As Isla watched him, she knew that Flora was right – it was possible to love two men, to want to be with one as much as the other.

He looked up just then, and the broad grin that was never far away spread over his face when he saw her.

'Hi there – I got an unexpected afternoon off, so I thought I'd get some work done on this ground before the weeds take over.'

'You shouldn't have bothered.'

'Why do the Scotch always say that?' Gregg asked.

'Scots. Scotch is the drink.'

'We learn something every day. You look very nice.'

Isla looked down at the suit she was wearing, a misty blue-grey check that Colin particularly liked. 'I always try to look smart when I visit Colin's mother. She expects it of me. I'll get changed.'

Later, working alongside him, sharing his countryman's pleasure in the good dark soil that slid from their spades, she felt soothed by his companionable silence. One day, she might have to face up to her feelings for him. But not yet.

They walked round to Flora's for tea, then returned to finish the digging, completing the task just as dusk brought out the clouds of tiny midges that made life outside unbearable. Then they drank cocoa in the kitchen and listened to the news broadcast on the radio, then to *ITMA*, which Gregg loved. He was roaring with laughter at something Tommy Handley had said when the back door burst open and Betty erupted into the room, heedless of the need to prevent the lamplight from spilling out of the door.

'Thank God you're still here, Mr Marshall.' Her face was as white as paper. 'It's Miss Currie, I think she's fallen in the bathroom and I can't get the door open—'

Gregg was on his way out of the kitchen before she had finished. The two women caught up with him just as he put his shoulder to the locked bathroom door. It flew open to reveal a small slight figure huddled on the floor.

'Let me by!' Isla pushed past the Canadian. Flora

was unconscious but still breathing. Her pulse was erratic and the area round her mouth had gone blue.

'Betty, telephone for the doctor.' Isla deftly drew Flora's nightdress and dressing-gown, which had rumpled up in her fall, down over her skinny legs, then Gregg carried the old woman across the hall and laid her gently on the bed.

'He's coming right away,' Betty said. 'He should be here in ten minutes.'

Isla, her fingers on Flora's pulse, laid her friend's hand down very gently on the bed, then tucked the blanket round Flora as though to protect her from the chill that was already on its way and would not be denied. 'There's no hurry,' she said.

32

Flora's family had been Baptists, and had worshipped at the Coats' Memorial Church, the church with the great sweep of stairs that Isla vaguely remembered passing on her way to visit Kenneth McAdam's grave, the first time she came to Paisley. That day seemed to belong to another life entirely, she thought, as she climbed the stairs to attend the funeral service, Gregg by her side.

The church's interior was beautiful and spacious, but even so it was quite well filled with people who had come to pay their respects to the last member of a family well respected and remembered in the town. Isla spotted Charlie Blayne, the auctioneer, among them and later, after Flora had been laid to rest in the imposing family plot not far from Kenneth's grave, she introduced him to Gregg.

The auctioneer's hair, a mixture of brown and grey when Ainslie had worked for him, was now a mass of tight silvery curls. He beamed at Gregg and shook his hand enthusiastically, then introduced his wife, a small neat woman almost hidden by his big sturdy body.

'How's Ainslie?'

'Very well, and busy looking after my two as well as her own boys. The twins'll be eleven next month.'

Charlie shook his head in wonder. 'Time flies when ye measure it against youngsters growing up. Give the lassie my regards the next time ye write, and tell her we still miss her at the auction-rooms. She could've done very well as an auctioneer if she hadnae lost her head and run off to Canada.'

'I think it was her heart she lost, Mr Blayne,' said Gregg, amused.

'Call me Charlie, son, everyone does. Aye, well, I suppose we all let our hearts away with too much.' Charlie put an arm about his wife and hugged her. 'Eh, Lizzie?'

'Aye, we all have a daft streak in us,' she said dryly, then to Isla and Gregg, giving Charlie a dig with her elbow, 'this is mine, and the older he gets the dafter he gets.'

Once again Gregg had borrowed a car from someone at the aerodrome. As it moved down the cemetery drive Isla asked him to stop for a moment. 'I'll not be long,' she said as she got out.

It was only a short walk along a side path to where Kenneth and his son lay. Catherine, at her own wish, had been buried in Dumfries. Isla stood for a moment, wishing that she had thought to bring flowers, even a single blossom, from those heaped round Flora's grave.

'Someone special?' Gregg asked as she went back to the car and settled herself beside him.

'Someone very special.'

The nieces whom Flora had never been able to give dolls' houses to were at the funeral, and so were the nephews. Because none of them belonged to Paisley, Isla had offered to hold the reception at her own house where, by dint of a lot of careful planning, and help from Betty and from Gregg, who brought provisions from the PX at Prestwick, she managed to provide everyone with food and drink.

Nobody stayed long, for many of the mourners had come from outside Paisley, and were anxious to get home before dark because of the blackout.

'We're grateful to you for all your help,' one of the nieces said as she was leaving. 'We'll be back next week to clear the house out and see Mr Forbes about selling it.'

Betty, who was going back to her family in Bishopton, a nearby village, was the last to leave. 'I'll never forget Miss Currie,' she said at the door, tears in her eyes, then she left, and Isla went back to the living-room, where Gregg was gathering up cups and plates.

'I'll help to clear things up,' he offered. 'I don't have to be back at the airbase for a few hours yet.'

After washing the dishes, they put the living-room to rights and Gregg got out the carpet sweeper while Isla made tea. It was growing dark, and he made sure that the blackout curtains were all in place before joining her in the kitchen. 'She had a very happy time, that last day,' he said gently, after a long silence. 'We all did, remember?'

Isla nodded, remembering how Flora had had them both laughing, Gregg until the tears ran down his cheeks, with some story of friends of her parents. 'I'm not being malicious, you understand,' she had said, her green eyes gleaming. 'Just a wee touch wicked – but that makes for a better story, doesn't it?'

'It's good to spend your last hours in life with friends,' Isla said now, summoning a smile.

'Are you sure you'll be all right on your own tonight? You look worn out. I can phone the base and tell them I can't get back until morning.'

'Of course I'll be all right,' she said at once, and knew by the way the colour rose in his face that her voice had been too sharp.

'I didn't mean . . .'

'I know. I'm sorry. I'll be fine.'

'Take some whisky before you go to bed, it'll help. Here . . .' he started to reach into his jacket pocket for his flask, but Isla stopped him with an upraised hand.

'Not brandy in my tea again, thank you, I remember the taste from last time. I've got some whisky, I'll make myself a hot toddy before I go to bed.'

'Okay.' Silence fell between them, companionable at first, almost like the old days, then gradually taking on a meaning of its own. It couldn't be allowed to continue, Isla thought, and jumped up to switch on the radio. A man's voice came through, talking about architecture in Italy. She twirled the dial in search of some music, or a comedy programme, but tonight every station she could find had people talking. All except one, but it was playing gloomy funereal music that she knew would reduce her to tears on such a day. She wished that she had thought of sitting in the living-room, where there was a gramophone.

Instead of sitting down at the table again she picked up her cup and drained it, then took it over to the sink.

'I'm so tired that I don't think I'll need that whisky,' she said over her shoulder.

Gregg brought his own cup to the sink. 'In that case, I'll clear out and leave you in peace.'

Isla took the cup from his hand, almost dropping it in her eagerness not to let their fingers touch, and started washing it vigorously, listening to the sounds he made as he picked up his jacket and put it on.

'I'm going to miss Flora a lot,' he said, his voice sombre. 'You've both been family to me since I came over here. She was like a favourite aunt, and you . . .' He stopped, then said slowly, 'Isla, we have things to talk about.'

'Not tonight.' She swung round from the sink, and pulled the tea-towel from its hook so roughly that the material caught and tore.

'You know what I mean, don't you?' Gregg asked. 'We've been scared to look at each other ever since the dance.'

'I don't know what you're—'

'For God's sake, Isla,' he suddenly burst out. 'Don't start behaving like a flirty teenager! That's not you at all. We're grown-up people, old enough to face up to what's happening.'

'We're married people too, with growing children, and responsibilities.'

'I know that.' He sounded so defeated that she wanted to go to him and hold him and comfort him. Instead, she folded the towel with great care, hung it over the back of a chair, and sat down at the table, so weary that she could no longer stay on her feet.

'I know,' Gregg said again, quietly, letting his lean

body fold down into the opposite chair, resting his curled fists on the scrubbed wooden table. 'I love Pat – but now I love you too.' The fists tightened. 'I never thought there could be room in my life for another woman, but there is. A great empty hole I knew nothing about, just waiting to be filled to the brim by you.'

'I wish I'd never gone to that dance!'

'I wish I hadn't asked you. I wouldn't have, if I'd had any idea of the harm it was going to do. But there's no use in wishing the past away. One kiss,' he said in wonder. 'One little friendly Christmas kiss between friends. That's all it was supposed to be. But I've not been able to get you out of my mind since, not for a minute.'

'It would have been better if you hadn't come back.'

'I know, but I couldn't have stayed away. Isla . . .'

He looked up from his hands, catching her gaze before she could turn away. His look seemed to light up the kitchen, his love was like a soft blanket, waiting to enfold and cherish her. She wanted to draw its warmth around her and stay in its folds for the rest of her life. But she couldn't, she mustn't.

He read her thoughts, and tried to lighten the tension between them. 'Of course, there was another reason why I couldn't stay away. I knew that the vegetable bed needed digging.' For a moment, as they laughed together, the clock was turned back and everything was all right again. Then, watching the laughter fade from Gregg's eyes, seeing the bleak despair that replaced it, Isla knew that, like her, he knew what must be done.

'There's no future for us, is there?' It was a statement, not a question.

'No future at all, Gregg. My Colin, your Pat – they don't deserve to be hurt.'

'I don't want to hurt you either.'

'At least I'll know why, and I'll know it's for the best.'

Gregg suddenly lifted his fists then slammed them down hard on to the table. 'God damn it, how can it be so wrong to love somebody and want to be with them? I could wring Adolf Hitler's damned neck! If it wasn't for him, I'd never have come to Scotland, or met you . . .'

'If you want to wring his neck, you'll have to stand in a very long line,' Isla said wryly, and he gave a grunt of laughter that was almost a sob. The sound of it hurt her unbearably.

'Right. Anyway, I guess I'd prefer knowing you and losing you to not knowing you at all.' He put his hands flat on the table and studied them. 'We seem to have talked ourselves into a decision.'

'Yes, we have.'

He got up, reached for his cap, then turned, his eyes pleading. 'Isla, can I stay here tonight? Just one time, once to remember for the rest of my life?'

It would have been so easy to say yes. Nobody need ever know, nobody would be hurt. But against all her own instincts, Isla shook her head. 'I think you should go now, Gregg. And I don't think you should come back.' It struck her that this was the second time she had sent a man away. The last occasion had had a happy ending, but that couldn't, wouldn't happen again.

Gregg gave a long defeated sigh, then got to his feet. Isla stared down at the table, praying that he wouldn't touch her, knowing that one touch from a finger-tip would be enough to destroy the wall she had managed to build round herself.

'You know something? I'm glad I took you to the dance,' Gregg said. 'At least I got to hold you in my arms, even though there were about a hundred other people round us.'

The door opened, then closed swiftly, to keep the light from spilling out. Isla got up and fumbled her way through the dark hall and into the living-room to the window, bumping into furniture as she went. She drew the blackout aside, but it was so dark outside that she could see nothing. She stood clutching the folds of material, hoping that he would change his mind and come back, but at the same time praying that he would just go away and get it over with.

Outside, a car engine hiccuped, then roared into life. The sound dwindled away into the distance, and faded to nothing.

The days trailed by, each just like the one that had gone before it. Gregg stayed away, and didn't make any attempt to get in touch with her, and with the house next door lying empty, Isla felt completely alone. Several times she found herself hurrying down the path on her way to visit Flora, and had to turn and trail back to the house. The only bright moments in her life came when she received letters from Colin and the children and Ainslie. She carried their letters and photographs around with her, reading and re-reading the written words until she could have recited every single one of them in her sleep, running the tips of her fingers hungrily over the photographs. Her longing for the children, assuaged a little by Gregg's descriptions of them, came back as strong as ever, to torment her.

Flora's relatives returned to clear everything out of the house, and a 'For Sale' sign went up in the garden.

'Heaven knows why,' Gilchrist Forbes said when Isla paid her weekly visit to him and his wife. 'It's not a through road, so there's no passing traffic to see the sign. But it's what they wanted, and the client is always right.'

Isla fell heir to Flora's dolls' houses, because nobody else wanted them. 'I don't know what she collected them for,' one of the nieces said when she made the offer. 'They just gather dust. I understand that you like that sort of thing, Mrs Forbes, so perhaps you'd care to take them. I seem to remember that there was a very nice Victorian house – you don't happen to know what happened to it, do you?'

'It was refurbished and auctioned to raise money for the families of the children killed in the Glen Cinema disaster.'

'Oh yes, I remember hearing about that,' the woman said vaguely. 'What on earth made her think of selling the little house, though? It must have been worth quite a bit – why couldn't she have just donated a pound or so to the fund and be done with it?'

The houses, together with a few boxes containing a jumble of furniture and dolls, had to be stacked on the upstairs landing, because Isla couldn't get them up into the loft by herself, and Gregg was no longer around to do it for her. One of them, Isla noticed, looked quite like the house next door. She took it into her bedroom so that she could study it, and decided that once the war was over, she would furnish it and turn it into a copy of Flora's house, just for herself.

The thought cheered her and gave her something to do in her spare time, sketching the rooms in Flora's home from memory, and sorting through the boxes of odds and ends in search of pieces she might be able to use for the task.

In May, the Allied forces, Colin among them, took Tunis, and it began to look as though the war was beginning to swing, slowly, in the Allies' favour.

Drew came home on leave, and as soon as Isla opened the door and saw him standing in the porch she knew that there was something wrong. He was wearing civilian clothes this time, and all his jauntiness had vanished. He followed her through to the kitchen, but declined her offer of a cup of tea.

'Mary's married,' he said bluntly.

'Married? Oh, Drew, I'm so sorry!'

'Not half as sorry as I am,' Drew said between clenched teeth. 'She met up with some damned Geordie soldier in the NAAFI and off she went. She'd only known him a matter of weeks, her mum said. I knew she should never have gone to work in that NAAFI, I said so at the time. But she wanted to do her bit.' He drooped over the kitchen table, the picture of misery. 'She did that, all right. Sent me one of those "Dear John" letters.'

'Mary's not the only girl in the world. You'll find somebody else, somebody more worthy of you.'

He wasn't impressed. 'That's what my mum says, but I don't want anyone else, I just want my Mary.

She'll be sorry, you know. I reckon she married the uniform, not the bloke. He'll look a lot different in civvies, doing a nine to five job and moaning because his tea's not ready.'

In an attempt to take his mind off Mary, Isla asked him to store the dolls' houses in the attic for her. He agreed in a lackadaisical way, but had brightened up a little by the time the job was done, even going out to his workshop to give some of his tools a good cleaning. Standing by the door, watching him at work, Isla was able to pretend for a little while that the war had never happened, that Nan was bustling around the kitchen and Colin was in his office and the children were due home from school at any minute, fighting to be first through the gate.

When Drew had finished they went back into the house, where he downed a mugful of cocoa and ate a jam sandwich as they made plans for future dolls' houses once he was back on civvy street.

Drew liked the idea of the Flora Currie house. 'She was a nice old soul, Miss Currie. I was sorry when Mum told me she'd gone.'

On the doorstep on his way out, he stopped to say, 'Mum and me are going to have a slap-up meal before I go back, with the coupons she was keeping for the wedding. And I've given her some money and told her to go out and put the clothing coupons she was keeping towards a fur coat for herself. They'd have been wasted on that Mary anyway.' And he went off with the slightly rolling step common to all seamen, leaving Isla to struggle with the mental picture of little Mrs Brown, thin and stooped, creeping along George Street in a fur coat.

Colin had survived the desert, and the taking of Sicily, and his letters had grown confident and cheerful, certain of victory now that the list of Allied victories was steadily increasing. In Canada, Barbara had gone on tour with the band, to Isla's consternation, though Ainslie's letters were reassuring.

'Phil and I felt that it would be wrong to insist on her staying here instead of going. She'll be nineteen in two months' time, Isla, she's not a child any more. The band leader's wife is travelling with them, a sensible soul who can be trusted to keep an eye on Barbara. Anyway, you've got a level-headed daughter, and I'm sure she's well able to make her own decisions.'

It seemed to Isla, who still tended to think of Barbara and Ross as she had last seen them, that she was caught in a time warp. Even with the photographic proof before her, she found it hard to think of Barbara as a young woman and Ross, now fifteen, as a youth on the brink of manhood.

Gilchrist Forbes sold Flora's house in September to a couple with a young family. A lot was done to it before they moved in, and the quiet road, which had once known the roar of Gregg's motor-cycle, now echoed to the sound of hammering and sawing, and workmen calling to each other.

Another letter came from Ainslie, a thick envelope. Isla knew, just by looking at it, that it carried bad news. She had recently received Ross's usual fortnightly letter, but nothing from Barbara, who had fallen into the habit of sending cards from wherever she and the band were playing, and photographs of herself and the grinning musicians. There were usually some fans in the photographs too, young men, and the occasional young woman, autograph book in hand.

She carried the envelope into the kitchen and laid it on the table. If Flora had been alive, she would have gone next door to open it, but Flora wasn't there any more, Colin was far away in Sicily, and Isla was on her own. After five minutes, during which her imagination ran riot, she opened the envelope.

Ainslie's writing, normally neat, sprawled across the pages, launching into the story she had to tell without wasting time on chat about the weather. Because the Canadian government had become somewhat edgy about the number of British children evacuated to their country and left there for much longer than had first been anticipated, they had recently been checking on all the British people temporarily resident in their country. Ainslie had explained that Barbara and Ross were not technically evacuees, but her half-sister and half-brother, visiting her on an extended stay.

This had been accepted without comment, but unfortunately, now that Barbara required a work permit in order to travel with the band, she had had to deal with some paperwork on her own, and had seen, in black and white, the details about her relationship with Ainslie.

'She managed to get time off, and came here in quite a state,' Ainslie wrote. 'I explained that you had thought it best to leave things alone until you were able to tell her in person, but I'm afraid she was in no mood to accept that. She's very hurt, Isla – she wouldn't discuss it with me, just went storming back to Ottawa. She's since written to Ross, but not to me. Ross, by the way, is quite pleased to find that he's related, through me, to Phil and the boys, and not in the least bothered. I suppose Barbara's just more emotional than he is.'

Isla groaned softly as she reached the end of the letter. She should have told Barbara the truth earlier, but by the time the girl reached the age when she might have started asking questions about her real father, she was in Canada and involved in a new life.

She waited and worried for a few weeks, hoping that her daughter would write, reluctant to burden Colin with her problems when he was so far away and engaged in the day to day business of just staying alive. But there was no word from Barbara. Ross wrote, bubbling over with the joy of discovering that he had a whole set of relatives. 'I think it's great,' his untidy scrawl said. 'It makes me feel as if I'm really part of the Hannigan family. I expect Ainslie's told you that Barbara's not so happy about things, Mum. I can't think why, because she really likes Ainslie. I suppose it's something to do with being female. Don't worry, she'll come round to it.'

But Barbara didn't come round to it. Eventually, deciding that she could wait no longer for a letter from the girl, Isla steeled herself to sit down at Colin's desk on one of her days off, and start writing a long letter to Barbara.

The only way, she thought, chewing the end of the pen, was to tell the whole story, from the first day she had set eyes on Kenneth McAdam in the men's surgical ward of the Edinburgh hospital where she was a probationer. She wrote steadily for several hours, keeping nothing back, forcing herself to go once again through all the pain of Kenneth's death, and the discovery of his other marriage and the first, terrible, meeting with Ainslie. It was even harder than she had expected it to be, but Barbara already felt as though she was being deceived, and now she needed, and deserved, every bit of the truth.

She stopped to eat and to rest her hand and wrist, which were stiff and painful, then drove herself back to the desk. 'I meant to tell you and Ross when you were old enough to understand, but by the time you both reached that stage, you were in Canada. Your real father loved you very much, Barbara, and so do I. Colin thinks of you as his own daughter. I know it must be hard for you to discover that your father and I were never legally married, but surely you must see that the important thing is that you're part of a family, and nothing will ever change that.'

It was late when she finished, signing and sealing the letter without reading it over, partly because she was afraid that she might then lose the courage to post it, partly because having just relived years of her life on paper, she couldn't bear to go over it all again. She had even taken Kenneth's final letter, the letter Gilchrist Forbes had given her when he came to tell her of Kenneth's death, from the tiny drawer below her jewel box, and copied it out word for word.

She slept badly that night, and went out to post the letter as soon as the post-office opened, before walking to the sanatorium.

It was a difficult day. For some unknown reason, the patients were all irritable, and two of the nurses on her shift were ill and off work. A group of officials chose that day of all days to inspect the place, and the matron took her nervousness out on her staff. Worn out though she was, Isla welcomed the hard work, because at least it kept her from fretting about Barbara, and reliving the submerged memories that had been released by the letter, and thrown up to the surface of her mind.

She stayed on duty for a few hours longer than necessary to help the night staff, also short-handed, to settle the patients down, then walked slowly home through a dark night lit, now and again, by the moon glancing through scudding clouds. She was halfway down the hill when she saw a sudden tiny flare of light appear then disappear as someone at the foot of the hill pulled on a cigarette. Isla stopped, listening, but there was no sound of footsteps either approaching or walking away from her, and no voices. She stared into the night until her eyes were aching, and eventually glimpsed another tiny glow, just where the first had been. Someone was standing near the wooden door she had to go through to reach Low Road.

Isla fumbled for the torch she always carried in her bag. She hadn't used it on the walk because the batteries were low, and she knew the way from sanatorium to Low Road so well that she could have walked it blindfold. She switched the torch on, but the light was so weak and wavery that it was no use to her at all.

She bit her lip. The moon had been hidden for the past few minutes, and she was in total darkness. She was on her own, faced with the prospect of trudging back to the hospital, or going on. Home was nearer. It had been raining when she left the house that morning, and she was carrying her folded umbrella. She gripped it firmly and walked on, the tap of her heels on the roadway loud in the silence.

She had almost reached the door when she heard the sound of movement, the heel of a shoe scraping on the pavement as someone turned. Just then the moon slid out from the clouds and shone on the man turning towards her. It was Gregg Marshall.

'Isla,' he said, 'I couldn't stay away.'

33

Gregg lit a fire in the living-room and they talked half the night, sitting on the rug before the fireplace. He had applied for a transfer to an air base in England, and it had come through. He was leaving in a few days' time.

'When it came to it I couldn't just leave without seeing you, just one last time,' he said, and Isla, happy for the first time since Flora's death, unable to believe that he was really there, really with her, reached out and allowed her fingers the luxury of touching his face. He put his own hand on hers, turning her hand so that his mouth could brush over her palm. 'How've you been?' His eyes travelled over her face. 'You look worn out, Isla. What's wrong?'

She told him about Barbara, the words spilling out. It was such a relief to be able to talk about it. He listened in silence, and when she had talked herself out, he took his handkerchief and dabbed gently at her face, drying tears that she hadn't even noticed.

'Isla, Barbara's a very nice girl who's growing up to be a very nice, very beautiful, very sensible woman. I've got no doubt of that. You're going to have to give her time, honey – as much of it as she needs. She'll come to terms with everything, and while you're waiting, just keep on writing to her. She's been hurt, but she needs to know that this doesn't make any difference to the way you love her. What does Colin have to say about it?'

'I haven't told him. He's got enough to worry about.'

Gregg's eyebrows rose. 'Honey, he's the only father Barbara's ever known, and she's his daughter now. Don't try to cut him out of what's happening; if you do he'll resent it when he finally finds out.'

Isla looped her hands about her knees, staring into the fire. 'Oh, Gregg, I've made a terrible mess of things!'

He shifted so that he could put an arm about her. It was good to be able to lean back against a man's shoulder again. 'You haven't made a mess of anything, you've just been trying to save other people from grief. You've been so used to coping on your own all the years you were raising your kids that you've forgotten how to let others help.' He squeezed her shoulder. 'You need to loosen up, lady. Nobody can take the cares of the world on their shoulders, not even Isla Forbes.'

'Oh, Gregg, I'm so glad you came to Paisley tonight.'

She felt a laugh rumble through his body. 'I aim to please, ma'am.'

They sat together in silence for a long time, looking into the fire. Then Isla stirred, turned, and found his mouth waiting for hers.

Loving Gregg in the firelight, being loved by him, was inevitable and natural and, in its own way, right. At the beginning they were hungry for each other, hungry for contact, demanding and taking, almost devouring each other. Then, with the first urgent need satisfied, their lips and hands and bodies gentled into true loving and giving and receiving in mutual pleasure, both anxious, in this first and last time together, to give as much happiness to the other as possible. They spoke to each other with their bodies, their mouths, their hands. Questions were asked and answered, pledges made, assurances given, without a word being spoken aloud.

The years seemed to drop from them, and they loved like teenagers, rather than the parents of growing children. Isla felt no self-consciousness at all over exposing her aging body to his gaze and his touch, nor was there any guilt. Colin had always been an enthusiastic lover, though considerate; Gregg brought a form of poetry to his lovemaking, worshipping and celebrating their union with every part of himself, finally flowing into her and around her, enclosing her, merging the two of them into one being.

She sensed, as she responded with a fluidity that she had never known before, that this was not the way he and his wife made love, just as it was nothing like the way she and Colin coupled. This was unique, belonging only to the two of them, and only for this one magical night. It was a primitive celebration of their meeting at a time when their great need of each other surpassed everything that had been in their lives before, or would come again.

At last, they slept in each other's arms, lying on cushions, wrapped snugly together in the large woollen shawl that was normally draped along the back of the couch. Isla wakened to find Gregg kneeling by her side, his lips moving slowly, gently, across her breasts. The fire had gone out, and because of the blackout, the room was dark, but she could hear birdsong outside.

'It's five o'clock, honey,' he said against her shoulder. 'I'll have to go.'

She wrapped her arms about him, drawing him close. 'Not yet . . .'

'Not quite yet,' Gregg agreed, his body responding to the movement of her limbs. This time the magic of the night before had gone, and they made love comfortably, completely, like a man and a woman who were dear friends, as well as sharing a mutual physical attraction. But his leaving couldn't be put off for ever; they dressed swiftly in lamplight, then walked to the door, their arms around each other. It was almost daylight outside, the air fresh after the previous day's rain.

'Are you sure you won't have something to eat before you go?'

'If I stay any longer, I'll never leave.' He kissed the tip of her nose, and said, 'I'll wheel the bike to the end of the road, otherwise the neighbours'll start talking about you.'

They looked at each other, a long look that they both knew would have to last the rest of their lives. 'I won't write,' Gregg said. 'I mean, I will, often, but I won't send any of the letters. Best to end it here and now.'

'When the war's over, we might go to Canada to visit Ainslie.'

'If you do, I'll stay away. I don't think I could bear to see you and not be able to touch you.' He kissed her, his mouth hard on hers. 'Take care,' he said, then she was alone, straining for one last glimpse of him through the bushes as he kicked the bike off its stand and wheeled it along the road.

When he had gone, Isla bathed in the few inches of tepid water allowed by the war regulations, dressed, and had breakfast before going into the living-room to open the blackout and restore the spilled cushions and shawl to their rightful places. She cleaned the ashes from the fireplace, washed the mugs and plates they had used, then set off for the sanatorium.

Although she had had very little sleep she strode briskly up the hill and along the road, ignoring the heavy rain-filled clouds that had begun to gather overhead. She felt fit and well, refreshed and renewed by Gregg's loving. Catching sight of her reflection in the glass panel of the sanatorium door as she was about to go in, she made a face at herself, then smiled.

She was forty years old, but she felt as young as Barbara. She would never cease to be grateful to the big Canadian for blessing her life, reminding her what it felt like to be young again, and happy. A mere fifteen hours earlier she had felt old and tired and depressed. Now, stepping into the sanatorium, she felt strong and optimistic. Although she had no knowledge of what lay ahead, she was sure that everything was going to be all right.

At last, in September, Barbara sent a letter. It was brief and somewhat cool, but at least it was a letter.

'I feel as though after all these years of being me, I'm not me at all,' she wrote. 'I'm a different person altogether. You should have told me, or Ainslie should have told me, instead of leaving me to find out the way

I did. I still don't know right now how I feel about it all, but I guess I should thank you for finally telling me everything.'

Although she wanted to reply at once, Isla restrained herself for a week, then wrote a chatty and affectionate letter, making no further reference to Kenneth other than to assure her daughter that she understood how Barbara felt, and would leave her to sort out her own feelings in her own time.

Christmas came and went, bringing with it bitter-sweet memories of the dance at Prestwick aerodrome the year before, and Christmas Day with Flora. This year Isla worked during Christmas Day and visited Colin's parents in the evening. On Boxing Day she went to Magret's to admire Greta's new engagement ring and meet her fiancé, a plump, fair-haired, shy young man content to sit in a corner and watch his beloved with adoring brown spaniel eyes. He and Greta didn't plan to marry for a year, at least. They had already put their names down for a Corporation house in one of the housing schemes built before the war.

'We don't mind which,' Greta told Isla. 'Whitehaugh, or Lochfield, or Ferguslie Park. The houses are all very nice.'

The Gillespies, the couple who had bought Flora's house, had moved in just before Christmas. They had two young children, a boy and a girl, and Isla welcomed the sound of the children's voices as they played in the garden. Early in January Janice Gillespie appeared at the dividing hedge as Isla walked up the path to her own door and invited her in for a cup of tea that afternoon.

Isla hesitated. 'I've got rather a lot to do,' she lied, reluctant to go back into a house which held so many memories.

The young woman looked disappointed. 'Just for a little while,' she begged. 'I wanted to ask you about something.'

So Isla agreed, then discovered when she nerved herself to step over the door lintel that it wasn't so difficult after all, because the house had changed out of all recognition. All Flora's dark wallpaper had been stripped off and replaced by pale distemper, 'stippled' with clusters of colour applied by dipping a sponge in paint then dabbing it over the walls. The furniture was modern and lightweight, and the couch and chairs in the living-room were covered with dark brown material, heaped with small cushions in vivid colours and patterns.

Janice Gillespie, pouring tea from an elegant, pale green fluted china pot into matching cups, suited her surroundings. She, too, was smart and modern, with short, well-cut dark hair, and red fingernails. She wore a dark green linen dress beneath a short-sleeved yellow coatee. Isla had heard that Mrs Gillespie came from a wealthy family, and her husband held down an important job at the munitions factory in Bishopton.

'Won't you have a biscuit? You'll probably think this is very impertinent of me, Mrs Forbes,' the young woman said a little nervously, putting the plate down. 'But I understand that you run a very successful business, furnishing dolls' houses.'

'I did, before the war. I'm nursing at the Craw Road sanatorium now, but I intend to start the business up again when I can.'

'Oh, I see.' Janice Gillespie looked disappointed. 'My daughter Angela's going to be six years old next month, and my sister's offered us the dolls' house her own daughter used to play with. But it's all very shabby now, and I'd hoped to persuade you to furnish it for her.'

'I do have some furniture, but it's rather ordinary,' Isla said hesitantly. 'I usually use specially made pieces, but my craftsman's in the Navy.'

Hope came into her neighbour's face. 'We wouldn't want anything too elaborate at this stage. Angela's too young to appreciate it, so we thought – just an ordinary little house that she can enjoy—'

'Ask your husband to bring it round tonight, when she's in bed,' Isla told her impulsively, 'and I'll do my best.'

Clearly, there was a genuine mother beneath Mrs Gillespie's sophistication. She beamed her delight. 'That's so kind of you!'

Later, showing her visitor out, she said, 'I understand that you knew the previous owner well. It must be strange to see how much we've changed the house.'

'I'm glad you did.' Isla looked round the hall and said, 'I think it rather likes the changes.'

'Really? We loved the place the moment we set eyes on it. It has a good feeling about it. I hope the children haven't disturbed you, playing in the garden. They're thrilled to be able to get out – we were in digs before, and there was nowhere for them to go. We had to spend most of the day in the park.'

'I enjoy hearing them – it brings back memories. My own children are in Canada for the duration of the war.'

'How dreadful for you, being apart from them!'

'They're not really children any more, almost grown up. But yes, I miss them very much, so it's good to hear your youngsters. And I think,' Isla said warmly, 'that the previous owner would be pleased if she knew that there was a family in the house again.'

Walking home, taking the old familiar route down one path, along the pavement, and up the other path, Isla was glad that she had thought of doing a copy of Flora's house eventually. Although the real house had changed out of all recognition, she would have her replica full of memories.

Mr Gillespie brought the dolls' house round that evening. When he had gone Isla eyed it thoughtfully. It had four rooms and an entrance hall and a flight of stairs to the upper floor, and once it had had a cheerful red roof, now scratched and faded. She ferreted in the cupboard in the workroom, unearthed some small pots of paint, brushes, items and furniture and scraps of material, and got to work.

The little house kept her happily occupied in her spare time over the next four weeks, and when she handed it back to the delighted Gillespies, fresh and colourful and furnished, she began work straightaway on what she now thought of as the Flora house, doing what she could and leaving the more difficult tasks until the day when Drew would be back in his workshop.

Another letter arrived from Barbara, still cool, but a little longer than the last letter, with some news of the band tour. Ainslie wrote to say that Barbara had asked her for photographs of Kenneth, which had been sent to her.

In March, Colin came home on leave, and insisted on taking Isla to Largs for a holiday by the Clyde. He booked a comfortable room in a comfortable hotel, and they spent most of their days braving the weather, walking along the front, wrapped up in their warmest clothes. Colin looked, on those outings, as though he was about to set out on an expedition to the North Pole. Largs, an attractive and very popular holiday town, was noted for its stiff sea breezes and Colin, used now to a much warmer climate, felt the cold intensely.

Isla had wondered, nervously, in the time between hearing that he was coming home and his actual arrival, if Gregg would come between them, if Colin might somehow taste the Canadian on her skin, read about him in her eyes, sense him in her touch. But once she was with him, held in his arms, she knew that there had been nothing to fear. Like Flora, she had learned that it was possible to love two men deeply. What had happened between herself and Gregg had come about because they had had a great need of each other at a certain stage in their lives. It had been written into their stars at birth, and it had also been written that, physically, their union would be brief. In every other way, it was real, and lasting, and guiltless.

Gregg would always be with her, locked away in a deep, secret compartment that nobody else would ever know about. But Colin was her husband, her love, her future, her life. He had asked, casually, about Gregg, and Isla had told him, just as casually, that the Canadian was in England.

'I dreamed of wet streets at night,' he said as they leaned on the rail on their first day in Largs, watching the waves race each other down the Firth of Clyde and the small boats at anchor rocking and tugging on their cables like horses trying to break free, 'with lamplight shining on puddles, and of the way falling rain dimples water, and sometimes I dreamed about snowball fights and zooming down a hill on a sledge. We must take the children sledging the first winter we have together.'

'They'll probably feel that they're too old for that sort of thing by then. Anyway, they've had lots of snow in Canada. Ours might be a comedown.'

'I don't care what they think – we're all going sledging in the first peacetime snow, and that's that,' Colin said stubbornly, then shivered and pulled the brim of his soft hat down as another gust of wind came chasing along the front towards them. 'I can't say I missed the gales, though.'

'We should have stayed at home.'

'No we shouldn't. You badly needed a holiday, and I wanted us to spend some time alone together. If we'd stayed in Paisley my mother would have been knocking at the door every day.'

'She's missed you, too.'

'I know, and I promise that I'll make a fuss of her when we get back, but you come first,' he told her. 'I want you to get the sea air into your lungs. Breathe deeply, or you'll end up as a patient in that sanatorium of yours.'

'I'm perfectly well!'

Colin put an arm about her and held her close, bending to nuzzle his cold face against hers. 'I don't know how you've been able to stand it. At least we're well fed, and we get the feeling that we're getting things done, bringing an end to this damned war. It's you and the other folks left at home who've had to bear the brunt of it – not knowing half the time just what's going on, coping with rationing, worrying about air-raids and about whether I'm all right and not seeing your kids for years.' His other arm wrapped itself about her and he kissed her. 'I'll make it all up to you one day, darling,' he whispered when he lifted his mouth from hers. 'I promise!'

'Colin, people are looking at us!'

'Let them,' he said, and kissed her again.

Later, in bed, he started to laugh. 'No wonder people were staring at us this afternoon. I'm as brown as a berry and you're white as a ghost.' He caught her hand and raised their bare arms in the air, pressed together. 'The two of us must look like a half-eaten chocolate cream when we're out together.' Then, as their hands, still linked, fell back on to the bed he added, 'Isla, I'm not going back to Sicily. I've to report to a unit down south.'

Relief swept over her. 'You're staying in Britain?'

'For a while, anyway. There's something special on the way, and they're reorganising things so that the older men can relieve the youngsters to prepare for it.' He turned his head on the pillow and kissed her shoulder. 'In military terms I'm a has-been. God, the very thought makes me feel old.'

Isla raised herself on one elbow and looked down at his tanned face, familiar, yet not familiar. There were lines there that she had never seen before, some caused by laughter, some by squinting into a fiercer sun than she had ever known. But most of the lines were grim

and hard, engraved deeply into his skin by sights and
sounds and experiences he would probably not talk
about for many years.

'You're not old. You'll never be old,' she said
fiercely, and he reached up to pull her close.

'If this war's taught me anything, Isla, it's how much
I love you and treasure you.'

The week in Largs was like a honeymoon. They spent
every minute together, talking, walking, loving, rediscovering each other.

Following Gregg's advice, she had told Colin about
Barbara. Now that they were together, they were able to
talk about it in depth. Colin, like Gregg, believed that
the girl should be left to her own devices. 'I don't think
you'll lose her, darling. You did the right thing, telling
her the whole truth once she'd found out about it.'

'If I could just talk to her face to face, answer all her
questions, I'd feel better. Oh, Colin, it's been so long
since I last saw them both!'

'I know, love, but I don't think it's going to be much
longer now.' He gave her a sidelong glance, then said,
'Has it occurred to you that they might want to settle in
Canada? They've both enjoyed their stay, and Barbara
seems to have established a career there.'

She looked at him in dismay. 'They wouldn't do
that, surely?'

'They might. If they do, it's not the end of the
world. We could settle there ourselves if it came to it.'

'But what about the business?'

Colin gave a short, grim laugh. 'After what we've all
been through in the past five years, the business doesn't

seem to be all that important any more. Not nearly as important as being with you and Barbara and Ross, and being happy. If it comes to it, I'm game.'

Isla thought of Gregg, of living in his country, perhaps meeting him, seeing him with his wife and his sons. He had said that he couldn't bear a meeting under such circumstances, and she knew that she felt the same way.

'They'll want to come home, I know it,' she said obstinately, and Colin shrugged.

'No sense in crossing our bridges. I just thought I'd mention it.'

34

In June, Allied forces stormed the beaches at Normandy, the 'something special' that Colin had spoken of in Largs, and began to drive the Germans back. British losses were comparatively light, but that meant little to Isla, because Drew Brown was among them. Her letter to Colin was smudged with tears that had refused to stop trickling for days.

'I went at once to see Mrs Brown, but the place was filled with neighbours, so there wasn't much left for me to do. The poor woman was just sitting there, huddled in her chair, lost and bewildered by what's happened. Drew was all she had. The only thing she said while I was there was that perhaps it was for the best that he hadn't got married after all. I'm not so sure. At least if he had, she would have had a daughter-in-law to share her grief. Now, she's got nobody.'

She stopped writing in order to dab at her eyes with a handkerchief that was already damp, then, seeing that some tears had splashed on to the paper, she tried to blot them and only succeeded in smudging the ink. She contemplated starting the letter over again, but it was almost time to set out for the sanatorium, and she wanted to post it on her way there. She sniffed hard, gave her eyes another swipe with the handkerchief, and went on.

'Magret has done a lot for Mrs Brown since the news arrived, and Mrs Leach was a tower of strength while I was there, so gentle with Mrs Brown that I could scarcely believe it. She's older now, of course, which might have mellowed her. And poor Mr Kelly's death in Italy might have had something to do with it. Magret says that since then, Mrs Kelly has become much stronger, and won't allow her mother to bully her any more. Her little boy is a beautiful child – completely spoiled by his grandmother, who looks after him outside school hours when his mother's at work. Would you believe it, Colin, Mrs Brown even managed to rouse herself when I was saying goodbye, and thank me again for getting her roof mended all those years ago.'

Although the war was swinging in the Allies' favour now, the Germans were fighting back viciously. At the end of June, flying bombs started ravaging London.

'It must be like being attacked by a swarm of bees, only a million times worse,' Magret said, shaking her head and showering Isla's kitchen with the white fluff that always clung to the mill workers' clothes and hair. 'Bees don't stop buzzing then start exploding. These poor souls down south, they've had the worst of it!'

The Allies marched into Paris, then on to Belgium, while rockets being fired from Germany and Holland added to the misery of the flying bombs for the London civilians, and set Isla fretting afresh about Colin. She had thought he was safe in England, but now he was involved with anti-aircraft guns and, she knew from his letters, rarely able to enjoy a trouble-free night.

Unable to do a thing to help him, she concentrated her spare time on doing as much work on the Flora dolls' house as she could. That helped her a little, though every now and again dark depression swept over her as she recalled that once the war was over, Drew wouldn't be there, after all, to create miniature replicas of Flora's massive, dark furniture.

Eventually she set it aside and, buying a plain little house from Mr Leckie, who was still running his toyshop, she turned to copying the room she and Barbara and Ross had inhabited in George Street.

'I didnae know that there were this many folk in Paisley,' Magret bawled into Isla's ear. The two of them stood on the bridge spanning the River Cart at Paisley Cross, at the exact spot, Isla suddenly realised, where she had stood looking down at the river on her first visit to the town.

Only this time she wasn't alone; it was VE-Day, and every inch of the Cross and the gardens on the riverbank was crammed with people singing, dancing if they could find the space, hugging and kissing each other, celebrating the end of the war.

A group of soldiers to one side were bellowing out a Welsh song, on the other, a bunch of girls and servicemen, arms linked, were jigging up and down, singing, 'Pack up Your Troubles In Your Old Kitbag'. Cars and buses caught in the crowd shrilled their horns in celebration, people leaning from the windows of the surrounding buildings waved Union Jacks and cheered, and all the statues in the gardens, even Queen Victoria's, were being used as footholds and handholds for folk trying to get above the crowd.

A burly man in naval uniform, a beer bottle in his hand, set up in competition with other singers with 'Roll Out The Barrel!' in a powerful voice that was soon joined by others, including the Welshmen and the girls and their escorts. Magret roared the tune out lustily, beating time in the air with clenched fists, then broke off and grabbed at Isla's hand. 'I'm dyin' for a cup of tea. C'mon, we'll find the lassies and go home.'

Half an hour later they had only travelled a few yards, to the other side of St Mirren Brae, and there was no sign of Greta or Daisy.

'Hell mend them,' their mother said cheerfully. 'We'll just go on home and let them come back when they're good and ready.'

Together the two women battled down St Mirren Brae, Magret stopping to hug every man she met, with an extra warm hug for anyone in uniform. 'Take yer chances where ye find them, that's what I say,' she said cheerfully after a particularly enthusiastic encounter with a good-looking naval rating. 'There's none of them'll bother tae pass the time of day wi' a middle-aged biddy like me once we get used tae the idea of peace again.'

The crowds were thinning by the time they had reached the end of George Street and begun to walk up its length towards Magret's new home. They stopped at the old tenement to visit Mrs Brown, and Magret tried to persuade her to go with them, but she shook her head and said with an apologetic smile, 'I'd just as soon stay here on my own today.'

'All right, hen – but ye know where I live,' Magret patted her hand. 'Ye'll be welcome there any time ye feel like it. Any time at all, mind.'

They covered the rest of the distance in subdued silence, both thinking of Drew, and young Mr Kelly, and finally arrived at the flat to find that Greta and Daisy were already there, holding an impromptu party with Greta's fiancé and Daisy's boyfriend and several other people, the gramophone the girls had bought between them thumping out a Glen Miller tune.

Magret's usual high spirits returned at the prospect of a party. Towing Isla behind her, kissing and hugging to left and to right, she fought her way through the crowd to the tiny scullery, which she called a kitchenette. 'Won't be long before your two are back, Isla,' she shouted above the noise as she set the kettle on the gas stove. Then, with a swift glance at her friend's face, 'Are ye still frettin' about Barbara?' Isla had told her about Barbara's discovery, but had withheld Kenneth's name. Although there were no longer any McAdams living in Paisley, she couldn't bring herself to betray him. For once, Magret hadn't pried.

'I can't help fretting.'

'Ach, she'll get over it. She'll have tae. And when all's said and done' – Magret, heedless of rationing on this special day, spooned sugar generously into both their cups – 'you're her mammy. It'll be fine, just wait and see.'

In July the blackout curtains were pulled down and the street lights went on again. Isla packed the hated gas mask into a cupboard and out of sight, relieved beyond measure that she had never had to find out whether or not she would have used it in a gas attack, and prepared, nervously, for the return of her son and daughter from Canada. To her relief, Barbara had decided to fly back with Ross, and Ainslie was coming with them.

'I'm more than ready for a reunion,' she wrote. 'Phil, bless him, will stay here with the boys. He reckons that on this occasion, we should be on our own. I can't wait to see you again. Prepare for a shock when you see Ross, he's so like the McAdams, though I would say that he has your temperament, thank goodness. Every time I look at him I'm reminded of poor little Innes.'

Isla, who was still at the sanatorium, and would go on working there until the local Hospital Board got everything sorted out and their nursing staff up to its required level, arranged to take time off on the day they were due to arrive. It had been agreed that they would come to Paisley from Prestwick Aerodrome by train, then get a taxi to Castlehead, where Isla would be waiting. As the expected time for their arrival came near, she was so nervous that she couldn't sit down, but had to pace the ground floor, going restlessly from room to room until she was certain she must have worn a track in the carpets. When at last she heard the taxi stopping at the gate, she rushed to the door, then paused at the top of the porch steps, terrified. It had been so long, and so many things had happened since she had last seen her children.

Ainslie was first out of the vehicle. Sophisticated though she looked in a tailored navy skirt and fur jacket, her red hair still fiery beneath a smart navy and white hat, she nevertheless gave a Red Indian whoop of excitement as she spotted Isla. She fumbled with the gate, then ran up the path as Isla ran down the porch steps. They met halfway along the path, thumping straight into each other's arms.

'I thought today would never come! You look—' Ainslie held Isla back for a moment. 'My God, you look as though you've been through the mill,' she said with brutal honesty, then gathered Isla close for another swift, hard hug before turning towards the two young people coming in at the gate.

'Come on, you two – let your ma see what a disaster I've made of your upbringing.'

Ross came forward first, grinning, and Isla saw with a catch of breath what Ainslie had meant. It was almost like seeing Kenneth again, though Ross's eyes were a darker blue and his face rounder. He caught her up in a bear hug that almost squeezed the breath from her. At sixteen, he was a good head taller than Isla herself.

'You've grown!'

'No, you've got smaller.' His eyes were bright, his voice deep, with just the trace of a drawl to it.

Then it was Barbara's turn. In spite of the photographs, Isla had been unable to think of Barbara other than as the leggy schoolgirl she had last seen going up the gangplank of the steamer at Greenock. Now she was confronted by an elegant young woman in a tan and cream checked costume, her lovely face carefully but lightly made up, her shoulder-length hair a glowing mass against the cream hat perched like a halo on the back of her head. For a moment mother and daughter eyed each other warily, then Isla opened her arms and

Barbara came into them, briefly, dropping a light kiss on Isla's cheek before freeing herself.

'Hello, Mother.'

'It looks so small!' Ross broke the awkward moment, staring up at the house. 'I remembered it as a big house.'

'Your mother's right, you daft lump – it's you that's grown,' Ainslie told him. 'Didn't I keep saying that you were eating too much?'

The taxi-driver, still waiting by the gate with a pile of luggage, cleared his throat loudly, drawing their attention to his patient presence. There was a flurry of activity, paying the man, getting the luggage into the hall, then they were all indoors, the door shut, grinning self-consciously at each other. All except Barbara, Isla noticed, avoiding eye-contact, looking around as she drew her gloves off.

'Same room?' Ross asked, and when his mother nodded he scooped up two cases and ran up the stairs, calling back, 'I'll fetch the others in a minute.'

'Ainslie, I've had to put a bed for you in Barbara's room.'

'Oh, no,' Ainslie said in mock horror. 'The indignity of it, having to share a room at my age with my kid sister!'

Barbara grinned at her, and for the first time, Isla caught a glimpse of the daughter she had known. 'First there gets the best bed,' she said, and ran lightly upstairs after her brother.

'She hates me,' Isla said in a panic.

'No, she doesn't.' Ainslie put an arm round her and gave her a swift hug.

'But she's so formal with me, and so relaxed with you.'

'She hasn't seen you for years, and anyway, she's inherited the McAdam pride, that's for sure. You'll have to give her time, Isla. Come and make me some tea, I've been dreaming about a cup of tea all through the flight.'

As they sat at the kitchen table waiting for the kettle to boil, they could hear Ross running up and down the stairs collecting the luggage, the thump of footsteps above, Barbara and Ross calling to each other, the slam of doors.

'This house has been so quiet, for so long,' she said in awe. 'And suddenly it's come alive again.'

'Everything'll soon be back to normal.'

'It'll never be the same again, but if we're lucky, we can start all over again.'

'Any word of Colin coming home?'

'Next month, he hopes.'

'You'll be pleased about that.'

'So will his father – he's worn himself out looking after the office. This time, he's looking forward to retiring.'

'Gregg Marshall arrived back just before we left, much to Pat's relief. She's missed him terribly. They've always been a very close family. It was good of you to give him hospitality while he was based in Scotland.'

'He's a very nice person.'

'That's exactly what he said about you,' Ainslie said. 'You'll be looking forward to getting back to your dolls' houses.'

'Mr Leckie's had some enquiries already. And Mabel's written – she'll be demobbed soon, and she wants to come back to work for me. I'll have to find another furniture maker.' She swallowed, then said, 'There'll never be anyone like Drew, though.'

'I know.' Ainslie reached over and touched her shoulder. The kettle began to whistle and Isla got up and poured some boiling water into the teapot, then emptied it out and reached for the tea-caddy.

'I was thinking of asking Mrs Brown if she'd like to be our housekeeper.'

Ainslie went unerringly to the right cupboard to fetch cups and saucers. 'Drew's mother? D'you think she'll want the job?'

'I think she might. It'd be good for her to be part of a family. If we are still a family,' Isla added, a tremor in her voice, as she set the empty kettle down.

'Of course you are. It's funny how things that happened years ago keep affecting our lives, isn't it?' Ainslie sat down again, putting her elbows on the table and leaning her chin in cupped hands. 'It's been over sixteen years since my father died, and yet when Barbara started asking about him, and the two of us spent hours going over the photographs I'd found for her, I could almost see the change coming over her. She matured, Isla. She's found qualities in herself that she'd never noticed before. Even though he died when she was little, Father shaped her, just as he shaped us. Remember when we talked it all over years ago, and I said that we were McAdam's women?'

Ross, yelling to his sister to hurry up, came thundering down the stairs and into the kitchen, a camera in his hand. He stopped suddenly, then said, 'I almost expected to see Nan here.'

'So do I, every time I come in,' Isla told him.

'It must have been awful for you.'

'It was – but now you're back home, and everything's going to be all right.'

Ross blinked rapidly, swallowed, then opened the back door. 'Outside, everyone,' he said briskly. 'I want to take some pictures.'

'But I want my tea,' Ainslie wailed.

'Later. I'm preserving this moment for posterity.' Ross tossed the words over his shoulder as he plunged into the garden.

Ainslie, groaning, got to her feet. 'We gave him that for his last birthday, and right now I wish we'd never thought of it. He's camera mad, I warn you. Come on, we might as well fetch Barbara and get it over with.'

They found Barbara in the workroom, standing over the dolls' house that Isla was working on. She turned as they went in, wonder in her eyes. 'This looks just like our old room in George Street!'

'You remember it?'

'Of course I do. That was where I learned to play peevers.' For the first time, Barbara gave her mother a genuine smile, and Isla, heartened, went to stand by her.

'I wanted to keep my hand in, and I thought it would be an easy one to do.'

Barbara reached into the little house and withdrew a matchbox tray, painted creamy yellow to resemble an orange box. Gently, she drew back the scrap of cloth hung on a thread across the opening. 'You've even put the little dishes on the shelves. Can I have it when it's finished?'

'Of course you can.'

Barbara gently replaced the little makeshift cupboard

in the dolls' house, then her index finger, tipped with pink nail polish, touched each of the dolls in turn. 'A mother doll, a girl doll, a boy doll. I insisted on having a daddy doll, didn't I?'

'Yes. You were quite right,' Isla said. 'There should have been one. I'll make one.'

'No, don't.' The silky fall of Barbara's red hair hid her downbent face. After a moment she straightened. 'We seemed to manage well enough without one,' she said matter-of-factly, and swung out of the room.

'She's thawing,' Ainslie whispered as they followed her through the kitchen and into the back garden, where Ross was standing by the edge of the vegetable patch, staring round in amazement.

'The swing's gone. Where's my swing?' he asked in his man's voice.

'You're old enough to make your own now,' Barbara said, and he made a face at her.

'I might just do that. Now, over against the garden wall, the three of you, with Mum in the middle.'

They grouped themselves, and he studied them through the viewfinder, then flapped a hand at them. 'Closer together.'

Barbara's scent, fresh and flowery, wafted towards Isla as they obeyed, arms about each other.

'That's good. Hold it,' Ross instructed.

'McAdam's women,' Ainslie murmured, just as the camera shutter clicked, freezing the three of them, Isla, Ainslie, and Barbara, entwined in an embrace for all time.